CAITLYN P. TAJON

Double Crossed

The Wring Bearer #2

First edition

ISBN: 9798873663408

Editing by Raistlyn Camphuysen
Cover art by Harbinger Designs

This book was professionally typeset on Reedsy.
Find out more at reedsy.com

Contents

Trigger Warnings

DOUBLE CROSSED is the second book in "The Wring Bearer" duet. It should be read **after** DOUBLE STANDARDS. It contains strong language, mature content, mental health issues (depression, anxiety), explicit sex scenes, alcoholism, mention of abortion, abuse, and divorce, unhealthy relationships, miscommunication, religion, kidnapping, death/murder, and guilt. **If any of these topics makes you uncomfortable or triggers you, <u>please do not read this book.</u>**

I prioritize the well-being of my readers and believe in transparency about the themes explored within this narrative. Some of the content may include sensitive topics that could be distressing to some individuals.

I encourage all readers to review the provided trigger warnings before diving into the book to safeguard their mental health. It is essential to note that nothing in this book is intended to offend, but rather, it aims to explore complex themes. The content is meant for mature audiences aged 18 and above. Your mental well-being is important to me, and I want you to have a fulfilling reading experience.

Dedication

To those who toggle between true crime podcasts and daydreams of fake marriage and forced proximity plots, who love the idea of no way out but together, and relish a bit of a praise kink with their coffee – this book was written for you.
-Caitlyn

"Double Crossed" Official Playlist

1. So Good - Halsey
2. Happier Than Ever - Kelly Clarkson
3. Better Man (Taylor's Version) [From The Vault] - Taylor Swift
4. Haunt You - Social House
5. On It - EMO
6. Heat Waves (with iann dior) - Glass Animals
7. I Quit Drinking - Kelsea Ballerini & LANY
8. Liability - Drake
9. Rent Free - 6LACK
10. Thru These Tears - LANY
11. Cave - Zoe Clark
12. obvious - Ariana Grande
13. Sparks Fly (Taylor's Version) - Taylor Swift
14. Till There's Nothing Left - Cam
15. SexyBack - Ilkan Gunuc & Clara Stegall
16. Like This. - JoJo
17. Afterglow - Taylor Swift
18. self sabotage - Maggie Lindemann
19. august - Taylor Swift
20. Ruin My Life - Zara Larsson
21. Call It What You Want - Taylor Swift
22. gold rush - Taylor Swift

Book Cover

WRING BEARER DUET #2

double crossed

"Second chances that leave you breathless. Redemption
and rekindled love collide when fate reunites
Callie and Liam in this gripping finale."

CAITLYN P. TAJON

One

Callie

"Oh my *God,* Liam!" I screamed, my head tipped back in ecstasy. The cold surface of the table I sat on was no match for the heat coursing through me.

Liam's stubble scraped my inner thighs, his tongue flat against my clit. He stared hungrily up at me with green eyes dark with lust. I could get off from that look alone.

I rode his tongue hard. When he slipped a finger into me, my back arched, the dual stimulation building an electric sensation in the depths of my belly. I moaned his name again, my insides quivering as my orgasm built and built and built until—

I bolted straight up in my bed, sweating from my lost release and panting like a damn dog. I looked around my room, heart sinking as I realized that Liam was not, in fact, here with me. It shattered a little bit more when I remembered he never would be with me again.

Collapsing back onto the mattress, I stared at the ceiling and swallowed thickly. I fucking missed him so much, both physically and emotionally. How had it only been a week since I saw him last?

The last time I had a wet dream about Liam, he hadn't broken my heart and ripped my soul in half. Hadn't stood in front of me and refused to say *anything* while I poured my heart out to him. Apparently I couldn't escape him, even in my dreams.

I'm so fucked.

* * *

2 weeks later

I stared stoically at the TV, watching *Sweet Home Alabama* for the fourth time this week. I tossed an extra buttery piece of popcorn in my mouth, then another, then gave up and shoved an entire handful in. Barely breathing as I inhaled the salty snack, it still wasn't satisfying the emptiness in my stomach. Or my heart.

I picked up a candy bar from my bedside table, greedily unwrapping it and taking large bites. The gooey chocolate coated my taste buds and brought me a temporary comfort—probably because I hadn't allowed myself to gorge on these snacks in years. Not since before I went to the Police Academy.

That life felt like it belonged to another person.

I was not the Callie Eden I left behind in Newark.

My eyes involuntarily rolled every time they showed New York City in the movie, as if I was subconsciously pretending I didn't miss living in a city. I did miss it. The absence of the place I called home for nearly a decade left a void in my soul that I was desperate to fill.

In the movie, Jake made a comment about people not meeting their soulmates in their childhood, about to sign the divorce papers as he looked up at Melanie.

Grimacing, I threw the now-empty popcorn bowl across the room. It hit the wall with less gusto than I hoped. "Soulmates don't *exist!*" I shouted.

Yikes.

The heartache rarely ebbed, leaving me feeling distressed even on the best of days. I felt bad for my family, who had been dealing with me for too many days now—days I didn't deserve from them. No one ever said there was a time limit on recovering from heartbreak and trauma. At least, that's what I told myself.

Jake and Melanie bickered on the screen some more, reminding me all too much of *him*. My refusal to say or think his name may have been immature, but doing so gave him too much power over me.

I was weak at the mere thought of him.

Maybe it wasn't too late to crawl back to him. Take him any way he'd let me—even if it only offered brief glimpses into a relationship that could never exist between us.

There was a soft knock on my bedroom door, pulling me from my dark thoughts. It swung open to reveal my sister, who looked a scary amount like me. Sometimes I thought about how she would be a prime target for a certain serial killer, but then I reminded myself that we were hours away from the city now. And I wasn't a cop anymore.

"What do you want, Leah?" I grumbled. I was perched in the middle of my bed, lounging against half a dozen goose down pillows, in the room I grew up in. The walls were painted a pale blue and lined with floating bookshelves. White furniture complimented the Berber carpet, and white gingham curtains hung over the arched windows on the far wall. Completing my teenage room was a photo collage of my high school years pinned to the wall beside my vanity. A younger version of myself grinned back at me from a trip to the lake—the trip where I met a green-eyed stranger who broke my heart ten years later.

And even though my room had been surprisingly untouched all these years of never coming to visit, I still felt out of place here. As if I never even belonged in the shoes of the girl who once occupied this room.

Probably because these four walls portrayed the innocence of a blue-eyed girl who so badly wanted to leave this town that she was willing to leave her family, and her dignity, behind to do so. It wasn't as honorable as I remembered it being.

No wonder I had caught my family off guard when I suddenly appeared in the entryway, looking fresh out of hell.

Two

Callie

3 weeks earlier

I inhaled the familiar fragrance of roses and lemon-scented Lysol wipes, the unexpected comfort of home washing over me. The relief nearly brought me to my knees right in the foyer.

Light flooded in from the tall windows by the front door, and the heater was on, warming the chill I feared had indefinitely rooted itself inside of me.

"Mom?" I croaked. "Dad?" My first instinct was to worry that they didn't immediately check to see who had waltzed in their front door. Then again, we were in a rural town in Pennsylvania where everyone knew each other.

Finally my mom rushed through the living room on the right side of the entryway, shock written on her face and her blue eyes wide.

"Callie?" She gasped before throwing her arms around me. As soon as I felt that familiar embrace, I broke down in tears and held her close. So many years of suppressing my emotions had me realizing how much I missed her. The guilt of never visiting threatened to swallow me whole.

I dropped the keys to the moving truck, my knees finally buckling. My mother surprisingly had the strength to hoist me up and half-carry me to the couch.

"Baby, what's wrong?" The worry in her voice only made me cry harder. Her gentle fingers brushed away the strands of hair that stuck to my tear-stained cheeks.

I shook my head. "N-not ready to t-talk about it," I sobbed. I needed a momentary break from the mess I'd walked away from in Newark.

I spent so long trying to be strong and independent—and for what? What was I trying to prove? That I could? That my career could make my family *proud?* That I didn't need anyone else, not even my family?

Fucking stupid.

Mom didn't press the issue. She gave me a single nod and rubbed my shoulder affectionately before rising to her feet and wiping her hands on her apron. "I'll be right back, sweetie." She disappeared into the kitchen and out into the backyard. She returned with my dad in tow.

"Sugar Plum!" He exclaimed, eyes bright until he got a good look at my face. He scooped me off the couch, spinning me around like he did when I was a child. A giggle bubbled out of me before I could stop it. "You're home just in time. Your sister just moved back since her internship abroad ended, and your brother's in town getting things in order for his wedding next month."

Guilt wound through me once more as he set me on my feet. *Wedding?* I didn't even know he was *engaged.* What an awful sister I was.

Biting my tender lip, I glanced up at my dad. I could only imagine his disappointment when he pieced together how I'd been handling things.

Give it three... two... one...

He frowned, wrinkles appearing in his forehead that matched the ones that were starting to form on mine. "What's going on, Sugar Plum? You look..." his voice trailed off, saying everything without even speaking. *Like shit, Dad, I know.* It was the nicest way to approach the subject without insulting my current appearance. Between the busted lip, black eye, bruised throat, and wounded ego, I looked every bit a dead girl walking.

"Have you been drinking again?"

I blinked. "Daddy, I—"

"Callie-Ann!" my sister screamed as she barreled down the stairs. Her use of my full name took me by surprise; I hadn't heard it in so long, not even from our parents. She leaped over the couch in true Leah fashion and damn near tackled me in a hug. Her agility rivaled that of any officer in training.

I huffed from her forcefulness, swaying back and forth. I couldn't recall the last time I was with my family like this. Hated that it was under such morose circumstances. Hated myself more knowing I had neglected my familial duties for so long.

Taking a tentative seat on the edge of the couch, I prepared myself to tell the story. I'd tell it only once, then never again.

Three

Callie

Present day

Leah slammed the door behind her, her eyes full of pity instead of the anger I expected to see.

"I can hear every time you yell at the TV," she scolded. "What did Reese Witherspoon ever do to you?"

Just like high school. I bit out, "I'm kinda going through something. Give me a break."

She rolled her eyes, the blue in them identical to my own. "So you got your heart broken. It happens to all of us. You don't get to just sit around indefinitely."

I scowled, which felt more natural than smiling these days. "It's not *just* that, but thanks for undermining my issues."

Leah snorted and jumped onto my bed, then tucked her legs under herself like she was preparing for a hot gossip session. "That kind of mentality is so toxic. The sooner you realize that there are greater things in your life than," she gestured at me and my current state, "*this,* the sooner you can heal from it all. Don't be the victim. Accept what happened and grow from it."

I stayed quiet for a moment, scrutinizing her. It was sage advice, even if I didn't want to hear it.

"I can't relate to all the work stuff and the domestic abuse," she added, a little too casually for my comfort. "But the dating stuff? I've *definitely* been there before. My senior year of college, my boyfriend Thad ended things after cheating on me with a girl in another sorority. He and I were together for two years, but everything changed when he became President of Kappa Psi Kappa." She heaved a sigh, her eyes going distant.

I crinkled my nose at her. "You dated a frat guy named *Thad?* Probably a good thing you're not still with him."

She smirked. "Look at you making jokes. That's more like the big sister I know."

My lips flattened. I wasn't trying to be funny. "How did I not know you dated someone for two whole years?"

She raised a shoulder. "You haven't exactly been…" she paused and frowned, "present."

The truth stung. "What are you talking about? Just because I haven't visited in—" I cut myself off as I tried to mentally count how long it had been. *Jesus.* When *was* the last time I had come home?

"Here's a hint: my high school graduation."

My eyes swung to hers. "There's no way."

"That's the last time you were home. It was right after you graduated from the Police Academy." She puffed her cheeks out, her shoulder-length hair swinging forward. "We all went to the lake house for the holidays for the next two years, and you did attend Thanksgiving both years, but after that… every holiday you stayed in the city to work."

I rubbed my forehead. She was remembering it correctly. After the Academy and my placement into Newark's Third Precinct, I was attending the Twin City Christmas Gala every year. I couldn't afford to miss those—or was that just the excuse I had made to avoid coming back here?

I groaned but didn't respond, which elicited a punch in the arm. "Ow, what the hell?"

"I'm pissed at you!" she yelled. "You abandoned me after high school. You always promised me a girls trip to the city, but you were too busy for me. That was the excuse you used for years, until I got the hint to stop asking. And now you don't even live there anymore, and my opportunity is gone. You'll never want to go back there after what you've been through."

I swallowed the lump in my throat. I didn't want to think about the growing list of people I had let down recently, my own sister included.

Shit.

"Leah, I'm… so, *so* sorry."

"I don't want an apology. I want you to get your life back together so we can actually do those things together someday. I won't be asking you for permission, either. I'll just show up one day and force you." She flashed a crooked grin. "You don't belong in this town. Not after what they did to you. You belong back in the city."

"You used to be so badass," she continued. "Witty and funny and fun. But now… you're not. You're a mirage of my sister, and you've really let a couple of men ruin you. So, let's use this temporary setback as a stepping stone to get you back there again." Her eyes glimmered with hope, but her honesty felt like a bucket of ice water being poured over me.

My lower lip trembled. "My job has changed me, Leah. I'm not the same woman I was a few years ago."

She shook her head, as if to tell me I wasn't getting it. "I wouldn't expect you not to change. I can't imagine seeing half the shit you have. But this isn't about your job. It may be a part of it, but we both know it's really because of your relationship choices."

I gulped, fixating on my hands in my lap and the feeling of the soft fabric of my leggings. "Maybe you're right."

"It's time, Callie-Ann." I tried not to cringe at the name—I was still adjusting to hearing it again.

"What am I supposed to do for work? I left my job and have no other skill sets."

Leah smiled. "First of all, you can get any job with your qualifications. You have so much office experience. Second of all, there's a sergeant position opening at the Springcrest Police Department."

I felt my lips tug downwards. "That's a promotion."

"You're more than ready for it."

I shrugged and stuck my tongue out to faux gag. "Being a cop here? God, that's the opposite of what I was doing in Newark." A bitter laugh escaped me.

"It doesn't have to be permanent. Just give yourself a chance at a better future than… whatever this is."

I sighed. "Fine. But you have to get a job, too. We both need to pay rent while we're living here."

She grinned mischievously at me. "Deal. Now, we start with your glow-up." She sat up on her knees and grabbed my arm, pulling me into an upright position.

"I'm not in the mood right now," I said with a grunt. She continued to tug until I was tumbling off the bed. "Leah! Knock it off!"

She put her hands on her hips as I crawled to my feet. "Get your lazy ass up. We're going on a run."

We leveled with each other, which felt pointless since we were the same height, until I finally caved. I waved my hands in the air.

"Alright, let me get dressed."

She smirked smugly and flounced out of my room. I threw a dirty look at her back and changed into exercise clothes, hating every second of it. I caught a glimpse of myself in the mirror as I stripped, and cringed at my appearance. My black eye had faded to a yellow bruise, the swelling gone, and my busted lip had healed. My hair was in a messy bun that admittedly hadn't been washed in days, and the dark crescents under my eyes made it seem like I hadn't slept in weeks. My posture sagged forward. The bullet graze that would forever mark my arm had healed into a shiny pink scar—just another painful memory.

Needless to say, I was in rough shape. I had avoided all mirrors these last few weeks.

I met my sister out on the landing, and she nudged me down the stairs. Our parents looked up at us, shock written on their faces as we passed them in the living room.

"What are you two up to?" Mom asked, skeptical.

"Callie and I are going on a run," Leah announced, dropping the *-Ann* from my name in front of Mom and Dad for the sake of preventing them from calling me by my full name. If they started, they would never stop.

Dad cocked an eyebrow. "Be safe."

I almost snorted in response. How could going on a run in Springcrest *not* be safe? But as they returned to reading their books, I knew I would be forced to go on this run.

My sister yanked me into the cold, not releasing me until we were jogging side by side. Comfortable silence wrapped around us.

While my cardio was in overall good health—the nature of my job, and all—I was feeling the effects of all the snacks and booze I'd dumped into my body the last several weeks. I felt... sluggish compared to my sister's lightweight bounding.

"So, tell me about Liam. You haven't talked about him at all."

Liam.

His name hurt to hear.

"He's hot. Gorgeous green eyes. Dresses well. Into the finer things, I suppose," I told her, thinking about Liam's nice watches and clothes, which were probably a result of his family's wealth now that I thought about it. The last thing I wanted to do was talk about his personality, or what he'd meant to me, or all the things he'd done—both good and bad.

"Like you do, and totally your type, then. What's he like?"

I cast my eyes skyward. "He's..." I searched for the words to describe him. My heart was pounding heavier now, the blood rushing through me and warming the ever-present chill in my bones. "Witty and charming. Thoughtful. He always forced me out of my comfort zone by getting under my skin. Before things got bad, he treated me like I held the sun and stars in my hands." I fought the urge to cry in the middle of the neighborhood and focused instead on my feet pounding the pavement.

"That's... good," she panted as we rounded a corner, passing cookie-cutter homes with well-manicured lawns and blossoming garden beds, creating a picturesque backdrop to a seemingly sleepy little town. "Now tell me what he did to you."

"You've heard… this story."

"It's not… for me. It's… for you."

I grunted and pushed myself to run a little faster. "He… broke my heart. He left me when I… needed him the most. Couldn't… commit to me." I stopped as my side cramped, doubling over. Leah paused, resting her hands atop her head as she panted at my side. We were stopped at the edge of where the homes turned into local businesses, maple trees lining the sidewalk and providing some much needed shade. "This is pointless."

"Is it? At least you're talking about it. Progress is progress."

I straightened and brushed past her, noticing we were approaching the small downtown area of Springcrest. I forgot how close everything was here. We wove around the small gatherings of people on the sidewalk.

"When you were with him, how did you feel?"

I wrapped my arms around myself self-consciously. "Alive," I admitted distractedly as I caught sight of a familiar face. I slowed as we passed one of the local coffee shops.

"Callie-Ann?" he called out as I came nearly face to face with him. "Is it really you?" He glanced between Leah and me before nodding resolutely. "Yeah, that's definitely you."

I halted, a grin breaking out across my face—my first real one in weeks. "Jason! Oh my God!"

He pulled me into a quick hug, just like he used to when we were teenagers, before releasing me to turn and kiss my sister on the lips. I blinked in surprise as he grinned fondly at her, then shifted his hazel eyes to me.

My high school boyfriend, who I only broke up with because I was moving to Newark and he intended to stay in Springcrest for good.

I tried not to notice how well he had aged—from his golden hair cropped into a Caesar cut, his jaw angled and strong, to his worn flannel and muscular forearms—because his arm was draped around Leah's shoulders, and the smile on her face said it all.

There was something between them that made my heart twist in my chest: *love.* No secrets or hiding of feelings.

I cleared my throat to hide how jarred I was.

"I have to admit, I never expected to see you again," Jason said, flashing me a cheesy, lopsided grin.

I shrugged, my gaze dropping to my sneaker-clad feet. "I didn't expect to come back here very often."

"She's back for the time being, just until she gets back on her feet," Leah said proudly—so sure that I'd make it back to the city.

"You didn't tell me she was back," he murmured to her. She gave him a little shrug. The simple interaction made it seem like they were in their own world, oblivious to the people going about their lives all around them.

I smiled awkwardly at both of them. "Leah, do you want to stay behind? I can finish—"

"No." She ducked out from under Jason's arm. "We're in this together."

Jason grinned at the both of us. "I see you on the news from time to time. You really did it. Became a city cop, chasing down the bad guys. Just like you always wanted."

I felt my cheeks warm, then instantly chastised myself. The last thing I wanted was my sister thinking I was into her guy. "Yeah, that was… it was everything I dreamed of. But I quit my job and moved back here. I needed a break from everything. What about you?"

He raised his eyebrows. "I'm working on my parents' vineyard. I manage all their social media and run their operations now."

"Wow, you're doing everything you talked about and more."

He grinned again before leaning in to kiss my sister's cheek. "I won't keep you two, but we should all grab drinks sometime."

My skin crawled with the sudden itch for a drink, but I'd sworn off booze after my most recent bender. I was done with alcohol until I could learn to control myself.

"I'd love to, but I'm sober." I gave them a feeble smile.

Leah patted my arm. "We can all go to dinner instead. See you later, babe." She grabbed my hand, pulling me back into a light jog. I caught a whiff of Jason's scent—pepper and pine. For the briefest of seconds, I was reminded of our blind teenage love, of a young man who saw a genuine future with me.

He had shown me what it was like for someone to love with all their heart. He had created a safe environment for me to share parts of myself, especially at a time when it felt like the whole town was against me.

He was my first, and he was special to me. He hadn't broken me.

It made sense that I was caught off guard by my sister dating him. She knew what he had meant to me, but that was an eternity ago. And judging by the looks of it, they had been together for a while—long before she moved back to Springcrest.

I ignored the jealous feeling in the pit of my stomach—not from the knowledge of who she was with. But because she was getting the kind of love I wanted from Liam—the kind of love he couldn't give me.

Four

Liam

My tongue was leaden as I tossed back yet another drink. I stopped counting some time ago—there was no point. That number didn't fucking matter. I grimaced at my empty glass and wished I had another, but I feared no amount of liquor in the world would mend my wounds.

Three weeks. Only three weeks had gone by without her, and yet it felt like a lifetime.

I let her down in so many ways. I broke her heart—not just once, but *twice*—and I had the audacity to be surprised—angry, even—when she skipped town.

Not to mention I had made zero progress on her prized case. The one thing she left behind for me to do, and I stopped putting in the effort because I couldn't bring that bastard to justice. I couldn't even prove he was the killer.

Instead I stayed up every night mulling over every fact in my brain but doing nothing to help.

I was failing her again.

I would never be the man she deserved.

I motioned for another round as the thought crossed my mind. I hoped she was healing and getting happier each day. And the way *that* made me feel had me turning to scan the crowd for tonight's conquest. If I couldn't have her, then I'd need someone to help me not feel so dreadfully alone.

It was a short reprieve for the long nights ahead of me.

I spotted a beautiful woman and smirked as we made eye contact.

That's all I'd been doing for the last few weeks.

Pretending. Pretending I was okay. Pretending to not think about her. Pretending I was preoccupied with my work.

I was nothing but a fucking fraud. I wasn't okay, I thought about her constantly, I was distracted at the precinct, and being in this stupid fucking city was only making it worse.

Picking up my refilled glass as soon as the bartender set it down, I sipped on the vodka as the woman made her way toward me. I gave her a coy smile—one that didn't reach my eyes—as she shimmied up to my side, purring her drink order to the bartender. I didn't care to listen—they were all the same. If someone asked me tomorrow what this woman looked like, I wouldn't be able to tell them. That was just another shitty thing about me.

I tipped my head toward the woman, earning a small giggle. I tried not to cringe. She was only trying to stroke my very bruised ego. So instead of making half-hearted jokes, I made small talk with her.

"You look like you need company tonight," she cooed.

My bitter heart twisted. "You could say that."

Humming, she sipped her martini and batted her eyelashes. "Want to talk about it?"

If snorting wasn't considered impolite, I'd have done that. "No."

She sidled closer, her shoulder brushing mine. The contact relieved some of the ache inside. "Straight to the point, I see." Her manicured finger traced a line down my arm, over the exposed tattoos on my forearm. My other hand clamped over her wrist to stop her.

"Not the tattoos," I damn near growled, drawing a line in the sand. That was reserved for one woman only, and I could never have her again.

Seemingly unoffended, she moved both hands to rest on my shoulders. "Fine by me. Just take me home."

Thank God that's over.

Nodding, I motioned to the bartender, then paid our tabs and led her away from the bar.

And even as we kissed when we entered her apartment, even as she rode me and I stared up at her bouncing tits, all I could think about was the woman who'd slipped through my grasp. For once, my mind wasn't littered with all the excuses I'd given as to why I wasn't ready to be with her. I could only think about how I'd let her go.

The woman whose eyes followed me into my dreams, whose voice lulled me to sleep like a serene lullaby, whose smile encouraged me to press forward each and every day. Her very existence reminded me that there was something good in this world, even though she would never be mine again.

So, I let this stranger ride me until, for a few short moments, I felt nothing but bliss.

And just like that, it was over. I gave her a few smiles and told her I'd see her around. She laughed, knowing it was a courteous lie, and walked me out. I shuffled home, not bothering to hail a taxi. I let the spring breeze whisk through my too-long hair and whisper against the facial hair I'd let grow out.

Not like my clean-cut appearance mattered anymore. Nothing really mattered anymore. Not without her.

I passed by the bar we used to frequent with our mutual friend, Sophie Reyes, for after-work drinks. But Sophie wasn't talking to me, either.

I didn't blame her.

I chuckled under my breath as I entered my apartment, the warmth curling around me like her arms used to back when things were good.

I missed her so goddamn much.

For yet another night, I lay awake, lost in that fucking case and stuck on every little mistake I made, contemplating how I was supposed to move on from it all.

Five

Callie

4 months later

I tucked a few wayward strands of my slicked-back ponytail away from my face as I read through one of my detective's reports, checking for errors and fighting an oncoming yawn. I loved paperwork, but damn, it was a lot less enjoyable when it was for small town crime. It didn't help that I'd been at the local police department for twelve hours today.

Not like I needed to be here that long. The other on-duty sergeant always claimed he had it under control, but his behavior said otherwise. He was immature, childish, crude, and outright sexist. And sometimes—*sometimes*—he reminded me of another detective I left behind in Newark.

"Hey, Dweeben, when are you leaving?" Dale Ferguson, the sexist sergeant, barked from across the room. We sat on opposing ends of the long room, our desks facing one another in the open space so we were accessible to other officers.

I scowled and raised my head to look at the scumbag before me. His mousy brown hair receded at the hairline and was balding in the back, and he sported a handlebar mustache that seemed to attract crumbs. When our eyes met, he lounged back in his desk chair and plopped his dirty boots atop his desk.

I curled my lip back in disgust. I could only imagine how messy his workspace was, and just the thought of that made my armpits prick with anxious sweat.

"First of all, I'd really appreciate it if you called me by my real name," I snapped, referring to the nickname he'd adopted for me: *Dweeben.* All because I corrected him one time with crime statistics my first week on the job, and rather than admitting he had made a mistake, he made a mockery of me and replaced my last name with the annoying nickname.

Asshole.

"Second of all," I continued slowly so his pea-sized brain could keep up, "you are more than welcome to leave any time you'd like. In fact, I'd prefer it. Your shift is over, and the night shift sergeants are here. I'm only here to wrap up the last of these reports."

Internally, I was pleading for him to clock out. I had very little patience left to deal with his misogynistic antics.

He grunted as he struggled to a sitting position. "Problem is, Dweeben, that if I leave, then you look better than me. And we can't have that," he sneered.

"Your work ethic speaks for itself. I look better than you all the time," I spat, tossing my long ponytail over my shoulder.

He raised his eyebrows, two thick caterpillars framing his dark eyes, and grinned wolfishly. "I wouldn't go as far as to say you *look* better than me, but I'd certainly tap that."

"You're married." It came out somewhere between a scoff and a snarl. I snapped the file shut and locked it up in my filing cabinet, unable to tolerate him for another minute without leaving a shoe print on his oily forehead. I grabbed my phone and purse hurriedly, and he wasted no time matching my speed. Probably just to annoy me.

"Marriage doesn't mean I can't appreciate a good lookin' lady." I fought the urge to gag.

"Fine, then you're a disgusting pig." I nodded at the night shift officers, not bothering to keep my low opinion of Dale a secret.

"Grease my bacon then, Callie-Ann." His voice dropped several octaves, a piss-poor attempt to seduce me as he continued his relentless pursuit despite me trying to escape his presence.

Joke's on him. I had already fallen prey to one coworker, and he was hot and a zillion times more charming.

I whirled on Dale, punching his arm as hard as I could. His eyes flew wide as he covered the spot with his hand, the smug look on his face temporarily wiped off. That alone made me internally smirk.

"Don't you ever say shit like that to me again." I threw open the front door of the building and strolled out into the night, beelining straight for the restaurant where I had a date with no one but myself.

* * *

I spread butter on the free bread at Sicily's, Springcrest's finest establishment and only Italian restaurant. Dating myself was oftentimes harder than I cared to admit, but I knew I needed time to get to know myself, without trying to please a man. I'd lost myself in recent years, focusing heavily on my career and a failing relationship. Now I needed to remember who I was… not that I even knew what that looked like anymore.

I was happy at one point, I think. Witty, as Leah had said. Ambitious.

It was embarrassing at first, eating alone or sitting in a movie theater by myself, but each time I forced myself to do it, the easier it seemed to get. The most difficult part was learning to enjoy my own company and being comfortable enough in my own skin to actually like myself.

My road to recovery the last few months had been long and treacherous— at times utterly unbearable—but here I was. Taking each day as it arrived.

Emotions came and went in waves. One day I was fine, then the next I missed city life, my old job, and worst of all, Liam. I'd be heartbroken all over again, wanting to stay in bed and hide from my feelings. Life didn't work that way, though, as I dragged myself to work day after day.

After Leah coerced me into pulling my shit together, I kept the ball rolling.

I exercised daily, resisted the frequent urge to reach for the bottle, and forced myself to apply for the sergeant position at the Springcrest Police Department.

While I expected the interview process to be more lax than Newark, I didn't expect it to be *so* casual. I showed up in a pantsuit only to find many of the detectives dressed in jeans and t-shirts, the chief of police included. He took one glance at my resumé and asked me about my experience. He questioned my leave of absence; *I was taking care of some personal issues during my administrative leave, but have since recovered* is what I told him. And that was all he deemed necessary before he all but handed me a badge and gun.

So now I was one of two day shift sergeants overseeing both the uniformed officers and the detectives—unlike Newark, who separated the two types of sergeants. But since this was a small town, it wasn't necessary.

Just as my bowl of Alfredo was placed in front of me, my sister slid into my booth. I cocked an eyebrow at her as she plucked a bread roll up from the basket.

"Howdy, Sergeant," she greeted cheerily, her cheeks flushed from what I could only assume was kissing Jason. "How was your day?"

I smiled at her. "I punched Dale for making a lewd comment to me," I said. "In the arm, sadly."

She laughed. "So it was good, then."

I nodded. "What are you doing here?"

"I was walking by when I saw you here. Figured I'd stop in and see how you were doing. You were out the door early this morning."

I shrugged and dug into my food. Did part of my "recovery" include burying myself in long days at work? Absolutely. There were some things about myself I couldn't—and wouldn't—change. My ambition *had* gotten me this far in my career.

Leah rolled her eyes at my silent response and propped her chin on her hand as she leaned on the table. "Do you ever miss it?"

I frowned around a bite of pasta. "Miss what?"

"The city. Your job there," she clarified. "I bet it was loads more interesting than here." Her eyes were distant, her shoulders stiff as if she worried what my answer would be.

I hesitated. I usually diverted my thoughts when they went down that road, because I knew if I spent too much time thinking about it, I'd inadvertently reopen the floodgate of emotions I worked so hard to keep at bay. I allowed myself to revisit that place now—to the memories of the glittering city lights, the sound of traffic no matter the hour, the nightlife, the office I spent so much time in, the friendships…

The answer she was hoping for was a big fat *no*. Ever since I'd come home, we had rekindled a sisterhood that had fallen out of place a long time ago. If I gave her a completely honest answer, I risked her emotionally distancing herself from me, the way I did when I was hurt. And I wasn't ready to lose the friend I'd found again in my little sister when I needed her the most.

I took a deep breath and thought of the magical, balmy summer nights in Springcrest, where birds greeted me at all hours of the day and the sidewalks were lined with cobblestones and maple trees. The pure, uninterrupted darkness when the sun went down, the unchanging houses decorating the neighborhoods, the whistling of the trees that lead into a forest beyond—

"No," I half-lied. "Well, sometimes. There are parts I miss. But I don't miss the person I had become, or what my job was doing to me. I certainly don't miss the temptation the city gave me. This," I gestured to the town outside the window, "is all I need right now. I didn't have *this* when I was there. I didn't have peace. I wasn't Callie-Ann, big fish in a little pond that gained the townspeople's respect through hard work. I was just… Callie. A city cop who made a lot of foolish decisions that nearly killed her. More than once." I met my sister's eyes to make sure she understood what I was saying. Tension still bracketed her mouth, but her shoulders seemed to relax.

"Would you ever go back?" she questioned after a moment.

I exhaled sharply and twirled my pasta with my fork. "I don't know. It would have to be under the right circumstances, I think." I motioned at my waitress for the check and looked at Leah again. "I have a lot of baggage there, you know? I missed it a lot initially, but now I've…" I searched for the right words. "Grown. Healed."

Leah bobbed her head and gave me a sad smile, like she didn't quite believe me. But she accepted the answer for what it was, watching as I paid and rose to leave.

"Whatever happens, I'm grateful for the time we got to have together," she said suddenly, her tone soft.

I turned to her as we left the restaurant together. "Why are you talking like this?"

She shrugged as we walked side by side, taking the long way home. "It just dawned on me. I lost you once, and I'm not dumb enough to think it couldn't happen again. You were always destined for things greater than this podunk town, Callie."

I didn't know what to say, so I chose silence. I wondered what was going through her head and if my parents felt the same way. Why refer to me as my legally changed name rather than my birth-given name, despite what I had just said? Everyone else here—including Leah, most of the time—called me Callie-Ann, because that's who I was to them.

Callie-Ann Eden, protecting and serving Springcrest.

Maybe I wasn't doing a good enough job of reassuring my family.

The thought weighed heavily on me as we continued on in silence.

Six

Liam

I dangled my hands between my legs, gazing out at New York City from the skyscraper I now worked in—NYPD's Major Crime Division. This division was located on the twenty-third story of a government building, towering over the smaller businesses and apartment buildings below. My office had an entire wall of windows and a wicked view of the city.

A soft rap on the door drew my attention away from the view. My assistant poked her head in and gave me a tentative smile. "Hey, Sarge. Alejandro Ramirez's husband is here."

I was still adjusting to the new title, even though it had been a few months. *Sergeant Liam Chandler.* A detective sergeant in Major Crimes. It was technically two promotions rolled into one, thanks to the help of some higher-up connections I had made over the years—my former boss and old family friend, Terry Levinsky, included. Not entirely unheard of, but my test results were high enough that government officials were willing to make an exception for me to transfer back to the NYPD despite their current hiring freeze.

I waved Krishna in, my gaze snagging on the white picture frame that adorned my glass and steel desk. Callie's blue eyes stared back at me, happy and glowing. She and I were each holding a champagne flute in the air, posing for the picture. The magical moments just before I broke her heart for the first time… after I realized I was in love with her. The photograph was an ever-present reminder to not take the good things in life for granted.

My chest squeezed, and I rubbed a palm over it, hoping it would minimize the pain.

It didn't.

But at least I was able to think of her name without wanting to drink to forget. That was progress, right? Eventually I would have to move on.

The door opened again, and a tall gentleman with straight black hair and dark eyes sauntered in. His shoulders sank as though he already knew the news I was about to break to him. I fought to keep a straight face and moved to stand in front of him. These conversations never got easier, and in fact they were arguably one of the biggest burdens of this job.

I took a deep breath and delivered the heart-wrenching results of the investigation: his husband died of asphyxiation and had been stabbed thirty-two times postmortem by a close friend. And there was nothing he could have done to save his husband.

* * *

Tracing my fingers over the photograph once more, like I did every night, I left my office. The elevator was empty—a rarity in a busy place like New York. The ride down was long and solemn. I closed my eyes and took a deep breath, to just be… present.

I too often lived in the past these days.

It was hard not to when I was in this city, when my old friends lived across town and my parents were upstate. New York wasn't quite what it had been before I moved to Newark, the familiarity of it having dissipated the moment I left to begin with, like a vapor in the wind.

It didn't feel like home anymore.

If I was being honest, I missed the coziness of Newark. I may have made comments to Callie about disliking her small city, but it had started to feel like home.

But I had left there, too, just to make the heartache a little easier.

No, I had actually left because I was a coward and didn't want to face the aftermath of my own actions.

As I stepped out into the humid summer evening—courtesy of the Hudson River—my heart yearned for the life I had all those months ago. The friends, the work partner, the woman I fell in love with. The future I may have had was nothing but a pipe dream now.

My feet carried me through the bustling city as my mind wandered. What was Callie doing tonight? Who was she with? Was she in as much pain as I was, or… had she moved on? Did she have new friends, a new job, a new life?

As much as I didn't want to, I thought about her often. She was still the bane of my existence, and if given the opportunity again, I would tell her just that. I'd tell her everything.

Like how all my mistakes haunted me, and how I also ruined myself when I ruined her. Or how sorry I was for failing her when I gave up on her case—*our* case—and gave it to her best friend when I left that job only a matter of weeks after she did. All because I couldn't endure the constant reminders of her.

I would tell her I loved her. Would *always* love her.

I slowed as a familiar glossy brown head of hair came around the corner, that captivating smile stretching from ear to ear. My breath hitched, and suddenly I was hyper aware of the sweat rolling down my spine, the stagnant air that clung to me. I raked a hand through my hair, hoping that it was enough to make me look presentable.

She's here. Why is she here? Did I manifest this?

She hated it here. She—

I blinked hard, face crinkling with the effort. When I reopened my eyes, she was gone, replaced by rippling air. People shoved past me on the street in true New York fashion, causing me to stumble. It was just a heat wave, and my desperate imagination was manipulating my vision.

That gave me an excuse to stop at the nearest liquor store and mindlessly grab a bottle of *something*, understanding now more than ever why Callie had turned to alcohol when she wanted to forget, be numb, not cope. I was abusing it the way she had, and I didn't have anyone to hold me accountable.

In those early weeks after she left, I was a less than honorable man, sleeping around as much as I could, becoming the very thing I hated when I was younger: a man-whore. I had even told her at one point that I was *not* that.

After a couple of months of attempting to curb my loneliness with meaningless women, one of my previous hook-ups approached me in a bar when I was talking to another woman, splashing her drink in my face.

It was a startling realization of the path I'd gone down. So, I cleaned up my act and refocused on my career.

I could deal with being alone every night if the world was at least a little bit fuzzy.

I may never be the man she deserved, and I may never be the man she called hers at the end of the day, but at least I was doing something for myself.

Seven

Callie

I bit into my chocolate croissant, struggling to balance my cup of coffee, purse, and phone as I did so. A group of teenagers rushed by me and I sidestepped to avoid a catastrophic tumble. I wanted to roll my eyes at them, but I had to keep a straight face in this small town. I couldn't let anyone see Sergeant Callie-Ann Eden losing her cool.

God forbid I have any negative emotions in public.

Sometimes I missed the bold, moody woman I was allowed to be in Newark. One that could express what she was feeling whenever she wanted.

The crowd separated as I made my way down the sidewalk. I did my usual smiling and greeting the townsfolk, when something familiar caught my eye. Nearly choking, I craned my neck to get a clearer view, and sure enough, across the town square sitting outside the other café in town, was none other than Owen Fisher.

My ex. I'd recognize that mop of curly hair anywhere.

He was angled away from me, the smallest bit of his profile visible.

I halted in my tracks, blood freezing in my veins and skin going cold despite the hot summer morning. For a moment I forgot to breathe. I forgot who I was, where I was—all I could remember was what my life was like five months ago.

Trapped in a toxic, albeit fake, engagement. Hunting a serial killer. Pining over an emotionally unavailable man. Depressed. Suffering from alcohol abuse. Pushing away everyone who tried to help.

The past made my breath strangle in my throat, threatening to close my airway just like Owen once tried to do with his bare hands.

But that was all before I found myself back in my small hometown. Which begged the question: why was he here, and what did he want from me?

My phone buzzed in my hand, breaking me from my reverie. I snapped my attention to the screen and saw it was a text from the Chief, telling me to meet him at Fountain Park as soon as possible. I hesitated, keeping Owen in my line of sight as I opened my camera, snapped a few photos, and headed through town.

* * *

I ducked under the police tape, astonished that there was a murder to solve in Springcrest. The little bit of crime we got here mostly dealt with robberies and the occasional drug problem, petty theft, drunk and disorderliness, animal abuse calls, and the rare domestic abuse case.

But never homicide.

Ferguson stood near the body. A dreadful feeling settled over me with every step closer. The scene unfolded before my eyes, my heart dropping to my knees and bile rising in my throat. One of the officers I oversaw, Paulette Genaro, handed me a file.

I warily took it from her, resisting—refusing—to look at the crime scene behind her until I had all the facts. I could see the body from where I was standing, and I wasn't ready to relive this. Not yet.

"What's this?" I questioned as I scanned her paperwork. My heart lurched at the handwritten report, already prepared for me per my specific instructions.

"I've never seen anything quite like this, ma'am. It's… unique. Gruesome. Doesn't seem like his first attempt at killing someone," Genaro informed me. I swallowed. *Because it's not.* "It was called in a few hours ago. Dirk and

I responded to the call, so we secured the scene and waited for everyone else to arrive. I just finished my preliminary report."

I flipped the pages. Each sentence solidified my theory more and more. *Fuck, fuck, fuck.* "Shit," I swore under my breath, my mouth going dry. "No sign of the killer?"

Genaro shook her head, her brown curls bouncing in her high ponytail. "None. Aside from the witnesses who found her, there was no one to be seen."

I rubbed my forehead. "Damn it. *Fuck.*" My head was spinning. I was suddenly regretting that croissant and sugary coffee.

How could this be? How—

"Are you okay, ma'am?"

I cleared my throat and gave Genaro a tight smile. "I'm fine. Thank you for this." I nodded at her once before willing myself to walk in the direction of the body. By the time I was standing next to the victim, I was certain my insides had twisted themselves into pretzel shapes.

"Hey, Dweeben, snap a pic of me next to this chick," Ferguson said as I came to a stop next to him. He shoved his phone in my face.

"This is a corpse, Dale. A *corpse.* Have some damn respect," I reprimanded, pushing his phone away from me.

He laughed. "It's not every day you see a dead body. Come on. Don't be such a stuck-up."

My hand curled into a fist at my side. "The answer is no. Please try to focus—" I was cut off before I could finish when he snorted and held his phone out to one of his beat cops.

Unfortunately, this officer looked up to Ferguson and his inappropriate, misogynistic behavior as if it were the only way to live. "Dweeben, she was a prostitute *and* an addict who lived south of the tracks and had a massive gambling debt," he said, as if that justified her death, and by association, his actions. "It's not like she went to heaven." He squatted to pose beside the poor woman's dead body as the beat cop snapped a plethora of photos of Ferguson in different poses.

I contemplated emptying the contents of my stomach on him. I was at my wit's end with him, especially when it came to this behavior. My lips peeled back from my teeth in a snarl as I retorted, "That doesn't make her any less *human,* Dale. She still had friends and family, not to mention her two sons."

Another snort. "And how do you know that?"

I took a deep, calming breath. *Composure, Eden. Keep it together.*

"Seriously? You didn't look at the report Genaro wrote up? It's all in here." I waved the file in front of him.

He shrugged nonchalantly, as if we were discussing whether or not he should've worn a jacket today. "Great, that's what she's there for. Now I'm here assessing it for myself."

"How would you feel if your children lost their dad this way?"

Dale stood, taking notes in his notepad as I spoke. "If I died this way, then I failed as a parent. Plain and simple. God, Dweeben, you're particularly uptight today. Are you menstruating?"

Oh. My. God.

My face heated in anger. "You are equal parts idiot and asshole. Genaro could do your job better in her sleep."

He chuckled, looking over his aviators. "Oddly enough, people still like me around here. Not sure how you got here, though. You're so young, pretty. How many dicks did you have to suck?"

"Watch it—"

"Oh, that's right," he interrupted, snapping his fingers like he just had an epiphany. "Just your old partner's. Lucky motherfucker. You can suck mine any time."

My breath hitched. I paused to scrutinize him, taking in his demeanor and facial expression. Yep. He definitely knew. But how the hell did he know about—

"Nice one," the beat cop complimented, holding up a fist for a fist bump which Dale quickly reciprocated with a cocky grin.

"What? No snarky remark to that?"

Glowering at him, I growled, "Keep your nose out of my personal life."

"But you aren't denying it? I watched a press conference of you and

Detective Liam Chandler," Dale said coolly, circling me.

I stilled as I heard his name. This case, the reminders of Liam, it was too much, too fast—

"He's a handsome guy. I see why you couldn't keep it in your pants. Did he put in a call here to get you a promotion?"

I whirled on him, shoving a finger in his face. "Back off, Ferguson. Whatever you think you know, you don't. Don't push me."

He just laughed, those cold, dark eyes glittering with amusement. The bastard was getting off on this. "Next thing you're going to say was that it wasn't an affair. You guys were in love. Yet you came running back home to mommy and daddy when things got hard. It's like the plot to a bad movie."

Feelings of fury, embarrassment, and shame wrapped their claws around me. How he knew these things about me, I wasn't sure. But to flaunt this information in public? That was a new low, even for a snake like him. I was mortified—but I had to save face somehow.

Squaring my shoulders, I quietly responded with, "No. We weren't in love. But I was. And then the man I was engaged to nearly strangled me to death, and I almost let him because I wanted to die. Eventually I fought back, and you know why?" I paused to let my words sink in. The smirk slowly melted off Dale's face.

"Because I was in love with another man. One who gave me hope. I saw a future with him, even if he couldn't with me. If it hadn't been for Liam, I probably wouldn't be standing here annoying the shit out of you today. You think I ran home because things got *hard?* A man laid his hands on me, and I let him almost kill me, and the man I ran to didn't want me. I was depressed and addicted to getting drunk to cope. So, yeah, I came back here, Dale. To save my goddamn life."

When I finished, I shoved past both him and the beat cop to look at our victim. I flicked my eyes over her; I knew her. She went to a different high school than I did, but we graduated the same year. People always said we looked similar.

Cheyenne Womack. Twenty-five years old. Divorced with two kids.

My throat constricted as I squatted beside her. She did, indeed, have fresh track marks in the crook of her elbow, bringing with it a hint of sadness, a twinge of horror.

Even though she was a prostitute with a drug addiction, that wasn't her cause of death. She was a victim of something much darker, much worse, much more terrifying. From the awkward tilt of her neck—her throat decorated with small bruises—to the ragged white gown she wore, it was clear as day who killed her.

Somehow, and for some reason, he was chasing me.

The Wring Bearer had come to Springcrest, and I had led him here.

Eight

Liam

Scrolling on social media while drinking is never a good idea.

I knew this, even as I sipped my glass of cheap whiskey while sprawled on my living room couch with the news on, eyeing my phone with temptation. The whiskey was far from enjoyable, but I didn't drink scotch anymore—correction, I couldn't drink scotch anymore.

Caving, I opened Facebook for the first time in months, wondering if Callie ever deleted me off it. When she left, I tried calling and texting her many times, but she had rightfully blocked my number.

I respected her enough to not attempt contact through social media, even though it killed me. She deserved to move on in peace.

I scrolled past pointless posts, selfies, and ads before finally typing her name in. Her profile was the first one to pop up. My heart skittered to a stop. It showed we were still friends.

I nearly dropped my glass from the force of throwing myself forward, trying to focus my blurry gaze on her profile picture.

She looked so breathtaking, so… happy. Her skin was bronzed, her cheeks rosy, her eyes glittering, and her smile wide. She sat on the edge of a fountain, the background not giving away her location, grinning fondly at the person snapping the photo. I wondered if she had met someone else—jealousy instantly tugged on my heartstrings.

My fingers itched to message her, but that wasn't fair of me. She was moving on. The last thing she needed was for me to pop up after months of silence.

Fuck this.

I groaned audibly and stumbled into my bathroom. My apartment here was smaller, older, and not as updated as the one in Newark, but I guess it could be considered homey. I often missed the extra space, though, and the chic, minimalist design of my previous apartment.

One look in the bathroom mirror had me flinching. My facial hair had grown out quite a bit, and was just groomed enough to be acceptable in the workplace. Strands of my hair tumbled forward, and the dark circles under my eyes were as permanent as tattoos at this point. My skin needed sun exposure but I hadn't cared to get out and actually do anything besides make it to the precinct.

I crawled into bed, returning to Callie's profile picture to remind myself that she had moved on, and therefore so should I.

I fell asleep looking at her smile.

Nine

Callie

I sprinted the five blocks from Fountain Park to the entrance of a hiking trail about half a mile away, hair flying behind me wildly. My stomach churned with the urge to vomit. If it didn't come out now, surely it would later.

Just after I had retrieved a small note from Cheyenne Womack's mouth—scribbled with the letters *EN*—we got a call that there was another body. I had all but shoved the bagged evidence into Genaro's hands; I trusted no one else to care for it properly. I tore off my gloves and shoe covers and took off running.

No time wasted.

I was there before someone could say "Catch me if you can."

I immediately caught sight of the slumped over male body and the young couple off to the side clutching each other as they gaped in horror. Coming to a screeching halt about twenty feet from them, my chunky-heeled sandals barely giving me enough traction to remain upright, I surveyed the scene before pulling on another set of shoe covers and gloves.

I carefully tiptoed over to the couple, my breaths coming out short and clipped from my sprint. I politely asked them to step back so I could secure the area until backup arrived, no more than a few minutes later. I spent those few minutes reassuring the frightened teenagers that everything would be alright and that we would handle it, doing my best to ask them questions as I did.

The girl kept sobbing that they were simply trying to go on a romantic hike together while on summer break before the boy finally locked eyes with me. He was putting on a strong front for his girlfriend, but his lower lip trembled when he spoke and his face was pale. He told me they had just arrived when they saw the body. They had called 911 right away.

That's it.

That's all the information they had.

The swell of disappointment was inevitable. The victim's skin still had color, so he hadn't been dead for long. I was so close and yet still too late.

Damn it.

Once the area was taped off, I walked over to the young man's corpse, dressed in a cheap tuxedo and decorated with fresh bruises. He was slouched against a rock, his head hanging limply over his shoulder and mouth wide open, revealing none other than a damp piece of paper. I reached in and pulled it out.

EI.

I swore under my breath. *What are you spelling, Leemore?*

Always a step ahead of me.

My pulse quickened as dread set in, forcing me to rock back on my heels as a shadow appeared over me. I didn't have to look up to know who it was.

"Gnarly," Dale said with a chuckle. "One hell of a wedding night, if it has anything to do with the last one."

So much for getting through to him with my confession.

I pursed my lips and shot him a dirty look. My resentment grounded me, prevented me from going off the deep end.

"Do you watch the news at all, dumbass?"

He held his hands up defensively. "Whoa, Nelly. Why are you so riled up? Try getting laid every once in a while."

My teeth clenched so hard my jaw ached. I wanted nothing more than to punch him in the nuts so hard he wouldn't be able to reproduce again.

"This has nothing to do with my personal life, Dale. I'm referring to the very distinct M. O. of these murders."

He rolled his eyes. "I don't see what the problem is here. He's already dead, M. O. aside."

I shook my head. How did this guy even get his credentials?

I supposed it was easy to forget about his lack of exposure to homicide and his overall incompetence when it came to actually doing work. Crime in Springcrest was often so menial that grisly cases like this meant law enforcement was woefully underprepared.

Plus, who knows, maybe Dale Ferguson was young and ambitious back in the day, and he just got comfortable in the job without caring about improving his bedside manners.

I shifted the victim's body to reveal the wedding band I knew would be there and waved a photographer over. After they snapped a few photos, I plucked the ring off the ground, the morning light gleaming off it.

Dale's eyes widened. "How did you know that would be there?"

"Because I'm really fucking good at my job." I dropped the ring into an evidence bag. "That, and I've seen this M. O. before. This case has been reported on nationwide news outlets. Killer's been at large for months. This is the work of a serial killer nicknamed 'The Wring Bearer,' but his real name is Vincent Leemore. Previously convicted of aggravated assault of his former fiance's lover."

A familiar rush of adrenaline flooded my veins. It was a sensation that had been missing since I left Newark, and one I feared I had left behind for good. This was the kind of work that made me feel alive, made me feel like I was making a difference.

Dale merely snickered. "These are drug-related cases, honey. The homicide was just a fun perk."

A fun perk.

Dale Ferguson specialized in narcotic crimes. It made sense his monkey brain wouldn't see past that.

"No, these are the victims of a serial killer," I repeated. "The drugs are a…" I paused, damn near choking on the word I spoke next, "coincidence.

They were easy targets because of the part of town they were from. These are… these were to get my attention."

"And what makes you think you're so special, honey?"

Truth be told, part of me hoped I wasn't special and that this was maybe even a copycat killer.

I knew better than that, though.

I cocked my head to the side and rose to my feet. "You've asked me countless times before what makes me so uptight. This was the first case I took on when I became a detective, but it went cold. My former partner and I reopened the case, and shortly after, the murders started up again. Turns out I met the killer by accident. He began taunting me by killing women who looked like me."

Ferguson blanched and awkwardly shoved his hands in his pockets. "Callie-Ann, I had no idea."

Finally, a breakthrough.

Taken aback by the use of my first name—after all, he was only one of a few who called me anything but Callie-Ann in this town—I murmured, "If you spent a little less time provoking me and a little more time getting to know me, you would've known this months ago." I looked at the victim's body, my stomach knotting once more as I realized what I had to do.

"I need to go write my reports. You know where to find me." I sauntered off the crime scene, having seen all I needed to.

* * *

I typed my notes furiously into my report, pausing only when I had to pull out my old work notepad from Newark. It was intentionally tucked away at the bottom of my desk drawer, for emergency use only. I flipped through the pages until I found the previous letters stuffed into victims' mouths.

EC. AD. LL.

And now, today's: *EI. EN.*

EC. AD. LL. EI. EN.

My eyes flitted over the letters, something in them as familiar as the back of my hand. Something spoke to me, something—

I gasped, my pen clattering to the floor. I pushed back from my desk as if the notes were on fire and ignored the concerned looks from the few officers in the building. One hand flew to my mouth at the realization—seemingly so random when we first discovered the pieces of paper at the crime scenes.

It was glaringly obvious now.

All these people killed, necks snapped as if it took hardly any strength, and it was all directed at me.

Me.

I clutched my chest, my heart trying to claw its way free of my rib cage. I was somehow hot and cold all at once as the revelation threatened to make me sick.

And then… then an image rose to the surface of my mind.

One I had forgotten about as I got swept up in a double homicide in Springcrest—a town where rarely anything changed, where the same faces greeted me every day, where I was slowly beginning to feel at home again.

But today? Today had started differently.

"No," I mumbled to myself. I *wanted* to be in denial. "No, it can't be."

I lunged for my phone, my fingers trembling as I opened the photos app and tapped on the most recent photo, confirming that today I had, in fact, spotted my ex in the town square. He hadn't seen me, but I had seen him. I had even stopped in my tracks out of fear as I recalled the most miserable year of my life. I sank back into my chair before my knees gave out.

No.

Glancing once more at the letters as the pieces fell into place, every single piece of evidence, every shred of doubt I ever had suddenly coming to light, I choked on a sob.

It had never been Vincent Leemore. He ran because we were chasing him for no reason and he didn't want to be incarcerated again. He wasn't responsible for these murders at all. He didn't even have a reason to come after me. But—

Those stupid fucking letters rearranged themselves, the message clearer than ever: *CALLIE EDEN.*

Ten

Callie

My hands were clasped in front of me to conceal their trembling while the Chief reviewed my case. He arched a brow at me as he flipped through each page. My mouth dried when he set the file down and turned his eyes to me.

"You're absolutely certain, Callie-Ann?"

My heart lurched. I wished he'd call me by my title: *Sergeant.* Or at the very least, *Callie.* Callie-Ann was endearing at first, but I left that woman behind when I first fled this town and all its hurtful secrets—not unlike how I left Newark.

Damn. Maybe running away from my problems was becoming a problem.

"I wouldn't be so adamant about this if I weren't. I have Genaro requesting a federal background check on him and everything we know about his existence."

He heaved a sigh as he lifted up one of the pages again, cringing. It must be one of the crime scene photos. "And you don't want any company?"

I shook my head. "No, sir. There's no sense in putting anyone else in harm's way if I'm the only one being targeted. I'll remain in close contact with you until I get there."

He puffed out his cheeks and closed the file. "Fine, but I'm sending someone in a few days once this is in the right hands. It gives you enough time to lure him there, but then I'll have another set of eyes there."

"Sir—"

"That's final. My leniency only goes so far, especially since I need to make sure you'll be okay. Not just as one of my few sergeants, but for your family."

My family.

I conceded and agreed to his conditions, leaving only once I got signed permission to depart the next day.

Back home, I found my parents and siblings sitting in the living room chit-chatting over glasses of wine. I hated that I was disrupting this moment—they all seemed happy and at peace.

My brother's eyes widened when he saw me, alerting the rest of my family to my presence. They looked at me with concern, and I realized they had heard about the double homicide.

"I'm fine. It's nothing I'm not used to," I assured them, and joined them all on the couch. A glass of wine sounded… refreshing. But this was not the optimal time to break my sobriety, so I shoved the thought aside as I looked at each of them individually.

My dad, who forced me to go outside for fresh air in those initial weeks home and distracted me as much as he could. My mom, who tended to my wounds—both physical and emotional—and let me weep as much as I needed to. My sister, who coerced me into exercising and putting myself back out there despite my pushback. My brother, who continued to pick on me just to give me a hard time, to give me a sense of normalcy while I healed.

They saved me when I thought I was beyond repair.

I had taken them for granted in recent years because I didn't want to return to this place. The very same place that had saved me when I needed it most.

I swallowed the lump in my throat and told them my plan, promising I would be back as soon as possible. That promise was the only thing that kept me from crying—the only thing that gave me the strength to go upstairs and pack my bags.

* * *

A quiet knock came from my open bedroom door, my sister's silhouette filling the frame. I quickly wiped away the tears that were steadily streaming down my face. It was pointless though; my eyes were swollen, my nose red.

Leah's eyes were sad.

I broke down again. Maybe this whole plan was foolish, maybe—

"Don't, Callie," she said gently, as if reading my mind. "Don't go there. Don't turn back now. This is everything you've been working toward."

I shook my head. It was about leaving my family behind after I spent so much time repairing my relationships with them. It was about returning to Newark as a new person. It was about facing what I had left behind and accepting what had happened with Liam. It was about how I had shared a home with a serial killer and was one step away from being the next victim.

"I'm scared, Leah," I admitted, my sobs quieting.

She sat down on the bed beside me. "I can't imagine a world where you wouldn't be. You're going back into the lion's den. And it's okay to be afraid of it all."

I sniffled.

"Besides," Leah continued, slinging an arm around my shoulders, "who else deserves to slap Liam across the face for what he did?"

I laughed, and for a brief moment, the memory of it all wasn't piercing my heart.

"That's true."

Leah giggled before her face turned serious once more. "I think we all always knew that something would summon you back there. And when you do get back to the city, you'll realize it's where you belong."

I bumped my shoulder against hers, my tears subsiding.

"I wish I could promise you that I'll come back here," I whispered, thinking of our conversation the night before.

Sighing, she said, "I know, but you can't let yourself make more empty promises. There will always be some form of disappointment if you do that."

"You're right. Thank you." At the cock of her head, I added, "For talking me through this."

"Crying isn't a weakness. Stop pushing people out. You need to accept help. It may have taken you a while to get there, but the point is that you got there."

She was completely right.

Eleven

Callie

My nerves were shot after the four-hour drive back to Newark. Looking into my rearview mirror every few seconds, as if Owen would magically appear in the car behind me, made me restless. He never did, and even if he had, I was armed with multiple weapons.

Not that that had ever stopped him from trying to come after me before.

I was parked in front of the Third Precinct, clambering out with as much grace as a newborn calf. My legs weakened further when I craned my neck to look at the building before me.

Still made of white marble, still bustling with officers, still surrounded by the noise of the city—it was all as familiar as my own mother's voice. I closed my eyes, trying to focus on the sound of passing cars, the rustling of the trees planted alongside the sidewalks, the chattering of citizens, the radio chatter from police cars. The smell of fresh coffee and pastries and flowers, yet still the indescribable and distinct smell of the city.

A shaky breath tore through me, and then—

A girlish scream sounded from the top of the steps that led into the precinct. My eyes shot open, my mouth stretching into a wide grin as I spotted my dearest friend. Her raven black hair shimmered in the sunlight, her slender body clad in a black jumpsuit—her signature color.

Sophie raced down the stairs, nearly knocking me back as she threw her arms around my neck. I let out a surprised laugh as I folded her into a tight embrace. I'd only seen her once since I left; she visited me in Springcrest to prepare me for my interview, and frankly it had been too long.

She pulled back, happy tears glimmering in her dark eyes. "I can't believe you're actually here, *chula.*"

My smile melted into a sheepish half-grin. "Temporarily," I corrected.

She cast her eyes skyward. "Right. *Temporarily.*" She giggled and looped her arm through mine, prepared to guide me up the stairs, but I halted, looking up at the building once more.

There was a sudden roaring in my ears as all the air whooshed from my lungs. For a few deep breaths I could only hear my own inhale and exhale. Was I really ready? Was I prepared to face—

"Whenever you're ready, Cal," Sophie murmured.

Cal.

My throat tightened as the nickname sunk in. *My* name. The name I had earned through the friendships I'd made here in Newark. Not Callie-Ann.

Maybe it was stupid. It was just a name. But it was also my identity.

I tilted my chin up. "I am." My voice was resolute. No more hesitation. I was ready for this.

We walked up the steps together, arms around each other's shoulders. When we reached the top, I stepped out of her half-embrace and reached for the doors myself. I needed this moment—this *I'm a new person and I've healed from all the bullshit* moment. I yanked the doors open, the force blowing my hair back in a model-like fashion as I entered the Third Precinct.

The booking clerks looked at me; I recognized them both and gave them a wide smile as I passed.

Sophie followed, hot on my heels as I made my way through the building. Just before we entered the bullpen, my phone blared from my purse. I stopped abruptly, realizing I was slightly breathless from my power walk as I pulled my phone out. Genaro's name was on the screen.

"Tell me good things, Genaro," I said by way of greeting.

She gave me a nervous laugh. Oh no. "Well, the good news is that the background check came back, but we're having an issue with the fax machine and scanner. The repair guy won't be here until tonight, so we won't be able to get the documents over until the morning."

I closed my eyes. Leave it to a crappy small town to fuck up sending over something as simple as a background check. "No problem. Thanks for the update." I hung up and glanced at Sophie. "Slight change of plans. There's an issue with their scanner, so we may have to delay the meeting until tomorrow. I can fill in some details today."

Sophie patted my cheek endearingly. I almost rolled my eyes at her antics. "Take your time."

I winked and proceeded to enter the bullpen. I missed the constant energy that seemed to buzz through this place. And as I surveyed the room, my eyes settled on Terry's assistant, Hailey, who was beaming and waving at me. I simpered and made my way to her.

"Is he in there?"

Hailey nodded and told me it was great to see me before shooing me and Sophie in.

Terry glanced up, then returned to his paperwork before doing a double take; as if he didn't quite process that it was me in his doorway. I didn't tell him I was coming, and if I was being honest, it was because I had a gut feeling he would insist I stay in Springcrest and have someone come to me.

I wasn't going to subject my family to that.

And also, maybe a small—*teeny, tiny*—part of me, wanted to come back.

"Callie?" He jumped to his feet and pulled me into a tight, father-like embrace. I let out a breathy chuckle as I returned the hug. "Sophie, did you know she would be here today?"

"I only found out yesterday, sir. She wanted to keep it on the DL." I could hear the smile in her voice.

Terry looked at me with wide eyes, wonder sparkling in them. "What are you doing here?"

"It's work-related," I admitted.

Understanding washed over him, his expression turning cool and calculated. "The Garrison case?"

I dipped my chin in response. "You know I wouldn't be here if it wasn't important. Not after everything that happened…" I loosed a heavy breath, "with Liam."

"He's not here anymore," Sophie murmured, voice laced with quiet concern.

My head whipped to pin her with an incredulous look. "He's not?"

She shook her head. "He moved back to New York."

I opened my mouth to respond, but snapped it shut again. I spent hours preparing myself to face him, to see him again, to have to say his name God knows how many times… I blinked back both my relief and disappointment.

I didn't realize I would feel either of those things.

My brain started working again. "When did that happen?"

"A few weeks after you left. Three, maybe four weeks. He works in Major Crimes now," Terry told me.

"Sergeant Liam Chandler," Sophie muttered under her breath. I could sense the bitterness rolling off her in waves. *What happened?*

My brain jolted at hearing my best friend so casually drop his new title, enough to rattle me for a moment. Sergeant in Major Crimes? That was a huge promotion… one that shouldn't even be possible.

It wasn't my place to judge. After all, that was my title now, too, even if it was overseeing a smaller staff in a tiny town.

Fighting to keep my reaction at bay, I offered a single nod in acquiescence.

"Well, I never thought I would say this after what transpired," I muttered in a slow drawl, "but I'll need him here to debrief everyone. And I only want to explain this once, so it's probably best I wait until he's here to brief you guys."

They both looked at me as if I was insane.

As if he hadn't shattered my heart and caused my life to fall apart a handful of months ago.

Terry hitched a thumb over his shoulder. "Want me to call him?"

I shook my head, already making up my mind. "No. I'll go get him, stay overnight in a hotel, and come back in the morning. The paperwork won't be here until tomorrow anyway, and he and I should probably set some parameters before we strike up any sort of work relationship again."

Sophie let out a sound eerily like a yelp. I gave her a sidelong glance. "Do you want me to come with you? I can be a buff—"

"No," I interjected with finality. "I'm a big girl. I've done a lot of growing up; I've healed and moved on. I appreciate your concern and discretion with the severity of the situation, but I assure you both that I can handle this just fine." I shot them both an admonishing look when they exchanged nervous glances.

They relented. Not like they had much of a choice.

* * *

After checking into my hotel room, I couldn't help but worry about my appearance. What kind of woman would Liam see after all these months? And why did I even care?

I endured so much, saw too much shit, almost let myself die at the hands of another man, and had to learn to cope with all of that. I wasn't the same person I was a year ago—hell, six months ago.

Maybe I wanted to prove a point: he fucking wrecked me, derailed my life, and I bounced back like a motherfucking *queen.*

Straightening my pale blue blazer and matching dress shorts and adjusting the straps of my white bodysuit, I was ready. I gathered my purse, spritzed myself with perfume, and tousled my hair so it looked fresh and voluminous. Then I headed out to walk to Liam's building.

It was late in the afternoon, and I hoped I wasn't too late. Sophie confirmed his schedule, but for all I knew, he could be out on a case and not in the office.

Fuck if I knew anything about his life anymore.

Humid air greeted me as I stepped outside, my baby hairs curling on the nape of my neck. My heels—stilettos, as was appropriate for the city, and a welcome change from the chunky sandal heels I wore in Springcrest— clacked on the sidewalk as I made my way down the few blocks that separated us.

I tried focusing on anything but that, and I was doing a decent job of it until I came to a stop in front of his building. Suddenly I was thankful I had used my vibrator to settle some of my nerves. And if I was completely honest with myself, it was also to get ahead of any wayward hormones that might threaten to bubble to the surface when I saw him again.

After all, I knew myself when it came to him—knew my body's inevitable reactions to his mere presence, and I definitely knew I could very well be doomed if I didn't at least try to get a handle on my libido before seeing him again.

I don't need sex. I don't need a man. All I need is myself.

I pulled the tall glass doors open and welcomed the air conditioning on my suddenly flushed skin. Okay, maybe part of me regretted using my trusty vibrator, because as I strolled to the security guard stationed in the entrance, I felt a slight wobble in my knees.

I pressed forward anyway, refusing to talk myself out of this just to have Sophie come save me.

One step at a time.

I was directed to the twenty-third floor. I held my breath as the elevator doors slid shut and my stomach released an entire flood of butterflies. I wanted to throw up the small salad I had eaten earlier.

The elevator came to a smooth stop. My breath mangled in my throat as the doors opened.

Here goes.

Twelve

Liam

"Sarge, I need you to sign off on this report before I take off for my weekend," one of my detectives, Brookins, told me as she handed me a file.

I raised an eyebrow at her before taking the pen and file from her grasp. Brookins was a decade older than me, and I knew she hated that a twenty-eight-year-old man was now the one signing off on all her reports, even though she'd been serving on the force for fifteen years.

But maybe I was just jaded since she had a constant attitude with me.

I quickly scanned her report to check for any errors or potential holes in her version of events, asking questions as I went. As soon as I finished signing my name, Krishna scurried around the corner, wringing her hands nervously.

"Sir, there's a sergeant from the Newark Police Division here to see you."

My ears perked up at this tidbit of information. *Newark?* I wondered who it could be before it hit me—*Sophie.* Even though we had a strained relationship these days, we still checked up on each other from time to time. She'd never shown up at my office, though, so my palms pricked with sweat at the idea of her visit being in regards to the Garrison case.

But Sophie wasn't a sergeant, so maybe Krishna misheard.

I gestured to the receptionist entryway she stood in. She looked like she wanted to say more, but I didn't let her. "Bring her in." I turned back to Brookins.

"Ms. Krishna didn't say they were a she," she snarled.

I picked up my glass water bottle off her desk as I snapped the file shut and thrust it back at her. "All good, Brookins."

She snatched the file back with a grumbled thanks.

I bit my tongue. I was cranky and irritated today.

But all that changed a second later, when I heard a lilting, feminine voice pipe up from behind me.

"Hey there, stranger."

I froze for the briefest of seconds before whirling and pinning my gaze on the woman in the doorway Krishna had just vacated. I couldn't quite believe it.

After all, just yesterday I let the heat waves fool me into believing I saw her.

Surely I was once again being delusional. Maybe exhaustion had finally driven me to the brink of insanity, or maybe I missed her so badly that my brain decided to give me some reprieve by conjuring her up in a realistic form. Except, if that were the case, my brain wouldn't have changed so many details about her. Details I wouldn't know unless she was, in fact, standing mere feet from me.

Like how her hair was still that rich glossy brown, now streaked with golden highlights. The same, but different.

Or how her skin was sun-kissed and glowing, hydrated and healthy, rather than the pale and unwell color it was all those months ago. The same, but different.

Maybe it was her eyes? Still that striking blue that haunted me, but what was once guarded like a vault was now replaced with a sparkling fondness. It nearly brought me to my knees. The same... but different.

And suddenly I knew what it was with every fiber of my goddamn being.

It was her *smile.* Wide and contagious enough that I felt my own lips tug into a grin that I had started to think no longer existed. Her teeth caught the overhead lights, bright white and perfectly straight, and I noted that there were no signs of stress or tension bracketing her mouth. Only unbridled freedom, charisma, and joy.

It was just an unadulterated smile greeting me as if we ended things on a good note, and that did crazy things to my heart, like sending it into an uneven *pitter-patter* in my chest.

My water bottle slipped from my hand, colliding with the ground a second later. My brain hardly registered the water splashing onto the hems of my dress pants. It didn't matter, not with her standing fifteen feet from me.

Her smile never once faltered, her gaze glued to mine like she was just as happy to see me as I was to see her.

"Callie," I breathed, my voice hoarse and raw, like all those months of trying to forget meant nothing.

And they didn't. Not anymore. I would redo the past five awful months if I knew I would see her again.

I wasted no time—even though it had only been a few seconds—and rushed over to her. My shoes crunched through glass and water as I closed the distance between us, wrapping my arms around her, not caring about our history or what brought her to me or anything else in that moment. I only needed to feel her in my arms once more. I folded her into my chest and pressed my face into her hair, relishing the soft tresses that tickled my cheeks. She was warm and healthy in my arms. Every inch of me was on edge as I held her, her arms careful to avoid my weapons as she hugged me back.

I was aware of all the eyes on us, carefully watching the entire interaction, but I didn't give a single fuck.

My heart tumbled—she was laughing. Callie Eden was *laughing* as I picked her up and spun her around. The sound was so familiar yet so foreign.

I wanted to know everything that had happened in the last few months.

Setting her down, I managed to pull away just enough to look at her up close—really look at her. Her cheeks were tinged pink, lips pouty and glossy. Our proximity had her scent curling around me like a comfort blanket. Something about that citrusy, sweet, spicy scent filling my lungs. And good God, her summer wardrobe—

I blinked, forcing myself to take a single step away so I didn't get a hard-on at work. "What are you…?" I had to break my silence but I couldn't finish the question. I wasn't even convinced she was actually here. I wanted to ask her so many things, but I bit my tongue, not wanting to ruin the moment.

Callie's smile slipped; it made my stomach flip nervously. She tilted her head ever so slightly, her eyes dimming infinitesimally. "Sadly, it's not a personal visit."

That was all she needed to say. I knew what it was about: the only reason Callie would go to Newark or brave New York City just to find me after all that transpired, after months of being away… The understanding hung heavy between us.

I inclined my head toward my door. "Let's talk in my office."

She nodded solemnly. "Lead the way, Sergeant." There was a playful tone in her voice. I threw a wicked grin over my shoulder as I held my office door open for her. As it swung shut behind us, I said, "So, you have an update on Leemore?"

It sounded like such a casual question. How was that the topic I decided to open with the second I had her alone?

She hesitated as she glanced around my office, her eyes almost immediately falling on the white frame on my desk. Even though the photo faced away from her, I saw the recognition flare in her eyes before she turned her attention to the view before us.

"I do have an update on the case," she responded slowly, her voice wary. *No mention of Leemore.*

I stepped around her to stand by the windows. "Have you been working the case while you've been away?" Translation: *Where have you been?*

My curiosity was eating me alive. Her response could answer so many questions, like if she was seeing anyone, how she had been, what she was doing for work…

"No." The answer was instant, firm. "Not until yesterday."

I swung my head to look at her when I heard her heels clacking against the floor. Oh, how I missed the sound of those.

I mulled over her words—*yesterday.* Clearly she'd stayed close enough that she wasn't too far from the city.

Callie came to a stop next to me, close enough to be friendly but far enough to not be intimate. I resisted the urge to reach out and take her hand.

"Did you move back to Newark?" I blurted. I was curious since Krishna mentioned a… I sucked in a breath. "And are you also a sergeant now?"

A small smile graced her lips. "I moved back home to Springcrest, where I did get a promotion. I'm only in Newark for this case, and then I'm going back." Something in her voice told me she didn't completely believe herself—or maybe it was the tiniest of frowns on her face that gave it away.

I was shocked. From the many late nights she and I had spent together, I knew she hated that place. She had always wanted more for herself than what people there told her she was capable of. I recalled her despising everyone knowing every little detail of her life when all she wanted was privacy. It was part of why she never went home, even for holidays.

In many ways, I think that town was why Callie was the spitfire she turned out to be.

"I came here to bring you over to Newark. I need to brief everyone at the same time." Her voice went quiet, soft even, as she clasped her hands behind her back and peered down at the busy streets below. My skin prickled—I didn't like the sound of that. "I'll have all the details to fill everyone in by the morning."

I raised my eyebrows at her. As much as I wanted to say yes and take off from my job just to help her out for old times' sake, I couldn't risk my position without going through the legal motions to work in Newark—a different jurisdiction and state.

"My job—" I started to explain.

"Is already taken care of," she finished, her eyes meeting mine with a sincere, lopsided smile. So many sweet smiles in a short period of time. It was an unusual amount of friendliness from her. "Terry already contacted your Captain to explain the urgency and request your assistance. She approved it immediately."

"You didn't really leave me a choice then, did you?"

It was meant to be a joke, but she gave me a reprehensible look, as if she felt guilty for forcing my hand on this. I couldn't blame her. The last time she tried to force me into something, I broke her heart and royally fucked up a good thing.

But the truth was that I didn't have any remaining dignity when it came to her. And I would happily walk barefoot across a field of broken glass just to be shot down if it meant a chance to stand by her side one more time.

I would honor her and shower her with the praise she deserved, even if it was just as a friend.

I would do anything for her.

"I would've done it in a heartbeat anyway," I admitted softly when she didn't say anything. I felt vulnerable and… chagrined. Maybe a little ashamed at how I couldn't even put on a poker face to conceal my feelings. I despised how little I cared that I just played right into her hands, but I reveled in the comfort it brought me to be with her again. In whatever capacity.

And I knew she could see it all over my face.

Then those beautiful blue eyes flickered with something I struggled to pinpoint. Sadness? Remorse? No—something worse. *Much* worse.

Pity.

It was as though she knew that I hadn't moved on… that I would go back with her no matter what it was for. She was fully aware that I had broken myself as badly as I had her, perhaps beyond repair in my case, and would do anything for redemption.

The man staring back at her was somehow both exactly what she expected and the complete opposite—that much was apparent from the way she looked at me. I was a shell of the man she once knew and loved. The sarcasm was still there, sure, and maybe some of the wit. But… also as different as she was, and not entirely in a good way.

While she had grown from heartbreak into a beautiful and more confident version of herself, returning to the glory of the woman she was before life threatened to strangle her light, I had further shattered myself.

I didn't even know it was possible after my divorce. Between that and losing Callie, I had learned to heal in angles, reopening old wounds that refused to close properly, and was merely hanging on with Scotch tape and Band-Aids and Elmer's glue. Partially put back together like a patchwork quilt, whereas she had been finely sewed and repaired.

Heartache had done her a favor.

At least one of us had walked out of the fire. Now she looked like the sun itself.

I deserved to be the one at rock bottom, stumbling through the dark and withering away.

"I know," Callie croaked, her voice hoarse and equally quiet. "I thought maybe I was making this easier for you," she paused, taking a deep breath, "but really I think I was just finding ways to distract myself."

I was stunned at her honesty and willingness to be open.

There had been a point in time when we agreed on full transparency. I still didn't know when that changed.

My lips thinned. I didn't need her pity, and I certainly didn't want her feeling sorry for me. I bit back the urge to snap a snarky remark, the way we used to when we loved to hate each other. I had to remind myself not to be that man again. Our relationship—in whatever form—had evolved from that. And I would never treat her that way again.

"How are you holding up?" I probed. She may have been withholding information on the Garrison case, but she was still standing here, and I had to know she'd be okay with revisiting this thing… again.

Callie gave me a shy smile, one that stirred naughtier thoughts—thoughts I had to battle to push down. After all, we were alone in an office, together… wasn't that how our whole affair started?

Affair.

The word made it sound so wanton, but that's what it was.

All the sneaking around, the weeks of tension, the innuendos and butting heads… the list could go on. Unfortunately, if I didn't divert my thoughts now, I'd be feeling a lot more embarrassed.

I only hoped she couldn't see where my mind had wandered.

"As well as I can," was all she said before turning to face the city again. The somber note in her voice was enough to keep those thoughts at bay.

And suddenly all those women I used as a distraction, all the random fucks and one-night stands with hollow women, faded away. None of that existed in this moment with Callie Eden.

Thirteen

Liam

"I'm staying in a nearby hotel for the night," Callie told me as she continued to stare out at the horizon. "I was planning to leave here around seven in the morning to go back to Newark, if you want to join me."

My heart soared. "Sure. Where should—"

"I'm staying at the Harrison," she said before I could finish my question.

I couldn't help my lips curling upward. She always was one to plan ahead, quick to provide necessary information, be the one in control. Some things hadn't changed.

She tilted her head and looked at me curiously, finally tearing her gaze from the city. "What is that look for?"

With her blue eyes on me so intently, complimenting her pale blue blazer and matching shorts, white tank top, nude heels adorning her manicured feet…

I shrugged and managed to finally look away from her, sliding my hands into my pockets. I didn't tell her what was on my mind: that I loved how neurotic she could be, or how I was reminiscing on fond memories, or how fucking beautiful she was.

I knew I was putting myself out there when I said, "If you want, we can grab a drink and catch up. No strings attached. Just two… friends." The word made my stomach turn.

Her face dropped, and I instantly regretted asking. She quickly smoothed out her features. "I'm sober, Liam."

Liam. My name sounded like a love song on her lips.

God, she had turned me into such a fucking sap.

Wait. Sober?

"That's amazing, Callie. I'm so proud of you," I breathed, allowing myself to speak her name and relishing in how it didn't feel like razor blades on my tongue. My pride for her was stronger than the pain of her rejection.

The ghost of a smile graced those glossy lips of hers. Not like I was paying any attention to them.

"But dinner is a good start."

There was a wicked gleam in her eyes that told me she knew what she did to me.

I loosed a breath. "God, Callie, no need to kick a man while he's down," I teased, giving her my signature smile that I reserved only for her, dimples and all. One that hadn't made an appearance in a long, long time.

She snickered as her eyes drifted to my mouth for a fraction of a second before meeting my eyes again. "Meet me outside my hotel at eight." She started to turn, took a few steps toward the door, and then threw over her shoulder at me, "And if you're running late, you have my number."

All too soon she was at the door and my heart was slamming against my chest, urging me to stop her, keep her here just a little bit longer, because any amount of time with her wouldn't be enough. I was tempted to give her another hug, and hold her face in my hands, and kiss her, and just feel her warmth.

As if sensing it, Callie paused once more, her hand hovering over the door handle. "It's really good to see you, Liam. Pick a good place to take me tonight. I'm in the mood for pasta."

I was so caught off guard by her parting words that all I could do was chuckle. I was left alone with my thoughts, the knowledge that she unblocked my number, and that damn picture of us, looking as in love as ever.

Fourteen

Callie

As soon as I was alone in the elevator, I sagged against the steel wall behind me. My heart was racing and my legs were Jell-O, but those were no match for my mangled breaths and somersaulting stomach. I squeezed my eyes shut.

Seeing Liam was way harder than I expected.

From the second I entered Major Crimes, my eyes had found him, as if they were trained to do so. His back was facing me, his sandy blonde hair glinted in the overhead lights. It was longer than he usually wore it, and—*why do I remember that?*

He wore a white Oxford, the sleeves rolled up to his elbows to reveal his muscular forearms, decorated with tattoos that I once traced my fingers over—*hello, forearm porn.* A brown dual holster was slung over his shoulders, complimenting his muscular frame. Tailored slim dress pants and dress shoes and—

I had willed myself to speak so I could focus on something else.

Yet I couldn't refrain from scrutinizing the way his head inclined as he spoke to another officer, or the way he stood tall and confident and broad-shouldered, or the way his badge fit snugly against his hip.

And as he turned to look at me, his familiar green eyes blinking in confused astonishment, I knew what he had been through. It was all too similar to my own painful experience; one I was still struggling with.

At that moment, I realized the man wore a facade when dealing with his colleagues.

I desperately wanted to throw my arms around him, but my legs bolted me to the ground… all because those fucking green eyes had found mine, and even as shadowed as they were, they were beautiful and they were *his*. The glass water bottle he held clattered to the ground, shattering. I didn't care, not one bit, because I was just happy to see him. He crossed the gap separating us in a matter of long strides, and I nearly sobbed in relief as he tucked me into him.

My own little slice of heaven, however brief my stay might be.

Suddenly he was spinning me, then pulling away to look me up and down—and oh damn, I missed the way he looked at me.

I missed being looked at like I was wanted and desired.

Jesus, Callie, reign it in.

When he invited me into his office, I contemplated running away. I could take Terry up on his offer to call Liam instead, but I was already here. I was a big girl. I could handle this myself.

Liam had grown his facial hair out in our months apart—it was trimmed and it suited his masculine jaw. A shudder ran through me as I recalled exactly how it felt between my thighs.

He was clearly not sleeping well, and his pale skin was an indication that he wasn't as okay as he acted. As rough as he looked… it didn't matter how he looked, actually. I forced myself not to notice, or pay attention to his irresistible dimples when they made their appearance. I cursed my traitorous body when those wobbling knees turned to trembling, weak legs at the sight.

But his eyes. They reflected so much pain, so much—

He's a grown man. He'll be okay. The subconscious reminder was an attempt to quell the agony thundering in my chest.

I had turned my attention to the tall windows adorning one wall of his impressive office, feeling at home beside him. Conversation was just as easy as it had always been. That longing tug in the air between us felt alive, the sensation that we both maybe wanted something that wasn't a smart idea was almost palpable.

But if I caved to those feelings now, then that meant maybe I hadn't moved on. And admitting that hurt more than I wanted to think about.

I shook the interaction from my head and straightened as the elevator came to a smooth stop on the first floor. I half-ran to get outside, needing the city breeze to lift my damp hair off the nape of my neck. Willing my legs to carry me to my hotel, I tried to think of anything except the invitation I gave him for dinner.

As *friends*.

What the hell was I thinking? Was that even possible for us?

I mean, I pretty much locked us into having the awkward post-break up conversation. If you could even call it a break up. We were never dating, just… Well, it was all in the past now.

I huffed as I entered my hotel room, crawling onto the bed and staring up at the ceiling until I had to get ready for dinner.

Fifteen

Liam

The next few hours crawled by agonizingly slow, taking their sweet ass time as I anxiously awaited meeting Callie.

God, that was weird to say after all this time.

As I was packing up to leave, Krishna slipped into my office, a nervous look on her face. I hesitated asking her what she needed out of fear that maybe Callie had canceled on me.

"She's the woman in the photo, isn't she?" she asked me.

I paused, my gaze drifting to the picture in question. I nodded once.

"What, um, what was she to you?"

I sighed. "It's complicated."

Krishna cocked a brow at me, silently pressing for answers.

I sighed again. "Right person, wrong time. We loved each other, but… didn't really know how to tell that to one another. Complicated love lives, poor communication, time consuming jobs." I gave her a sad smile. "Also, we butted heads a lot since we were partners."

"Partners?"

"Yeah. We were both detectives in Newark, but then things went sideways, and… well, she moved back to her hometown, and I came here."

She hummed. "Are you seeing her again?"

I slung my bag over my shoulder. "Yes. I'm picking her up for dinner." Krishna gave me a knowing look and I rolled my eyes. "*Just* dinner. I think that ship has sailed." I thought of her profile picture on Facebook, and my heart sank. Yeah, my chance was long gone.

"Well, enjoy your night, sir. I hope you get some closure."

* * *

I cringed at my appearance as I got ready for my *just-friends* dinner date with Callie. My hair was a touch too long, so I settled for styling it back for now. I also decided to shave, hoping I looked more put together than I felt.

There was nothing I could do about the dark circles under my eyes, though.

I rolled up my shirtsleeves, glancing at the new tattoo on my forearm that I'd gotten at the peak of my heartbroken misery.

I only hoped she'd recognize me somewhere behind the strong front I was putting on.

By the time I made it to her hotel—right on time—the seconds ticked by too fast. Now I felt like I didn't have enough time to prepare to see her, when that's all I'd been dreaming about for months.

I exhaled sharply and let my eyes flutter closed, and when I reopened them, she was standing there. I blinked, thinking it was some sort of magic trick.

My heart beat loudly in my ears as she approached me, chin held high with a sexy confidence that hadn't always been there. I raked my eyes over her. Hair twisted into a simple, elegant updo; a style she'd worn many times before, and one she knew made my knees weak. And the red dress—God, why'd she have to wear red?—that clung to her waist and hips, fell to her knees and tied at the side.

I should look away.

But I couldn't.

Jesus Christ. Her lips were glossy and cherry-colored, drawing my attention before my gaze dropped to those signature nude heels.

She was giving me every goddamn reason to believe she was doing this on purpose: driving me absolutely fucking wild.

I swallowed thickly, withholding the inappropriate groan rising in my throat along with the flashbacks that seemed to flood my mind.

When I had pushed her back against the wall in my bedroom after taking her to dinner, in the cold months before things had gone awry. With one hand on the base of her throat to tilt her head and the other tangled in the same updo she wore now, whispering in her ear how much I loved her hair this way because it made it easy to kiss her neck.

The image of her in a similar colored dress two years in a row at the Christmas Gala. Coincidentally the same color she wore when I realized I was in love with her.

The many times she'd left red lipstick marks on my skin, my lips, my shirts, and my cock during our heated moments of passion.

The instances where she wore those exact red bottoms she had on now, except then they were propped on my shoulders.

Friends.

Dinner as friends.

That's all this was. Nothing more.

Sucking in a breath to break my trance, I gave her a friendly smile. I leveled with her as I realized that's where her mind went, too—further confirming that her showing up this way was intentional torture. I may have made a lot of stupid decisions as a man, but I was a smart detective.

I didn't voice it. That's not what tonight was about. Instead, I shoved my hands in my pockets and inclined my head. Callie fell into an easy stride beside me as I led her down the few blocks to the Italian restaurant where I'd made a reservation.

"You look great, by the way," I complimented.

"Thank you." She glanced up at me. "You shaved."

I chuckled and responded with, "Those kinds of observations are what make you an excellent cop."

An homage to something she once said to me.

She tilted her head back and let out a laugh. It was mesmerizing to watch.

Then, she was quiet for a couple of minutes as we wound through the city crowds. At one point she reached for me, and I let her loop her arm through mine so she wouldn't lose me in the throng of people.

"I hate this city," Callie muttered under her breath.

I snorted. "You always have." I snuck a glance at her to see a small smile. Looked anywhere but her hand resting on my forearm. It didn't mean anything.

"Too many damn people."

We came to a stop in front of the restaurant, where I reluctantly pulled away to open the door. She gave me a bashful smile and entered first, with me on her heels, my hand on her lower back as I gave my name to the hostess.

We sat at a table in the back overlooking the streets. Candlelight flickered a little too romantically between us as we settled in. And now, up close in this lighting, her skin glowed. She looked like summer personified. I had to ignore my dick stirring at the swell of her breasts, visible under her nearly too-low neckline.

I nonchalantly draped the linen napkin across my lap to cover the evidence.

"So, Liam, what's good here?" Her lilting voice broke through.

I blinked and glanced down at the menu. "You said you wanted pasta, so I assumed you were in the mood for your favorite. Alfredo."

It was her turn to blink, her eyes twinkling with pleasant surprise. "You remembered."

I smiled at her. "I remember everything."

Sixteen

Callie

I clutched the menu so Liam couldn't see my trembling fingers.

I nodded at him to order his drink first. He ordered a glass of red wine, and as badly as I wanted to do the same, something possessed me. My next words came out like word vomit as I gave him a stern look.

"We'll actually both have water," I told the waitress, whose eyes shifted between us before she dipped her chin and scurried away. When I returned my gaze to Liam, his head was cocked to the side and his eyes were narrowed.

"What was that for?" he wondered. Not angry or upset, just... curious.

I refrained from squirming in my seat. I had to maintain some level of composure—the portrait of confidence I had perfected—so I pinned him with an admonishing glare. "When was the last time you went a day without a drink?" I prompted.

Okay, maybe it was a low blow. And it definitely wasn't any of my concern nor was it my place, but... all the signs of alcohol abuse were there. I would know better than anyone. From the sallow color of his skin, to his overall lower energy levels. I knew it from the moment I saw him, because I was still recovering from using alcohol as a crutch myself.

God knows our line of work didn't make alcoholism easier to fight.

A muscle in Liam's jaw feathered as he examined me. I could tell he was teetering on telling me to fuck off and being polite. The problem was that he and I were *never* polite with one another. That had been established early on: always transparent, never afraid to speak our minds… with the exception of our feelings for each other.

So… that must mean he was biting his tongue because he was afraid I'd disappear again.

I leaned forward. "Don't be coy with me, Mr. Chandler."

That earned a half-smile from him, one dimple revealing itself. I squeezed my thighs together and pretended not to notice. Fucking hell, he was so hot it physically hurt me to look at him sometimes.

"I haven't gone a day without one since you left." He shrugged and added, "I've been a mess."

I sat back in the booth. What he was going through? Yeah, I understood.

The waitress reappeared with our waters and took our order. When she left, my eyes lingered on his glass.

"Drink it. You broke your water bottle earlier when you saw me."

Slowly, he picked up his glass and drank half of it. With a clean-shaven face, I could see every detail again; the way his throat bobbed when he swallowed, his dimples when he smiled, his chiseled jaw.

When he was done, he ran a tongue over his lips, and I couldn't bring myself to look away.

"You're concerned about me," he noted.

I played with the linen tablecloth. "So what if I am? I've been there before."

"And you expect me to believe that's the only reason?" he pressed, leaning forward with eyebrows raised.

My breath hitched as I met those inscrutable green eyes. Remembered how they looked when the sun hit them, how they made me feel when his attention was only on me.

"If there's something you want to ask, then ask. You've never been one to not ask the difficult questions, babe." The pet name slipped past my lips before I could stop it. Warmth took over my whole body, but I didn't acknowledge my slip up.

Liam analyzed me again, an amused smirk gracing that talented mouth of his. This side of him was more… calculating than I was used to. Quiet. Broody. There was a filter that hadn't always been there.

"Okay, fine. Why dress like this for me? Do you not have someone waiting for you at home?"

I sucked in a breath, utterly caught off guard.

Not because he was wrong. He was goading me, trying to figure out who I had been with since I left. I glanced down at myself. I couldn't lie and say it wasn't intentional; it absolutely was. I spent a solid half-hour mulling over my wardrobe before deciding on this. And if I wasn't so keen on being honest with myself, I would've told myself it was muscle memory.

But I knew—I knew that sliding on a red dress that hugged me in all the right places would attract him like a moth to light. I also knew that he'd give me attention in ways I shouldn't want, yet part of me craved anyway.

I hadn't stopped myself, even with this awareness.

I ran his questions over in my mind and snorted. "Someone at home? Don't be ridiculous. Do you really think, after everything, that I would be ready for something else?"

Liam's eyes narrowed ever so slightly before his shoulders visibly relaxed. I made a mental note of his behavior. "I was just asking." Cold, hard words.

It was my turn to scrutinize him. "What made you think that?"

Silence.

"You never reached out to me," I said softly.

He shrugged. "When you blocked me, I owed you at least the decency of giving you space. I respected that."

My stomach flipped. I was dying to ask follow-up questions, but now was neither the time nor the place. I kept my mouth shut as I lowered my eyes.

"If we're going to work together in any capacity, no matter how long it's for, we need to talk about it." His tone changed, now soft, and… gently reassuring.

I shook my head, nimbly running my fingers over the silverware on the table. "I don't want to talk about that."

"Like hell we're not."

My gaze snapped to his, my blood trilling at the sound of a fight in his voice. "That's not what tonight is about, Liam."

He took a deep breath. "That's not what tonight's about? We never set boundaries or rules on this dinner aside from being here as *friends.*"

My lips pursed. If I changed the topic, we wouldn't have to revisit this conversation. At least, not tonight. My emotions had been through the wringer today, not to mention the last few days. I was exhausted.

"When I went back home to Springcrest, I ran into my high school sweetheart. For a brief moment, I wondered what it would be like to give it another shot." Liam bristled. "That thought lasted all of ten seconds before I found out he was dating my sister," I told him.

Shame made my throat close. I hadn't admitted this to anyone. "I realized then that I needed to spend some time alone getting to know myself and figuring out what it was that I needed. So to answer the question you never really asked: no, I don't have anyone waiting for me at home."

Liam opened his mouth to respond, but I cut him off.

"I don't know how long this will last."

I hesitated continuing as I searched for the right words; ones that wouldn't give away the very vital pieces of information I had gathered over the last couple of days. Then I realized I had momentarily forgotten why I even came back here.

It was a sobering thought.

Damn it, Liam. Always distracting me.

"But I swear to you, Liam, that I will not leave again before we have that conversation."

He clenched his jaw before dipping his chin in understanding. Before he could respond, a pretty young woman approached our table. Not our server—no, not with the way Liam's spine went ramrod straight. My gaze flicked up to the woman batting her eyelashes at the man across from me. I almost rolled my eyes as I realized exactly what had happened while I was gone.

Liam had slept with her, and she couldn't have made it any more obvious.

"Liam, hey," she cooed, shimmying closer to him. He shifted away from her. God, the nerve of this woman. No shame that he was having dinner with another woman.

"You never called me. I had such a great time that night and thought you felt the same."

I sucked my lips into my mouth and pressed them tightly together to keep from laughing. Instead, I peered down at my phone in distraction, thoroughly amused. And given my earlier response to him, I was surprisingly not jealous of the stranger who stood at the head of our table.

Liam cleared his throat. "I'm sorry, now really isn't a great time to discuss this."

I checked my email to give them as much privacy as possible, but there was only silence. I lifted my head. The woman's eyes were sizing me up, growing colder with each passing second.

"Are you planning on doing the same things to this poor woman?" she demanded, not taking her eyes off me.

Liam flushed. The sight had me almost bursting at the seams in laughter. I couldn't contain the twitching of my lips as I met the woman's stare, raising my eyebrows expectantly at her.

"He's the pump-and-dump type," she hissed. "This is where he brought me before he took me back to my place, fucked me, and then didn't call." She pouted for dramatic effect.

Something in her story comforted me, but I couldn't place what it was.

I could sense Liam's discomfort from across the table. I'd gotten my entertainment; I came to his rescue by reaching into my purse and pulling out my badge.

"I apologize for his behavior. He was left heartbroken and hasn't learned to love again." I managed to reign in the grin—the cackle—that threatened to break free. Liam narrowed his eyes at me. "However, I do believe you are mistaken. Mr. Chandler and I are colleagues in separate police departments and are currently working on an active serial killer case."

The woman's eyes widened, her mouth opening and closing like a fish's.

I smiled sweetly at her. "We're actually on official business right now, and you're disrupting something incredibly crucial to the case. So unless you'd like us to arrest you on charges of harassment, obstruction of justice, and direct interference of a police investigation, I suggest you humbly turn back around and leave."

She looked back and forth between us. "I'm so sorry. I had no idea." She turned and speed-walked through the restaurant. I trailed her until she bolted past the host stand, then slid my badge back into my purse.

When I finally looked at Liam again, there was an arrogant curve to his lips. The discomfort from mere seconds ago was long gone. "Jealous, Eden?"

My heart lurched. The inside joke rang clear and true, and I returned his smile with an innocent one. "You were floundering and it was painful to watch, so I decided to put an end to your misery. Next time, try to keep it in your pants."

He snickered and shook his head, but the lump forming in my throat betrayed me.

Maybe I was jealous.

Shit.

How many women had he been with since I left?

Seventeen

Liam

Spending the evening with Callie wasn't what I expected—like having dinner with a ghost from my past. The way she warded off one of my one night stands reminded me just how much of a spitfire she was. Like when she told off my ex-girlfriend after being assaulted by her. Part of me wanted to smile at the memory, while another part wanted to curl up in a ball and weep.

That was the last night I had spent with her.

The last night I had called her mine.

To make matters worse, I didn't even remember one-night-stand's name, let alone telling her that I'd call. Shame burned my cheeks as I looked at Callie.

"Thanks," I croaked, finishing off my glass of water so she wouldn't see the flurry of emotions pouring through me.

She just nodded in response.

There was very little talk of anything truly important for the remainder of our dinner. I asked her about her family—*They're good.* Her new job—*The job is fine, except the other sergeant.* What it was like being back in Springcrest—*It feels more like home now than it did when I grew up there.* Her answers were clipped yet genuine, and I knew that the unexpected visitor

77

had put a damper on the evening.

More silence between us as I paid and we walked back to her hotel. There was no touching this time, just inches of distance between us. She looked lost in thought. I didn't want to disrupt wherever her mind was at, so I kept my mouth shut as we came to a slow stop in front of her hotel.

I had the sudden urge to reach out and take her hand, press it to my chest so she could feel how wildly it was beating.

Callie swiveled on her heels. The whole night she had been the model of cool confidence and radiant smiles. Nothing that alluded to the troubled sorrow now swirling in her blue eyes—a certain deep-rooted sadness that I knew all too well. It made my stomach roil to know she felt it, too.

"Thank you," Callie murmured, "for entertaining me tonight. I think I would've gone crazy in my hotel room all night." A crooked, half-hearted smile that didn't reach her eyes.

This time I didn't stop myself from grabbing her hand. She didn't pull away. "I wouldn't have had it any other way."

Her smile turned more sincere. A few tendrils of her hair had come loose, and the light summer breeze blew them across her face. I reached up with my other hand and tucked them behind her ear, earning a slight blush on her cheeks. I couldn't help but grin at her. Her lips parted, her breath visibly hitching. I don't know what possessed me, but I cupped one side of her face, leaned in, and pressed my lips to hers.

And I'll be damned if it didn't make my body feel as electric as a live wire.

I probably shouldn't have been so brash. It would set things off on the wrong foot between us. But seeing her standing there, not saying anything, staring at me with those doe-like eyes, as if she were discontent about something, but not rushing to go back inside…

I couldn't help myself.

She moved her lips against mine, gently—so gently. *Jesus,* it was like being kissed for the first time. Then her tongue swept across my bottom lip. My dick stirred and I fought the urge to press myself against her.

I knew the kiss was a mistake the second she pulled away. Callie tore her lips from mine and took a step back. I didn't reach for her.

"We can't do this, Liam."

Something about the way she said my name nearly made me crumble.

I could taste her cinnamon lip gloss burning my lips, feel the heat that had started to spread through me. My heart thudded so hard I thought it might break through my rib cage, and my fingers ached with my restraint. I wanted her all over me, wanted to be with her just one more time, change the narrative of the last time we were together. I wanted to apologize for everything—what a stupid fucking fool I had been and what an asshole I was to her.

I wanted so many things, but I was walking on very thin ice.

I gulped. "I-I'm sorry. I shouldn't have done that," I stammered.

She remained a few feet away, still panting. "It won't work," she mumbled, almost to herself.

Callie was probably right. It wouldn't work; it didn't before, and now our relationship bore so much damage. Too much scar tissue to move past, despite how badly I wanted to be wrong.

I inhaled sharply and shoved my hands in my pockets, straightening and looking down at her impassively. "I should go. Sounds like we'll both need rest for whatever news you're breaking tomorrow. I'll be back here at seven." My sentences were firm. The way they needed to be so she knew I respected her decision to shut this down before it started.

I turned on my heel and melted into New York's crowd.

"Liam!" I heard her call out, as if she had changed her mind.

But she hadn't. I knew if I looked over my shoulder, if I turned back, she would only be confusing herself.

Because if there was one thing Callie Eden had mastered, it was not knowing exactly what she wanted.

Eighteen

Callie

I shouldn't care that Liam didn't turn around after I rejected him and told him we wouldn't work out. I winced—of course he didn't turn around.

Truth was, I didn't realize just how hurt from the past I still was. I had denied it for so long, and tonight it had been glaringly obvious.

But my body and my brain wanted two different things.

That too-short kiss left my head reeling. I wanted to allow it to lapse into something more, but my brain told me otherwise; Liam needed to clean up his act, and we had too many conversations to have before we attempted anything. I don't think either of us could afford to get hurt like that again.

His shutters flew up to deflect my rejection, taking it as respectfully as one could. That alone made me want to change my mind. It took an unbelievable amount of willpower to ignore my wobbling knees from seeing him smile, to disregard my stomach twisting from the tenderness of him brushing my hair out of my face. My stupid heart sputtered and misfired from how gently he spoke to me—how gently he hung onto every word that fell from my lips.

So I stood there for several moments after I called out his name, hoping he would come back, but I knew he was long gone and probably hadn't even heard me over the noisy streets.

Tears pricked my eyes as I raced up to my hotel room. I needed some time to myself. Not just tonight, but in general. I needed to be single, and Liam did, too. Maybe once we both found ourselves again, we could be together.

I wasn't in charge of his life, though. Sure, I could tell him to figure his shit out, and he'd probably listen, but would that type of controlling behavior win him over?

Something else tugged at my heart: if I was already considering what needed to happen for us to be together, wasn't that just setting the precedent that I *wasn't* going back to Springcrest?

I threw myself onto the bed, haphazardly pulling off my expensive Louboutins and ripping the pins out of my hair.

All the progress I thought I made and I still couldn't avoid the throbbing between my legs. Clearly the idea that we couldn't be together turned me on.

I huffed, wriggled out of my dress, and reached for my vibrator, needing to do anything to relieve the ache. I had to banish these thoughts so I could be on my A-game tomorrow.

Damn it.

One dinner with the man and I was rethinking my entire plan.

Again.

* * *

I was struggling to zip up my jumpsuit when a knock sounded the next morning. I was surprised to see Liam standing there when I opened the door, looking hotter than the sun in a white Oxford and khaki dress pants.

"I'm supposed to meet you outside," I grunted, still fighting with that tiny zipper.

Liam shrugged and gave me a smile that was too dazzling for the early hour. "I figured this would be easier."

Translation: *I couldn't wait to see you.*

I rolled my eyes and stepped aside. "You can zip me since you're here." I turned so he could take over the seemingly impossible task, pretending like I wasn't fazed by his presence. Like I didn't remember the time he'd secured my bra in our office one morning after I'd fallen asleep there and had to change my clothes.

There was a hint of hesitation in the air before his familiar hands were on me. One held the bottom of the zipper near the base of my spine while the other tugged the insipid thing up my back.

Sweet agony.

I stepped away the moment it was done.

"Carry my suitcase?" I asked as I lunged for my purse.

"Of course."

He followed me into the hallway. I was still recovering from his touch, however momentary it was.

"Are you ready for today?" Liam asked when we stepped into the elevator.

If he was trying to kill the mood, he was succeeding.

I heaved a sigh. "As ready as I can be."

"I don't even get a sneak peak into what news you're delivering today?"

I snickered. When I glanced up at him, he looked dead serious. I straightened. "I don't want to talk about it longer than I have to. As it is, everything changes after today."

His eyebrows tipped toward each other in confusion.

I turned to face the elevator doors, dread settling into my gut.

After today, I was no longer a free woman.

* * *

It's just the summer heat, I told myself as a flush came over me while watching Liam lift my bags into the trunk of my car. His forearms flexed, back muscles shifting. Not even breaking a sweat.

Images of him, naked and dripping as he positioned himself between my legs, popped into my mind. I remembered what it felt like to have his mouth on me, his tongue delving into my center, his fingers working my nipples.

Sure, I could get myself off, but it lacked romance and passion.

I suddenly regretted turning him down last night.

I tried to quell the wayward thoughts, but they momentarily consumed me. Just like they had when we worked together every day.

Ugh. I wanted his fingers in my hair and his hands tracing every inch of my skin as though they were trying to memorize me. Bending me over, pressing me against the wall, kissing me with the taste of me on his lips.

God, I was a weak woman.

I let out a soft whimper and pressed my legs together.

Liam threw a quizzical look over his shoulder, and I realized the noise had been audible. My cheeks warmed.

"You okay, Eden? You're acting strange this morning." His teasing tone, signature smirk, and dimples just about sent me into overdrive. He was being so graceful, despite being rejected the night before.

This definitely wasn't the same man I had left behind, and no part of me was disappointed.

I nodded and headed for the driver's side. I needed to pull my head out of the gutter. "Just slept weird," I grumbled in response.

The moment the air conditioning hit me, I felt myself coming down. Good. Maybe it was just the heat of the city making me act crazed and depraved. I leaned back against the seat, my back slick with sweat.

I could do this. I could survive this car ride and get through the debriefing with my former colleagues. Easy peasy.

Liam got in the car. The smell of him was enough to keep my mind off the dreadful news I was soon going to break.

"I, for one, slept like a rock all night," he said with a smug smile as he looked out the window while I backed out and left the parking garage.

Fuck.

It was going to be a long ride across town.

Nineteen

Liam

Had I slept well? Sure, after I jacked off a handful of times as I imagined Callie in truly wicked ways. I may have been a decent enough man to step back and accept her gentle letdown, but I was still a man with needs.

And those needs ran rampant whenever I was in the presence of Callie Eden.

This morning, though, I woke with a clarity I hadn't had in months—and I hated to admit that it probably had to do with being sober.

Callie, on the other hand, had also slept well, despite her saying otherwise. It was evident in her bright eyes, radiant skin, and graceful poise. Even if there was something distracting her, something… something that had nothing to do with work. I had a sneaking suspicion as to what it was, and I intended to play on it.

Just to mess with her. Like old times.

So if she wanted to be as open and honest as we were before, then kissing her last night had been me doing just that. Except she didn't want that, so I'd have to be more calculating.

She sat restlessly in the car, stuck in city traffic. I snuck glances at her at every opportunity, part of me still not convinced she was actually here.

She kept biting her lip, her eyes flitting over the congested vehicles but not really seeing. She was lost in thought again, and we were only halfway there.

"Penny for your thoughts?"

Callie stiffened. "Just the case. As always. It's… well, it's not good, Liam." She took a shaky breath.

I shifted toward her. "What else?"

She looked at me and raised her eyebrows, the morning light catching all the different shades of blue in her eyes. "What makes you think there's more?"

I chuckled. "Callie, sometimes I think you forget how well I know you. We may have both changed these last few months, but fundamentally we are the same," I explained, examining her body language as I spoke. Back straighter than yesterday, baby hairs damp as they stuck to her neck and temples, a slight rosy tint to her cheeks, her thighs pressed together—*that's it.*

This time, speaking her name felt oh so sweet.

Callie just rolled her eyes, and my dick stirred in response to her stubbornness. "It's nothing."

Now I just had to tread carefully. I tugged a hand through my hair, a gesture I knew always snagged her attention. It worked like a charm; she tore her eyes from the road momentarily to watch.

I wish I could say I was the only one affected. But here she was looking catastrophically beautiful. I had never seen her in her summer wardrobe, and it did not disappoint. She was all pastels and summer hues and everything bright and shiny, with her lavender jumpsuit caressing all her feminine curves and her cleavage just barely showing. It was hard not to stare.

"Summer suits you," I said.

She tilted her head to the side, a small smile appearing. She opened her mouth to respond, but I beat her to it.

"You're beautiful."

That earned me a bashful grin. The same one she had given me at my office yesterday.

"You don't look too bad yourself, you know."

I placed a hand on my chest. "Are you… are you *complimenting* me?"

Callie laughed. "Don't let it go to your head. The last thing we need is your ego stroked more than it already is."

I grinned deviously. I missed our banter. "I can think of another head I'd rather you stroke," I purred.

"*Liam,*" she hissed, eyes wide.

We weren't far from Newark now, which meant our time as something other than professionals was almost up. When would we get another moment like this?

Depending on the news she delivered this morning, there wasn't even a guarantee we'd *ever* get a moment like this again, so I had to make it count.

I reached over and pushed her hair behind her shoulder, intentionally not touching her. I watched as she took a deep breath, her chest rising with those perfect, perky tits.

"You know how much I love hearing you say my name." A seemingly innocent statement laced with suggestive promise.

Callie's cheeks turned a little more pink as she squirmed. I almost lost it then; I was way past half-mast at this point. Maybe I should have been embarrassed with how easily she turned me on, but it had always been this way with her. No point in hiding that fact now.

"I see your mind is still in the gutter. Some things never change," she quipped.

I snorted, that shit-eating grin still plastered on my face. She was in the mood to play, it seemed. "With you, Callie Eden, my mind is always in the gutter."

Her hands tightened on the steering wheel. I was really affecting her, and it was only verbal foreplay.

"You're being awfully distracting this morning."

"How? I'm just sitting here. The portrait of innocence, my dear."

She bit down on her bottom lip to stop a smile. She was enjoying this as much as I was, and she wanted me to see it.

"Your brain can't even keep itself in its pants, Liam. You may have a problem."

I barked out a laugh as she pulled onto the bridge connecting the two cities. "The only problem I have right now is how hard I am knowing I'll have to face our old colleagues very, very soon." I hoped the cheeky comment wasn't too reckless, but it was a risk I was willing to take. I let my eyes close in hopes I could will my hard-on away.

Her gaze flickered down to my crotch and smirked. "I could take care of that, you know."

My eyes widened. Of all the things she could say, that was the last thing I expected. My cock approved of her statement as all the blood seemed to flood the extremity. Okay, so maybe my "harmless" flirting had backfired.

"What, no snarky remark to that?"

I swallowed. "Now you're just teasing me."

She giggled, and *fuck*, that was my undoing. I looked out the window again. Maybe if I stopped gawking at her and pretended I couldn't smell her, maybe—just maybe—I could shift my train of thought.

Yeah, just focus on the glittering water under the bridge and the passing cars. That would help.

"Who said I'm *just* teasing? Don't put words in my mouth."

I groaned, side-eyeing her. "You know what you're doing, and it's borderline evil."

Callie sucked her lower lip into her mouth. I told myself to look away again, but I couldn't. The second I let my gaze dip to her cleavage, where I could see how hard her nipples were, I stopped caring if I made a stupid fucking decision.

Was it bad that I took pride in knowing I still turned her on?

With a soft exhale, I managed to look out the windshield. I noticed how close we were to the precinct.

"Show me, then," Callie urged.

My head snapped back to her. "What?"

"Show me how much you want me. What you want to do to me right now. I know you're thinking about it, thinking about me. Show me. *Tell* me." It was nearly a plea with how breathy and strained her words were.

Jesus.

I only hesitated a moment before I all but threw myself at her. I slipped my left hand into the hair at the nape of her neck while my right hand slid over her thigh and slowly inched its way up. I pressed my lips to her neck; I could feel her warm skin under my touch, feel her breathing accelerate from the pulse point near her throat, hear her sigh of relief.

Her thighs clenched tightly together, trapping my hand. The heat between them was enough to make me want to burst. I hissed through my teeth. *Has she been like this all morning?*

I traced the curve of her neck with my tongue, from the base all the way to the tender spot behind her ear. She whimpered when my teeth clamped down on her earlobe, her head falling back against the seat. How she was still driving was beyond me.

If it were the other way around, we would've crashed already.

My hand continued its journey up her thigh until I reached the apex, where I was greeted with her damp heat. I groaned against her skin, my fingers involuntarily gripping her hair and tugging gently. I wanted her so badly, wanted her more than I had ever wanted her, and that was saying a lot given our history.

I teased her with my touch, my fingers grazing her clit through her clothes. She gasped and tried to press her hips forward into my hand. I traced my hand up her stomach, up to graze her nipples in a feather-light touch before slipping beneath the hem of her jumpsuit. The warm swell of her breasts greeted my awaiting hands, and goosebumps scattered down her arms. I bared my teeth and left gentle bites along her neck.

My dick was throbbing so hard it hurt. I shifted so I had better access to her… and to give myself some friction.

Callie cried out when I pinched one of her nipples, her right hand leaving the steering wheel to rub me through my pants. A guttural groan escaped my throat, and I swore her touch was like fire through my clothes. I couldn't stop myself from thrusting forward into her hand.

She released me seconds later to park the car. The lustful fog in my brain couldn't even comprehend that we'd arrived at the Third Precinct.

I raised my head, giving her a break from the smothering kisses I had been planting along her shoulder, collarbone, and jaw, so that I could sit back in my seat and gather my thoughts. I attempted to shove my unadulterated, very X-rated desire for her to the recesses of my mind. Tried so hard for her sake, because if I had no leash on my self-control, I'd fuck her here and now.

Callie was obviously only doing this to get under my skin. And I had let her. I showed her all my cards: how I still wanted her, how *badly* I yearned for her.

I looked over at her to see how she was faring, only to find her taking deep breaths, her body trembling with arousal.

The chemistry hung heavy in the air between us, crackling and zapping as if it were alive.

Look away.

Look away, because if you don't—

Twenty

Callie

I thought I could handle a little fun, lighthearted teasing with my ex-flame.

I was so, *so* wrong.

"Dating" myself was useless; the second I was put in a situation where I was susceptible to seduction, I was visibly quivering with what little willpower I had left. It's not like I would never be touched intimately again… no, it was because of who sat next to me.

Him and his big dick energy.

And his big dick.

I was looking for a distraction as much as I was caving to every deep desire I still had for Liam. And honestly? I could think of no better way to relieve some of that pressure.

My legs were clamped tightly together, my knuckles snow-white from how hard I was clutching the steering wheel.

What was I *thinking?*

I knew the effect his touch had on me the moment I met him two Christmases ago—and that wasn't counting the time we'd met as teenagers.

I could tell myself that my next actions were out of my control, but I would be lying. It was my own volition that willed me to pry fingers off the steering wheel, my own will that had me lunging toward him and gripping handfuls of his shirt to pull him into me.

It was so fucking stupid of me to not bring him up to my room last night.

Our lips crashed into each other's, all tongues and teeth for a few seconds before I twisted, folding my legs underneath me so I had better access to him. I moaned into his mouth shamelessly, dry humping the air with the hope that I could get myself off.

No such luck.

Liam's hands rested on each side of my neck possessively, and I was pure putty under his touch. His fingertips plunged into my hair and held me tightly to him. Heat spread through my core, writhing and twisting through my every nerve ending. My skin tingled where he touched me, and I wanted more, more, *more.*

I stopped thinking about whether or not I would regret this later. I needed this. Needed *him.*

Some things never changed.

I crawled over the center console gracelessly, stumbling into his lap to straddle him. Liam groaned against my lips, his breath warm and heavy and so fucking delicious. The rise and fall of our chests had them brushing on each inhale, and I felt him shudder under me.

"Callie, if you don't stop—" he started, his voice low.

"I don't want to," I interrupted with a growl, kissing him again and gyrating my hips against his rock-hard erection. We were a mess of lips and tongues and hands.

He pulled back suddenly and opened his eyes. I gasped softly at the color that greeted me. I wished I could say that I didn't miss the way he looked at me—how he fixated on me because he saw only *me.*

I leaned in to kiss him again. Our lips brushed momentarily before he gently pushed me away with trembling hands. I sat back and gaped at him, utterly confused. Did he... did he not want me like that anymore?

"I can't do this," he admitted, his cheeks flushed and eyes dark with desire. His words were like a slap across the face. "I don't want you to hate me again. Or yourself, for that matter."

How was he thinking about this in the throes of passion? My mind was on everything *but* that.

Fuck him for taking that decision away from me.

Except… there was something there that made my breath catch a little. It was the raw emotion in his voice, the regret etched into every line of his face. I knew then why his mind had wandered: he recalled the times he'd fucked me and ended things right after.

In other words, the times he'd broken my heart.

It was a sobering reality check.

Whatever moment had been there was long gone.

I ran my hand over his toned, bare chest, trying to commit the feel of his muscles to memory, how every ab rippled under my touch and how warm he was and how goddamn good he smelled.

I took a shaky breath. I wasn't sorry for leaving or for taking care of my health when I hit rock bottom. I rebuilt myself day by day to become the woman sitting in his lap now.

Finally meeting his gaze, I deadpanned, "I have never stopped wanting you, Liam. But okay." I climbed off his lap, still feeling a little perplexed. What a turn of events.

Twenty-One

Liam

Callie was in my lap, her lips on mine and her tight little body grinding against me. It was all I wanted—all I had thought about for what felt like an eternity. I should be happy, right?

Wrong.

As good as it felt to have her in my arms, and as badly as I wanted to do this with her, I couldn't. Somehow, through the haze clouding my mind, I managed to push her away. My hands were shaking as I used every ounce of willpower to just *stop*.

She blinked at me, waiting for an explanation and squirming so deliciously against my cock that I almost forgot what I was doing.

"I can't do this," I told her, surprising even myself with the declaration. "I don't want you to hate me again. Or yourself, for that matter."

Not when I just got you back, was what I left unsaid.

I refused to fall prey to the same mistakes I made before. After all, she had just rejected me the night before, and it was for a reason. She would regret this later. So if that meant waiting, at least we'd both be ready to be together.

I watched as realization washed over her before she nodded once.

Her next words made my blood freeze.

"I have never stopped wanting you, Liam. But okay." A blush crept across her face as she scrambled out of my lap. Her embarrassment hung in the air as much as my stupidity.

I suddenly regretted ever saying anything, but there was no coming back from this.

Callie started smoothing her hands over her hair. I caught her wrist and turned it over to press a kiss into the soft skin there. She paused and looked over at me.

"This isn't because I don't want it," I said softly.

She gently withdrew her hand from my grasp and faced forward. "I know what it's about, and I understand. I just..." She paused and took a deep breath. "Well, I guess you'll see when we get inside." She got out of the car, and I had no choice but to follow suit.

I adjusted myself as I straightened, then took her bag from her. She handed it over without so much as a second glance in my direction.

Judging by the way her shoulders were rolled back and her chin was tilted up, she was in full work mode.

That made one of us.

I watched as she pulled her shoulder holster on and tucked in her guns. God, she was fucking hot when she was packing heat. She could bring an entire precinct to its knees if she wanted to.

Lord knows she had already done that to me.

I followed her to the elevator, and as the doors closed us in together, for once there was no electric charge in the air between us.

Only a feeling of dread for what was to come.

Twenty-Two

Callie

I shook my hands out, hoping it would expel some of my nervous energy as I paced back and forth in the bathroom. I had a room full of people waiting for me, but I needed a moment to collect my thoughts after receiving some ill-inducing news from Genaro. The information she faxed over was worse than I expected, and now I wanted to hurl and break down and scream all at once.

It was a miracle I held it together with breathing exercises alone.

Inhale, two, three, four. Exhale, two, three, four.

I couldn't—wouldn't—let my emotions bleed into other areas of my life. Not again.

Even though it would be a hell of a lot easier to take it all out on Liam for rejecting me and setting a boundary between us, instead of compartmentalizing and processing each individual event.

But I wasn't that woman anymore.

Inhale, two, three, four. Exhale, two, three, four.

I wished he knew that I needed one last release, one last moment of normal… one last time with him.

I shook my head and took a final deep breath, squaring my shoulders and tipping my chin up. *Think about it later.*

I glued a smile on my face and left the bathroom, strolling across the bullpen to the briefing room. This place was once somewhere I considered to be home; now it felt foreign.

Inhale, two, three, four. Exhale, two, three, four.

The second I crossed the threshold to the briefing room, I breathed a sigh of relief. So many faces there to comfort me: Liam, Sophie, Terry, Hailey, Marcus, and Officers Dodson and Gerard… that's it. Those were the only people I trusted.

Centering myself at the podium, I was well aware of all the eyes on me as I hooked up my slideshow. I picked up the remote with trembling fingers and turned to face the small gathering before me.

I cleared my throat. "First of all, it's great to see everyone again. I didn't expect to be back so soon, but…" I paused, flashing my best smile and earning a few in return. "Well, second of all, I wish this were for a personal visit. And it's not exactly what you think it's for, either. I…" Hesitating, my chest squeezed as I fought the discomfort of anxiety. I sought comfort in the room, for anything that could soothe—

My gaze met Sophie's first. She gave me an encouraging nod. Then my eyes flitted to Liam's to find he was already watching me intently, and to my surprise, it was his presence that brought me solace.

"As you all know, we have a warrant out for Vincent Leemore's arrest, but we've had trouble tracking him with our limited resources and jurisdiction. We've also struggled to place him at a few of the crime scenes. When I moved back to Pennsylvania, I gave up on this case. Until two days ago."

I pressed a button on the remote and the photos of the Springcrest homicides appeared on the large screen behind me. "We thought Leemore was fleeing because he knew we were onto him, but we were wrong. He's not the killer." I forced myself to swallow the lump in my throat to buy myself a few more moments before I had to admit it out loud.

"My ex-fiancé, Owen Fisher, is the killer."

I clicked the button again, and the photo I took of him in Springcrest appeared next. I couldn't bring myself to look at anyone's faces. I was ashamed and embarrassed as I heard Liam choke, and the whole room seemed to gasp.

"Except his real name is Oliver Frankford, and he lied to me the entire time we were together."

Twenty-Three

Liam

I gaped at Callie in horror, unable to comprehend the bomb she just dropped on us.

The whole room, myself included, held their breath in response.

Wait.

That name sounded familiar. Oliver Frankford. It rang a distant bell, but why? I had a nagging feeling—

"While I don't think anyone in this room but Liam will recognize his name," Callie was saying. The second she said my name, my attention returned to her. "This is a combination of aliases he's used, specifically Ollivander Francis. Back when Liam and I discovered the connection between the victims, Marcus and I uncovered that Hanna Garrison was looking to make extra cash unbeknownst to her husband, so she worked for Madame Lefevre. The night she was set to meet her very first client, who went by Ollivander Francis, she was abducted."

Ollivander Francis.

The name clicked immediately, the pieces starting to fit together.

"He always keeps the initials the same. I can only assume it's easier for him to keep track of his identities that way." Callie switched to the next slide, and her ex's punchable face appeared before us. "Oliver Frankford, also known as Owen Fisher and Ollivander Francis, is an accountant at Hitchcock & Walt. He's been employed there for five years."

Out of the corner of my eye, I saw Sophie raise her hand. "How did you discover this, Cal?"

Callie's lips formed a mirthful smile. She switched slides again to a photo of Owen—Oliver—sitting outside a café on a sunny day. "Two days ago, just before I got notified of the homicides, I saw him across the town square. He didn't spot me, but I saw him. I thought it was odd that he wound up in my small town with no plan to come visit me," she explained. "It didn't click until I finished my examination of the crime scene and was writing up my report."

We all leaned forward with anticipation. I couldn't tear my eyes off of her. The way she held a room was… captivating, to say the least. The softness of the lavender color she wore was disrupted by her shoulder holster. Every bit the sergeant she was.

God, I would love to see her in her new position.

The next slide was a picture of her handwriting spelling out her own name. "If you remember, shortly after Liam and I re-opened this case, the victims had notes rolled up in their mouths, which was different from the early killings. This escalation in M. O. revealed his message after these last two murders."

When the next picture slid into view, my heartbeat faltered for a moment. Above her name were jumbles of letters in sets of two.

I recognized them instantly.

I also knew what it meant: he was targeting her, and had been for quite some time. While we had been unaware of that until now, who knew if she was safe now? He was done spelling out her name, so surely that meant she was next.

Fuck.

My throat constricted. It explained why she came back here—why she crossed over to the Big Apple to come get me. She knew she was safer here.

With this new information, all I could do was stare at her, drinking her in as my gut clenched. I had this primal need to protect her at all costs, even if it meant risking my own life. I didn't care. All that mattered was that she was safe from that bastard.

It was Marcus's turn to speak. "I don't understand what made his attention shift to you. It wasn't always his original intention, right?"

Callie shook her head and motioned to the next photo: her ex with another brunette woman. "Oliver was engaged and walked in on his fiancé sleeping with her coworker a week before their wedding. I believe this is what triggered his initial spree. Why he targeted me..." she took a deep breath, and for the first time since she'd reappeared in my life, I saw the strain in the set of her shoulders, the stress lines bracketing her mouth. "After we found Hanna Garrison, my old partner and I did a series of press releases. And shortly after that, I met Oliver, who I believed was Owen Fisher. I think he went after me because I was one of the detectives in charge of his case. I was new to the job, single... easy."

"So how do you explain the break between kills?" Terry asked. "And why the shift in M. O.?"

Callie smiled meekly and met each of our gazes in turn. "Isn't it obvious? The kills didn't start again until *after* Liam and I became partners. He realized he had competition. At that point, it was about sending a message, but now that he's reached the end of it, one can only assume my life is well and truly in danger." She fidgeted with her hands. "I did what his ex did to him. I cheated on him with a coworker, even after we got engaged. Despite our engagement being under false pretenses."

"But didn't he cheat on you, too? Even though he was 'celibate?'" Sophie said.

Callie's eyes widened at her friend, her mouth opening and closing before she settled on a frown. "Yes..." her voice trailed off. "That's the one piece of the puzzle I can't figure out."

But I could.

I spoke up for the first time since she entered the room. "You were never who he wanted to be with, Cal," I told her softly, giving her a small smile to help break the chill in the room. "Being celibate was an easy out for him to not sleep with you, that way he didn't have to do so out of obligation to you. So, he found a sense of justification in his actions because he was only with you to throw you off his scent. Meanwhile, he knew you were with him by choice. You were a loyal partner to him and he had no reason to suspect otherwise."

"Until you," she responded gently, her features softening.

I flashed my dimple at her. "Until me."

For a brief moment, there was an intimate silence that followed, the energy in the room charged. I shouldn't have found a sense of pride in being the reason a serial killer was now hunting her. Yet I was, because that meant something had been there between us and that it wasn't all for nothing.

Terry cleared his throat. It cut through our moment.

"What did you need from us, Callie?" he asked.

She looked around the room once more. "Well, clearly this is beyond our capabilities. He was able to fly under the radar while living with a cop. And worse, he was actively killing while I slept in the next room. Right now he's evading law enforcement easily with multiple aliases and changing jurisdictions, so… I think it's time we call in the FBI."

Twenty-Four

Callie

It was done. The truth was out, and I was okay.

As okay as I could be given the circumstances.

At the very least, I was relieved to relinquish the responsibility of this godforsaken case to people more qualified to deal with a serial killer. Swallowing my pride was easier than I anticipated.

Now I just had to anxiously await the two days until the FBI arrived.

I was walking across the bullpen when someone grabbed my elbow and hauled me into a nearby investigation room. I whirled as soon as the door was shut, only to find myself face to face with Liam.

I gulped. This was the first time we had been alone since the elevator ride down from the parking garage, and I wasn't entirely prepared to be alone with him again. Settled into the aftermath of our moment earlier, I felt… embarrassed. I threw myself at this man once again only for him to—shocker—shoot me down.

Even as I thought it, I knew how hypocritical it sounded.

"Liam, what the hell are you doing?" I whisper-shouted.

"I wanted to talk to you," he responded, giving me a look that said that should have been obvious. "And not… not in a way like we were in the car." His cheeks flushed, and I hated how damn cute it was.

I crossed my arms. "Well, you have my undivided attention now."

He leaned back against the door. "I wanted to apologize for making a move last night. It was wrong to do that to you. And after how this morning transpired, I wanted to make sure things wouldn't be awkward between us."

I blinked and then laughed. "How can things *not* be awkward? Even if you set aside a few innocent kisses, it's not like we ended things on a good note."

He cocked an eyebrow. "*Innocent kisses?* Come on, Callie, we both know those were far from innocent."

Damn it. He was right.

"I consider them to be innocent because nothing else came from them."

Except my heart was beating way too fast and my body was a little too warm.

And he knew it.

Liam's gaze darkened ever so slightly. My breath hitched. The air in the room seemed to hike up a few degrees.

"Anyway, if that's all you wanted to talk about, then I'm glad we cleared that up," I said, averting my eyes so he couldn't see how his expression affected me.

He pushed away from the door and stepped toward me. I stilled. "No, that's not all. Are you okay? You're going through some pretty heavy shit right now."

I looked away from him and shrugged. "I'm trying not to think about how I feel right now." I paused, then added, "I don't want to think about how I feel about anything."

He was quiet. I glanced up to see a calculating look on his face.

"What?"

"That's why you made a move on me this morning, huh? You wanted a distraction."

I raised one shoulder in response.

"Can you understand why I couldn't go through with it?" he asked, his voice low.

I wasn't in the fucking mood for this conversation. "Can we talk about this later, Liam?"

"I think we should talk about this now since we're going to be working pretty closely for God knows how long," he insisted as he took another step toward me.

Fuck. From here I could feel his warmth, could reach for him if I wanted to. And God, did I want to.

"What do you want me to say?"

Liam raked a hand through his hair. I watched a few locks tumble over his forehead; it took everything in me to not reach up and push them away. "I want you to tell me how you really feel about… well, everything. You had no problem being honest with me earlier this year."

My blood started to boil. As if I wasn't humiliated enough from a similar conversation with him. I sure as hell wasn't about to have it again. In a police precinct of all places.

"I'm not talking about this right now," I snapped and tried to reach around him for the door handle, but he pushed my hand away. I glowered at him. "Let me leave."

"No. We don't get to have this conversation only when you want to, Callie. I deserve answers, too."

This back and forth bickering felt like old times. I almost laughed.

I stumbled back a few steps. His scent wafted over me and made it hard to concentrate. Once there was more distance between us, I grimaced. "You want the honest truth? I'm embarrassed from this morning, and I'm somewhere between wanting to fuck you just to release some of this pressure I'm feeling, and not being ready to see you yet. I may have moved forward but that doesn't mean I've moved on. I still remember everything. *Everything.*" My voice was breathy at the end. Almost suggestive.

His eyes softened, the green so penetrating it felt as though he could see right through me. "I haven't, either. Those feelings haven't just gone away."

I put my hands on my hips. "What feelings, Liam? Hmm? Because, as I distinctly recall, you couldn't tell me yours. So please, enlighten me."

It was a low blow.

God, and *this* was exactly why I didn't want to have this conversation. It was messy and emotional and so not the time for it.

"I want you to consider giving us a fair shot. Neither of us are in relationships and we've been given a second chance. You can't look me in the eyes and seriously tell me you haven't felt anything. Even now, in this very moment."

Damn him.

I wanted him to be wrong, but he wasn't. My stomach had bottomed out when he pushed me away this morning, and even in the briefing room I was comforted by him.

I knew there was a solid chance those old feelings could resurface; I just didn't expect it to happen so quickly. Neither of us was ready for that.

"I can't lie to you and say I've felt nothing," I whispered, my voice wary as I eyed his every move. We were cloaked in the dim light of the room, as if a whole precinct didn't exist just beyond the door. "But I've been back for one day. We're both different than we were all those months ago, and life is about to shift on its axis for me. It's not really optimal timing."

"Is timing ever right? Callie, I'm standing before you telling you how I feel, like you asked me to. I'm here to help protect you. You know I would give my life for yours in a heartbeat."

Okay, so he *had* done that before when he saved me from a bullet to the skull. I was lucky to have escaped with only a scar.

"All I'm asking is for you to keep an open mind. Since you left, all I have thought about is what I'd give to have you back."

My heart crumpled. These were words I would've given my last breath to hear, but they were so late, so full of promises I wasn't sure he could keep. He seemed to sense this, because he sighed in defeat and stepped aside.

He's letting me leave? Just like that?

This wasn't typical Liam behavior. Usually this would escalate to an argument, and we'd be so caught up in the moment that we'd both be reeling and maybe—if I was lucky—we'd have passionate sex after. But this Liam... this was the Liam I saw at dinner last night. Calmer, more collected.

As I went to leave, both relieved and disappointed, he caught my wrist.

Twenty-Five

Liam

We weren't getting anywhere with this conversation. I put feelers out on where I stood, and she didn't bite. For once, I wasn't upset with Callie's dismissal—I respected it. She was going through enough. My intention wasn't to make her life more difficult, so I wasn't going to push it.

I stepped out of her way so she could leave. There was a slight look of hesitation on her face before she shuffled around me. Her shoulders were slumped in defeat. I gently grabbed her wrist before she could leave. She paused her retreat.

My fingers trailed down to interlace with hers. "I'm proud of you," I murmured. "You're handling all of this with an amazing amount of strength and grace. It's important you know that."

Her eyes misted over. It was the first time she'd shown any real emotion over this whole situation. "You really think so?" she whispered.

I turned toward her and slowly backed her against the wall by the door. "Yes, and everyone else here would agree." I brought my other hand up and caressed her face. "And also, about us? I hear you, and I understand. I'll be here when it's the right time."

Her lower lip trembled. I stepped away, flashed her a smile, and left the room.

Despite what I told her, my heart still yearned for her to be mine. But I knew I couldn't put that kind of pressure on her. That pressure is what drove us to fall apart in the first place. The more she put on me, the more I felt like pushing her away. I couldn't explain why—maybe because I wasn't ready until it was too late. And now it was her turn to not be ready, and I was certain a relationship was the last thing on her mind right now.

As for me?

I needed some fresh fucking air.

If I didn't clear my head, I'd be sent right back to New York, and right now Callie needed people she trusted to take care of her.

I needed to be one of those people.

Twenty-Six

Callie

It was a relief when Sophie and I strolled into the Third Precinct two days later. The FBI had arrived. My anxiety released its chokehold on me—it was finally going to be out of my hands very, very soon.

"Sorry if you heard me and Dean last night," Sophie said a bit sheepishly.

I laughed and refrained from sticking out my tongue. I had been crashing on her couch the last few nights, and Dean had come over to spend the night with her. Things got a little bit… *loud* in her bedroom.

"I'm just happy to see you guys are doing so well. He looks at you like… you're his whole world." I slung my arm around her shoulders, breathing in the smell of freshly brewed coffee.

She sighed in contentment, but her eyes flashed with uncertainty. "Yeah, he is pretty amazing. I love him."

I frowned. *Who are you trying to convince, me or yourself?*

I didn't press the issue, and instead said, "That much was clear in the wee hours of the morning, Soph."

She tilted her head back and laughed. We paused in front of her office. "Love you, *chula.* Keep your chin up today. I'll see you in a few hours when the feds arrive."

"Love you, too."

Out of habit, I turned and strolled toward my old office. I paused in front of it, half-expecting to see new detectives occupying the space, but the door was shut and the lights were off. I frowned and tried the handle; it swung open. I flicked the light on, and the familiar harsh fluorescent lights poured over stacks of boxes. I was surprised to find they were filled with unused office supplies.

Standing in the center of the room, I took a deep breath. As I turned in a slow circle, I found remnants of my old life—sticky notes with my handwriting and case suggestions still on the board, my mega-sized calendar on my former desk, left on the month of February with a heart drawn around Valentine's Day. I sank onto the couch and closed my eyes.

I was utterly exhausted; sleeping for a week before facing the feds sounded appealing.

"I thought I could find you here," Liam's voice chimed from the doorway.

Twenty-Seven

Liam

Callie jumped. "You scared the hell out of me!"

I gave her a lopsided, boyish smile. I'd barely seen her the last two days while I helped pull the archived files and prepare the investigation room for the feds.

"It's weird being in here again," I admitted.

She looked around the room with fondness in her eyes. "I was just thinking that. A lot happened within these four walls."

I raised my eyebrows. "That's putting it lightly."

She rose to her feet with a heavy sigh, and I finally got a good look at her. She had dark circles under her eyes.

"Is everything ready for the feds?"

I nodded and crossed my arms. "Now we just wait."

Callie stared down at her feet and wrung her hands.

"What's wrong?"

"You mean, besides the obvious?" she half-joked, but there was a cold undertone to her words. "Terry broke the news to me yesterday that the feds want me to stay here in protective custody until further notice."

"A cop being kept prisoner in a police precinct. Seems a little ironic," I teased.

She rolled her eyes but I saw a small smile tug the corners of her lips. "What's ironic is sleeping on this couch every night knowing the activities that have taken place on it."

I chuckled. "I didn't realize you meant *here* here."

She spread her arms wide. "Welcome to my new home."

"I think that's a little dramatic."

Callie scowled. "Coming from the person who gets to leave here at the end of the day."

God, I missed her.

"If you don't want to be stuck alone here, I can bring takeout like the good ole days."

She sat back down on the couch. "As much as I'd love to say yes, I think I need to be alone tonight. I spent most of last night trying to drown out Sophie and Dean."

I held back my laughter. "Whatever's best for you, Cal." I winked at her before turning on my heel to leave, but her next words stopped me.

"Wait. I-I've been thinking. You know, about our conversation a couple of days ago."

Slowly, I turned back around without saying anything. Her eyes glimmered with an unnamed emotion, lips pursed.

"Listen, I..." her voice faltered as she searched for words. "I really appreciate you giving me the time and space I need. I don't want you to think that, you know... *we* are off the table. I just know that I have to get through this before I can think about that."

Even though my heart twisted at her words, I understood where she was coming from. I assumed that we wouldn't be having this conversation again so soon. And this time, I was the one who wasn't ready.

I leaned against the door frame and crossed my arms. "Like I told you the other day, I'll be here waiting when this is all said and done. I'm not here to rush you." I held her gaze so she'd know how serious I was.

Callie frowned, and that adorable little V formed between her brows. "So that's it? No pushback?"

I blinked. "I guess I'm not understanding what you're looking for. You're telling me you're not ready. Wouldn't I be an asshole if I didn't respect that? The last time I pulled shit like that, we argued—a lot—and you pushed me away."

She scoffed, and a part of me deep down was growing angry. What did she want from me? I was doing my best to respect her wishes, and that didn't make her happy. But trying to push her into something serious before *also* didn't make her happy. Was I missing something?

"Yeah, I guess you're right," she said finally, conceding as she bit her lip.

I looked away, focusing on the notes we had both left on the board on the wall. The last thing I needed was to think of all the things I wanted to do to her.

"Will you answer something for me?" she asked.

I shrugged. "Sure."

"How many women have you slept with since I left?"

Shock rushed through me. I almost turned and walked away without answering her. It was a trick, right?

I shrugged again. "I don't know. Several," I admitted, then added, "I never expected to see you again."

Callie nodded. "I figured."

I frowned. "What the hell does that mean?"

"Last year, I was… in dire need of human connection, and you were substituting me because you didn't want to be alone."

I gaped at her, and not in a good way. I couldn't wrap my brain around what she was implying. How she had whittled what we had down to practically nothing.

It fucking *stung*.

"I mean," she continued, as if she couldn't stop herself, "you were with your ex-wife for most of your adult life. And as soon as I left, you turned to all these women. Now you're using alcohol to curb that loneliness. I'm used to being alone, and I'm sober now. I think it's helped prepare me to be in a relationship once we've put all this bullshit behind us. So I'm just wondering, do you really feel like you're ready?"

I dragged a hand down my face. "Jesus, Callie. I've been catering to your every whim since you walked into my office, done everything you've asked and respected every choice, and yet you *still* choose to call out my indiscretions as if I'm not. You could've just left things as they were," I snapped.

And the reality was, she had no idea what she was talking about, but I wasn't going to get into that with her right now. For the first time maybe ever, I wanted to get away from her. She twisted the knife just far enough that now I was the one who needed space.

"I'm just saying, I think it's important for you to take time to sober up and learn to be on your own without a crutch before we give this a shot."

My blood simmered in my veins. She blindsided me with these questions and then weaponized my answers against me. It was premeditated; it had to have been just to pick a fucking fight with me. I bit my tongue to prevent myself from lashing out at her. I closed my eyes and took a deep breath before looking at her again. "Right. Should I add anything else to my list of things to fix before I'm good enough for you?"

Callie's eyes flashed with hurt, maybe a little bit of remorse, but I didn't have it in myself to apologize. I left before things could go any further.

As it stood, she already poked enough holes in my confidence that now I was second-guessing one glaringly important thing: maybe I *wasn't* ready. Not if that's how she was going to act every time I screwed up.

Twenty-Eight

Callie

⚜

"I may have fucked things up," I lamented to Sophie as I waited for her to accompany me downstairs to meet the feds.

"Don't tell me you tried to hook up with Liam again," she quipped, rifling through the papers on her desk with a small frown on her face.

I shook my head and groaned. "No, worse. I told him he needed to be sober and learn to be on his own before we could be together."

Sophie winced and gave me a quizzical look. "Why? Was he being pushy?"

I put my face in my hands. "No. The opposite, really. He's been completely respectful of my boundaries and… I don't know. I can't help but feel like I… intentionally picked a fight with him?" I sputtered, trying to put my thoughts into words.

She leaned back in her desk chair and looked at me expectantly.

"Everything was going great. Like I said, he was receptive to everything I asked, he even set his own boundaries. That's great progress for us. But then… ugh, I don't fucking know! Maybe part of me misses the passion from our fights."

"Callie, that's *so* toxic."

"I know," I muttered. "He's different. He isn't caving to it like he used to."

"Of course he isn't. The last thing that man wants to do is drive you away.

And quite frankly, I agree with his course of action."

I frowned. "Whose side are you on?"

Sophie leaned forward. "The right one. And right now, you're fighting against literally nothing. You guys aren't together, and you've probably offended him by telling him he needs to change." She paused and quirked a brow. "He's already changed so much in light of what went down. You weren't here to see what it did to him. He, at least, is being mindful of what he did to you."

I flinched. Her words stung. Her taking Liam's side stung even more. Clearly, I was still making a lot of poor decisions on how I was navigating this non-existent relationship with Liam.

"Now, shall we go pass the baton to the feds?" she prompted, as if she hadn't just put me in my place.

* * *

Sophie and I stopped at the bottom of the stairs. The first floor of the precinct was pure madness. The building's normal chaos had shifted. Officers and suits bustled about. Nervous chatter floated down the hallways, dark energy flooding every empty corner. It felt like a completely different building than the one I entered this morning.

My stomach lurched. This was the atmosphere of a manhunt—one to track down a prolific serial killer who managed to disappear into the shadows at the drop of a hat.

I spotted Terry, his dark hair and rich brown skin a stark contrast against the white shirt of his uniform.

Wait. *Uniform?*

I hadn't seen Terry in his uniform in years, save for the rare event we were mandated to attend.

Terry stood next to Liam, who was looking over a file with two other people I didn't recognize.

"This is a tad insane," I remarked, wide-eyed at the crowd.

Sophie nodded in agreement. We wound through the throngs of people as we beelined for Terry and Liam. When we broke through, the loud babbling of voices seemed to quiet some.

"Ah, there's the woman of the hour," Terry greeted, draping his arm around my shoulders to pull me into the small circle he'd formed in the middle of the bullpen. "Sorry, Callie, I know it's wild in here, but these guys are amazing, and they have access to the coolest technology."

That wasn't really the point of them being here.

I refrained from rolling my eyes; I threw him a meek smile instead.

"I want you to meet these two agents. They'll be the ones taking your statement. Drew and Madelyn, this is Sergeant Callie Eden and Detective Sophie Reyes. This is Supervisory Special Agent Drew Matthews and Special Agent Madelyn Carver," he introduced, referring to the two other people with us.

They were pretty young for their titles, probably around my and Liam's age. The man had deep gray eyes, captivating and secretive, and curly coppery-brown hair that was longer on top and short on the sides—stylish. The woman was short, quite a bit shorter than me, but stood taller than everyone in our circle with her presence. Her rigid demeanor made me feel small, especially with her curly platinum hair and glimmering amber-colored eyes. She was strikingly beautiful, but had a hard set to her jaw.

I was mildly terrified of her.

"Who are all these other people?" I asked the agents as I looked around.

The two agents shared a brief look, and I watched them carefully. It was Agent Carver who said, "They're here for backup. We need as many hands on deck as possible. After our team reviewed the case and saw just how dangerous this killer is, we realized it could unravel much quicker now that he's completed his message to you. We decided to bring on a dozen of our own team and SWAT members to be on standby. We've officially put Oliver Frankford on the FBI's Most Wanted List, and he is now classified as a national threat." Her voice was lilting and serious all at once.

I blinked.

"Wait. Why didn't you guys take it this seriously last year? Was it because he stopped killing?"

Agent Matthews arched a brow. "We've never reviewed this case before."

The world tilted. Slowly, I looked up at Terry, who covered his mouth with his hand and looked at me apologetically.

"You... *lied?*" I rasped.

"Callie, I-I admit that I lied," Terry confessed. "To be honest, I didn't think you'd get anywhere with the new piece of evidence you found, and by the time you did, you guys were making great headway and I really believed you'd close it."

I felt like the wind had been knocked out of me.

This man... I had looked up to him for *years.* And here he was being dishonest about something that destroyed my life. Because of his fucking lies—

"You mean to tell me," I seethed, "that all of this could have been avoided."

"Why don't we take this into another room?" Agent Matthews prompted, gesturing to the room we had set up for them.

"That's a great idea," Liam chimed in. He rounded Terry and put a hand on my shoulder, gently pushing me forward.

I shrugged him off. "I can escort myself." I stormed toward the investigation room.

Agent Carver was the first one in the room with me. "You should really watch how you speak to your Captain."

I glowered at her. "He's not my Captain. I came here as a courtesy because they have all the case files."

She narrowed her eyes at me as the rest of our small group filed in. "You know, Drew, I think we should take her statement now."

Twenty-Nine

Callie

I settled into the interview room that the feds had ushered me in to. The cold metal chair bit into the backs of my thighs and was slightly wobbly by design—a tactic we used to make suspects uncomfortable and antsy. Facing the two federal agents, I felt like an actual suspect.

The light above me seemed too harsh, the corners of the room too dark. The tiled walls needed to be cleaned, and the grime on the grout was more noticeable from this side of the table.

All that was missing were handcuffs around my wrists.

I glanced up at the one-sided mirror, knowing who was on the other side watching my every move like a hawk. I wanted to squirm, though I had no reason to.

"Couldn't we have cleared out an office and done this in there? It's much more comfortable," I muttered. I felt guilty of a crime I hadn't committed and didn't want to give my statement under these circumstances.

Agent Carver's smile didn't reach her eyes. "This is fine. Now, Sergeant Eden, why don't you tell us when this whole thing started?"

I gulped. *Why am I nervous?* This was standard for any investigation, and it wasn't the first time I'd been interviewed by the feds on a case I assisted. "F-from the beginning?" When she dipped her chin, I began to tell the story, from start to finish. I willed my tongue to cooperate, channeled that confidence I worked so hard to display in front of others. I knew my qualifications and my personal involvement, my own faults in this case, and all the details in between. I knew what I had gone through and had no choice but to be steadfastly comfortable with all my decisions leading up to this point.

When I was done, I was nearly out of breath. Admittedly, I felt rattled, but on the outside I was the portrait of a composed woman who had gone through hell.

"Sergeant Eden, why didn't you follow up with your former Captain about involving the FBI?" Agent Matthews inquired, cocking an eyebrow at me.

"To be frank, we thought we had it under control. We were also under the impression the FBI did not deem it urgent enough to take over. The case had gone cold, but new information came to light about the nature of Hanna Garrison's disappearance. And then there was a breakthrough on the connection between the victims. Even when the killings picked up again, it was isolated to Newark. The Manhattan cases had ceased entirely. We did our best to treat this as a typical homicide case given the circumstances."

I tried my hardest to remain calm, but the news that Terry had lied was still fresh, the wound sore. How much collateral damage could have been avoided had he been honest?

The agents exchanged a look.

"Are you aware that at any point in time, you could have tried to reach back out to us?"

I took a deep breath to center myself and collect my thoughts. *They're just trying to get the full picture,* I reminded myself. "Yes, I realize that now. At the time, I was not comfortable going around my Captain to do so. That, and also my pride and personal attachment to the case stopped me."

"Hmm," Carver murmured. "And why do you think Frankford is targeting you?" She gave me a look of skepticism that made me uncomfortable.

I pinned myself to the chair, refusing to fidget even though I wanted to. "Were you not apprised of the details?"

"We want to hear it from you."

I raised my eyebrows. "He was with me to keep tabs on the investigation. I can only assume he knew who I was from press interviews I'd given. After Sergeant Chandler became my partner, Frankford was threatened and that's when he started killing again. He grew more hostile at home, and at some point became aware of my own… indiscretions, if you will."

She leaned forward, her bouncy hair falling over her shoulder. "So you were having an affair?"

I cleared my throat. Why they were having me recount these events *again* was baffling. Were they trying to prove I did something wrong? Ethically with the affair, I had; but legally with my job? Never.

I didn't like that I couldn't get a read on the stone cold robotic agents before me.

"Yes," I confessed. "I was having an affair with Liam Chandler, a former detective here."

"Interesting," Matthews said quietly. I remained impassive, but inside a flicker of irritation sprung to life. "Do you ever feel like your involvement with your partner hindered your ability to solve this case?"

I didn't like his implication.

"Not at all," I said. "If anything, it gave me more insight into the victims. Liam and I had our fair share of differences, sure, but we always prioritized work over everything else. For you to imply anything else is completely out of line."

Agent Carver seemed to instinctively reach for Agent Matthews's hand, but she retracted it before they could touch. "There's no need to be defensive, Sergeant Eden."

I gritted my teeth. "I don't appreciate my character being called into question. The only thing I did off the books was fake an engagement to Frankford so I could find out what he was hiding. And yes, it did put my own safety at risk and resulted in a life-threatening physical altercation. That's not a secret and I take full accountability for my actions."

"Right, but that plan of yours involved two other law enforcement officers to participate without legal permission, correct?" Matthews asked.

I looked between the two of them, sensing the protective fondness they had for one another, and used that to my advantage. "Let me ask you both something. Have you ever cared about a person, maybe *people*, so much that you would be willing to put it all on the line for them?"

Carver's eyes widened a fraction of an inch, and I knew I struck gold.

"That's what Sophie and Liam did for me. They trusted me so deeply when I said that something felt off with the man I knew as Owen Fisher, they were willing to stand by me and help any way they could."

Silence greeted me. I noted the haunted look that passed over Agent Carver's face.

"Any more questions, or am I free to go?"

Agent Matthews was looking at Agent Carver, concern written all over his face. I wasn't sure what kind of nerve I struck, but I rose to my feet anyway and left the room.

Terry was waiting for me in the hall. It was all I could do not to shoulder him when I passed. I wasn't sure I could ever forgive him for what he'd done.

"Have I done something wrong, *sir?*" I sneered mockingly when he blocked my path. "Is that why they're interrogating me as if I'm the one under investigation?"

He shook his head and ran a hand down his face. "No, Callie. They're turning this place upside down. They're looking for anything that could suggest case negligence or obstruction of justice."

I crossed my arms.

"I'm sorry, Callie. My job is now on the chopping block because of what I've done."

Good.

"Major Crimes *and* the FBI could have taken this over if you had done your job."

He rolled his shoulders back. "Careful, Callie. Remember your place."

"I no longer work for you. You deserve to know how badly you fucked up."

"You think I don't know that?" he snapped. "It's why I was so lenient with you for so fucking long. I was hoping you'd have a sense of loyalty to me. Clearly, I should have straightened you out as a rookie."

I gasped.

"Handing a case like this over to Major Crimes or the FBI doesn't look good for the precinct. It would have brought our clearance rates down and likely an audit with it. It was the last thing we needed. We would've faced extensive budget cuts and God knows what else."

I scoffed. "So money was more important to you than doing the right thing?"

Terry was silent.

The door to the investigation room opened. "Sergeant Eden?" Agent Matthews piped up. "We'd like to finish your interview now."

I didn't tear my eyes off Terry. "If you're going to charge anyone with obstruction of justice, it should be myself or Terry. Don't blame Sophie and Liam for being emotionally invested in my well-being or for trusting their superiors."

"We're not your enemies. We're merely here to help."

I finally looked over at the two agents in the doorway. "Then help," I snarled. "Don't just interrogate me; acquaint yourselves with the evidence and the facts."

Thirty

Liam

2 weeks later

Once the feds got settled, I headed back to New York and went back to work, only returning to Newark every few days to check in on the progress and to see how Callie was holding up.

Things were in utter disarray back in Newark. Callie felt trapped in protective custody at the Third Precinct. There was tension between Callie and Terry, both refusing to speak to one another. Terry's entire career as Captain was being investigated with a fine-tooth comb. Sophie and I were on slightly better speaking terms, but nothing more than being professionally cordial. Callie and I sometimes spoke in passing, but things were awkward after our last conversation.

And worst of all, the feds were no closer than we had been.

I was packing up early for the day to head back over to Newark when Detective Brookins knocked on my door. I glanced up to find her looking around sheepishly.

"Brookins. What can I do for you?"

"I, uh, wanted a word with you before you left," she said.

I waved her in.

"Listen, I know I haven't been exactly, um," she paused to clear her throat, "welcoming of you as my boss, and I wanted to apologize. I thought you were just another man receiving a leg up while I've worked my ass off to get to where I am."

I raised my eyebrows and waited for her to continue.

She was a damn hard worker; that much I could admit.

"Donaldson just filled me in on what you're going through back at your old precinct in Newark. I had no idea you were working with the feds."

"Brookins, I don't need nor want your pity," I deadpanned.

Her dark eyes widened. "Oh my God, sir, that's not—," she paused. "That's not where I was going with that. I just meant that, I haven't had the privilege to work on a case quite like that. I was wrong about you; I was unaware of your qualifications."

"Not like my qualifications are any of your business," I said quietly, leaning across my desk, "but thank you. The involvement of the FBI was long overdue, and an unexpected visitor decided it was time to bring them in."

"The woman from a few weeks ago?"

I nodded slowly. "Yes."

"You changed after she arrived," Brookins noted.

I cocked my head to the side. "How do you figure?"

"Well, for starters, you shaved. And you have this look in your eyes I've never seen before. You look… happier. You have a history with her, perhaps a romantic one?"

"Brookins…" This was getting too personal for me.

She held her hands up defensively. "Sorry, sorry. Not my place."

"My involvement with Sergeant Eden was at one point a romantic one, but I don't foresee that happening again anytime soon," I decided to tell her, because I could tell her curiosity was eating at her from the purse of her lips and her shifting from one foot to the other.

She gave me a small smile. I wasn't sure I had ever seen Brookins crack a smile before now. "That certainly explains a lot, sir." Realization dawned on her as she asked, "Sergeant Eden… as in Callie Eden?"

"You know her?"

"I know *of* her. She was my brother's old partner. Charles Hale? He moved north a few years ago, but I remember him talking highly of her. Said she was a smart kid with a promising future."

I smiled. "He wasn't wrong about that."

* * *

"You can't seriously leave after you've torn this place apart," I argued with Madelyn and Drew—the two federal agents in charge of taking this whole thing over.

"I'm sorry, Liam, but we've already spent a lot of time without getting anywhere. This guy's a ghost. We'll take everything over and work it from our home base," Madelyn replied as she shoved files into a box.

I pinched the bridge of my nose. "And what are your plans with Sergeant Eden? You've kept her captive here for the last two weeks because you felt she wasn't safe."

"She's not," Drew interjected. "She'll have to remain in protective custody."

"I'm sorry, have you met Callie?" There was a hint of laughter in my voice, because I could already imagine that conversation.

"I'll talk to her," Madelyn said with a sigh.

"It doesn't matter who talks to her. When you tell her that you're heading back to Quantico, she's going to lose it."

"Well, then you explain to her that we've exhausted our resources here."

"Try to have some compassion for the poor woman, Maddie. It wasn't that long ago that you were in a similar position," Drew chided.

Over the last couple of weeks, I'd gotten to know the two agents pretty well. They were dating and had been through some pretty fucked up shit. We were all friendly with one another now, and part of me would be sad to see them go.

"When are you guys leaving?"

"Day after tomorrow. We'll try to find a better solution for Ms. Eden in the meantime," Drew told me.

I heaved a sigh of relief. "Thank you. That'll spare me at least a little bit when I break the news to her."

Drew barked out a laugh. "With that temper of hers? Good luck, buddy."

Madelyn scowled at him. "Careful, Drew. Don't underestimate a woman with a temper."

"Oh, so now you're on her side?"

"I'm just saying. You did that once or twice and groveled for days."

I chuckled. "Well, I better go check in with her."

* * *

Callie returned to the precinct a few hours later. I was reviewing CCTV footage with Marcus and trying to find any trace of Frankford while I waited for her. So far, it had been a whole lot of nothing. I put in a call to Callie's department in Springcrest to obtain footage from the café Frankford was at that day she saw him, but had yet to hear back.

When Officer Dodson informed me of Callie's return, I thanked Marcus for letting me join him before I headed down to our former office—AKA Callie's new home. I found her rifling through one of her bags in frustration.

This will be fun.

"Hey," I greeted her.

She looked up with an adorable scowl on her face. Her blue eyes softened when she saw me. "Hey, yourself. Is it your shift to come babysit me?"

I rolled my eyes but gave her a small smile. "We aren't babysitting you. But, I am here to check in on you. Can I do anything to help?"

She straightened. "Get me out of this godforsaken place?"

My smile split into a grin. Some of the tension eased off my shoulders; things weren't as awkward as I expected after the last couple of weeks. "I don't have that kind of authority, but I can keep you company, if you're feeling up to it."

"I thought your new job made you a hotshot," she teased, the ghost of a smile on her lips. "Maybe you can put in a call to release me from this prison."

I chuckled. "It'll be over soon enough."

Callie puffed out her cheeks. "Right. Look, if you want to keep me company, you can help me review these reports from my officers. Work is about the only thing keeping me sane right now."

"Yeah, I'd be happy to." I hiked a thumb over my shoulder. "Want any tea before I join you?"

"I'd love some, thanks." She sat down and pulled a folder into her lap.

I smiled at the sight, even though she couldn't see it. It all just felt so familiar. Like… home.

Shaking the thought from my mind, I wandered down to the break room to make us some tea. I returned several minutes later to find her in the same position but in pajamas now, intently reading the pages in the folder.

I set her mug down on the coffee table in front of her. She glanced up, those big blue eyes catching mine. My heart squeezed. "Thank you." She picked up the mug and took a grateful sip.

I sat on the floor on the opposite end of the couch and leaned back, then grabbed a folder from her stack. It took me a moment to get used to the different format and overall lack of flair in these reports. After all, these were all based on small town crimes.

An unknown amount of time passed in silence. After several files, I felt her eyes turn to me. I tried to ignore it for as long as I could.

"Why are you just staring at me?" I asked without looking up from the report I was now pretending to read.

"This just… feels like old times."

This time I did look over at her, but I didn't say anything. I just took in her beauty for the first time in a while. Her hair was pulled back into a ponytail, her skin free of makeup, her body clad in tight pajamas.

Callie flushed as I scrutinized her. I missed how cute she was.

"How did things get so fucked up between us?" Her voice was almost a whisper as she distracted herself by picking at her nails.

I snickered. "A couple of people making rash fucking decisions based on emotion alone."

She giggled. "That's a nice way of putting it, I suppose."

Now would've been a great time to break the news to her about the feds leaving, but she scooted closer to me, until her knee was touching my shoulder. I couldn't think straight when she was this close—especially as she lowered herself to the ground beside me, and my eyes wandered to the swell of her breasts under her tight-fitting shirt.

Jesus. It had been a while since I allowed myself to look at her this way; I did my best to keep naughty thoughts hidden given the current state of, well, everything.

But damn it, I couldn't stop my dick from hardening.

I swallowed thickly, forced myself to focus on how confusing she was. One minute she's adamant about it not being a good time, and the next she's making a move.

At least, I thought she was making a move. She'd turned off the bright overhead lights quite some time ago, so the room was awash with warm light from the two desk lamps in the room. Now she was sitting beside me, lightly running a finger down my arm.

Then the air was charged between us, the raw chemistry almost palpable in the air, and I wasn't sure who leaned in first but suddenly her lips were on mine and all was right in the world. I tossed the report to the side and grabbed her waist to pull her closer. She let out a soft whimper against my mouth and *fuck*, it was sexy as hell.

I missed her warmth, how her body fit so perfectly against mine, and I missed her noises and her irresistible smell and the way her kiss made me want to bury myself deep inside her.

I swept my tongue across hers, and any remaining logic flew out the window. I was suddenly consumed by the idea of taking her on this couch. Nothing else mattered, least of all my boundaries. To hell with it all.

Callie's hands slid up my stomach, my chest, my shoulders, leaving trails of fire as she went. I was melting under her touch.

I cupped her face in my hands as she climbed into my lap to straddle me, and held her there. As much as I was tempted to rush into ripping her clothes off, I wanted to enjoy the feel of her pouty lips on mine. Maybe it was juvenile, but it felt like fucking nirvana to kiss her.

She ground her hips against my hard length, and I growled into her mouth. I didn't know how much longer I could resist her.

My hands slipped under her shirt, skating up her ribs and cupping those perky tits of hers, earning another moan from her.

Yeah, this was going to progress fast.

Suddenly a soft rap on the door had us springing apart. Drew stood in the doorway, looking back and forth between us with amusement. A quick glance at Callie revealed her reddened face and swollen lips.

"Chandler, I need to speak with you." He included his head to the hallway behind him.

"Sure, I'll be right out." Drew disappeared and I focused my attention on Callie again. "I'm sorry."

"Interruptions are a common theme with us, huh?" she retorted half-jokingly.

I rubbed the back of my neck. "Seems that way." Tucking a loose strand of her hair behind her ear, I added, "But trust me, when the time is right—and it will be eventually—I will fuck you any way you'd like."

The color in her cheeks darkened.

"And that's a promise."

Thirty-One

Callie

As soon as Liam left, I shut and locked the door. I didn't want to be bothered for the rest of the night. Plus, I was left high and dry and needed some alone time with my vibrator.

I only got to see Liam once every few days, and every time I did, he took my breath away. His strikingly handsome features were a refreshing change, and even awkward small talk with him felt more normal than my current day to day life.

And as much as I knew we needed to work on ourselves, I still craved physical intimacy with him. Besides, we had tried the whole friends-with-benefits thing before and it had gotten messy. *Fast.*

But now my body was buzzing with arousal and my lips were tingling from his passionate kiss. My head was reeling from his words: *I will fuck you any way you'd like. And that's a promise.*

Sighing, I tossed my now-used vibrator into my open duffel bag and collapsed on the couch. It had been a mentally exhausting few weeks, and tomorrow I was going to have to act surprised when someone broke the news to me that the feds were leaving. They all acted like it was some big secret, but I was smarter than they gave me credit for.

At the very least, maybe they would release me from sleeping in a police precinct. I just wanted my own space and privacy back. Even being back in the field sounded like a nice change of scenery.

I curled up on my side and looked at all the missed calls from my family. I didn't want to talk to them and tell them I had no update or a day I would be returning home. It was just easier to text them and say I would call them back later.

Sleep soon pulled at my tired mind, and I let myself drift off into a much needed rest.

Thirty-Two

Liam

I found Drew leaning against the catwalk railing and joined his side.

"I take it you didn't tell her that we were leaving?"

I laughed. "What gave it away?"

"Gee, I don't know. Just a hunch," he teased, a smirk on his face.

"Right. Sorry you had to walk in on that," I apologized, feeling only mildly apologetic. Not that it was a secret Callie and I had a history... not like people weren't already speculating that we had rekindled our flame.

Drew shrugged. "If anyone understands a complicated workplace relationship, it's me." He heaved a sigh, his gaze locked on someone down below. I followed his line of sight and spotted Madelyn talking with another officer. "But when you know, you know."

"As messy as it can be, I'm sure it all pays off," I said.

"It's all about how you navigate those twists and turns. And how you deal with a strongly opinionated woman."

I grinned. "I hope you're right about that."

"Well, what are your thoughts on long distance relationships?"

I straightened and turned to face him, eyeing him skeptically. "What are you getting at?"

"I found a solution for Ms. Eden."

Arching a brow, I silently urged him to fill me in.

Drew took a deep breath. "I made a few calls, pulled some strings. I'm having a US Marshal meet us here the morning we leave to get Callie settled into WITSEC."

I took a step back and blinked. "Wait, *witness protection?* Are you fucking kidding me?"

He hesitated. "It's either that, or she stays here. At least with WITSEC she has the opportunity to build a new life."

"Yeah, with a new identity surrounded by no one she knows."

"Look, there's no happy medium here, and you know that. Oliver Frankford is a national threat and he's playing dangerous games with a law enforcement officer. We do not take that lightly. Quite honestly, I think WITSEC is a better and safer option than protective custody. She'll have freedom and the chance at a normal life. It's the less shitty of two shitty options," he explained.

My throat was dry as I tried to swallow. That meant… that meant for as long as Frankford stayed out there, Callie would be gone. For good. No contact, no communication at all. Her life as Callie Eden would be over until further notice, and I… I would lose her again.

I leaned against the railing again and dropped my head into my hands. How—*when* did all of this happen? How could we not see how serious this was?

"I'm sorry, man. This is the best I can do," Drew stated.

"Yeah, man, I know. It's just… right when I get her back," I mumbled.

He clapped my shoulder sympathetically. "We've notified her family that beginning tomorrow, she can make final phone calls. That being said, I think she'll respond best hearing this from you or Ms. Reyes, but she's not here, so…" his voice trailed off.

I groaned. "I'll take care of it."

* * *

Callie was asleep when I got back to the office, her knees tucked into her chest on the couch. I loosed a breath and pulled a blanket over her. It seemed like the WITSEC conversation would have to wait until the morning.

I drove to Terry's, where I stayed in the guest room during trips to Newark. While part of me was angry that he had lied, I realized I needed to pick my battles. We all had enough going on, and I still trusted Terry despite one bad call.

Even if his bad call had now cost me an indefinite future with Callie.

I crawled into bed and attempted to sleep, but try as I might, I couldn't manage it. I tossed and turned, the sheets damp with my sweat. Anxiety burned a hole in my chest. I was tempted to wake Callie up and tell her, but she needed to rest. I could suffer one night.

After all, the past five months had been spent suffering. What was one more night?

My restlessness nagged at me. The more I willed myself to sleep, the worse it got. This usually only happened to me when I was so invested in a case that I wanted to stay awake to solve it.

But I couldn't solve this. WITSEC *was* her best option. I knew that. I just didn't want to accept it.

Huffing, I kicked the sheets off and crawled out of bed to get dressed. I wouldn't be getting rest any time soon, but I could at least make the most of the night.

I quietly left, the warm summer heat greeting me as I stepped outside. I wasn't super familiar with his quaint, family-friendly neighborhood, but I stalked off toward the direction of the city. After some time, the lights and sounds of downtown greeted me. I came to a stop in front of a bar and hesitated.

Sure, Callie had told me to clean up my act—and I had done that. I hadn't had a single drink in the last two weeks, but frankly I thought the circumstances called for one.

My feet carried me in before I could talk myself out of it. Before I knew it, I had downed a drink and savored the way it felt on my tongue. I waved at the bartender for another round. Another glass was set in front of me and I blinked at it. I didn't realize I had ordered a scotch. The amber liquid glimmered in the dim lighting. I was suddenly reminded of why I hadn't drank it in months.

My eyes shut. I couldn't escape her. And that made this all the more painful.

Picking up the glass, I tossed it back in one go, motioned for another round as its smoothness hit the back of my throat, and took my time on the third one.

* * *

The walk back to Terry's was peaceful and quiet. The alcohol had done the trick and quieted the buzz in my mind.

I didn't track how long I walked, but I knew at one point I glanced around and noticed I was in a nice park strolling along a stone path. It was humid, the air thick and the breeze hot. I let it sober me up, let myself feel whatever rose to the surface, let myself enjoy the solitude…

Before I came to an abrupt halt when something caught my eye. I blinked several times in an attempt to clear the drunken fog that had clouded my mind.

No.

I panted as I raced over to the pale heap on the ground twenty feet from me. I fell to my knees in front of her and felt my heart plummet when I pressed two fingers to the side of her still-warm throat.

Lifeless eyes stared back at me, her jaw hanging open with a piece of paper peeping out from between her lips. Neck angled in an unnatural way, bruises decorating her throat, dark brown hair spilling over her shoulder. Her slim frame was clad in a stark white wedding dress, bright in the darkness of the night hanging over us.

And the dress of choice? It looked identical to the one my ex-wife wore on our wedding day.

Fuck.

The fresh work of the Wring Bearer. He was back in Newark, hot on Callie's heels and wasting little time in his killing game.

I staved off the relief that filled me when I discovered it wasn't Callie, as I had originally thought when I saw her. The relief was quickly followed by guilt. This poor woman.

It was all I could do to not reach out and look at that note in her mouth. It had to be reported first; I needed gloves and shoe covers and not to disturb the crime scene.

My tongue was leaden from the scotch. She hadn't been dead for long. With trembling hands, I pulled my phone out and called the Third Precinct to dispatch officers to the scene, rambling off my badge number, title, and location. Then I dialed Terry.

The call to Callie lasted less than fifteen seconds before she hung up. I knew it would be only a matter of minutes before she arrived.

Thankfully backup got here first, the red and blue lights following the blaring of sirens around the corner before they haphazardly stopped in the closest parking lot. I remained standing there to ward off any late-night walkers passing through the park; they gawked at the victim's limp body before scampering away in horror.

There were no witnesses, as expected; no one hanging around who saw the mop-headed fucker who took this woman's life and carelessly dumped her here. Nothing for me to go off of, and in the limited light of the dark park, there were no obvious clues that would allude to Oliver's whereabouts.

A few uniformed officers, including Dodson, rushed to me, gloves, shoe covers, and flashlights in hand.

"Sergeant," Dodson said by way of greeting. "Fill us in."

I relayed the story to them, and they immediately got to work flagging down a crime scene photographer and tech, placing markers as I gathered supplies from them. It felt strange to work an active crime scene in Newark again, but with my current dual-municipality approval, it was allowed.

When I asked the officers if they had any water with them, they frowned at me. But I flashed them a warning look, and Dodson promptly rushed back to the cars, returning a moment later with a bottle of water. I drank the entire thing.

I needed to sober up before other people arrived.

Surprisingly, Callie arrived before Terry. I was only alerted to her presence when I heard Sophie's voice call her name.

"Callie, slow down!"

I turned and saw Callie running toward the scene, ducking under the crime scene tape as if nothing in the world could hold her back.

Honestly, I wasn't sure anything could.

Seconds later she was in front of me, her eyes wild and frantic, her chest heaving as she caught her breath. She wore a pair of biker shorts and the same T-shirt I'd left her in a few hours before—the one that hugged her breasts in a delicious way.

Not like I noticed at a time like this.

"Were you the first to arrive?" She tugged on latex gloves and did a quick assessment of the crime scene.

"I found the body," I told her, taking a few steps away. Anything closer than three feet was much too close, for too many reasons.

Callie gave me a questioning once-over and twisted her lips. "Why were you out walking around at this hour?" Then she smirked. Yes, *smirked.* How she managed to do so under these circumstances, I wasn't so sure.

I blinked at her slowly. How was I supposed to tell her I went to a bar and got damn near drunk hours after making out with her?

"Have you been the *real* killer this whole time?"

A joke. From Callie Eden. When her serial killer of an ex was stalking her. Standing in front of his most recent victim. And she had the gall to make a *joke.*

Normally, the roles were reversed.

But my brain was still a little buzzed, and I wanted to fade into the darkness rather than admit to her what I was out doing.

I was saved from answering when a few of the officers around us stopped and looked at us. Callie waved them off and told them she was kidding before training her eyes on me again, her face mirthful and curious at the same time.

"Well?" she urged, a bit more seriously.

"I couldn't sleep." My words were clipped as I gritted them out. They weren't technically a lie.

Sophie sidled up next to us, throwing Callie a dismayed look. "Neither could I." Then, by way of explanation, added, "Dean and I had another fight, so I went and woke Callie up at the precinct. She nearly dragged me here by my hair after you called."

I gave them a half-hearted smile. "Doesn't surprise me."

"I only half dragged you here," Callie defended.

"Why are you so damn chipper?" Sophie teased her friend, her frown playful as she examined Callie.

Callie shrugged. "This is the best way to escape protective custody for a few hours!" She threw her arms out wide with a dazzling smile.

Fuck. Fuck fuck fuck.

I had momentarily forgotten about WITSEC. She had no idea yet. I could just imagine how that conversation would go down, how she would take it out on me.

My heart—and admittedly, my dick—throbbed at the thought. Maybe I wouldn't mind that so much. Her temper was one of the many things that I loved about her, and I hadn't really seen that side of her since she'd shown back up.

Sophie raised her eyebrows. "I'm very concerned about you right now."

"Don't be concerned about me. Be concerned about *him.* He's the one who was out walking at night like an old person with insomnia, *and* he found the body."

Another joke.

No part of me could bring myself to laugh. Mostly I just felt a little sick to my stomach.

Sophie's gaze swung to me. "She has a point. Care to explain?"

I glowered at both of them. I was in no mood for fun and games. I was worn down. My emotions had been on a roller coaster, I had to break shitty news to the woman I was still in love with, and I was not entirely sober while having to investigate a crime scene.

Whoa.

It was the first time I had admitted to myself that I was still in love with her.

I inclined my head toward Callie. "Care to do the honors of reading the note?" I carefully evaded the question by speaking as little as possible.

She gladly squatted beside the body and pulled out the piece of paper, unrolling it at a painfully slow pace. He'd already spelled out her name, what was next? Her middle name? Her job title?

As the paper revealed faint black writing, my heart nearly stopped. All three of us sucked in a breath as we silently read the note.

LIAM CHANDLER.

Thirty-Three

Callie

My good mood dissipated in an instant.

It was one thing when it was just me who had to worry about being hunted—obviously, aside from the victims. And therefore, it was easy to make light of the situation when I didn't have to worry about those I cared about.

But as I read Liam's name over and over, the three of us perfectly still as we processed it, I felt my legs wobble underneath me. I didn't want anyone else at risk because of my recklessness. Yet here we were. And why... why was *this* the victim Liam happened to stumble across? The one with his name written on a piece of evidence?

I hated to admit that it was a coincidence, given he was out at such a late hour. I wished he would tell me why.

I slowly rose to my feet and turned to look at him and Sophie. Liam's eyes were unfocused, a muscle in his jaw feathering as he stared at the small piece of paper in my hand. I wanted to know what was going through his mind; as much as I wanted to ask, it felt private. Personal.

And I wasn't sure we were at a place where I could ask those things.

Fuck it.

I placed my free hand on his arm, but he stumbled away from me. There was a surge of hurt, the taste of rejection bitter in my mouth. This was shockingly different than a few hours ago when he willingly sat in a quiet room with me and helped me with my work. Who kissed me with passion and promised to do unholy things to me.

I glanced at Sophie, who hadn't torn her eyes off Liam. She fixated on him with a concerned look, and I wondered if there was something I was missing.

There probably was.

I knew they had a strained friendship, but in my months of absence, they kept in touch. Saw each other occasionally, had deep and honest conversations, and occasionally consulted one another on cases. No doubt she knew more about his state of mind these days than I did.

"Liam—"

He waved me off and stormed away. I watched as he ripped his gloves and shoe covers off, his broad shoulders sagging in defeat.

"Should I follow him?" I murmured, not realizing at first that I said it aloud.

"No," Sophie responded right away. "He needs a minute. He's just as affected as you are."

My brows knitted together. "By the case, or by… me?"

She shrugged. "Both."

As that fact settled, I let the photographers take the note from me, place a marker, and snap photos. I stood there, feeling completely numb. It was bizarre working this case again, alongside the same people. As if nothing had changed, and yet *everything* had changed.

Maybe the third time's the charm.

At some point, Terry joined us. He didn't speak nor look at me, only asked Sophie for a briefing. I ignored his cold shoulder and gave him my own.

"Where are the feds?" Sophie asked him.

"They'll come check out the scene in the morning once it's been processed," he told her. "Where's Liam?"

I was tempted to answer, but I feared something harsh would come out of my mouth if I spoke to him at all.

"He stepped away after we saw the note," Sophie said. I was impressed at how gracefully she answered. "Do you know what he was out doing so late?"

Terry looked at us quizzically, for the first time acknowledging my presence since he arrived. "He didn't tell either of you?" We shook our heads. "He couldn't sleep, so he walked to go get a drink. He was on his way back and came across this victim."

I took a step back as if he'd shoved me. I couldn't believe what I was hearing—he went out to *drink?* No—*no.* Hours after kissing me, knowing what I asked of him, he went to a bar?

I pushed past them both without saying anything, following the path I saw Liam take earlier. I found him speaking to a few officers when I approached him in the parking lot. My hands balled into fists, my jaw clenching tighter than a vise.

"What the hell is wrong with you?" I demanded, breaking through his little circle to shove him backward. I didn't mean to be violent, but he had to know he crossed a line.

Liam caught himself as he fell back a few steps and straightened, training a very cold, dark look on me as he did. I couldn't read the emotions in his eyes as he said, "I was just wondering when I'd see this side of you."

My nostrils flared. In my peripheral, I saw the officers disperse as if they were afraid of becoming collateral damage. "What are you talking about?" I bit out.

He cocked his head to the side, one brow arching. "Your temperamental side. The one you reserve mostly for lashing out at me."

My hands twitched at my sides. The *audacity.* "If you weren't such an asshole, maybe I wouldn't be temperamental," I snapped.

Liam laughed, cold and heartless. "You and me, Callie? Fundamentally we have not changed in the last several months. And this?" He gestured between the two of us. "Me screwing up for a reason you have yet to reveal while you get pissed at me defines our dynamic at its core. So please, *Ms. Eden,* enlighten me on what I've done wrong this time."

Ms. Eden.

How dare he call me that in a time like this? My shoulders shook. I hadn't been this angry and upset since… well, since the day I left. I hadn't felt my temperature rise, my body buzz in so long… hadn't felt so *alive* in ages.

"Where were you tonight? Before you wound up here?"

Slowly, a devilish grin crept across his face, those dimples deepening as he realized what I was getting at. "You already know the answer, so why ask?" he prodded. He was intentionally trying to get under my skin.

And damn it, he was.

I ripped the gloves off my hands. "I want to hear you say it."

Liam cast his eyes skyward and stalked past me. I half expected him to admit it, but I certainly didn't anticipate him walking away in the middle of our conversation.

If that's what you'd even call it.

My stomach was doing somersaults as I chased after him. "Hey!" I called, not caring that it was the middle of the night. "You don't get to just walk away while we're talking!"

He halted and whirled toward me. I stopped a few feet from him. I could finally read his expression—anger, irritation, and something far more vulnerable swirling in them. Something I hadn't seen before. "First of all, we aren't talking. You're coming at me with useless accusations. Second of all, my whereabouts are none of your concern. We aren't partners anymore. We aren't together. And whatever moment we had earlier? It was exactly that: a *moment*. You made it very clear a couple of weeks ago that I'm not good enough as is. So why do you care?"

Something like a snarl tore from my throat, surprising us both. "You tell me you want to be with me and that you want me to give us a fair shot. I tell you what you need to do to help us get there, and then you do the exact opposite. That is why I care!"

I wanted him to cave, to admit that I was right. But in typical Liam fashion, he didn't.

"To hell with all of that, Callie!" he yelled, and I gasped. He rarely raised his voice at me. I was usually the one to do it while he sat back and goaded me with snarky remarks.

But then, he closed his eyes and took a deep breath. When he looked at me again, the anger was gone, and part of me was disappointed. Where was the fight that had been in him before I left? How far did I have to push him to unleash that side of him? Because damn it, I wanted things to feel like they once did.

"I'm sorry. I shouldn't yell at you." He put his hands on his hips and tilted his head back, as if trying to clear his head. A light breeze blew his hair back. The sight of him under the stars made him look like a fucking angel asking heaven for guidance. I clenched my thighs together, hoping the sinfully good-looking man didn't notice.

After a moment, he grabbed my elbow, and the butterflies in my belly erupted and spread lower, somewhere more sensuous. This new calm, humble Liam did dangerous things to my insides, made me see him in a new light. And I'll be damned if it didn't make me more attracted to him. Languid heat spread through my core, my skin tingling with anticipation as he guided me through the parking lot.

God, what was wrong with me? Why was this such a turn on?

Sophie was right: I *was* toxic.

"Get in your car. We aren't airing our dirty laundry out for everyone to see," Liam said quietly, his voice low and commanding as we rounded the driver's side. He opened the door for me, and I climbed inside without looking at him. I was as equally frustrated as I was aroused, and being in a small space with him wasn't going to help. I started the car and turned on the cold air as he slid into the passenger seat.

Liam sighed. "I'm... frustrated and confused, Callie," he said slowly. "Those are ground rules you set, not me. I have done nothing but respect your space and where you are at, but you sure as shit don't care about *me*. Not a single time did you ask what would work for *me*. You just assumed that I needed to be sober because that's what you needed. You're just as much a control freak as ever, and you seem to think that extends to relationships, that it's your way or the highway, rather than a compromise. And, by the way, in the last two weeks, I didn't have a single drink until tonight."

I was dumbfounded, chewing on my lip as I contemplated his words. Sure, he had some valid points, but I wasn't letting him off that easily.

I could get out of the car right now, let us both cool off, but I couldn't relent. Not now, not when we were being honest with each other and finally getting to the nitty gritty stuff we usually avoided.

"All I want is for you to take care of yourself and spend some time alone—"

Liam held up a hand and looked at me with such purpose that I paused with bated breath. "Why? You think you're just a rebound? Is that why you think I need to 'figure out how to be by myself?' Is that the newest excuse you've made?"

I hesitated. Was that why? Or was I just afraid to finally give him my heart and risk him shredding it to bits again?

The searing look in Liam's eyes made me squirm, made me feel hot and bothered everywhere. I rolled my hips slightly to give myself some much needed friction.

He looked out the windshield.

"Let me tell you something, Callie." His voice was so low and deep and quiet and so, so delicious as it scraped over my skin. I refrained from shuddering, tried to withhold the blush that crept up my neck. "You think I haven't had any time alone with my thoughts? You're so incredibly wrong. And maybe that's my fault for keeping you in the dark about what I went through after my divorce. All I did was spend every fucking night alone. Sure, I slept with a few meaningless women, but that's it. I stopped hanging out with the friends I made when I got married and wallowed in my misery as I grieved the loss of my future. My life, my wife, what I pictured would be my family. I couldn't face *anyone*."

Liam turned to me again so I could see it all. I watched his frustration fade as sadness settled into the shadows of his face. It was unlike any emotion I had ever seen on him before. And I felt my stupid heart pitter-patter in response, the fight in me beginning to leave my bones as I realized that perhaps *I* was the problem.

"I faced my emotions head-on," he continued, his voice gentler now as he searched my face. "I had to. Maybe I overcompensated by rushing into things with Kelsey when things were complicated with us. But when I had the chance to be with you, baby…" He paused to take a deep breath, and God, I was a pile of goo when he called me that. "It's not that I didn't spend enough time by myself. It's that I spent *too much* time by myself, that I talked my way out of it. Made excuses because I was scared and traumatized by what happened with Victoria.

"So when you left, I couldn't be alone again, Cal. I didn't have anyone around to help me move on. Everything reminded me of you. I moved back to New York, and that helped some. I found distractions in my daily life, and slowly started to heal from it all. But I never expected to see you again. Honestly."

Tears sprung to my eyes, and I forced myself to look away from the crushing devastation on his face. How could I have been so ignorant to not have thought about his side when I came back into the picture unexpectedly? What, I expected him to still be head over heels and ready to fight for me after disappearing for so long, without so much as a text to him? Did I really think he had magically escaped it all unscathed? God, how selfish and stupid of me.

"One of the many mistakes I made the first time around was not telling you how I felt about you. I have that chance again, but I don't think you're ready to hear that. Just like I wasn't ready when you told me. I'll be here because you're not a fucking rebound, Callie. You're my endgame."

My lips parted in surprise.

"All that being said, I don't know how much time we have left together. I was informed after I left our old office earlier that you'll be admitted into WITSEC, effective the day after tomorrow. You should contact your family to say your goodbyes. They've already been informed." He paused. "Once Frankford's in custody, we can resume whatever this is. If we're both ready."

Liam climbed out of the car, and this time I didn't chase after him. I sat there, taking in his words and wondering how I didn't see it all before. The only sound in the car now was the air blowing through the vents, cooling my skin after our heated discussion. Drenched in darkness, I felt… lost.

Like I didn't know where to go from here.

Then the last part of his declaration hit me.

I gaped at his retreating figure through the windshield as he walked toward a wooded part of the park. *WITSEC?* Oh my God. That meant that everything he said… those were his parting words.

Now I had such little time to wrap my life up in a bow before I had to leave. I had no idea when I'd be back.

Shit. I had promised my sister trips to the city. Sophie and Dean were in a tumultuous place; what would she do if I was gone and they broke up? She didn't talk to her mom about those things. Would she be all alone?

And what about Liam?

Oh God.

What if he moved on while I was gone? What if everything he just said didn't matter by the time I got back? What if I was in WITSEC for years, and *I* decided to move on? Would I always feel like he was the one who got away? The right man at the wrong time?

Fuck, would I be full of regrets?

Wait.

Liam had essentially told me what I had waited so long to hear, without actually saying the words, because… because…

I screamed and hit my steering wheel, once, twice, three times before it felt like my hand would bruise, the last one honking the horn and startling me. I felt so fucking overwhelmed by all the emotions crashing into me at once.

A few lingering officers in the parking lot looked over at my car, and I waved awkwardly, embarrassed by my loss of control. My cool facade was nowhere to be seen.

A hollow pit in my stomach threatened to swallow me whole as embarrassment morphed into devastation. I'd have to say goodbye to everyone—for good this time.

And maybe some anger accompanied that. Why did Liam have to be the messenger?

And oh, I was definitely feeling heartache. After all this time, he chose to declare his love when we had absolutely no time to work it out.

I choked out a sob and buried my face in my hands. Just when I thought this situation couldn't get any worse, the universe went and proved me so, so wrong.

Thirty-Four

Callie

After letting myself wallow for a few minutes too long, I wiped away my tears and flipped the visor down. Mascara pooled under my eyes; I swiped it away before I stumbled out of the car. Taking a deep breath, I allowed the clean night air to brace me, calm and center me. So I had less than thirty hours to wrap up any loose ends in my life. That was doable. There weren't that many now, but there was one person I needed an intimate moment with.

Half-running to the forested part of the park, the moon providing just enough light to guide my way, my focus drifted to slowing my erratic heartbeat and uneven breathing. Just because I had a minor meltdown in my car didn't mean my body had settled afterthe high that came from fighting with Liam.

And, well, just being in his presence.

I slowed as I approached the trees and found him seated on a bench in the middle of a small clearing. His hands were in his hair, elbows on his knees.

The slump in his shoulders and tense set to his jaw made him look defeated. My heart sank as I realized I was partly responsible for that.

"I'm not in the mood to fight with you, Callie." His voice was hoarse, husky. I shivered as I took a tentative step forward.

Then I frowned. How did he know it was me?

"I'm not either."

He dropped his hands and lifted his head, scrutinizing me before rising to his feet. I walked until I was right in front of him, my head tilted back to look at his face. He was so goddamn tall. I always loved how delicate and feminine he made me feel.

There was a shift in the air then, an understanding that passed between us. Between our equally heavy breaths, our chests almost touching, the intensity of the look in his eyes...

Liam grabbed the back of my neck with one hand and backed me up until I was flat against a tree. The rough bark scratched against my shirt and the ends of my ponytail. I let out a soft whimper as he lowered his head, his lips brushing mine. My breath hitched in anticipation of his touch, heat pooling between my thighs, and my God, if it wasn't the most intoxicating feeling.

I was going to let myself get lost in this moment, even if it was the last thing I ever did.

His free hand played with the hem of my shirt, his lips skimming my jaw. "Why do you insist on driving me to my breaking point?" His voice was equal parts gentle and raspy, like he was straining to get the words out. Maybe he was, if the erection pressing into my hip was any indicator.

I exhaled and nipped at his earlobe. "Because it makes me feel *wanted*."

His fingers traced tantric circles on my skin as they inched their way up my torso. Goosebumps spread down me like wildfire, and I felt myself swallow, trying to focus on his words but instead tumbling down into an abyss of blind desire that I only felt when he was around.

Liam pulled back just enough to meet my gaze. "Don't you know by now that you're the only woman I want?" He removed his hand from my nape and hitched one of my legs up around his waist, cupping the back of my knee and holding me so I was at the mercy of the friction between us. "Don't you know that I have wanted you from the very moment we met?"

My eyes fluttered shut as he flexed his hips into mine. A moan escaped me; my teeth clamped down on my lip. His heat burned through our clothes. Electricity pulsed and radiated from the apex of my thighs.

Liam ran his hands around my waist to grab my ass. I arched into him, just for his hands to drift up, over my ribs… *Fuck.* As he brushed his thumbs over my nipples, his name falling from my lips, he pinned me with his hips, keeping me exactly where he wanted me. He was deliberate in how he caressed me, as if he knew the exact ways I *needed* to be touched. He probably did. Despite all the time apart, there had been a time when he knew me better than I knew myself.

A sobering reality broke through my haze of desire. "We only have one more day together."

His gaze narrowed, his jaw clenching before he smirked. His signature dimple popped out and made me wetter than I already was. My mouth went dry. He was so fucking hot. "Then we better make it count."

Liam pulled my other leg up so I was completely wrapped around him, my hands in his hair, ankles locked against his lower back, back pressed into the tree. He kissed me fervently, his tongue sweeping across mine. I sighed into his mouth as my body melted into his, as if I had belonged here all along.

He wrapped my ponytail around his wrist and gave it a gentle tug, tearing my lips from his as my head tipped back, baring my neck to his white-hot kisses. He groaned against my throat, the vibrations sending a shiver down my spine.

"Jesus, Callie, you smell so good."

The way he said my name had me involuntarily pushing my hips forward, trying to grind against him, to tell him I approved of his praise.

I didn't realize how much I had missed hearing my name. More so from him, because it sounded like a precious prayer falling from his soft lips. Maybe in trying to find myself again, I lost a different part of myself too— just plain *Callie.*

He unwound my hair and lowered me to my feet, my pussy rubbing against the length of his cock the whole way down. I gasped at the delicious sensation.

"Turn around."

The gruffness in his voice made a shiver slither down my spine. My insides clenched and I whimpered. I did as I was told, and he gripped my hips and pulled me tightly to him. I could feel his own staccato breathing as he returned to nuzzling my neck. I was hot and itchy everywhere from his touch, his kiss, his mere *presence.*

"How wet are you for me?" His teeth tugged on my earlobe as one hand slipped under the waistband of my shorts, the other creeping up my belly to my breasts–not doing anything except torturing me. Every inch of me was on fire as I writhed against him, needing to feel him pressed against me. He groaned. "If you don't stop, this will be over much faster than either of us would like."

"I need you, Liam," I moaned, my voice breathy and pitchy. If I wasn't so caught up in the moment, I would cringe at myself.

His thumb found my clit with ease, and he pressed down while simultaneously palming one of my nipples with his other hand. I arched my back into his touch, consumed by him. His hand moved lower so he could insert two fingers into me, and he hissed through his teeth at the liquid heat he met.

I was overstimulated, my nerves tingling everywhere he touched—my nipples, tits, neck, lips. His hands on me, *in me.* And it was so, so erotic. He moved slowly but deliberately, taking his sweet time. Driving me insane.

"Liam—," I breathed, and as if sensing I needed more, he sped up the pace of his fingers as they moved in and out of me. He pulled them out briefly, spreading my wetness up to my clit and circling it. Waves of pleasure crashed through me, causing my legs to quiver. He repeated this, in and out, circling me.

"Put your arms around me," he panted.

I reached up and looped my arms around his neck. He nuzzled me deeper, biting and suckling on my throat and collarbone, his stubble scraping across my skin in a way that made me shiver. That much needed pressure was building fast and strong. I pushed up on my toes to brace for my impending release, unable to stifle my high-pitched moans. Liam stopped fondling my nipples to clamp a hand over my mouth.

"Hush, baby. Come for me."

His words tipped me over the edge, that pressure finally bursting and spreading a sense of euphoria to every nerve in my body. My vision fragmented, my insides pulsing around his fingers, his scent enveloping me like a blanket.

As I slowly came back down to earth, I realized Liam had pried my arms off of him and retracted his hands. Is that all he would give me? I swallowed my protest as he put his hands on my hips and nudged me toward the tree I'd been flattened against earlier.

I barely had time to catch my breath before he growled, "Hold on to the tree and don't let go." He nudged my thighs apart as I obeyed, even as I questioned the publicity of our indecency. All I knew was that I would do anything he asked of me because *fucking hell*, everything he did was pure ecstasy.

Who needs drugs when you could get fucked by Liam Chandler?

Liam grabbed my biker shorts and underwear, pulling them down and letting them fall to my ankles. I heard the sound of his zipper being undone, and the thought of him inside me had my arousal dripping down my thighs.

He had one hand on my hip, the other positioning himself at my entrance. My breathing stopped as I anxiously awaited him, but he paused. I couldn't see him, not with his command to hold onto the tree. Just as I was about to ask him what his hesitation was, he rolled my shirt up from the hem, pulling it up to my mouth.

"Bite down on this. I'm going to fuck you hard, and I don't want anyone to hear you. It's for my ears only."

I shuddered and took the fabric into my mouth. This was a new side of Liam, and no part of me minded him taking the reins this way.

"Good fucking girl."

I whimpered at his praise, and he rewarded me with the sweet sensation of entering me, filling me until I was certain I couldn't take any more.

He wasn't joking about fucking me hard.

He thrust into me, deep and forceful to the point it was nearly painful, yet I couldn't get enough. I gritted my teeth into my shirt and squeezed the tree harder with every relentless thrust. He hit that delicious spot inside me over and over, my body climbing toward climax once again.

My nipples rubbed against the lace of my bra. My ribs and cheek scraped against the tree bark—my overly sensitive skin had tears springing to my eyes and spilling onto my cheeks, in the best way. I was distinctly aware of how everything inside me sizzled as if I was ready to combust.

And God, was I.

With that pace, his grip in my hair, and his own sounds of pleasure, I caved to my rising orgasm. Couldn't think around the intensity of it. My toes curled in my sneakers, my thighs shook, my knees wobbled.

And then liquid dripped—no, *sprayed*—out of me. I barely had time to register it before a rush of heaviness settled into my core, and then erupted like a glitter bomb. I dug my fingertips into the tree as the orgasm took me, spiraled me into oblivion and rattled my very existence. Yet somehow, I was vividly aware that my muffled noises made Liam shudder and curse as he finished inside me.

My legs finally gave out. While still inside me, he wrapped an arm around my waist to support me, squeezing me tightly to him. Then, he rested his forehead on my shoulder while we both struggled to catch our breath.

There was something so… sweet about that.

My heart did a little flip. Because despite the naughty public act that would incriminate us if we were caught, or how rough and demanding he was—something he wasn't typically like—I felt safe.

He made me feel *safe*.

Despite everything, he still grounded me.

And I knew once all of this passed, he was the one. The *only* one.

Thirty-Five

Liam

⚜

I wanted to give Callie a moment to remember, and fuck, I think I accomplished that.

There was something about being able to control the control freak that had me taking her in the exact way I'd pictured it since she'd started to pick a fight with me in the parking lot.

It was such a fucking turn on to see her stomp toward me, her face red and her eyes blazing. Even when she shoved me, when she yelled at me, all I could imagine was bending her over and fucking that temper out of her.

Truthfully, had she tried to keep me in the car, I would've fucked her in there. I may have poured my soul out to her, but that argument damn near broke my willpower before I could get through my sob story.

I spent the last two weeks being the nice guy and keeping my hands to myself. Then she followed me to a more secluded part of the park, and I knew it was game over for the both of us. She stormed in there *ready* to be fucked. All my restraint evaporated in the wind.

I also let a few things slip that I normally kept in my head, but she seemed to enjoy them. *A lot.*

Fuck.

I felt the slickness on our thighs and reached a hand around her to feel it, sucking in a deep breath.

"Jesus Christ, Callie, you *squirted.*"

It was probably the biggest turn on ever.

She stilled before breaking out into laughter. Her face was still pressed against the tree as she sighed blissfully. "Yeah, I did. First time for everything."

Fucking hell, I made her squirt for the first time.

That did wondrous things for my ego as I blinked in disbelief. "Well, this will be fun."

Callie slowly pushed away from the tree and backed into me. I slid out of her gently with a wince, but let her back rest against my chest for a few moments. We separated at the same time to catch our breath, and I got a good glance at her.

Her ponytail was a wreck, her eyes wild, her shirt covered in dirt, her lips swollen, her thighs glistening.

She was a literal goddess in her full glory. I couldn't look away, and that seemed to catch her attention. She gave me a small smile, a look of gratitude shining in her eyes.

It only made me want to fuck her mouth so she could look up at me with those eyes.

I forced myself to take a deep breath of the warm night air to ground myself. It'd been months since I was this aroused and thinking so filthily about someone—about her. No one ever elicited these feelings except Callie.

Before we could part ways, I pulled her into me and kissed her slowly, passionately. I took my time with this kiss, spelled out her name in cursive with my tongue and cupped her face. She sighed against my lips and melted into me. By God, this woman could do no wrong.

In fact, every thing she did made me all the more crazy about her.

I was still totally and utterly in love with her.

Thirty-Six

Callie

Okay, so one day left to process the fact that my life as I knew it was ending.

Cool.

Love that for me.

I didn't really know where to start. I wasn't ready to call my family. That needed to be last, to spare my emotions as long as possible.

They would understand.

I hoped.

What I did know was how jittery I was. I woke up feeling more energized than I had in years, and I could only attribute that to one thing: Liam. Yep, despite how badly he had broken my heart and driven me to abuse alcohol, I was still head over heels for the guy. And no, it wasn't just because he literally *fucked* me—the absolute definition of the act. Although, that was a major perk.

My body was still sore from last night, but that was the last thing on my mind. I was itching to do it again. If today was my last day seeing him for an undefined period of time, we both needed to get this out of our systems.

I paced back and forth in an old, unused copy room that had since been turned into a storage closet. There were a few racks of boxes, a copy machine, and counters with cabinets that were completely empty.

The door clicked open and I heard Liam's voice before I saw him. I was facing away from the door, slowly unbuttoning my dress. My shoulder holster was already off and on the counter.

"Hey, is everything okay?" he asked.

"Yeah, can you shut and lock the door, please?"

I glanced over my shoulder to see him frown but do as I asked.

I swore I was seeing him in a new light this morning, and I was immediately damp when I looked at him. Hair styled, eyes bright, well-rested… and those broad shoulders showing so much confidence that I could practically taste his demanding tone.

I slowly turned to face him as he locked the door.

"What was the urgen—" he cut off mid-sentence as his eyes swept me up and down, flickering with pleasant surprise.

Really, I couldn't blame him. I wore a short-sleeve black button-front dress, unbuttoned all the way down to my midriff, and underneath it was a strappy black lace bra. My hair was twisted up into a claw clip and my feet were clad in those nude heels he loved so much.

"Oh," he breathed, then blinked. He didn't come any closer, but I could see temptation wash over him. "*Oh.*"

I backed up until my thighs hit the back counter and smirked. "Yeah, *oh.*"

"There are people waiting for us downstairs," he said distractedly, not tearing his gaze from my body.

"They can wait." I released another button. "We don't work here."

Liam inclined his head to the wall on my right. "Clemens's office is right next door."

I tilted my head at him and pulled myself onto the counter, spreading my thighs and inching my dress up. "I guess we'll have to be quiet then, huh?"

He stalked toward me, seeming to accept where this interaction was going, and that primal walk had me squirming on the counter top. "You think you could be quiet like you were last night?"

I grinned deviously at him, pulling my dress all the way up so he could see I wore no panties. "You liked me so demure, didn't you?"

Liam arched a brow and smiled, stopping in front of me and resting his hands on either side of my thighs. "Do you know how fucking sexy it is that you obeyed me?"

"Probably the first time ever."

He chuckled, and *fuck*, those dimples appeared. My cheeks warmed, and I almost laughed. I sat, legs splayed and tits out, and I was blushing from his laugh?

I reached up and pulled my dress down my shoulders, letting it pool at my hips. His eyes widened as he first took in the love bites he had left behind mere hours ago that decorated my collarbone, shoulders, and neck; then, he examined the tattoo that splashed across my ribs. The one that I got during my recovery, too dark to have seen in the moonlight last night.

Enthralled, he ran his hand over the twisted tree with roots drooping toward my waist, the limbs in full bloom.

I met his gaze as understanding settled into his eyes.

I got it for you.

Thirty-Seven

Liam

It was official: Callie Eden was going to the death of me.

She had texted:

Meet me in Office Supply Room 207H ASAP!

And of course, thinking she was upset about something, I rushed through my conversations with everyone who stopped me so I could make sure she was alright.

She was.

More than alright, actually.

Mostly naked, what little part of her not exposed was clad in lingerie, on full display before me. The sight might very well have sent me into cardiac arrest.

But then my eyes snagged on the hickeys and the red patches from my stubble I had unintentionally left on her, and oh how I loved the branding on her skin. My gaze dipped lower, to that tattoo—the one I had been gawking at for several moments. The one that looked so similar to the one on my forearm.

I wanted to ask her questions, but knowing that my own ink held sentimental meaning, I didn't press her. I did, however, straighten and try to clear my head. I was having a hard enough time forcing the memories of the night before out of my mind.

"You're stunning," I told her in a soft voice, withdrawing my hand from her warm skin. I didn't realize I had been tracing it.

Callie caught my wrist and pulled my hand toward her thighs. I had every intention of pulling away, but my fingertips brushed the outer folds of her pussy.

"We—I—we should, um," I stammered, attempting to not notice how decadent the center of her thighs looked. "People could come looking for us."

Raising her eyebrows, she said, "And that's any different from last night?"

I huffed out a laugh, grateful that things weren't awkward between us this morning, though I desperately wanted to know where her head was at with it all.

She shifted then, and my fingers slid into her. She was so goddamn wet, I was met with no resistance as I involuntarily slid my fingers in as far as they could go. Her lips parted in a quiet moan.

Unable to refrain any longer, I dropped to my knees in front of her. She was my ultimate weakness, and there was no denying my desire to have her. I glanced up as she moved to the edge of the counter. I dove in, sliding my fingers in and out in time with my tongue swirling her clit.

Callie dropped her head back, one hand twining through my hair. She writhed against my mouth, and I groaned against her. She tasted so sweet—I could stay down here forever, drinking her up.

But too soon, her breathing shifted and her legs wrapped around my head, trembling as her insides quivered around my fingers. And as much as I loved it, I wanted to be buried in her. My dick was pressing against my pants so uncomfortably that I found myself thrusting my hips forward.

I rose to my feet and captured her mouth with mine, letting her taste just how delicious she was. A moment later she pulled back, tipping her chin down and looking up at me through her eyelashes.

"Like last night," was all she said.

It took a moment for my brain to process what she meant. I smiled at her. "So you liked that?"

A single nod.

I leaned into her ear and whispered, "Let your hair down."

She swallowed, a pink flush coloring her cheeks as she reached up and pulled the clip out of her hair. Her long tresses fell around her shoulders.

"Good girl." I fisted the hair at the nape of her neck and kissed her pouty lips. She tasted like cinnamon candy on my tongue, and my insides *burned* from how much I needed her.

Callie unbuckled my belt as our tongues danced, as if she couldn't wait any longer. My lips curved wickedly against her mouth. I grabbed her wrist as an idea crossed my mind, pulling away to see curiosity in her eyes, like she was dying to see what I was up to. I yanked her dress off her arms, took off my holstered gun and badge and set them on the counter. The handcuffs draped over my belt, however, were going to stay with me.

Well, with Callie, actually.

Her eyes widened as I released the cuff and met her gaze. I reached over her to hook the cuffs through one of the cabinet handles above her head, then grasped her wrists one at a time and secured her arms above her head. Now she was splayed before me, unable to move and completely at my mercy.

My cock throbbed.

Her chest rose and fell rapidly, her pupils dilated as she waited for me to touch her. Far be it from me to withhold any longer. I kissed her once more, rough and hard, before I unzipped my pants and let my cock spring free. I worked quickly at unbuttoning my dress shirt, wanting to feel every inch of her skin flush with mine.

The room was quiet, only the two of us existing while all our outside problems faded away. The look in Callie's eyes burned into me, and I almost blurted out my feelings for her right then.

But instead, I buried that thought and thrust into her, all the way to the hilt. She bit down on her lip to keep quiet, and I had to tuck my face into the crook of her neck to muffle my own groan.

Callie's familiar tight, wet heat squeezed me in the most addicting way. Sex with her had always been otherworldly, and this time was no exception.

"You feel so fucking good," I murmured, nipping at the base of her throat. Her pulse jumped under my tongue as a strangled whimper escaped her. I gripped her hips so tightly, wanting to hold her as closely as possible and knowing this was probably the last time I would get to do this with her. Unless we managed to squeeze in time later today, which I doubted.

"Please, Liam… I need—" she gasped as I picked up the pace, rough and punishing for the both of us. "*Yes.* Don't… stop."

"Fuck. You take me so well," I rasped.

A light sheen of perspiration coated our skin as we moved together, her hips grinding forward to meet me thrust for thrust. I was literally balls deep in her, loving the way her wetness dripped down me.

I slowed my pace and looked down at where our bodies met, hissing through my teeth at the sight. I moved one hand to grip her inner thigh, my thumb swiping over her clit, red and swollen. She arched her back and let out a stifled groan.

"Need to… come… *please,*" she breathed between heavy pants.

"You'll come when I tell you to," I growled, knowing now that she seemed to like a little bit of praise, and maybe the ability to let go of control during sex. "Your pussy is *mine,* Callie. Do you understand?"

She nodded, her eyes closed and head tilted back, exposing her beautiful throat and all those love bites I had left behind. What a sight to behold, with her arms cuffed above her head, unable to touch me.

"I want to hear you say it."

"Yes," she said instantly. "Yes, it's yours, only yours, Liam."

I grinned at how my name sounded like both a plea and a hymn. "Good." I circled her clit once, twice, three times, feeling her quivering as I increased the speed of my pumps inside her. She was close, and damn it, so was I. As badly as I didn't want this moment to end, I was eager to feel her come around my dick.

A tingling sensation sparked at the base of my spine, beginning to wind its way through me.

"Now come, baby."

I watched her fall apart, her body going taut and her arms tugging at the handcuffs, the way the movement of her hips became sporadic. Felt her muscles clench around me, pulsing again and again until I followed after her, my own orgasm making me spill inside her.

She sighed my name as she rode that high, and I took my lips in hers, wanting to catch every breath I could before this was all over.

"I fucking love watching you come," I murmured against her mouth. And it was all I could do to not tell her I loved her.

Thirty-Eight

Callie

Liam uncuffed me, and I rubbed my tender wrists. He trailed a finger down my sternum, his eyes following its path. I watched the infatuation on his face, my heart swelling. Maybe it was post-orgasm bliss, but when he looked at me like that, it made me want to lower my walls and just *be* with him.

But my current situation made that impossible.

So I just soaked in that look, and locked it away as a memory to relive when I missed him.

I already missed him, as strange as that sounded. After all, not even eight hours ago we were fighting, and after two days things were still awkward and tense between us.

And yet, a hunch told me that it was different this time, that we'd finally broken through a lot of our individual reservations and were ready to figure this thing out—*together.*

I ran my hands down his chest and abs, pushing the fabric away so I could see his tattoos. "You're very beautiful, Mr. Chandler."

He chuckled. It was a beautiful sound. "I could say the same to you, Ms. Eden." His hands rested on my hips.

I grinned, sliding my hands up his shoulders and admiring his tall, muscular build. "I missed you."

He sucked in a breath. "I missed you, too. If you couldn't tell."

Mmm, music to my ears.

He leaned in and kissed me again, soft and slow. I relaxed into him, feeling my blood stir. Sensing we were headed back into dangerous territory, he pulled out of me to tuck himself back into his pants.

I pulled the sleeves of my dress back over my shoulders and slowly buttoned it back up. Liam reached out to help me off the counter; I winced as I hit the ground.

"Are you okay?"

"You just made me a little sore with that magical dick of yours. That's all." The grin on my face felt permanent, my limbs light. I felt sated and… happy.

Liam tipped his head back and laughed. "That's a new one. Magical dick, huh?"

I smiled bashfully at him while I re-secured my shoulder holster. "You know damn well what I mean. With your come-fuck-me eyes and dimples and sexpertise and all that."

"I have come-fuck-me eyes?"

I shot him a dirty look. "You just got done telling me how well I take your dick and *that's* what surprises you?"

He gave me a cocky grin and crossed his arms. "And you loved every second of that praise, didn't you?"

"You loved every second of controlling the control freak, didn't you?" I threw back at him, matching his stance.

"So you've noticed it's different this time around, too? I thought it was just me."

I shook my head. "Not just you. The stakes are different this time. Makes it easier to be a little more… free."

Liam's dimples were on full display, and if we didn't leave soon, I would let him bend me over for another quickie. "Whatever it is, I'm not complaining."

I hooked my fingers on the belt loops of his pants and pulled him toward me until I was kissing him again. "Can't imagine a world where you'd complain about getting off."

He smiled. "Who are you and what have you done with Callie?"

I rested my head on his chest, reveling in his intoxicating smell. "She's choosing to mentally check out and just be in this moment with you."

There was a moment of silence. I let out a heavy sigh. "I don't want to leave."

"I don't want you to, either. I just got you back."

His words hit me like a ton of bricks. "Thank you for putting me in my place last night. I was being a selfish bitch by not trying to see things from your perspective."

Liam rubbed my back, and for a brief moment I allowed myself to picture being right here in his arms forever. "I wouldn't go that far. It's my fault for keeping you in the dark for so long."

"You don't need to make excuses for my behavior. I know I need to be better at communicating."

"Yeah, me too."

Another beat of silence, this time bittersweet.

"When did you get that tattoo?" His voice was so soft, as if he were afraid it would break this gentle moment.

"A few months ago, after I got my new job."

He kissed the top of my head before letting me go. I instantly missed his warmth. "Mmm, I like it. It suits you."

"I figured you would." I giggled and flashed him a coy smile that made him suck in a breath. There was something about the look he was giving me that felt so familiar, and suddenly my stomach was in knots. I knew that look—knew it very well, because I felt the same thing.

I wondered how long it would be before we said it... or if we would at all, now that I was leaving. It might hurt too much.

Liam chuckled and ran his hands down my arms as he turned me to face the door, our moment ending as he ushered me forward. "So you had intentions all along for me to see you naked?"

I blushed as I unlocked the door. "So what if I did?" I shot him a playful look over my shoulder before slipping out.

***

"You just missed them," Hailey, Terry's assistant, told me and Liam. "Agents Carver and Matthews had to speak to their agents in private before meeting with you guys."

I glanced at Liam and shrugged. "What now?"

He inclined his head behind us. "Coffee?"

I nodded, and we fell into an easy walk beside each other. He held the door open for me, and I stepped outside into the summer heat, the sun nearly blinding me. As I passed Liam, our hands brushed, his fingers curling around mine for a brief moment before he followed me outside.

As we descended the steps, there was a shrill scream followed by a girlish cry. "*Callie-Ann!*"

At once, the dozen officers littering the outside of the precinct stilled, hands flying to guns and attention snapping to the source of the sound. Liam instinctively put his hand on my lower back, his hand clutching the back of my dress as if prepared to pull me out of harm's way.

But I knew that voice, and my back stiffened as I came to an abrupt stop on the second to last stair. My sister rushed down the sidewalk excitedly.

What… the actual… fuck was she doing showing up here? Had I not made it abundantly clear how dangerous this was? Did she not get the hint when the feds explained that I was being put into *witness protection*? Instant irritation flooded me, clouding my vision.

I cleared my throat and looked around at all the frantic officers. "It's okay, everybody. It's just my sister. Sorry," I apologized, embarrassment warming the tips of my ears as she approached us.

Liam muttered from behind me, "Callie-Ann?"

"Don't call me that," I hissed.

My sister threw her arms around me. I hugged her back before I pushed her away to narrow my eyes at her. "This is a police precinct, Leah. Don't scream unless you're in danger," I reprimanded.

"Yes, Mom." She smiled feebly before her gaze shifted to the man behind me, her blue eyes widening. "Oh my God, is this him?"

As if he wasn't standing right there.

I hesitated before turning to half-face Liam, who was looking between us with curiosity. "Leah, this is Liam Chandler. Liam, this is my sister, Leah."

Leah looked starstruck as she gawked at him. "Jesus Christ, Callie-Ann, you said he was hot, but even pictures don't do him justice."

Oh my God.

I was going to kill her.

"You showed her pictures of me?" Liam teased.

"Can you blame her? You're hot."

I pressed my lips together, not liking this. "Leah, could you try to use a little discretion when it comes to our private conversations?"

She arched a brow at me, flicking her gaze between the two of us. Then a smug smile crossed her face, and she folded her arms over her chest. "You naughty little bitch. Even freshly fucked you're still uptight."

I blinked as shock washed over me. Liam sucked in a breath, and I snuck a glance at him to see him fighting laughter.

I glowered at my sister. "I don't know what you're talking about." I meant for it to sound flippant, laid back, but it came out all wrong, almost nervous.

Leah looked between us again and broke out into laughter. "You're joking, right? It couldn't be more obvious." There was a pregnant pause before she continued. "Callie, do you really think I don't know that you'd never leave home without your hair perfectly styled? You clearly just threw it up into that clip. Also, your face was pink and glowing when you walked out of the building." My hand subconsciously fluttered to my hair, which *was* styled perfectly this morning.

Liam snickered.

I felt like dying, I was so mortified. Did everyone we passed notice this as well?

She turned her eyes to Liam. "You're not in the clear, either. You're still giving her bedroom eyes every time you look at her. And did you think I wouldn't notice those handcuffs on your hips that match the lines around Callie-Ann's wrists? I had no idea that cops were into bondage."

Shit.

I forgot about that.

I crossed my arms and pursed my lips, choosing to plead the fifth.

"You're awfully perceptive, but then again, so is your sister," Liam remarked. He sounded completely unfazed. Actually, he sounded amused, and that annoyed me.

Leah grinned mischievously—she always was the pot-stirrer of the family. "I think I should've been a cop."

"It's never too late, you know."

I scoffed and hit Liam's arm. "Don't tempt her. She would do it just to mess with me."

"That's my job," Leah stated with a flip of her hair.

"Leah!" I heard Sophie call from the top of the precinct stairs. Next thing I knew, a flurry of dark hair flew past us and embraced my sister. I watched their reunion with cool indifference.

Sophie pulled back and assessed our group before grinning at Leah. "So, you've met Liam now."

Leah's lips tipped up. "Oh, yeah. We were just talking about how obvious it was that they'd just got it on."

I flinched. "Okay, that's enough—," I interjected, but Sophie tilted her head back and cackled.

"These two have *never* been discreet. Not a single time."

Liam wrapped his arm around my waist, as if sensing I needed more support. I looked up at him and saw his own cheeks were a little flushed.

"What can I say? Callie's hard to resist," Liam said, fixating his green eyes on mine. The familiarity brought me a sense of comfort, and I found myself leaning into him.

"Even last night? I'm pretty sure all of Newark heard that argument," Sophie quipped.

Kill me now. For fuck's sake, I just wanted to run away from this conversation.

Sophie noted my discomfort and did not relent on calling us out.

"You've gotta be kidding me. In public? At a crime scene?"

"You guys have proven your point," I snapped, scowling at them both.

"We're just teasing," Leah said. "Besides, it's nice to see you happy. Even if it is with… him. His dick must be magical for you to forgive him."

I raised my eyebrows at Liam, as if to say *I told you so.* He gave me a knowing smile, which I matched.

"Gross. You guys need to get a room," Sophie sneered.

"We're… working through things. That's all you need to know," I told my best friend and my sister.

Leah jabbed a finger at Liam. "Hurt her again and I'll castrate you. You hear me?"

Liam flashed his dimples at her, making Leah blink. *Yeah, I have the same reaction, sis.* "I don't intend to. She got away once. Biggest mistake of my life. I love her too much to let it happen again."

I whipped my head towards him. *He said it first.* He widened his eyes at me, realizing it the same moment I did, and silently pleaded *not now.*

I decided to brush past this before Leah could open her mouth to comment. "What the hell are you even doing here? I told you guys to stay put in Springcrest."

My sister's face fell and she fidgeted. I eyed her warily. "Well, yeah, but… look, we just wanted to say goodbye before you were put into wit—"

Liam, Sophie, and I shushed her.

Her eyes rounded. "Oh, shit. Right. Sorry. I forgot it's hush-hush."

I rolled my eyes. "What do you mean by 'we?'"

"Mom, Dad, and Sam are all at breakfast right now."

I blanched, my stomach bottoming out.

"And also Dale is here."

"For the love of God, why?"

"Apparently you have to sign some papers to hold your position?"

Liam stiffened behind me. I subconsciously grabbed his hand and squeezed it for reassurance. It felt so natural, so… comfortable.

I sighed. "I'll save the lecture for when everyone's here, then. Why aren't you with them now?"

Leah's demeanor changed then, her eyes growing soft. "I thought it'd be easier to tell you we're all here if it was just me. You know, so you didn't feel bombarded."

I swallowed thickly. As much as she got under my skin like the annoying little sister she was, she still considered my feelings. "Thank you."

"Also," she continued, turning and waving at someone leaning against a building I hadn't noticed before, "I forgot to mention Jason is here."

Jason.

He had a boyish smile on his face as he jogged over and planted a kiss on my sister's cheek, then turned and gave me an awkward hug.

"Callie-Ann, good to see you. Sophie, nice to see you again," he greeted, then raised his eyebrows at Liam.

I made a quick introduction. I didn't miss the realization in Jason's eyes, and I hated that my entire family was going to meet Liam *now.* The man who, in the last hour, had me handcuffed and on full naked display while he ate me out, fingered me, and fucked me.

You take me so well.

Your pussy is mine, Callie.

Now come, baby.

I fucking love watching you come.

I shifted on my feet, shoving those thoughts from my mind. I wasn't about to get all worked up again in front of the very people who just got done making fun of me for it. And I definitely couldn't be thinking about that when my dad shook Liam's hand.

Jason smiled at Leah as he draped an arm around her shoulders. "So, have you told her yet?"

I frowned. "Told me what?"

Leah chewed on her lip before digging into her purse. "Well, Jason and I are going to have celebratory mimosas since we're in the city and while everyone's at breakfast. He proposed last night, and I said yes!"

I inhaled sharply and gave her a dazzling smile, albeit a little forced.

"Oh my God, congratulations!" I exclaimed, pulling them both in for a hug. Sophie cried out in excitement and joined the group hug.

"Well, don't let me keep you two lovebirds from celebrating," I told them. *Holy shit.* My little sister was engaged, and I was beyond elated for her. A selfish part of me wished it wasn't when I was being forced to disappear. I wanted to celebrate with her and enjoy this time with her...

But life had other plans.

There was a pit in my stomach, and suddenly all I wanted to do was be alone in a booth at a coffee shop with Liam.

We said our goodbyes, congratulating them again, and Sophie returned to the building. Jason and Leah went the opposite direction we did, and I held Liam's hand like a lifeline as we made our way to a coffee shop we frequented when we worked together.

The streets were busy today. People were talking loudly, shouting across the street, and cars were honking. In the air, the scents of coffee and pastries swirled in the light breeze, and the sun was completely unobstructed. The heat had sweat dripping down my spine as it beat down on my black dress.

Liam pulled me to a stop before we crossed the street, tilting my chin up. He searched my eyes, and I just wanted to melt into the depths staring back at me. "What happened back there?"

I sucked my lip into my mouth and ignored how his gaze dropped to my mouth for a brief moment. "My little sister is engaged," was all I managed to say, as I realized maybe there was a little bit of envy unfurling in my chest.

Thirty-Nine

Liam

"Is that a good or a bad thing?"

Conflict was etched into Callie's features. Her mood had shifted as soon as Leah broke the news of the engagement, and I had been trying to get a good read on her reaction since.

Callie pulled her chin from my hand. "I'm happy for her." Her response was clipped as she turned to cross the street. I heard her mutter under her breath, "Even if it is with my ex-boyfriend."

I choked and hurried after her. "Wait, *what?*"

She turned when she reached the sidewalk on the other side. "Let it go, Liam."

I paused. The last thing I wanted to be when she was combative was her argumentative counterpart. Any semblance of my happy, loving Callie had vanished.

"I'm just trying to understand. He's your ex?"

She folded her arms. "He was my high school sweetheart. I lost my virginity to him." She scrutinized my reaction. I didn't expect to feel a surge of jealousy, especially when I had no room to talk. I tried not to let it show on my face, but she said, "He wanted to stay in Springcrest to work for his family's business, and I left because I needed to get away. There were no hard feelings, we both had our closure, and I've barely given it a thought since. I don't even know why I mentioned it just now. That part doesn't bother me."

Her words were reassuring, but they brought a whole new set of questions. "So you're okay with it, then?"

Callie sighed. "I am happy for them. Really. I swear it has nothing to do with my history with Jason. I just wish I was going to be around to help her plan. When I first left Springcrest, I promised Leah there would be trips to the city and shopping sprees and bar hopping, but… I got too busy and never made time for her. I guess I'm feeling like I can't make up for lost time now that I'm forced to leave."

I brushed a few loose tresses out of her face and tucked them behind her ear. "I'm sorry. I can't imagine how that feels." I gave her a small smile. "Wanna tell me about *Callie-Ann?*" I'd been dying to know since her sister called her that. I was pretty sure it wasn't her middle name. No, scratch that, I knew it wasn't her middle name. Maybe it was a nickname?

That lightened the mood. She brushed my hand away and rolled her eyes. "Don't even get me started."

I chuckled and stayed behind her with my hands in my pockets as she led us into the coffee shop. I admired the way her hips swayed and how the fabric of her dress moved so effortlessly with her. Her body really was perfect, and no matter how hard I tried, I couldn't shake some very naughty images of her from my mind. It was becoming a problem.

We waited in line near the doors, the familiar coffee shop ambiance surrounding us. I leaned down to speak to her so only she could hear me.

"We've got a lot of good memories here."

Callie shuddered. "You're thinking about that right now?"

She was referring to the time I followed her to the bathroom, pressed her up against the wall, dropped to my knees, and worshiped her with my mouth. It was after one of our many sleepovers together last winter, before we would go into work. So yeah, I was thinking about that now.

"It's hard not to."

She shook her head at me in mock admonishment. "You're naughty," she whispered.

"What's naughty is knowing you're not wearing any panties underneath this dress."

Her eyes flicked to mine, the blue so bright it took my breath away. I took the opportunity to subtly skim my fingers up the back of her thighs. A flush crept up her neck and into her cheeks. I paused just below her ass; she exhaled sharply.

Just as I was about to cup her delicious backside, the line dispersed and the cashier smiled brightly at us. I dropped my hand.

* * *

"Will you *please* tell me why your sister calls you Callie-Ann?" I begged as I slid into the booth next to Callie, turning toward her to give her my full attention.

She sighed loudly. "It's my real name."

I almost laughed. "You're fucking with me." She gave me a resigned look that said otherwise. I raised my eyebrows. "Why don't you go by it, then?"

Callie shook her head. "I left Springcrest wanting a new life. I feared people would find me, so I legally shortened my name."

"What made it so bad there?"

She ran a finger around the rim of her coffee mug. "It's a small town where you can't escape your mistakes."

I frowned at her vagueness. "Baby, I want to know. We've never…" I let my voice trail off until she looked at me. "We've never talked about these things."

She bit her lip, seeming on the fence about it. "Fine. Springcrest seems charming on the outside, and maybe to some it is. But when I was a senior in high school," she took a deep breath, "I went to a party with some friends. It wasn't often I did that, but I agreed to go because Jason and I had gotten in a fight and I didn't want to be alone. One of my friends and I were drugged."

My stomach plummeted. Callie took a sip of her coffee.

"I was fortunate enough to escape before anything too bad happened, but my friend wasn't. She was raped." Another sip. "I thought I was in the clear and was just recovering from the trauma of being roofied, but a few weeks later, pictures and videos were leaked of me performing some… acts on one of the most popular guys in school. The worst part was, I was clearly incapacitated. I had no memory of it, and everyone thought I was a lying whore. Faculty members and churchgoers included."

She looked ashamed with splotchy red cheeks and downcast eyes, her shoulders curling in.

"I'd known for some time that I wanted to leave Springcrest, but when that happened, I swore I would never go back. No one would let me live it down. People paint-sprayed my locker with filthy names. I was shunned in classes. Even the teachers looked at me differently. Law enforcement did nothing. Everyone had seen me intimately exposed, and no one could see past it. So I moved away after graduation. Callie-Ann Jade Eden ceased to exist, and I never looked back.

"I think I convinced myself I was okay with it all when I was back there. That I wanted to be hometown sweetheart Callie-Ann again, but it never… I don't know. I always felt like I was trying to prove that I was more than what the past had painted me as. Dale, who you'll meet today, made a lot of lewd comments and alluded to my history. He liked to make a game out of it all. I always found it hard to believe that such a disgusting human was sworn to protect and serve any community on the planet.

"Actually, it was the lack of care from local law enforcement when I was a teenager that made me want to be a cop. Dale just proved me right when I was there." She frowned.

"And come to think of it, what happened in high school is probably why I had some intimacy issues in my early twenties. Which you are, for lack of a better word, *intimately* aware of." Her laugh sounded forced.

My heart was pounding against my chest. *Fuck.* That wasn't what I was expecting. Honestly, it was a lot worse than I was expecting. I ran a hand down my face. "Jesus, Cal, that's… morbid. I don't even know what to say."

Callie smiled sadly into her coffee.

"You know the world is better having you on this side of the law, right?" I said softly.

She shrugged, as if that would erase the past. "Enough of that. Now you know."

I slid a hand over her thigh. That earned a sincere smile. "Can I at least mention how cute your middle name is?"

"I can't believe you never knew my middle name," she said as she spread her legs, and I glanced down in surprise. I wasn't trying to be suggestive in my hand placement, but I wasn't complaining. "What's yours?"

I moved my hand up her thigh. "Aiden."

She arched a brow. "It's basic."

I tipped my head back and laughed. "*Basic?* I don't know if I should be offended or not." I slid a finger across her center and dipped a finger into her, not expecting to find her wet already. I cleared my throat at the same time she sucked in a breath.

I withdrew my hand to leave her wanting more, and quickly reminded myself that there wasn't much time left to do these things with her.

My heart murmured. It was all happening too soon, too fast. She just came back into my life, and we were finally inching toward being on the same page. For the first time maybe ever. And that fact alone made my chest ache. I turned away, not ready to show her how bothered I was.

I was also grateful she hadn't brought up how I'd let the L-word slip out earlier.

Forty

Callie

The only person I'd ever told about my history in Springcrest was Sophie. Until Liam. I never felt safe enough to admit it to anyone, and our relationship last year was mostly just sex, basic life discussions, and learning one another's personalities. Now... Well, now we had seen each other at our worst, knew how bad it could get, and were both wanting to give it another go.

I came to terms with the knowledge that maybe my requests for Liam were a little outlandish and came from a place of insecurity. Maybe it's what I needed to hear to feel like I could be vulnerable with him. *Completely* vulnerable.

The sexual attraction was still there, more palpable than ever now that we knew we could act on those feelings whenever we wanted, but the emotional intimacy made it all the more special.

Liam, Sophie, and I stood in the lobby of the Third Precinct and awaited my family. I figured this was as safe a place as any for them to come say goodbye to me. That, and also the feds were finally ready to meet with us and said it would be good information for my family to hear so they could understand the gravity of the situation.

That alone made me want to roll my eyes.

Because of course my parents wouldn't take me seriously—just other people in this profession. Pretty sure they believed this job was just me dressing up in costume.

"Don't be so nervous," Liam murmured in my ear.

"It's not going to be pretty when I tell them who you are," I responded, my voice low.

"They don't need to know the specifics. All they need to know is that I'm here assisting with the case."

Sophie snickered. "Her parents, especially her dad, are going to know. You two smell like sex."

I shot her a dirty look. "You're as bad as my sister."

She raised a shoulder, a half-smile tugging on her lips. "That's not so bad. I love Leah."

I rolled my eyes. "You're not exactly innocent either, Soph. I've heard what happens with you and Dean before you come into work."

She smirked, but a tinge of pink splashed across her cheeks. "Oh, look, your family is here."

My attention shifted to the entry, where they were all looking around in awe before opening the doors. My parents looked relieved to see me alive and well as they rushed over and caught me in a tight hug.

"Hi Mom. Dad," I croaked as they squeezed the air out of my lungs.

"We've been so worried about you, Sugar Plum. You've barely returned our calls," Dad said.

Guilt squeezed my chest as they pulled back. "I'm sorry. It's been crazy. And overwhelming."

"Hey, sis." Sam gave me a half hug, flattening my hair. I swatted him away and patted my hair. Not like it was perfect to begin with, as Leah had so kindly pointed out earlier. Which, judging by the shit-eating grin on her face, she was recalling too. I narrowed my eyes at her; I didn't trust that look one bit.

"Long time no see," I heard Dale pipe up, and I had completely forgotten he was in attendance.

I scowled at him. "Can we sign the damn papers and get you out of here?"

"Callie-Ann, be nice," Mom hissed. I forgot I had to watch my mouth around my parents, let alone save face even with people I didn't like.

"Yeah, Dweeben, be nice," Dale sneered like a child.

I opened my mouth to retort when Liam chirped from behind me. "Dweeben? That's a new one."

I huffed as I said, "Don't encourage him, Liam. He's like a giant petulant man-baby."

My parents and Sam stilled when they heard Liam's name. They analyzed him.

Right.

All they knew about him was that I was madly in love with him, and he broke my heart.

Oh, and that he was the leading cause for me moving back home.

They had no idea that I had planned to involve him in this again the minute I arranged my return to the city.

I heaved a sigh. "Liam, this is my family. My parents, John and Helen. My brother, Sam. You've already met Leah and Jason, and behind them is my colleague, Sergeant Dale Ferguson. Everyone, this is my former partner, Sergeant Liam Chandler."

It was probably the most awkward moment in my life, with my parents scrutinizing the man who had sent their little girl running for the hills and my brother sizing him up, even though Liam had at least two inches on him.

I ushered everyone through the bullpen and into the investigation room where the feds were waiting for us. I was beyond relieved that someone else would be doing the talking.

Taking a seat at the large conference table, I rubbed my temples. Everyone was chatting among themselves, and a headache was beginning to bloom behind my eyes. I wanted to squeeze Liam's hand for comfort, but for the sake of my family's presence, he had the decency to sit across from me.

I hated the distance between us.

This really wasn't how I imagined today panning out.

Agents Carver and Matthews stood at the head of the table, their presence demanding and powerful. They didn't have to say anything to get everyone to quiet down. I closed my eyes and took a deep breath, feeling some reprieve.

"First of all," Agent Carver started, "it was extremely dangerous for all of you, with the exception of Sergeant Ferguson, to disobey direct orders and come here. When we spoke with you on the phone yesterday, we explained in great detail how Ms. Eden's life is at risk and how imperative it is that she cut all ties with her current life."

I gulped. Hearing it from a federal agent made it feel more real. Like a sucker punch to the solar plexus.

"That being said, we are putting a protective detail on all of you for the time being. Now that you're in Oliver Frankford's hunting ground, it's not unreasonable to assume you're all targets by association, even more so with Sergeant Eden going off the grid. Especially the younger Ms. Eden," Matthews said. All eyes swung in my sister's direction, who for once in her life, was speechless.

"Sir, with all due respect, I don't think we're in need of babysitters," my dad snapped.

Matthews cocked an eyebrow. "You have no choice. You made a mistake, and this is the price for it."

My dad shifted in his seat. "I think it's a little extreme just because we wanted to say goodbye to our daughter in person."

"That could have been arranged in a safe manner," Carver said, her voice cold.

I wanted to hug her. Ever since I became a cop, it was apparent my parents didn't take me—or my job—very seriously. Part of me believed they were in denial about the dangers surrounding my work, but in their eyes, I wore a badge and played pretend while all the boys went out and did the hard work. It wasn't until this very moment that I realized how much that had hurt me. And how that probably contributed to me not visiting for so long.

My gaze dropped to my hands, and I felt Liam's eyes turn to me. I couldn't bring myself to look at him, at anyone. Maybe my inherent need to always be right, overachieve, compete, take control of my work... maybe it stemmed from the fact that my parents would never fully understand me—that I was always trying to prove myself to them so that one day they'd be proud of what their daughter did with her life.

But God, it was so evident that they would never be proud of this career choice as long as I was in it.

"Listen to the agents, Dad. They're just doing their job," I mumbled without looking up.

"Callie-Ann, you don't find witness protection to be a little rash?" Mom wondered.

"No," I admitted, surprising myself. Last night I felt differently about that decision. "I lived with a serial killer in the next room." I cringed as I said it. Cue the *I told you this career wasn't for you* eye roll from my parents. "At one point he had his hands around my throat. I know what he's capable of. If I'm not vigilant now, it would be downright reckless. I cannot seriously believe you're fighting this. It's a done deal."

"Don't speak to your mother that way, Callie-Ann," Dad interjected.

"Don't call me that," I snapped at him. The room grew quiet, and I buried my face in my hands. I didn't want to be disrespectful to my parents, but I was so close to the breaking point. And they *knew* I didn't like being called that.

Sophie put her hand on my arm and glared at all the patrons at the table. "It's important that right now, we rally together to help this transition go seamlessly. For the safety of *everyone* in this room."

"Detective Reyes is right," Carver agreed.

Dad slammed his hand down on the table. I jumped. "This is bullshit!"

"*John,*" my mom chided.

"How are you not more upset about this, Helen? She's spent the better part of this year back home with us. Did you not spend the last seven years wishing she was closer? And just when we get her back in our lives, suddenly they're going to take her away from us?"

I didn't miss Liam dipping his chin in understanding, as if he felt what they felt. I tilted my head and looked at him, but he trained his eyes on the table.

"Would you rather her die?" Leah blurted. Meeting my sister's teary gaze, I mouthed, *Thank you.* "Because that's what she's facing. This isn't permanent. What is so hard to understand about that?"

Everyone began talking, speaking over one another. Voices were rising, people started arguing, and the only silent ones were me and Liam. We stared at each other across the table, all sexual tension gone. All that remained was raw emotion, specifically an unspoken one: *love.*

His eyes were rimmed red. It made my heart split.

I didn't want to leave, but more than that, I didn't want to leave *him.*

His next words caught the attention of the entire room.

"It's my fault she's leaving."

Forty-One

Liam

I must've had a death wish by announcing that I was the reason Callie was leaving. Maybe I subconsciously felt like I needed to be punished for my actions. Her family was already heated before I spoke up, but now those angry glares were trained on me.

"What?" Callie breathed, as if she couldn't comprehend what I'd said.

I didn't look away from her. I was leaning back in the conference chair, pretending I was self-possessed, but inside I was a complete shit show.

Speaking only to her, I said, "Carver and Matthews broke the news to me that they were leaving. I asked for them to find a better solution for you than protective custody."

She sat back in her chair. "That wasn't your decision, nor your responsibility, Liam." Her voice sounded defeated.

It felt like we were the only two in the room until I felt the weight of everyone's stares on us both. I had to tread lightly in my response.

"I know—"

"But it also wasn't your fault."

"But—"

Callie turned to face Carver and Matthews. "Would you have recommended WITSEC if it wasn't for Liam's interference?"

Carver tilted her head, her blonde hair glinting in the overhead lights. "Drew and I were already discussing next steps with you. We knew extended protective custody wasn't feasible here. The other possibility was bringing you to Quantico, but that would've limited your freedom further. This was the least shitty of all the options. All Liam did was force us to think outside the box a little more."

Callie turned back to me, offering me a forgiving smile. "See?"

"I just didn't realize the alternative until it was too late, and I apologize if I overstepped."

"Haven't you meddled in her life enough?" Callie's mother spat.

I turned to her. Callie clearly inherited her beauty from her mother.

"Don't answer that, Liam. My family has every right to be upset, but they don't understand your intentions."

"'Intentions?' You have *intentions* with my daughter?" Her dad seethed, turning red in the face.

Fuck.

This was new territory for me.

It was one thing to have in-laws and have my relationship with them start out on the right foot. This was… far from the right foot.

I had yet to get a word in to defend myself. The path of the conversation was complete chaos.

"If only he knew," Leah muttered from my right with a mischievous grin. I closed my eyes. There was no way her dad didn't hear.

"*Leah,*" Callie hissed, rising to her feet as if she might throw herself across the table at her sister. At this point, I didn't think it would surprise me.

"Oh, please. Let's not pretend you're innocent, Callie. Dad, you're smart enough to figure out what his *intentions* are."

Their dad turned furious eyes at me, but Callie flying off the handle saved me from a spiteful lecture from him. Her face turned bright red, and if looks could kill…

"I fucking knew you were going to cause trouble today. I saw it written all over your face," Callie snapped at her sister.

"Callie-Ann, watch your mouth," her mom said.

Callie rolled her eyes. "What I don't understand is why you just can't keep your mouth shut, Leah. You stood there in front of us playing nice this morning and then came in here to supposedly support me. What the fuck is *wrong* with you?"

"Fuck you," Leah hissed, planting her hands on the table and leaning forward.

Suddenly it was a showdown between the Eden sisters.

"Girls! Enough with the language," their mom said again.

"I can't believe you're going to stand there defending him!" Leah shouted. "I don't care how good the sex is, you can't change the past. We talked about this for months!"

I stifled a groan and put my head in my hands. I wasn't even man enough to sit there and pretend this didn't bother me.

"This meeting isn't about that, Leah." Callie's hands were shaking. She rested them on the table to hide it. "And of course I'm defending him!"

Oh. I snuck a glance at Drew and Madelyn at the head of the table, who were watching with cool amusement.

"No one gives him credit where credit is due!" she continued. "Has he made some mistakes? Yes, he has, but so have I. He's also sacrificed so much to help me. Do you know he's taking time out of his very busy job in New York to be here right now? Or how last night when we were standing over a dead body, we pulled out a note with *his name* written on it, yet he sits here today worried about *my* well-being? Or maybe how last year he saved my life from a bullet to the head?" She pointed to the large raised scar on her arm.

I gawked at her, completely in awe and caught off guard. I never knew she thought those things about me, and hearing it come out with such passion in front of all her family made my heart palpitate.

"And stop, for the love of God, calling me Callie-Ann. That's not my name. I'm going through enough of an existential crisis, and I'd really appreciate everyone respecting this one thing I'm asking for."

The room was dead silent.

Then, "I don't want to hear any more about your relationship with this young man. I can tell you're really emotional about all of this, Sugar Plum. Your sister is just looking out for you, as are we. Try to take a step back and see this from our perspective," her dad said. "Also, dear, that is your birth-given name, and we will call you that if we'd like."

Callie sighed. I watched as she reached the end of her rope, straightening her shoulders and rubbing her temples.

"Don't call me emotional. I'm allowed to defend myself and those I care about. *Also,*" she sneered, emphasizing the word, "I legally changed my name when I moved to Newark years ago. To *just* Callie. So no, that's not my name."

She spun on her heels and stormed out of the room, the door slamming shut behind her.

* * *

The room remained silent for several moments after Callie left. I exchanged an uncomfortable look with Sophie.

That was not how this was supposed to go.

Then again, I couldn't imagine how she was feeling with her family being here, with no warning, fighting every step of this process. I saw where she got everything from—each member of her family had dark hair, blue eyes, a beautiful smile, a quick tongue, and a hot temper. I could just picture how holidays were with all of them together.

I loosed a breath, preparing for a shitstorm to come my way.

"What should we do?" Leah whispered, seemingly to no one.

"She won't want to see you right now. You've insulted her enough. She needs a few minutes to cool off," I murmured back. Leah's eyebrows rose in surprise as I addressed her. Gone was the friendly playfulness she displayed earlier, now replaced with a bratty attitude.

Not unlike her sister.

"The only reason she'd want to see *you* right now is so you can fuck the anger out of her," she spat.

Everyone gasped, including me.

Jesus Christ, please save me now.

Her parents shifted uncomfortably, and I was tempted to get up and leave.

"Leah Irene, how many times do I have to tell you to *watch your mouth?*" her mother chastised, at the same time her brother jumped to his feet and leaned across the table.

Why Leah had thrown us under the bus like that was beyond me. I'd done nothing to this woman, and yet here she was stirring the pot for no good reason.

"You keep your hands off my sister," Sam threatened.

"Settle down, Sam," Sophie said, exasperation lacing her words. "Callie is a grown woman, and it's not your place to involve yourself in her relationships." It was the kindest Sophie had been to me in a long time.

"He can speak for himself," Sam snapped.

I rose to my feet and leveled with him. "I'm not going to sit here and talk about the private nature of my relationship with Callie, and quite frankly, I don't think anyone in this room cares to hear about it either. We're focusing on the wrong things right now. We're here to listen to the precautionary measures these agents have put in place."

"I can't believe you, Sophie," Leah said, ignoring me completely. "You saw what he did to her."

"Yeah, and I also saw what *she* did to *him*, Leah. It's not just his fault. I encouraged Callie to accept a proposal to a serial killer under false pretenses, and when everything fell apart, guess who was here picking up the pieces of their work life *and* the ramifications of their affair? *Me.*" I wanted to fall to my knees and thank her for standing up for me. That is, until she opened her mouth again. "Besides, it's not like it'll matter after today, now will it? They won't be together anyways."

Ouch.

"That's the best news I've heard all day," Callie's dad said.

I wanted to hang my head in defeat. It was hard to be in a room full of people who despised me, with the exception of Drew, Madelyn, and Terry in the corner, watching everything transpire with indifference.

Instead, I sat back down.

"Do you disagree with them, Liam?" Sophie challenged.

I met her dark eyes. "It's not like it matters after today, so why are you asking?" I shot back, throwing her words in her face. So much for her being on my side.

"Because no matter how hard she tries to move on from you, you find a way to worm your way back into her heart. And rather than being in here like she should be, she ran away because she expended so much energy on defending you."

I ran a hand down my face. "You and I both know it's more than that."

She cocked an eyebrow. "Is it? Because from where I'm sitting, this isn't the first time she's ran away from her problems. And those problems always lead back to you."

Well, fuck me.

She may as well have smacked me across the face. Maybe she was onto something.

"I'm not getting into this with you, Sophie."

"Oh, okay, so you'll have a huge argument in a public parking lot in the middle of the night, then sneak off to fuck her, but you won't have this conversation with me now?"

What. The. Actual. Fuck.

I groaned. "Oh my God, Sophie, you have no idea what you're talking about. Have you even *asked* her what that argument was over?"

"You pissed her off—"

"Because I went and got a drink after she asked me not to. Do you know why? Because I was the one responsible for breaking the news about WITSEC to her."

Sophie opened her mouth to respond when Terry cut her off. "Back off, Sophie. Leave it be."

She gritted her teeth. "You're not innocent here, either, *sir*. One could argue we're all sitting here because of *your* greedy actions."

"Whose side are you on?" I quipped. "He made a bad judgment call, but no one could have prepared an entire police precinct for this."

She laughed darkly. "Must be nice to be part of the good ole boys club, huh, Liam?" My spine stiffened. "Always having someone to pull strings for you."

I pushed back from the table, ready to leave the room. "I'm not going to get all the blame put on me. I'm not the only bad guy. We're all in part responsible for the severity of the situation, and I'll be damned if I sit here taking the heat for all of it. I can admit to my mistakes. I suggest everyone else do the same."

Sam snickered. "As if."

I narrowed my eyes on him, then took a turn looking at each person, despite the disdain on their faces. "A lot of you probably don't see it because Callie puts on a strong front, but she's scared as hell right now. For herself *and* for her family. She's about to leave everyone behind to keep you all safe. Not to mention, she just found out her sister is engaged—congratulations, by the way," I said, nodding at Leah and Jason. "And won't be able to participate in wedding activities. And speaking from personal experience, that's one of the most exciting times you'll ever have.

"Also, try to remember she's dealing with the fact that she was hunting the serial killer that lived in the same apartment with her for over a year. There are a lot of moving pieces to this. Stop hyperfocusing on my mistakes, and take a second to look at the whole goddamn picture." My chest was heaving now, my blood boiling in anger.

When no one spoke, I took my leave. "Now, if you'll excuse me, I'm going to find her so we can wrap this up."

Forty-Two

Liam

The precinct was stuffy when I emerged from the meeting room. I felt claustrophobic and flustered as I frantically rolled my shirtsleeves to my elbows. What the *hell* just happened?

I just knew I needed to clear my head and calm the fuck down.

That was one of the most embarrassing, degrading, infuriating experiences of my life.

I took the stairs two at a time until I was out of the bustling bullpen. The air felt clearer up here. I would go find Callie once the indignance in my head had faded, but right now I needed a goddamn minute to breathe.

Presuming she was in our old office, I made a beeline for the vacant supply closet we had been in earlier, knowing it would be private enough to be by myself. I swung the door open and paused when I found Callie sitting on the floor, leaning against the cabinets with her knees pulled to her chest. She raised her head as the door opened; eyes puffy and cheeks wet, her makeup smudged, and the look on her face somewhere between telling me to get the fuck out and begging me to stay.

Okay, maybe I didn't need a minute alone as long as she was with me.

We stared at each other for a moment as I closed the door behind me. *Lash out at me, baby. Whatever you need,* I pleaded with her silently.

She seemed to understand as tears welled in her eyes, her lower lip wobbling. She needed to break down, and she needed someone to hold her.

It broke my heart.

I locked the door. Whatever I'd been feeling moments before no longer mattered—my primal instincts had me needing to take care of her now. I sat down beside her and extended my legs in front of me, not forcing anything but letting her know I was here.

She threw herself into my lap and sobbed, covering her face. I swallowed thickly, hating to see her like this, and once again I felt like it was my fault. Apparently no matter how hard I tried to be a better man for her, I was still majorly fucking her life up.

"I'm sorry, baby," I croaked, forcing the words out around the lump in my throat. I ran a hand up and down her arm, then reached for the clip in her hair to pull it out so I could run my fingers through her soft locks.

After a few moments, she removed her hands from her face. "Please don't sit and blame yourself. You were only looking out for me." Her voice was hoarse.

"You should be mad at me. I shouldn't have tried to intervene. You're a strong woman and you voice what you want, when you want it."

She paused. "I am mad at you, but not for what you think. I'm mad that you didn't talk to me before you went to Drew and Madelyn about it. I don't care that things have been… awkward between us. You owed that to me."

I cleared my throat. "You're right. I'm sorry."

Callie huffed out a laugh. "It's not worth spending what little time we have left together being angry."

I smiled, even though she couldn't see it. But then something nagged at me, something I'd been avoiding telling her.

"It's not just you I'm mad at," she confessed.

"I know."

"My parents are complicated people. I don't think they understand the position I'm in."

"Maybe they don't want to believe it?" I offered.

She shook her head against my legs. "I thought that too, but honestly my parents have never understood my decision to join the force. I feel like they think I'm a pencil pusher who wears a badge with no real power and who occasionally sees dead bodies."

I didn't mean to laugh, but I couldn't help it. "Do they even know you? You're a force to be reckoned with." I meant it as a joke, but Callie sighed.

"I don't think I'm the daughter they expected me to be. They're pushing back on this because they don't take me seriously."

"Baby, I think they're just being parents in denial."

"How did your parents react when you told them you were joining the force?"

I blinked. I hadn't thought about that in a long, long time. "They weren't happy," I admitted. "But they understood why I chose this path. My mom thinks I'm dead if I don't call her at least once a week."

Callie caught my wrist to look at my exposed forearm now that my sleeves were rolled up. Her fingers gently traced over the tattoo of my mother's eyes, and a shiver went down my spine. "Are they proud of you?"

I paused. "Yeah, I think so. I know if they had their way, I'd be working for the family business, but they listen to all my stories and tell me they admire what I do."

After a moment, Callie nodded. "Good. That's what parents should do."

I realized that Callie's parents *didn't* do that for her. Leaning my head against the cabinets behind me, I stared up at the ceiling. So many layers to this woman that I was only beginning to see. Layers I'd only scratched the surface of last year. "I guess that explains where your praise kink comes from."

She laughed, loud and hard. It made me grin. "You're probably not wrong about that." I continued stroking her hair. "My sister really set me off."

I chuckled. "Siblings have a way of doing that."

She frowned. "No, I mean *really* set me off. As soon as I saw her enter the precinct with the rest of my family, I had a gut feeling that she was going to pull some unexpected shit. What I don't understand is why she would save face this morning just to turn around and cause a scene like that. I mean, she doesn't even *know* you. She has no room to be making such harsh judgments. And in front of our parents, no less!" She groaned. "I'm so fucking upset that she would throw out such personal information in front of all those people."

Something about this conversation, how raw and emotional and intimate it felt, being each other's safe places when everything else was upside down... It made me feel like Callie was *my home*. The one I'd been missing my whole life. "I think she's suffering in her own way, babe. You just told me earlier that you made all these promises to her when you moved to the city. You probably told her you'd be back soon, huh? Not knowing this was the direction it was going to go."

"Yeah. That makes sense. Fucking childish reaction, though."

I snorted. "You said it. She didn't exactly simmer down after you left."

She groaned. "I'm not ready to face the music."

"We don't have to go back yet."

We sat in comfortable silence for a few minutes before Callie turned onto her back so she was staring up at me. Those big blue eyes caught mine, and I swear the world stopped for a beat. These moments—this is all I had wanted with her for the better part of a year. All I still wanted.

"Thanks for coming in here. I didn't realize I just needed someone to be with me." She frowned, then added, "I didn't realize I needed *you* to be with me."

I simpered at her. "I think we both needed a break. Besides," I said, winking at her, "I'll never turn down alone time with you."

Her cheeks reddened as she sat up, and I instantly missed her warmth on my legs. "I'm still a little mad."

"You're entitled to your feelings, babe." My lips curved when that earned a small smile from her. "If you're mad, that's fine. You can take it out on me, if you need to. Whenever you want. I'm not fragile." Her shoulders dropped, but I pressed on. "You should know at this point that I will go to the ends of the earth to give you peace of mind. What you're going through doesn't scare me. And I couldn't care less that my name was on that piece of paper. We're going through it *together*." Okay, maybe now would be a good time to express that pressing matter she needed to know about.

Callie inhaled deeply, her eyes fluttering closed. She interlaced her fingers with mine. "Thank you. I know this isn't easy on you."

"I'd rather be here pining after you than back in New York with a stack of papers." She giggled and leaned into my side, resting her head on my shoulder.

"Can I be honest?" she wondered.

"Always."

"I was already feeling apprehensive today as the reality of it all hit me, that seeing my family show up just pushed me over the edge. And all I could think about was being with you."

My heart soared.

She tucked her legs under her and turned to face me completely, readying herself to say something big.

But I had to get that nagging feeling out.

"Before you finish," I breathed, knowing I was treading on thin ice. "There's something you should know." Her expression turned wary. "I went after you that day."

Several emotions flitted across her features—confusion, anger, sadness, heartache. "What?"

"I went after you," I repeated. "I realized what I'd done moments after you left, and I ran after you to tell you I was sorry and beg you to stay." My eyes burned as I confessed. She needed the whole story. "But I couldn't find you. I was going to tell you I loved—*love* you. And then Kelsey showed up and I broke up with her because I knew all I wanted was you and I wasn't going to spend one more minute with someone that *wasn't* you. I went to your apartment, back to the office just to see you'd packed up and left. I called, I texted. No one knew where you went, and—," I cut off my rambling, shutting down the word vomit as pure, unadulterated anger washed over her.

Callie pushed herself to her feet, her hands flying to her hair as she backed away from me. I wasn't expecting this reaction. Whatever she'd been about to say before was long gone.

I rose to my feet slowly. "Callie."

Because I realized I'd said those words again to her that she had waited so long to hear, twice in one day, this time in private.

"What am I supposed to do with that information, Liam?"

I sucked in a breath.

"All these months," her voice croaked, "could've been avoided."

I could blame it on her blocking my number, but I had resources to get in touch with her. Yet I chose not to, because I thought I was being honorable by giving her the space she deserved—*needed.*

I shook my head. "I disagree. You said it yourself: we needed this time apart to be ready for each other. Even if we *had* reconciled things that day, we still had our own shit to deal with. And who's to say we would've worked through it together? I think we both needed to find ourselves again before we could give each other our all." It was the first time I had admitted that to myself, and the truth was refreshing. Real. Relieving. All that pain… it wasn't for nothing.

Her shoulders dropped in resignation. She knew I was right. I could tell by the small smile ghosting her mouth. "Why tell me now? Why not tell me in any of the conversations we've had over the last few weeks? Why wait until the day before I leave? Why tell me at all?"

I raised a shoulder. "In the spirit of honesty? I didn't think it would change anything."

"Change anything?" she echoed. She stepped toward me, cupping my face in her hands and pressing a tender kiss to my lips before turning and leaving the room without saying another word.

I exhaled, long and loud. I didn't know what that reaction meant.

What I did know was in that exact moment as she shut the door in my face, that I had just given her my heart, and without her giving me hers, I couldn't give her my body again.

Because she clearly wasn't ready to return the sentiment. It wasn't fair to either of us until she could.

Guess I wasn't catching a break today.

Forty-Three

Callie

⚜

I haphazardly twisted my long hair back into the stupid claw clip that had caused me nothing but trouble today, grumbling as I went.

Re-entering the investigation room felt like stepping into a war zone. The tension was heavy, everyone avoiding looking at one another with either their arms crossed or their fists clenched. I wondered what had happened, but I didn't address it. Everyone was sitting except Madelyn, Drew, and a middle-aged woman who appeared to be discussing a serious matter in hushed tones.

Moments later, the door clicked open again. I folded my arms across my chest, studiously ignoring Liam as he brushed past me and returned to his seat at the table.

Was I mad that he decided to tell me that he chased after me the day I professed my love and he so obviously rejected me? No. I was mad that he was *right*—that even though we both went through hell from the fallout of our relationship, it made us both better individuals, which in turn would make us better partners to each other.

But the idea of having saved an endless amount of heartache was an easier pill to swallow.

"Welcome back, Ms. Eden," Agent Matthews greeted, his gray eyes twinkling as their small group approached the table. "You're just in time. Your Marshal arrived earlier than expected."

My breathing stopped. *Already?*

The middle-aged woman stepped around the two agents and held her hand out to me. Her voice sounded like it was underwater. *"Marlene Randall, US Marshal. Here in regards to a Ms. Callie Eden and a Mr. Liam Chandler."*

I blinked at her. "I'm sorry, I just wasn't expecting you until tomorrow."

She gave me a crooked smile. "Due to the most recent advance in this case, we felt it best that I fly out immediately. I planned everything on the plane. I've already disclosed all I can to your family, so I think it best I finish debriefing the both of you in private." Her brown eyes flickered to the conference table.

Confused, I glanced at everyone rising from their seats. My family lined up to give me a hug one at a time, saying their goodbyes and crying. My brain was so fogged, I hardly remembered telling them I loved them and I was sorry for what had transpired today.

After a few moments, it was just me, Liam, and the Marshal. She gestured for me to take a seat. I obeyed, feeling dazed.

"I apologize for the secrecy, but I'm sure you can understand the sensitivity," Marshal Randall said.

I nodded numbly.

"Let me start with you, Mr. Chandler. The US Government can't, in good conscience, let you return to your job while Ms. Eden is admitted into the Witness Security Program. We've already made arrangements for the both of you to enter the program together, departing later this evening."

Liam sucked in a breath and leaned forward. "I'm sorry, what?"

She glanced down at the open folder in front of her, a small frown forming. "Ms. Eden, have you or have you not been in a physical altercation with Oliver Frankford?"

I dipped my chin. "I have."

"And did you or did you not have an affair with Mr. Chandler that resulted in said altercation?"

I tilted my head back and forth. "More or less, yes."

She nodded.

"And Mr. Chandler, did you or did you not directly offend Oliver Frankford by having an affair with his fiancé?"

"I did," Liam said with resignation, steepling his fingers under his chin.

"Was your name associated with Oliver Frankford's most recent victim?"

"It was."

"Then it is with these findings that we deem it necessary that the both of you enter the WITSEC program, effective immediately. A joint cover offers additional protection to the both of you."

I cleared my throat. I wasn't sure I heard her correctly. "Where will we be relocating?"

Randall pulled glasses out of her suit jacket pocket and slid them on. "There is a safe house in the Rocky Mountains in Idaho where you will both be assigned. It's approximately five miles from McCall. Every two weeks you'll need to come into town to meet me. The first meeting will likely require you to make a trek down until we get approval for a vehicle."

Once every two weeks.

She made it sound like we were going to be there for the rest of our lives.

"Is there some sort of cover story involved that we need to abide by?" Liam urged.

The Marshal nodded. "I was getting to that. Whenever you are in the public eye, or outside the safe house, your names are Josh and Emily Blake. You've been married for five years and decided to move to the mountains and work remotely. Before that, you lived in Seattle."

A hysterical laugh bubbled out of me before I could stop it. This was all so ridiculous. "Married? Liam and I?" Liam rolled his eyes at my antics. I ignored him.

Another nod. "In public, yes. It's the easiest lie for people to believe, because marriages come in every shape."

"Okay... and what, exactly, are our 'remote jobs' and what kind of knowledge do we need to have for them?"

"Ms. Eden, you'll be entering a technology start-up as a data entry manager, 'transferred' from another company. It's straightforward work that requires you to check other people's work for clerical errors and to keep their deadlines on track."

Great. A glorified babysitter. At least it wasn't too far off from what I was doing in Springcrest.

"And Mr. Chandler, you're a freelancing editor for manuscripts. We've already provided a faux portfolio for you and have a couple of client meetings that are arranged for next week after you've gotten settled, with small indie authors. Both are easy enough to enter and require little to no discussion on your backgrounds while keeping you both protected in the confines of the safe house. You won't be prisoners there, but it will help."

There was a moment of eerie calm before someone spoke again.

"Will I be able to return to New York to pack some items?" Liam questioned, and he and the Marshal spoke back and forth for several minutes.

I couldn't process anything they were saying.

I stared at the table, my brain not comprehending any of the past fifteen minutes.

I was preparing to leave Liam behind after today and have to deal with the heartbreak all over again.

But this? Pretending to be married to him, not being able to run away from the emotions overpowering me, and getting the chance to truly give us a shot? That was fucking *terrifying*.

How was Liam so calm about this?

I don't know how long we sat there, but after some time, Randall rose to her feet and gathered her papers. She looked between the two of us and said, "I'll see the both of you back here in five hours." She paused for a moment before pulling a small bag out of a file she was holding, dropping it on the table. "Find one that fits. Your cover starts the moment you step off the plane." She left the room, leaving me and Liam sitting at the table in silence.

My chin was resting on my hand, while Liam was leaning back in his chair. I didn't even know what to say with him; we were both in shock. I reached for the bag and opened it, almost laughing when I saw wedding bands inside. I dumped them on the table and plucked a simple solitaire one, slid it on my finger, and thought how this was nowhere near what I imagined when I pictured a life with him.

With that thought, I pushed myself to my feet and moved to leave, half-expecting him to stop me. But he didn't so much as look up.

Forty-Four

Liam

Well, today turned into an absolute disaster.

I didn't even get to say goodbye to my family in person. I had five hours to drive to the city, pack my things, and come back. A FaceTime call to my parents was all I got, and I was forced to be okay with that in order to deal with what was to come.

I sat next to Callie on the private plane as it prepared to take off. The Marshal had explained that everyone placed into witness protection had to fly private in order to help maintain their identity. I wasn't going to complain; at the very least, I was comfortable.

Randall explained to us what would happen once we landed—where we needed to go, who we needed to be—before moving to the front of the cabin to rest.

So now it was just us. Callie had been stoic all afternoon. I didn't want to make her situation worse, but I wasn't sure how to prompt a conversation with her when all I felt was inner turmoil. We were both giving each other space.

I finally decided to reach for her hand. Her fingers curled around mine for a moment before she pulled it away as though my skin burned her. I looked at her in disbelief.

"Callie."

She gestured with her hand and turned to look out the window as if she were struggling with something.

I nearly scoffed.

Did she have grounds to be mad? Definitely. But this attitude? Unbelievable.

Actually, it was completely believable. This woman always did unexpected things; it was how she kept me on my toes.

I sighed and leaned my head back against the headrest. Next thing I knew, Callie was unbuckling her seat belt and climbing into my lap, her lips crushing against mine. A surprised moan tore from my throat. My hands gripped her hips to prevent her from grinding into me.

I wasn't confident in being able to stop her if she made any contact with my cock.

Pinned underneath her, though, I was nearly powerless. Her tongue invaded my mouth, and her fingers twisted in my hair before dropping to my chest, where she fiddled with the buttons of my dress shirt.

Jesus. The Marshal was fifteen feet away.

"I need you," she groaned into my mouth, her voice low and gravelly. She settled further into my lap, and I was nearly a goner at the sweet friction against my rock-hard erection.

"*Callie,*" I pleaded, though for what, I wasn't sure.

My moment of weakness gave her the opportunity to press her lips onto mine and rub along my length. I broke our kiss and tightened my grip on her hips to stop her from doing it again. She looked at me with wild eyes.

"Tell me you love me, and you can have me," I whispered.

She stilled, searching my eyes frantically before pulling back to a sitting position on my lap. "What?"

"You said you need me. Tell me you love me, and you can have me. All of me."

"You're giving me an ultimatum?" Disbelief flashed in her eyes.

I shook my head. "It's not an ultimatum. It's taking the next step in our relationship."

She scrambled off my lap just as we hit a patch of turbulence, careening right back into me. I caught her, but she tore away from me and took off down the aisle toward the bathroom. I sighed, taking this as a chance to corner her, and practically threw myself to my feet to follow her.

Forty-Five

Callie

I slipped into the bathroom at the back of the plane, relieved to be by myself for a second before I cried in front of Liam. But before the door could shut behind me, he stepped into the cramped space behind me.

I gaped at him in the mirror, unable to turn around in the limited confines of the bathroom.

"Liam, what the hell are you doing?" I whisper-shouted, annoyed that I had to hold back my tears, equally embarrassed at my stomach fluttering from our close proximity.

His gaze darkened. I knew how badly he wanted me—felt it myself when I was grinding on him—but he swiftly shut me down. Unless I professed my love. But my trauma stopped me. Not because I didn't love him, but because I was scared and swept up in a million other messy emotions from the tangled web that was my life.

My breath hitched as our gazes locked in the mirror. He leaned forward, his hands gripping the edge of the counter as he pinned my hips to the small vanity. His lips pressed into the crook of my neck. I let out an audible moan as my head fell back, his lush, spicy scent filling my head with inappropriate thoughts.

"You can't run away from me forever," he murmured, his deep timbre vibrating through my body. I shuddered.

"Watch me," I challenged, but my voice was tight, strained.

He cocked a brow. I was so very aware of his chest against my back, his heat mixing with mine as he said, "You and I are all we've got now." And this teasing was sending me barreling toward complete compliance.

As if I wasn't riled up enough before coming in here.

I pressed my ass into his crotch. His eyes closed as he groaned, pressing a hand against my belly to still me. I smirked. Maybe I could break him, after all, and he could forget this whole silly ultimatum.

"Don't," he breathed. "You're playing a game you won't win."

"I'd like to see you try to resist me."

Toying with him distracted me from my need to cry.

Liam grinned wickedly, his dimples popping out. My vagina tingled at the sight. He brushed the back of his knuckles over my breasts, my nipples, my waist… moving until he hiked the hem of my dress up to reveal the fresh bruises from his punishing hold on my hips this morning. He brushed over my center through my panties. I fought the gasp of air my lungs were screaming for and raised my gaze to meet his in the mirror.

Holy shit.

The view was utterly spectacular—my dress pulled up, one hand on my thigh tracing the marks he left on me while the other stroked me. My head rolled back on his shoulder, his lips brushing my ear.

Then, as I was getting antsy to feel his fingers in me, he withdrew his hands and curled them over mine on the counter. I whimpered in disappointment. To hell with being embarrassed. My desire for this man was no secret.

"I'll resist you for as long as it takes for you to tell me you love me," he rasped. "Because *I love you.*" With that, he pushed away and slipped out the door, leaving me breathless and reeling.

* * *

I returned to my seat after reaching a steely resolve. He wanted to play hard to get? Fine, I'd play his game.

No longer in the mood to cry about it, I slipped my drenched panties off and sauntered back to our area. After a quick glance at Marshal Randall confirmed she was sleeping, I dropped my discarded panties in his lap. His eyes flew to mine.

"Callie, what the fuck? Put these back on right now."

I smirked at him, leaning across him and bending over to grab my purse from my seat. I rifled through it, taking my sweet time so he could appreciate the full view of my naked bottom half, until I found what I was searching for.

Instead of taking my seat next to him, I fell into the seat across from him. His gaze seared into me, his hand clutching my underwear like a lifeline while the other gripped the armrest until his knuckles turned white. I smiled salaciously at him before spreading my legs, adjusting my dress so he had a nice view of my bare pussy.

Liam sucked in a breath as his eyes dropped down, watching my hands as I switched my small, portable vibrator on and trailed it up my inner thighs. They trembled in response, already so ready for what was to come. And in this case, it was *me* who would be coming very, very soon.

The sounds of my toy and my labored breaths were drowned out by the jet's engine, the rumbling of it only adding to my stimulation. I pressed the vibrator against my clit, then circled it, the way Liam did with his tongue. Then I moved it down, collecting my arousal just to come back up and circle my clit again.

I watched Liam's every reaction. His cheeks flushing, his eyes flooding with desire, his hands clenching and unclenching. He alternated between tugging on his hair with his free hand, and biting down on his knuckles, and god dammit, I was obsessed with watching him watch me.

He was losing his fucking grip right before my eyes.

That alone had me spiraling toward an orgasm, building and building until I reached an intense peak. I rode the wave as I tipped over the edge, my back arching off the seat and my teeth biting down on my lower lip to stifle my moan.

And as I came back down, I found my face in Liam's hands as he stood over me. "I could watch you come all day, baby." I met his gaze, then brought my hand up, still clutching the now turned-off vibrator, and slipped it between his lips. He sucked on it, his eyes fluttering closed as he groaned.

I pulled it out abruptly, whispering, "Enjoy the taste. It's the last you're getting. Remember that when you're jerking your cock off by yourself, since you're playing hard to get."

He blinked slowly before straightening and taking his seat again, running his tongue over his lower lip.

I just smirked at him.

Game on, baby.

Forty-Six

Liam

Callie was curled up in her seat next to me, sated as she slept soundly, but I was wound up tighter than a fucking watch spring. My knee was restlessly bouncing, my fingers were sore from keeping them clenched in a fist, and my dick throbbed painfully in my pants. I could feel precum soaking the ends of my tucked-in dress shirt, and I swore I was ready to blow my load from dry humping the air.

I don't know what came over Callie. It made me weak in the fucking knees watching her masturbate in front of me. And on a plane with the Marshal within sight, no less. The taboo aspect added an unmatched level of hotness.

Maybe my little plan would backfire... *quickly.*

I huffed in frustration. I probably *should* go jack off in the bathroom, but that was more pitiful than sitting here with a boner that refused to go away.

I think.

I wasn't exactly clear-headed since all the blood in my body seemed to be flooding my lower extremity.

I fisted myself through the fabric of my dress pants, and my hips involuntarily flexed upward. *Not good.* I was seconds from coming in my pants, the image of Callie's sweet little pussy clenching as she orgasmed taking over every other thought in my head.

Nope.

I raced down the aisle and locked myself in the bathroom, fumbling with my belt until my cock sprang free, red and angry-looking and dripping with precum. My chest heaved as I took the base in one hand and stroked up and down.

Callie moved her vibrator in a small circle around her clit, just like I wanted to do with my tongue.

"Fuck," I cursed under my breath as I braced my free hand on the vanity.

She dipped her cute little pink vibrator into that perfect, tight pussy, letting out a soft moan as she moved it back up to that swollen bundle of nerves.

"Fuck, fuck, fuck!" I came so hard at the mental image of Callie getting herself off that stars swirled in my vision, thick ropes of my cum coating the bathroom vanity as my cock emptied itself.

I pulled my hand away and looked down at the mess I'd created, including a few drops on my nice dress shoes.

Sighing, I tucked myself back into my pants and grabbed paper towels to clean up, feeling utterly spent and wondering how I planned on following through with my promise of holding out on her. I couldn't even handle her getting off in front of me, and I had fucked her twelve hours prior.

I'm so fucked.

* * *

The Marshal wasn't joking about having to make the trek up to the cabin. She was kind enough to drive us so we would know the route. The early morning sunshine was peeking over the mountain tops, and I couldn't tear my eyes from the scenery. I'd never seen anything quite like this.

The black SUV turned onto a sloping driveway lined with tall, lush trees. The road was secluded and bumpy, and after a couple minutes, a small wood cabin appeared.

So this was it.

I wasn't quite sure what to make of it, but it wasn't like I had much of a choice in the matter.

The car came to a stop, and we all climbed out. The air was much thinner and cooler, despite it being July. It took a moment to feel like I could breathe again.

Randall helped us unload our luggage and carry it to the front door. She handed me a set of keys and two SIM cards. "Welcome home. Around the back, there's a shed with firewood, but you'll probably need to collect your own kindling. Food has already been stocked in here. We are arranging for an internet provider to run lines here, but I don't have an ETA on that right now. Same with the car." She paused. "Just a reminder that you will need to make the hike into town two weeks from today to meet with me at Rotary Park. Groceries will be delivered to you then. When you do go into town, you can use these SIM cards with your new numbers. There's a plan set up under your aliases."

I took the keys and SIM cards from her, feeling a pit in my stomach for the first time. I had checked my phone on the way up to see we had lost service. So… this was really it. "And if there's an emergency before the internet gets installed? There's no service here."

She nodded. "There's an emergency phone in there that does, but you'll need to be cautious with it. It has a limited amount of messages and minutes on it."

I sighed and glanced at Callie, who was looking around the front porch impassively. No doubt at all the spiderwebs collecting in the corners.

"Be safe, you two. Rest assured we're doing all we can."

"We understand. Thanks for your help."

Randall gave us both a small smile before walking back to the car. I watched as she left, wondering what it was like for her to be able to return to her normal life after dumping us here.

After a moment, I turned and unlocked the front door, pushing it open with the toe of my shoe. I frowned down at them, realizing I didn't have a need for them in this climate. The thought made me sad.

Callie and I paused in the entryway of our new home. My heart pinged with bitterness. This was never how I imagined us living together.

Inside was cozy enough, with an open layout. To the right was the living room with rich brown leather couches, a stone fireplace, dusty bookshelves filled with books, even a TV. Off to the left was a small dining table and a kitchen, and in front of us was a hallway that presumably led to the bedrooms.

"Well this is…" Callie breathed, her voice trailing off. My head snapped to look at her. They were the first words she'd willingly spoken to me since the plane.

"Not what you were expecting?"

Out of the blue, she burst into laughter. Cathartic, infectious laughter that had me joining her even through my confusion.

"My life's a joke," she gasped as she calmed down, dabbing at her eyes. "This is almost comical. I'm a city girl. I don't belong in the mountains."

I chuckled. "I'm not really sure what to make of this, either. But we'll figure it out."

Callie dropped her bags. "I don't know about you, but I'm exhausted. My sleep was less than restful on the plane." She stretched her arms over her head.

I smirked at her, my mind going to all sorts of places… her getting off in front of me and then shoving her vibrator in my mouth, coated in her arousal. But I could see fatigue written all over her face, and I reminded myself of my decision. I gestured toward the hallway, picked up her bags, and followed her to the end. There was a bedroom on each side, and after a moment, she entered the one on the right. I set her bags down just inside the door.

"Get some rest," I said softly, and shut the door behind me.

Forty-Seven

Callie

❧

Damn, the nights were cold. The heat wasn't very efficient in our cabin; it mostly just warmed the living room, so the bedrooms were chilly. Both rooms had an attached bathroom, but of course I had chosen the one without a tub. I desperately wanted to soak in a hot bath, just to bring some warmth back to my body. But I didn't necessarily want to waltz into Liam's room to do that.

Two days in this remote cabin and I was already going a little stir crazy. There wasn't anything to *do* while we waited for the internet to be installed so we could work. Nowhere to eat—okay, that wasn't true, I just didn't want to make a five mile hike to eat at a restaurant just to work up an appetite on the way back.

Ugh. I couldn't wait until we got the approval for a vehicle. Randall didn't give us a timeline on that, so we stayed within the perimeters of the property. Much to my dismay.

I shivered and pulled my blankets up to my chin, but it didn't help the cold seeping into my bones. I was tired and cold and tired of being cold, even in my sweats, fuzzy socks, and long sleeve shirt.

Never feeling less attractive, my libido had locked herself away. She was nowhere to be seen, and frankly I couldn't blame her. We belonged in the city together, in the warmth of the summer, not *here*.

Not like my sex drive even mattered right now, because Liam wanted me to drop to my knees and tell him I loved him. I hadn't even pushed the topic any further while I adjusted to this new life.

Shivering violently again, my teeth chattering, I kicked the blankets off in frustration. Fuck this. I climbed out of my bed and crept across the hall to Liam's room, gently opening and closing the door so it wouldn't creak. In the moonlight filtering through the window above the headboard, I could see him lying on his back, his face turned toward the door, chest rising and falling in even, slumber-filled breaths.

He looked so beautiful and peaceful, and my deep feelings—the very same ones he wanted me to confess to him—slammed into me like a freight train. It terrified me that they came rushing back so quickly, stronger than before.

I slowly crawled into his bed, tucking myself under the blankets and sheets that smelled like him, and curled up by his side. Warmth radiated from him like a furnace. As tempted as I was to rest my head on his chest and let him wrap me in his arms, I could already feel sleep tugging at me. I gave into the pull and drifted off into a deep, dreamless slumber.

* * *

The sound of birds and the bright rays of sunshine stirred me awake. It took a moment before I opened my eyes and remembered whose bed I was in—and whose arm was draped over my waist, whose chest was pressed against my back. Liam was so fucking *warm*, I never wanted to leave.

And then, a sobering thought: I couldn't leave. If I chose to stay here all day, I could do that. Work was in limbo, our life was… well, this.

I rolled over to find Liam with his eyes still closed. Not sleeping. No, not with the way his hand drifted to my hip to hold me in place. I stilled, ignoring the heat pooling in my core, and refrained from squeezing my thighs together.

Well, there was my missing libido.

This wasn't the point of me crawling into his bed in the middle of the night. I just wanted to maintain some level of comfort with the chill.

My eyes drifted over his muscular body, taking it all in. The morning sun only did him favors, making him even sexier than he already was.

Damn it.

I was head over heels for him, and what better time to explore this relationship than when we were isolated in the mountains together?

I placed my hand over his on my hip and let my fingers trail up his arm, to the unfamiliar tattoo on his forearm. Half a compass that looked like the other half blew away in the wind, curling at the edges. An arrow speared through it with a small heart at its tip. Beautiful.

Liam's hand gripped my hip harder. "You're in dangerous territory, Ms. Eden," he mumbled, his voice thick with sleep. My eyes snapped to his face. He slowly opened his eyes, and I sucked in a breath. The sun hit them, and the unbelievable green of them made my panties damp, my heart rate kicking up a notch.

"I think I'm right where I belong," I murmured, giving him a bashful smile.

A slow grin crept onto his face. "Don't tempt me. I intend to make good on my promise."

I whined and jutted out my lower lip. Okay, so maybe it wasn't my *full* intention to just be warm throughout the night; maybe there was a bit of an ulterior motive with me being in his bed. My clit throbbed as I pouted.

"But—"

"No," he said sternly, a mirthful smile on his lips and amusement in his eyes. I flushed at his tone. I wasn't used to him being so… firm with me, but some small part of me liked that, liked feeling controlled. It was a nice break from always feeling the need to be in control of everything else.

Wanting to push the boundary, I moved my hand toward the waistband of his gray joggers. I wanted to feel how hard he was in my hand; he grabbed my wrist before I could get far.

I pushed myself to a sitting position and eyed him. "You're being serious?"

He sat up, and the sheets pooled around his waist. I couldn't help my wandering, hungry eyes. His devious grin, dimples and all, told me he knew exactly what he was doing to me. "I'm being serious."

I swallowed and looked away. I couldn't have a conversation while he was half-naked, knowing I couldn't touch him the way I wanted to. "You snuggle me and then expect me to keep my hands off?"

Liam raised his eyebrows, locks of his hair falling adorably over his forehead. "You crawl into my bed in the middle of the night, freezing cold, and expect me to *not* snuggle you?"

I pursed my lips. "Touché."

Now would be a perfect time to tell him how I really felt—but he was challenging me, and it made me want to play games.

He leaned back on his hands, his gaze flicking up and down my body, where evidently I had kicked my sweatpants off in the middle of the night, leaving me in just a shirt and panties. My whole body lit up under his ogling.

"Besides," he drawled, "you've barely spoken to me since we got here."

Shrugging, I said, "It's been a lot for me to process."

His eyes turned hard and unreadable. "Me too, but I'm not trying to shut you out."

I bit my lip and stared down at my hands. "I know. I've got some things I can improve on."

Liam's gaze softened as he reached up to push my hair behind my shoulders. Heat spread through me at the gesture. "Don't do that."

"Don't do what?"

"Don't tell yourself you're not good enough as is."

I winced, thinking about his words from a few weeks ago.

Should I add anything else to my list of things to fix before I'm good enough for you?

His words had stung, and they'd been stuck in my head since. I never wanted to make him feel that way, and here he was finding his own way to move past my hurtful words. He'd been constantly working on himself while I'd been stuck in this self-sabotaging loop that I didn't know how to stop.

Liam had said those three words to me already. I knew how he felt. I knew we were going to finally be together once I said them, too. So why couldn't I bring myself to say them now? There was no fear of getting hurt like last time, no putting myself out there and hoping for the best.

I needed to figure out my hesitations first, before I said anything to him.

"You are good enough for me," I whispered before I fled the bed and raced to my room, needing some space to think.

Forty-Eight

Liam

My willpower was holding on by a frayed threat, each day bringing me closer to the breaking point with Callie. Especially since every single fucking night, right around midnight, she'd climb into my bed and curl up next to me to keep warm. And every night, I spent at least an hour willing my throbbing cock to chill the fuck out as she fell asleep beside me. Her smell on my pillows, her silky smooth skin brushing against mine, her shirt riding up to reveal her in just panties.

But I held back. Somehow. I knew she was fucking with me, just to see how far she could take this, how far she could push before I caved.

And believe me, I was *so* fucking close to caving.

But it also hurt me that she would rather do this than tell me she loved me.

She would waltz around the cabin in minimal clothing, or find ways to brush against me while I was cooking, or flash me a heated look while splayed on the couch.

But she wouldn't say those three little words.

I very quickly had to develop a hobby just to take some of my frustration out—whatever I couldn't take care of by jacking off in the shower every day.

That typically included me going outside for fresh air, collecting kindling, chopping firewood, and learning how to start an efficient fire so that come the cooler months, I could keep us comfortable.

And when I wasn't doing that, I would hide in my bedroom at the desk, reviewing manuscripts for my new job and pretending to know what I was doing. Google was my best friend. Which was only possible to access because a week into our time here, a cable company miraculously showed up to run fiber optics to the cabin. Callie and I both celebrated the ability to connect with the world again, albeit with limited exposure.

But finally, life gave me some reprieve. The day came where we had to meet Marshal Randall in town, so we bundled up and packed a bag for the day. I couldn't wait until they granted us a vehicle, then we could pretend to have normal lives.

Well, somewhat normal lives.

I pulled out a pair of old hiking boots that I hadn't used in damn near a decade, lacing them up before tugging on a flannel and beanie. While I had been dressing casual since we got here, I hadn't broken these items out yet. It felt foreign to be in them, and until I had gone home to pack, I had forgotten that I even owned them. As Callie stepped out of her room wearing combat boots and a puffer jacket, she paused and took in my outfit. After a moment, she laughed.

I frowned. "What are you laughing at?"

"I've just never seen you dressed like this. It's different." She smiled. "I like it."

I cocked an eyebrow at her.

"You just… you remind me of home." A sheepish look crossed her face.

I grinned, not expecting that response out of her, and inclined my head toward the door. "Should we go?"

She nodded and followed my lead.

* * *

Nearly two hours later, we arrived at Rotary Park, spotting Randal's car almost immediately. It was hard to miss the large black SUV. We both climbed in, breathless and eager for an update.

She eyed the two of us, as if trying to determine whether or not there was something romantic happening between us.

"First thing's first. Names?"

"Josh and Emily Blake," Callie answered immediately.

"Good. Any contact with anyone since you've been stationed here? Even on the internet?"

We both shook our heads.

"Excellent. Now, onto the fun stuff. You've been granted approval of a vehicle. An SUV will be sent to the cabin with some groceries inside sometime today, so you won't need to haul it all back with you."

"Great," I muttered, wondering why they couldn't give it to us now so we didn't have to hike back.

The Marshal raised her eyebrows at me but continued. "There are no updates on your case, so for the time being, we will continue on this path."

Callie heaved a big sigh. "He hasn't killed anyone else, has he?" she asked as if she hadn't been monitoring the news for an update.

Randal shook her head. "Not that we've been made aware of."

Callie's shoulders dropped in relief.

"My best advice for the both of you now is to try to settle into this new life as much as you possibly can. Thinking of it as a long-term solution will help."

I met Callie's eyes. Something stirred in them, but I couldn't place what I was seeing.

We wrapped up the meeting with the Marshal, making our way back to the cabin we were slowly turning into a home.

* * *

Callie was quiet on the way back, seemingly lost in her head. I nudged her shoulder with mine, breaking her from her reverie.

"Penny for your thoughts?"

She hesitated before reluctantly admitting, "I was thinking about how Randall said we should be thinking of this as long-term."

"And?"

"And I'm not really sure what to make of that. How to go about creating a new life, in this new job pretending like I know what I'm doing, all under a false identity. It's weird." She gestured at the wilderness around us.

"You've done it before."

She stumbled a step. I caught her arm. "What?"

"When you moved away from Springcrest. You started a new life, changed your name and left it all behind. This isn't the first time."

She stared at me for a moment. "Yeah. That's true," she drawled.

"And besides, you and I both know the truth of our past. We'll keep each other grounded, prevent each other from losing ourselves by becoming *Josh and Emily Blake.*"

Callie snickered. "Maybe you're right. I guess we'll see what freedom is like with a car, right? Maybe it won't be so bad."

My heart squeezed. I knew she was struggling. When she wasn't trying to seduce me, I caught the sadness in her eyes.

"Either way, at least we have each other." I glanced down only to find her already looking at me, that same emotion churning in her eyes as earlier, the one I couldn't quite put my finger on.

"Yeah," she murmured distractedly. "At least we have each other."

Forty-Nine

Callie

6 weeks later / 8 weeks in WITSEC

Weeks passed. Flew by, actually, as I settled into my new job. Turns out, managing a whole team was time consuming and utterly exhausting. Both my fake and real identity were born for leadership roles, and while most of my knowledge in the technology industry came from faking my way through every interaction, I was killing it.

The weather started to turn, the world shifting into browns and reds and oranges outside. Autumn in the mountains was exquisite and unlike anything I'd ever seen before. If you stood on a specific spot on the property—right in the center of the driveway at its peak—you could see the sweeping vibrant colors that faded into white-capped mountaintops. And while it was freezing most days, I found myself curled by Liam on the couch in front of a fire every night.

We came and went as we pleased, unlike those first few weeks, and fell into an easy routine in this small town. Liam was right; we had each other, and while things were platonic between us, we had become known as the young, madly-in-love couple that lived in the mountains. We loved the local reputation we'd received.

"Liam, I'm *starving*," I groaned, pressing a hand to my grumbling stomach and balancing the other on the couch. We were getting ready to go to dinner to celebrate my birthday–*Callie's* birthday. Balancing on one foot, I grabbed my other heel from the ground and slid it into place.

"Yes, birthday girl, I know," Liam cooed as he stepped out of his bedroom. I inhaled sharply at the sight of him in a suit. It had been so long since I'd seen him dressed up like this; it made my lady parts wet with desire.

Liam held firm on *not* fucking me until I professed my love, despite my attempts. And at first, I refused to say it just to see if he would give up on resisting me. So around and around we went, until I was so dizzy on this merry-go-round that I crossed a boundary I shouldn't have.

I had masturbated in front of him again. Instead of him ravishing me like I had expected him to, he picked me up and carried me to my room, practically throwing me down on the bed. I was so excited as he went down on me, eating me like it was his last meal. Even though I had just come, I very quickly approached another orgasm. That is, until he had pulled away, his mouth wet with my arousal and his eyes gleaming with wicked intent. I was trembling with my impending release, reaching for him to finish what he started, when he rose to his feet and pinned my hands above my head.

I blinked up at him. He growled, "This is what you do to me every goddamn day. You tease me and fucking frustrate me and leave me wanting you more than I should, and I swear I am trying to be a gentleman, but you're not making this easy. I am begging you—*begging you*—to please stop until you're ready for the next step." Then he'd torn himself away from me, rushing out of the cabin before I could respond.

I hadn't come on to him since.

But now, seeing him like this made me horny, and that meant my vibrator and detachable shower head would be my best friends tonight. Depressing.

"You look beautiful." He leaned in to brush a kiss to my cheek, but I turned my head at the last moment so our lips could touch. He stilled before returning the kiss, his tongue gently sweeping across mine before he pulled away. It was much too short, but oh so sweet to taste his lips. He tilted my chin up. "Clever, naughty girl."

A blush crept up my cheeks as I looked up at him through hooded eyes. "Only for you."

Liam's eyes darkened. "Damn right. Now turn around."

I did as I was told. He reached around me to grab my coat off the rack by the front door, the scent of him wafting around me. He slid the sleeves over my arms, and I lifted my hair so he could pull the coat over my shoulders. His fingers brushed the bare skin at the nape of my neck, and damn if I didn't break then and there.

Just as I was about to let the words *I love you* fall from my lips, he said, "Shall we go?" in a low, delicious voice that sent shivers slithering down my spine.

* * *

"Happy birthday," Liam said to me, dipping his finger into the chocolate cake the restaurant had delivered to our table, then holding it out to me.

It's for the facade, I told myself as I leaned in and sucked on his finger, swirling my tongue around it. I enjoyed watching his pupils dilate, the way he shifted in his seat as he retracted his finger, how his gaze dropped to my lips.

I grinned at him. "Hopefully twenty-six will be better than twenty-five."

Liam chuckled. "It wasn't all bad. Or have you forgotten all the fun we've had?"

I cleared my throat and brought a spoonful of cake to my mouth, intentionally not responding to his question.

He caught my wrist, turning it over so he could look at the fake ring on my finger, inspecting it carefully. I swallowed thickly, remembering how much I detested it when I first put it on because of what it represented. Now it felt normal—felt normal to pretend that he was my husband, even if we weren't acting on anything romantically.

He was my best friend. I knew I could tell him anything, knew I could trust him with my life and my heart, knew we could have a beautiful life together, whether we were Josh and Emily or Liam and Callie.

And God, I wanted that more than anything.

There were words unspoken between us as we looked at each other, and I opened my mouth to say *it* to him, when the waiter gently set the check down between us, breaking the moment.

I internally sighed. Second time in one night, and I was starting to wonder why I kept getting interrupted. Maybe it was a sign.

Liam paid, and as we made our way outside the restaurant, he snaked an arm around my waist, pulling me close. I leaned into him and his warmth for the duration of the walk to the car. Before I could break away from him, he turned and flattened me against the car door. I blinked up at him in surprise.

"I'm going to kiss you, but that's *all* I'm going to do, because I can't wait another minute to do it," he growled. Then his lips were on mine, rough and harsh and demanding. I melted into him, matching his urgent pace, my fingers twisting in his carefully styled hair. Heat spread through me, my pussy throbbing at the sexual tension between us. I moaned into his mouth, arching my back to press my breasts into him. He responded by grabbing my waist with one hand and my hair with the other.

His touch left a searing trail behind, and I felt *so hot* everywhere that I half-expected to burst into flames. I wanted to rip our clothes off right here in the parking lot, let him take me any way he wanted without caring who saw. I didn't care anymore. I just needed him in every single way I could have him.

He pulled away, stepping back from me so he wasn't touching me at all, and I gasped for air. He closed his eyes, clenching and unclenching his fists, before he reached out and opened the door for me. I conceded and climbed inside, my thighs pressing together to alleviate some of the aching pressure.

* * *

The ride home was quiet, the tension tangible and intense. My body was still on fire.

Soon we turned onto our winding driveway, and I was ready to jump out of the car the second we came to a stop. Liam grabbed my wrist before I could get to the front door, stopping me from going in. He dipped his chin, meeting my heated gaze with one of his own.

I squirmed but let him unlock the door and flick the foyer lights on. Inside, he had set out an elegant display of roses and a single cupcake with a candle in the center. LED candles lined the counters and the hallway, and a couple of wrapped gifts were stacked next to the flowers. I slowly turned to look up at Liam. He watched my reaction carefully, as if unsure I'd like it.

"When… when did you do this?" I asked quietly, utterly astonished. No one had ever done something like this for me, and if I wasn't already madly in love with this man, I would be after this.

He put his hands in his pockets and shrugged, as if this was just some casual thing he'd done. "When I ran back inside after you got in the car."

I took my jacket off and hung it on the coat rack, then walked over to the counter to admire the display. I leaned in and smelled the flowers, ran my fingers over the gifts, took it all in for the grand gesture that it was. I whirled, only to find him standing inches from me. I sucked in a breath at his nearness, glancing up at him through my lashes.

"Thank you," I whispered.

"You deserve to feel special, Callie." He pulled me into his arms, tucking me in so perfectly to his chest. I breathed him in, listening to his steady heartbeat. How could I feel anything but love and adoration for him?

"You always make me feel special," I told him. "Like I'm the only woman in the world."

His fingers brushed through my hair. "You are to me. I love you, Callie." He hadn't said those words in weeks. I tilted my head back to look at him again.

Say it, Callie. Damn it, say it say it say it—

"Kiss me again?" I whispered instead.

He swallowed, his Adam's apple bobbing up and down. I knew he was considering it with the way his eyes dropped to my lips, how his fingers stopped their soothing motions. But then he stiffened, realizing I wasn't going to say it back even after such a monumental moment. He didn't act on it because of one big reason: I'd *hurt* him.

Frustrated, I pulled away from him.

"We've gone over this." Liam's voice was weary and soft.

I huffed and folded my arms across my chest. "I just—you do all of this for me," I flailed my hands around as I motioned at the room, "and I'm supposed to believe you don't want to make love to me? On my *birthday?*"

He sighed and looked up at the ceiling, resigned. "It's not about that, and you know it." So calmly, so seriously. Not an ounce of fight in him.

I bit my lip. I knew it wasn't about that, but maybe fighting with him would stir enough passion between us that he'd kiss me again. Maybe then I could bring myself to utter the words he wanted me to say.

Jesus, what's wrong with me?

"You understand my reservations… right?" I prompted quietly.

He shrugged his suit jacket off, and fuck if him in a dress shirt and pants didn't undo me when I was already unraveling at the seams. "Of course I do, baby." I groaned inwardly at him calling me that. He rarely did, and it made me weak every time. "But you can't really compare things now to what they were then." He pinned his irresistible green eyes on me.

I scowled.

"I just feel like I'm doing everything I can tell you *and* show you how different things are this time around, but you don't seem to care."

Finally.

Now this I could fight with.

"I *do* care, Liam. I just want to know that this is *it* this time, you know? That we're a sure thing and I won't get hurt again."

Take the bait take the bait take the bait.

His jaw feathered and he averted his gaze. "If… this," he glanced around the room, "doesn't convince you, nothing will. Thank you for a great night. Happy birthday." He set his wallet and keys in the bowl on the kitchen counter, then pressed a small kiss to my forehead.

Un-fucking-believable.

I snatched the keys out of the bowl and stomped toward the door like a petulant child, hearing him groan from behind me.

"Callie, what are you doing?"

"I'm going for a drive," I snapped, tears burning my eyes at his *nothing will* comment, and threw open the door.

Fifty

Liam

When Callie grabbed the car keys, I expected her to say she forgot something in the car, not that she was leaving the cabin.

I was exhausted from these same conversations—even if it had been a while since we'd had to have it—and quite frankly, I was losing grip on all my self-control. I wanted to go to sleep and pretend like waking up with her in my arms filled the void in my heart. Wanted to act like it was enough for me, that it wasn't a tease at what our future could look like if only she'd set her pride aside for one goddamn minute.

I caught the front door before it could swing shut and followed after her. "And where do you plan to drive, huh?" I demanded, my feet pounding on the steps. Icy rain fell in fat drops onto my dress shirt; her skin-tight black dress wouldn't keep her very warm.

"I don't know. I just need to clear my head," she threw over her shoulder, rounding the front of the car.

Grabbing her wrist, I spun her around. "I don't think it's a good idea for you to be leaving here at night by yourself."

She yanked her arm away from me, her blue eyes glittering with unshed tears in the flood lights of the cabin. I reeled at the sight of those tears— what did I say that caused this? How was this conversation any different than the ones we'd had in the past?

"I'm not a fucking prisoner here," she spat.

I rolled my eyes. "I never said you were. I just worry about you because your ex is fucking psychotic and loose on the streets God knows where, hunting you. So, if you're leaving, I'm leaving. Bottom line."

Raindrops ran down her bare arms. She glowered at me, but I didn't miss the shiver that ran down her. *Stubborn woman.* I stayed put in front of the car, hands on my hips as I watched her closely.

"Stop being so goddamn stubborn."

Now at that, Callie took me by surprise by smiling. It wasn't a happy smile; it was mischievous, and the devious glint in her eyes matched it. "What are you going to do about it?"

What am I—

"What am I going to do about it?" I repeated, appalled, then narrowed my eyes at her. "I'll carry you back inside over my shoulder, if I have to." Her lips parted, drawing my eyes to them. *Oh.* "But what I'd really like to do is break that fucking promise I made you and fuck you until you can't walk straight because of all the shit you've pulled since the moment we left Newark."

She swallowed.

"But I won't do that. So please, would you just go inside before you give yourself hypothermia?"

Callie pressed her lips together, tilting her head to the side with a calculated look. Her once curled hair now hung around her in damp strands. "I'll go back inside once the old Liam decides to make an appearance. I know he's simmering just below the surface."

I frowned. "What the hell are you talking about?"

She stormed to me, stopping two feet away. "You never fight with me anymore. You just… you shut down."

"I never…" my voice trailed off, perplexed. "I don't *want* to fight with you, baby. In case you haven't noticed, I've done some growing up since we broke up."

Callie laughed coldly. "You can't break up what was never a relationship."

Fuck, that hurts.

I took a step back. "Just because we didn't label it doesn't mean it wasn't a relationship."

"*Stop!*" she shouted, her hands balled into fists as tears fell down her cheeks. "Stop being so fucking calm and collected!"

I took a deep breath. Most people didn't want to expel their energy on petty arguments; it wasn't exactly healthy. "Are you seriously trying to pick a fucking fight with me about not fighting *enough?*"

She leveled with me. I scrutinized her, trying to find the root of this response. But here, with the cold rain falling around us, our clothes wet and hair soaked, I realized what it was.

I circled her, almost predatory. "Why is it that you're trying to pick a fight, hm? Is it because that's how our affair started out?" I paused, noting that she had frozen, and I knew I struck gold. "Does it turn you on to fight? Does it make your blood sing because when I fuck you, it's more intense?"

Callie swallowed thickly, a flush creeping across her face as I stopped right in front of her, closer than before.

And Jesus, it was even turning me on.

She arched an eyebrow and gave me silent attitude.

I lowered my voice and murmured, "Get your ass back inside. Now."

Callie shook her head defiantly. "No."

I clenched my jaw. "Why, Callie? Why are you doing this? This isn't *healthy.*"

"You think I don't know that?" she quipped. "I know how fucked up it is. It's toxic, but I don't give a shit." She licked her lips, her chest rising and falling. "Because even when you see me at my worst, you still want me, babe. And that is the most intoxicating feeling."

Something snapped in me then, as if I could finally express my real, raw feelings. As if the dam could no longer hold it all back. I gave her what she wanted—I put up a fight.

"Good*damn it*, Callie," I snapped, chuckling and shaking my head in disbelief. I probably sounded crazy. *She* was making me crazy. "There is never a time when I don't want you!"

"Then why don't you ever act on it!"

"Because I can't give you only half of me!" I yelled. "I can't give you only the physical intimacy you're asking for when I'm so fucking in love with you that when I touch you, the world stops moving. And when I look at you, I only see my future. That's not fair to me. If I only give you half of me, I'm giving you the wrong half. And that hurts because I can't have all of you. You're all I want! *That* is why I'm waiting until you just tell me how you fucking feel!"

Tears spilled down her cheeks again, a sob catching in her throat. She looked so fucking beautiful even as the mess she was. "I do love you, you idiot! I shouldn't need to tell you that for you to know!"

I blinked at her and tugged my hair. "That is the single most hypocritical thing you've ever said. If I had said that to you earlier this year, would you have stayed?"

She pursed her lips. "I don't know."

There was a pregnant pause, our argument hanging in the air between us.

"I love you," Callie said again, and this time the weight of her proclamation hit me.

Finally.

I almost cried in relief.

"And I love you. So why are we still fighting?"

She gave me that wicked grin again, except now there was a fondness in her eyes. "Makes you feel alive, doesn't it?"

I rolled my eyes, but I couldn't wait any longer. My heart was soaring; my hands trembled with emotion. I cupped her face in my palms, backed her against our SUV, and kissed her. *Really* kissed her. More passionately than in the parking lot earlier, or the time we kissed in a utility closet while on a case, or in our office for the first time.

The kiss said so many things.

I love you.

I'm sorry.

You're mine.

I'm yours.

And it was worth every heart-wrenching moment that had occurred between us.

This was it. This is what I had been yearning for—months of longing, heartache, dreaming of this very moment where we could finally belong to each other.

Our tongues danced, our hands roaming and groping and grasping, warm breaths mingling on this cold night and skin slipping from the rainfall. I didn't care, and I don't think she did, either. We were enough to keep each other warm, enough to satiate one another for the rest of our lives.

Finally, I broke our searing kiss to look at her, still cupping her face in my hands. Her eyes were wild and crazed, her lips red, her chest heaving.

I loved her with every fucking fiber of my being.

I bent down and hauled her over my shoulder. She shrieked and laughed. "Liam! This is hardly appropriate."

I grinned and smacked her ass, traipsing up the stairs and back into the warmth of our cabin. "Since when do you care about being appropriate?"

She groaned. The noise went straight to my dick. "Officially? Always. Secretly? Never."

I smiled to myself. "That's what I thought." I carried her through the cabin—our home—and straight to my bedroom. Not her room, never again.

I gently laid her on her back, her wet hair fanning around her.. My heart squeezed; I rubbed a palm over it to calm the sensation.

Her blue eyes were bright and warm, her mascara smudged from the rain. Cheeks pink and lipstick smudged. As gorgeous as ever. I paused so I could soak this moment in, so I could swallow the lump in my throat. This was what I had spent the last year pining for—for us to *be together*. No more sneaking around, no more withholding our feelings or our thoughts. Just… being together.

Everything I had been through… it was all behind me now.

The relief that crashed into me was so fucking powerful, it almost knocked me on my ass. My eyes burned.

Callie sensed something was off, propping herself on her elbows. "Liam? Are you alright?"

Her voice broke through my haze, reigning me back in. I focused on her face, letting her ground me like she unknowingly had done so many times before. Without answering, I climbed on the bed, kneeling as I took her face in my hands and pressed my lips to hers. I let myself get swept up in the heat of the moment as we stripped each other of our clothes, each piece of wet fabric landing on the floor with a splat.

I pulled back to admire her in all her naked beauty, my eyes lingering on that tattoo on her ribs. I ran my fingers over it, watching how it made her shudder.

She was all mine now.

I was sitting back on my heels when Callie sat up and crawled over to me, settling onto my cock as she sat in my lap. I sighed, my mouth pressing feverish kisses to her neck and collarbone.

I want to savor every second of this, I thought as I met her thrust for thrust. Because this was the first honest-to-God time that I got to make love to her—really, truly, whole-heartedly make love.

And I did just that as we fell into a tortuously slow but gratifying pace.

Holding the woman I loved close, our foreheads touching as we both looked down at where our bodies met, where our souls collided and we became one, I whispered over and over again how in love with her I was.

She came, moaning my name and kissing me with such fervor that I saw stars. I continued pressing into her, reveling in how her chest pressed against mine. She ground her hips into me until she came again, moaning louder this time. Her head dropped back, and I followed her into orgasmic bliss.

Fifty-One

Callie

Best. Birthday. *Ever.*

I snuggled in closer to Liam, feeling completely at peace for the first time in my life. Even if I was stuck living a second life with a different identity, at least I was doing it with the man I loved.

"I love you," I whispered freely, tracing lazy circles on his chest.

"I love you too, baby." Liam's fingers ran through my hair, now dried in frizzy tangles after standing in the rain and then being fucked into oblivion. He hugged me closer. "I'm sorry for all the wasted time between us. It should never have happened."

I tilted my chin to look up at him. "It's not like either of us were in a place to give a relationship our all."

He chuckled bitterly. "Sure, but I should have said it back to you that day. I had been feeling it for weeks and it scared me."

I sighed. "In hindsight, I agree with you that it was worth the wait. I had some shit to work out that you didn't need to see."

Liam stopped stroking my hair but didn't say anything. I looked at him again to see him giving me a curious look. I frowned. "What?"

He shook his head. "No matter what you're going through, no matter what you're healing from… your partner is supposed to be there for you.

Supporting you, loving you, lifting you up."

I mulled over his words. "I've never had that before," I admitted, so softly it was almost to myself.

"You do now. Just don't push me away anymore, okay? Your problems don't scare me. God knows I have enough of my own. I was lucky enough to be given a second chance with you."

I *hmmed* against him, running my fingers over all his tattoos. I stopped on the one similar to mine on his inner bicep, then trailed down to the bow and arrow on his forearm. "You once told me this was a story for another day."

Liam puffed his cheeks as he exhaled. "My best friend, Anthony Pullman. It was my senior year in high school, and my friends and I took a trip to Raystown Lake to camp. Which you know, because it's where we first met." I smiled as I recalled the two of us meeting briefly as teenagers. "Everything was going great until the second night. When we woke up, Anthony was dead." He frowned as he said this. "The responding officers didn't seem to care much since we were a bunch of rowdy, drunken teenagers. The coroner said it was due to alcohol poisoning."

"Liam," I murmured. "Hey, that couldn't have been your fault."

"It was, though. We always had one rule: watch after your buddy. I got tired, Anthony and I were pissed at each other about an ex-girlfriend we shared, so I went to bed. If I had just watched him…" his voice trailed off.

"You didn't know he would keep drinking."

"Well, I should have," he crooned bitterly. "Anyway, after that, I wanted to make sure no one else had an awful experience with law enforcement. We moved away after that, and I cleaned up my life so I could get into the Academy as soon as I turned twenty-one."

"So the bow and arrow…?"

"Is a reminder to keep going forward, and to not focus on the past."

"Well, that's rather apt right now."

Liam laughed.

"I had no idea."

"I know. It's not something I talk about often. Kinda like how you don't talk about Springcrest."

My face heated. It felt like a lifetime ago when I had told him about that, rather than two months.

"So what about your tattoo?"

I shrugged. "I was working through my newfound sobriety and putting myself back together. One night, I was just… inspired, I guess. I wanted to feel the pain of the tattoo to distract me from all the healing."

"Seems a little masochistic, don't you think?" he teased.

I giggled. "Exactly. Something about this design stood out to me. It stands as my own reminder that there's always more than what's on the surface, but that doesn't stop you from blooming."

"That's beautiful, Cal."

I licked my lips nervously. "It was cathartic for me. Even though I was reminded of your tattoo, the pain of getting it was like the closure I never got. The last time I was going to allow myself to truly hurt over what happened. So in a way, it was a double-edged sword."

Liam tugged my hair to bring my lips to his. I melted into him.

"And was it?"

"Was it what?"

"The last time you allowed yourself to hurt over what I did," he clarified.

I pressed my lips to a tattoo splashing across one of his pecs. "It was so much more than just what happened with you. There was a lot that happened behind closed doors between me and Owe—Oliver—that I never told you."

"Like what?"

I hesitated, but the safety net Liam was holding out for me gave me the courage to admit it out loud. "The night he put his hands around my throat," I whispered, "I almost…" I shook my head and started over. "I was tempted to let him kill me. But… then I pictured you and realized there were too many things left unsaid, and having you in whatever capacity I could was something worth living for." I clenched my fists to hide the trembling in my hands. "So in a way, I owe you for saving my life twice."

Liam absentmindedly brushed his fingers over the scar on my arm. When

I stole a glance at him, his eyes appeared far away. "You don't owe me anything." A pause. "When you showed up at my door that night, I realized I'm probably not the morally picture-perfect cop that I once prided myself on being."

My brows furrowed. "What do you mean?"

"If you hadn't needed me at that moment, I would have killed him."

"Liam—"

"It's true. And I would have gotten away with it too, because everyone would believe a cop defending themselves against a woman abuser. My moral compass hasn't been the same since."

I eyed him. The flutter in my stomach surprised me. Did I… *like* that? I never would have guessed that a man telling me he'd kill for me would be attractive. The by-the-books police officer in me was nowhere to be found these days. Probably because she hadn't been around in a long time. "I don't think that makes you a bad cop. I think it makes you protective. Isn't that what cops are supposed to be?"

He laughed but finally brought his eyes down to me again. "Always defending my actions, baby."

Sitting up, I interlaced our fingers, the familiar weight of the wedding band on my finger as comforting as his touch. I straddled his hips, rocking back and forth a few times and reveling in his hardening length beneath me. "For better or for worse, right?"

Liam's green eyes darkened, his lips parting. If only I could photograph that look. His free hand moved to the nape of my neck and pulled me down to him, the flash of silver on his own hand reflecting our special brand of insanity.

"You don't know what those words do to me, coming from you," he growled, kissing me hard. For a moment I feared I had crossed a line and sent him spiraling back into bad memories of his ex-wife, but when his tongue swept across mine and he held me closer, those thoughts flew out the window.

"If you're not careful, I'll think you mean them," he murmured against my lips.

Fifty-Two

Liam

14 weeks in WITSEC

Uncomfortable laughter tore out of me as I read the manuscript in my hands. I couldn't believe some of the shit I had to read. Not like Callie minded most of the time, especially when it was one of those smutty romance novels she had taken a liking to recently. Those gave us all sorts of fun things to do in the bedroom.

But this… no, this was most definitely not one of those.

"Oh no. What are you reading now?" Callie wondered from the leather armchair beside the couch I lounged on. It was dark outside, only our lamps bathing us in cozy lighting, the sound of rain and crackling fire a comforting background noise.

I groaned. "A man writing a woman." I quickly learned the difference between women writing men, and men writing women. The difference was astounding—and most of the time, painful.

She laughed loudly. "Can't wait to hear this one."

I took a long sip of my scotch. "It's so bad, babe. I don't think you want to hear it."

Callie put her phone down and rose to her feet, stretching before curling up in my lap. I kissed her temple. "Read it to me."

"I apologize in advance for the male species, for we know not what we talk about." She cocked an eyebrow at me, so I caved and lifted the manuscript up again, cringing as I found the part. "'*She was small and dainty, with legs that seemed to go on for days. Her small waist accentuated her curvy hips and breasts like a porn star. When she looked up at him with sultry emerald orbs, he realized she had no idea how sexy she was. He knew it was up to him to make her feel as beautiful as the way he saw her, doing what he did best: fucking.*'"

Callie covered her face and laughed before I could finish. "Okay, okay, please stop, I can't hear any more!" Tears leaked from her eyes as she continued to laugh hysterically.

I was more horrified reading it out loud. "God. I would never describe a woman that way."

Her laughter ebbed into soft giggles. "That's because you're a hopeless romantic at heart, my love."

I hmphed lightheartedly. "This guy just gave away that he's a virgin and has never made a woman climax."

"*Liam,*" Callie scolded, bursting into another fit of laughter while scrambling to straddle me. "That's not very nice."

I pinned her with a glare. "How would you feel if you were hooking up with this man and he couldn't make you come?"

She shrugged. "That's easy. I'd never hook up with someone other than you."

Rolling my eyes, I set the manuscript down on the side table, then tackled her into the couch and attacked her lips with mine. "I'd like to demonstrate what a man making a woman come looks like," I quipped, moving down the couch to tug her joggers down.

* * *

The next day, Callie slipped into our room. I put a finger to my lips to tell her to be quiet since I was on a work call. She flashed me a devilish grin that could only mean trouble. I narrowed my eyes at her as her fingers made quick work of the buttons on my flannel that she had spent all morning in. My mouth went dry as she dropped it to the floor and revealed her spectacularly naked body, and—*oh my God, is that a new tattoo?*

There was a curly scripted *L* on her left hip that was fresh and shiny from ointment.

It must've been where she wandered off to first thing this morning.

I almost groaned into the receiver; instead, I gripped my phone harder and tried to focus on the discussion of my call. Leaning back in the office chair, I said, "The second draft was much better, Stefan. I really enjoyed the changes you made to Dottie's character development. If you had kept her as is, I think that would've really detracted your female audience."

Stefan Dupree paused for a moment, deep in thought. My eyes drifted over to Callie, who now sashayed across the room and dropped to her knees in front of me. My jaw locked as she blinked up at me, doe-eyed. *Jesus fuck.*

"Are you sure? I had some great thoughts about the love story between Dottie and Harold—"

"*I'm sure,*" I pressed, my voice strained. I couldn't handle another re-read of his awful book. The first two times were hard enough. "I'm confident in you moving forward with self-publishing." But if I thought about his book, *Shadows of Her Essence*, it would at least distract me from my pretend wife.

Wife.

The word used to carry a negative connotation with it, but when I looked at Callie and thought of it, it did all sorts of things to me—like make my heart thud a little faster, like make my breath whoosh out of my lungs, like make my blood rush to my lower extremity with the primal urge to claim her as *mine.*

For better or for worse, right?

She'd said that to me on her birthday... The night everything changed.

For her, I would make those vows again. For her, I would keep them until the day I died. For her, I would kill anyone who hurt her. For her, I would do *anything.*

Her fingers deftly pulled my gray sweats down my hips. I planted my feet on the ground and lifted my hips to help her pull them down and—*What am I doing?* I was on a work call, for Christ's sake.

My cock sprang to life and she grabbed it greedily. I gasped.

"… back, Josh?" Stefan asked.

I blinked. "I'm sorry, I didn't catch that. What did you say?"

"I asked how long it would take to get another draft back. If I sent one to you."

"Oh." Callie's eyes locked on mine as she wrapped those perfectly pouty lips around me, taking the head of my cock into her mouth. I trapped the moan in my throat before it could escape. "Probably the same amount of time as the last two. Within a week."

"That's great," he murmured. "Okay, let's circle back. I need to discuss this with the other people on my team. Can I conference them in?"

"Callie." Her name slipped out before I could stop it, and the gleam in her eyes signaled her approval. *Shit shit shit.*

"Josh? Who's Callie?"

I tipped my head back in frustration, wishing this goddamn phone call would end so I could fuck Callie's mouth. "Callie is my wife's cat. She's a little… wily sometimes." Callie laughed, the vibrations on my cock sending a jolt of pleasure down my spine.

She is so going to get punished for this later.

"Oh, no shit? You've got a cat? What kind?"

I grinned. "Not sure. Feisty though. Brown hair, big blue eyes. Beautiful kitty cat."

"Huh. That's an interesting combination for a cat. Maybe part Siamese? I've got two Siamese. They're fun."

I rolled my eyes, partially in pleasure and partially in annoyance. "Is that so?"

Stefan chuckled. "Yeah. Anyway, hang tight for a few, I'm going to confer with my team to discuss next steps and whether or not I'll need you for another draft."

"Okay." I immediately muted my phone and released the groan I'd been withholding. Callie was fucking deepthroating me, the warm wetness of her mouth coating me gloriously. "Jesus, Callie, don't stop."

She didn't. Even as her eyes watered and she picked up the pace, she never relented. I felt a familiar build-up at the base of my spine, tingles spreading down my thighs as my balls tightened. "I'm going to come, and I want you to swallow every last drop. Got it?"

The flicker in her heated gaze told me she would.

"Good girl." I embraced the orgasm that assaulted every nerve-ending in my body, both hands in her hair. "*Fuck,* baby. What a good little wife you are."

I exploded at my own words, my mind fragmenting at the thought. She froze before slowly pulling away and licking her lips. The look in her eyes had changed, but she didn't rise from her knees.

Then my brain played catch up. My eyes widened. *Shit.* Too much, too soon. I knew that much. It didn't take a genius to put two and two together.

"Wife?" Callie whispered, her cheeks now pink.

Yeah… first time I had called her that in private. It was bound to happen at some point, right?

I opened my mouth to respond when Stefan spoke to me again. I glared at my phone on the desk before picking it up. "Yeah, I'm still here. Whatever you guys want to do, I'm on board with. Just let me know so I can schedule work accordingly."

Callie finally pushed herself to her feet and padded out of the room, grabbing my flannel as she went.

Fifty-Three

Callie

I shoveled ice cream into my mouth in an attempt to settle the butterflies in my stomach. *Wife.* Maybe Liam was blurring the lines between our new identities and real life.

But isn't this new identity our real life? My brain screamed at me.

I shut the thought out and took another bite of ice cream, leaning on the counter. I winced, my hip still tender from my new tattoo.

Wife?

Part of me still denied that this was our reality—because surely we wouldn't be permanent files in WITSEC, right? *Right?*

I was Josh Blake's wife, not Liam Chandler's. Not yet. I mean, I wanted to be, but nothing was, like, *official* until we were out of witness protection. It was important we continue to discern between the two, because otherwise it would be way too easy to believe our two storylines could blend together and not think there would be any fallout.

I mean, what would happen when we returned to life in the city and involved our families and friends?

He had to see that. If he was going to call me that in private, he needed to be serious about it outside of WITSEC. And it needed to wait until this was over.

Right? *Right?*

Or… did we not have to wait?

Damn it, I was confusing myself now.

Liam's footsteps sounded in the hallway, pulling me back to the present. Sweat gathered at the base of my spine when he stopped in front of the breakfast bar, his eyes sweeping over me warily.

"Callie, about what I said—"

I waved my hands to cut him off. I wasn't sure I wanted to know if he meant it or not. If he did mean it, then there were a lot of conversations to be had—as if there weren't enough already. And if he didn't… Well, then, dying a slow, painful death sounded more manageable.

Yeah, I didn't want to know.

For now, I wanted to live in the moment. This little bubble we had spent the last few weeks creating—getting to know each other on a more intimate level, making *lots* of love, domesticating one another… that was all I wanted.

All I needed.

"It's fine. We're good," I told him, jumping on the counter and crawling across it toward him. Liam's gaze dipped lower, the corners of his lips tugging up as he pulled me to the edge, spreading my legs so he could stand between them. The tips of his fingers traced the tops of my thighs under the flannel I wore. Heat pooled in my belly, and I wondered if that feeling would ever go away.

God, I hoped not.

"You're doing that thing again."

"What thing?" I feigned innocence as I tilted my head to the side to give him easy access to my neck.

"Where you don't talk about what's going through that pretty head of yours." He pressed a kiss to the fluttering pulse at the base of my throat.

A moan caught in my throat. "All I'm thinking about right now is how much I love you and how I want to spend forever with you." It wasn't a lie, per se. Because thinking about our future had *everything* to do with how much I loved him.

I felt Liam's grin against my skin, his hands inching north before he dropped to his knees. "Good, because you're mine. Forever and always. And I'm about to show you just how much I love you."

And then his mouth closed over my clit.

Fifty-Four

Callie

24 weeks (almost 6 months) in WITSEC

Winter in the mountains was a new kind of endeavor. Fall had come and gone a little too quickly, replaced by snow flurries and wind cold enough to burn my cheeks.

The days and weeks had flown by, and so had all our worries about Oliver Frankford, who remained a ghost and had seemingly disappeared into thin air. While he stayed on the FBI's Most Wanted list, the initial push to find him had slowed.

Which meant that our foreseeable future would be as Mr. and Mrs. Blake, and that every meeting with Marshal Randall was the same.

It wasn't bad, though. Neither of us minded it, because we had settled into our roles. Liam had taken to learning how to build fires and chop wood. Occasionally we would wander into the woods together to gather kindling, but mostly it was his job. I stayed in and kept our cabin warm and clean.

Usually because we thought it was fun to mess around in the woods, only for us to spend hours trying to warm up again.

We stayed active by heading into town to go to the gym. We were regulars, and at some point it was just as normal to be Josh and Emily in public as it was to be Liam and Callie in private. We both accepted it, even though there were times we wanted nothing more than to call our families.

For now, the occasional exchanging of letters sufficed, per permission from the Marshal.

I awoke one day in early December with an impending sense of doom. I couldn't explain it, and didn't know how else to describe it to Liam. To say he was concerned was putting it lightly; it put the both of us on edge the entire day. I had even gone to my old room to load my gun—something I hadn't done since the first week we had arrived. I tucked it back between the mattress and bed frame in the room we shared for easy access.

But like I said, I didn't know why I felt this way and I couldn't pinpoint where it came from. Maybe it was just my mind telling me to stay on top of my game.

We went into town to go grocery shopping, and Liam even put his shoulder holster on under his long wool coat. There was a twinge of pain in my heart at the sight. I missed work. I missed our life in the city and the familiar, comfortable weight of my gun and badge on me at all times.

As we pulled back into the long, winding driveway, that dread I'd been feeling dug deeper. I could tell Liam felt the same way, because the air in the car seemed to be sucked out, replaced by something heavier, darker. Liam's jaw clenched as he parked the car. We both stared at the dark windows of our home, knowing something was off.

He instinctively unholstered his gun, switched the safety off, and cocked the hammer. I gulped nervously, making him fix his green eyes on me, the look in them inscrutable. There was an exchange of understanding between us.

"Stay here." A simple command that I *really* didn't want to obey.

"Liam, you're not going in there alone."

"And you're not going in there unarmed."

"But—"

"End of discussion. It'll only take me a minute." He started to climb out of the car, and panic rose in my throat. He paused and leaned across the console to kiss me hard. "We'll be fine, okay? I love you. I'll be right back. Lock the doors."

"I love you," I whispered, and watched as he bounded up the steps. I did as he asked and locked the doors.

We'll be fine.

I love you.

I repeated his words over and over. We were both probably overreacting. I mean, we had spent months absorbed in our own little world that we had built. So much so that it was easy to forget why we were here to begin with. And many times, we did. We were just enjoying our time together.

So maybe this was our way of giving ourselves a reality check. So we didn't get too comfortable.

I kept my eyes trained on the door, waiting for him to come back out. More than a minute passed. Two minutes. Three minutes. And then a flash in the dining room window and a gunshot.

My heart sputtered a stop.

Fifty-Five

Liam

The second I stepped out of the car, I was grateful I told Callie I loved her. Truth be told, I had the same feeling as her all day, but I didn't want to stress her out more. Acknowledging her feelings and making her feel safe was all I could do, and it helped keep me busy.

I kept my gun in front of me as I tried the front door. *Locked.* Good. I unlocked it and slowly pushed it open, trying the lights. Nothing.

Fuck.

It confirmed my suspicions.

He was here.

I side-stepped into the cabin and shut the door behind me, waiting for my eyes to adjust to the sudden darkness as I raised my gun. Flattening myself to the wall by the door, I glanced to my left and right, not seeing anyone. I loosed a breath and crept into the kitchen, keeping my steps lights, when Oliver fucking Frankford launched onto my back, his arms looping around my throat.

Caught off guard, I stumbled, my gun clattering to the ground. I kicked it away from us as I grabbed his forearms and pitched myself forward until he flew off my back and landed on the ground. Our eyes locked, and he gave me a malicious smile. I pressed my boot into his throat.

"How nice of you to make an appearance," I sneered.

He gasped for air, but his eyes flared with delight. *Sick fuck.* "Don't be a pussy, Liam. Fight me like a man."

He didn't know how badly I wanted to. And if I did, I wasn't sure I could stop myself before I killed him. Oliver must've seen my moment of hesitation, because he shoved my foot off him and rolled away. I dove onto the ground after him before he could reach my gun.

"Shooting me is the easy way out. What happened to fighting like a man?" I grunted through clenched teeth.

"The quicker you die, the quicker I can get to Callie," he spat, wrestling with me. I managed to pin him underneath me and landed a punch to his jaw. "Fuck you!" He bared his teeth, now covered in blood.

"That's for laying a hand on my wife," I snarled, going in for another blow. I didn't miss the way his nostrils flared at the admission. Was it a lie? Sort of, but not really. In the legal paperwork with our different identities, it was true. And I was so accustomed to saying it now that it felt natural. "That's for calling her a whore."

"Doesn't matter what she is. After today, she'll be *dead.*"

I punched him again. "That's for cheating on her." I gripped the collar of his shirt with my other hand, slamming him into the floor as I pulled my fist back again, when suddenly a flash of silver caught my eye. I saw the knife in his hand just in time to throw myself out of the way and crawl across the kitchen to my gun. He lunged for me just as I wrapped my hands around it, and I pulled the trigger by accident before I could aim.

Fifty-Six

Callie

I scrambled to unlock the door, the sound of my blood roaring the only thing I could hear.

Fuck fuck fuck fuck fuck fuck—

I pulled my phone out to call 911, but, surprise surprise, there was no service.

Damn it damn it damn it damn it—

The door unlocked, giving away to my desperate attempts before I raced toward the front door.

Please be okay please be okay please be okay please—

My heart lodged in my throat.

Liam and Oliver struggled on the ground, Liam's gun in both their hands, while Oliver's other hand held a knife. I eyed it carefully, afraid that Liam wouldn't dodge a blow in time if he was hyper-focused on the gun.

I grabbed Oliver's arm and twisted it behind his back. He cried out in surprise, the knife falling to the floor. I scooped it up and threw it across the room, but as I did so, Oliver raised his elbow and hit me in the face. I fell back on my ass, and before I could recover, Oliver was on me. Hands around my throat, just like—

I squeezed my eyes shut as the memory flashed across my vision. He lifted me to my feet, and shoved me against a wall.

The clicking sound of Liam's gun misfiring reverberated off the walls. *Shit.*

This is what we get for not taking the guns out and shooting them, not actively cleaning them. *This* is what happens when you get too comfortable.

"Get your hands off her," Liam growled, and suddenly I could breathe again. It took a few gasps of air before I realized I needed to get my gun. *Now.*

I turned toward the hallway, but before I could reach it, Oliver had a fistful of my hair, yanking me back. I cursed at the sudden pain and lost my footing, which gave him the leverage he needed to throw me over the couch and into the coffee table. My back hit the edge of it, taking the brunt of the impact, but my head snapped back t as well. My stomach rolled as my vision doubled. One blow to the head and I was rendered nearly incapacitated.

But Oliver was back on Liam, and I heard my husband cry out in pain, and Oliver's twisted laugh.

It was all the motivation I needed to drag myself to a crawling position and round the side of the couch. I blinked, their figures blurry.

"Callie," Liam groaned. "*Gun.*"

I knew what he meant. I clumsily pulled myself to my feet and ran down the hallway to my old room, supporting myself on the wall to stay upright. My stomach churned from my disorientation as I pitched forward to grab my gun from its spot under the mattress, removing the safety. It was loaded and ready to go, and I thanked myself for trusting my gut.

When I emerged in the living room again, I saw Oliver standing over a bleeding Liam. My heart lodged itself in my throat, my eyes growing watery. It wasn't helping my already fuzzy vision. I probably had a concussion.

Turning an angry, hateful gaze on my ex-fiancé, I didn't hesitate in the slightest as I raised my gun and shot not once, not twice, but three times. Abdomen, leg, arm. I didn't miss.

I couldn't care less if he stuck around and died or took off. I just needed him out of the way to make sure Liam was alright.

Oliver yelped, his knees buckling. "You *bitch*."

"Move. Away. From. My. Husband," I bit out, then blinked. It was the first time I had said it outside of the public eye, and it scared me suddenly that Liam was injured and I may not get to call him that for real if I didn't get us out of here.

So not the right time for these thoughts, Callie.

"Let me live and I'll leave," Oliver pleaded.

My stomach flipped. The smart thing to do would be to kill him. Then I could get Liam to a hospital and Oliver would be out of the picture. But death would be too easy—he deserved to rot in prison for the rest of his sad, miserable life. I wanted the satisfaction of knowing he was behind bars, serving a sentence for all the people he'd killed. For terrorizing me.

Liam looked at me like I was crazy for even considering this. *"Don't,"* he managed. He didn't look good. In fact, he was turning paler by the second, and there was a growing pool of blood around him as he clutched his side.

So I made a deal with the devil.

"You have five seconds to get out of my sight before I change my mind," I seethed, aiming my gun at him again. Oliver wasted no time. Holding his abdomen, he limped out the front door.

I watched him leave, skepticism running through my veins. If we were his end goal, then why would he choose to leave us alive?

Unless he's getting stitched up and coming back for us.

But... How far could he really make it after three gunshots?

I didn't have time to think about that right now. I dropped to my knees by Liam, trying to look at him through my tears. "You're okay, baby, you're going to be okay."

He laughed bitterly. "You're... insane," he panted, sweat beading on his forehead. My heart broke. "Why did you... let him leave?"

"Stop worrying about that right now. Let me see." I pushed his hands away. He flinched, dropping his head to the floor. There was a deep gash, several inches wide, the kitchen knife a few feet away. I sucked in a shallow breath.

The sound of our car starting had my head whipping to the window in horror. I shakily rose to my feet to see Oliver flooring it down our driveway. That earlier panic rose once again in my throat.

No no no no no no no no no.

"What's wrong?"

"He—the keys. He took the *keys.* The car. It's—it's gone," I stuttered, falling to my knees again.

Liam swallowed, his Adam's apple bobbing. My chest hurt with every passing second. "That's why he wanted to leave," he croaked.

My eyes grew misty again. "There's no service. He cut the power and internet lines."

His bloody hand caressed my face. "I love you, and I'm so… so grateful for all this time we got… together."

I shook my head vehemently. "No. Don't do that. Don't say those things."

"I love you," he said again.

Fat tears rolled down my cheeks. "Stop it. You're going to be fine."

Liam nodded, but his eyes flickered. I knew he didn't believe me, but he was going to pretend, for my sake. "But just in case… I want you to know that I… see my future… with you."

I choked on a sob and lifted my trembling hand from the bleeding wound. "I refuse to believe this is the end. Not yet. Don't you dare give up on me now, Liam Chandler." I stood and fought to see straight through the throbbing pain in my head. "Where do you keep the liquor?"

He had kept it hidden from me for months, at my request.

"Above the refrigerator. Why?"

I ignored him as I climbed onto the counter and opened the cabinets, pulling out every bottle I found. Half a dozen, at least, but I didn't take the time to count as I scrambled down, gathered first aid supplies and the suture kit, and brought it all over to the coffee table. Then, I knelt down by Liam again.

"We have to get you to the couch."

"Callie—"

"*Please,* Liam," I begged. We stared at each other for a few moments before he nodded ever so slightly. I helped him up, hoisting him to his feet and bearing his weight on my shoulders. And slowly, so slowly, we made our way to the couch, his blood soaking through my clothes. A reminder that we were truly and royally fucked.

Carefully helping him into a semi-comfortable position on the couch, I helped him out of his coat and propped him up with pillows—focused on anything but the blood, anything but the pain on his face. I just needed to stay strong for him, just for a few more minutes.

I opened a bottle of vodka, tipping the bottle back and letting the familiar burn slither down my throat, then put it to his lips. I made him drink three mouthfuls, and when I pulled the bottle away, he coughed. More blood came out of the wound as he did so.

"God, that burned."

Next I tore strips of fabric off a plain white t-shirt and shoved the rest of it in his mouth. "Bite down on this. This next part is going to hurt like a bitch." He did as I instructed, and I poured the bottle of vodka over the wound to clean it. Liam gripped a throw pillow until his bloodied knuckles turned white. Color returned to his face as he yelled into the shirt. Guilt grappled at me, and tears pricked my eyes again as I mumbled heartbroken apologies to him.

I was so thankful for all my CPR and first aid training that was mandated in the Academy and every two years after.

I threaded the needle with the suture material, coating it in vodka to sanitize it, then positioned it against his skin. I met Liam's eyes once more, and he let me see it all.

Love and fear and sadness and remorse and *so much more.*

"I love you," I whispered before I focused on pushing the needle through his skin.

* * *

I sat back on my heels and wiped a hand across my sweating forehead, admiring my shoddy, makeshift stitches. The bleeding had stopped, but Liam had lost a lot of blood, and despite my tearful pleas for him to stay awake, he'd passed out.

Pressing the back of my hand to his forehead, I was relieved to feel his temperature was still normal, but I wasn't sure how long I could maintain that with the little bit of firewood we had left. The weekend was when Liam chopped wood, and it was almost time for that.

I cursed myself for making us go through extra wood since I was cold all the time.

Suddenly I remembered that there was an emergency phone, but to use it sparingly. *How could I forget?* Hope bloomed in my chest as I scrambled to my feet and ran to the kitchen, rifling through the drawers until my hands closed around the rugged black phone with a large antenna. On the back was a phone number scribbled on a sticky note. I went to dial it, and as I brought it to my ear, all remaining hope crumbled in my chest.

We're sorry, but there are no remaining minutes available. To purchase more, please go to your local—

I screamed and threw the phone across the room. Because why would it work in an *actual* emergency?

Exhaling a shaky breath, I opened a bottle of wine and chugged it, collapsing beside Liam once again.

Fifty-Seven

Callie

I raised my head from its awkward position on the couch, my back barking in pain as I sat up. The floor was hard beneath my knees, and the sunlight filtering through the curtains was harsh. I blinked at the brightness and winced at the accompanying throbbing in my head. My breath was sucked out of my lungs as I looked around at the ransacked room.

A handful of expelled shell casings littered the floor.

A bloody t-shirt, strips torn from it carelessly.

Spilled wine and a broken glass.

The first aid kit strewn across the coffee table, needles and gauze and other bandage materials.

I choked back a sob as I recalled the night's events. I whipped my head around to look at Liam's limp figure on the couch. His skin was pale and damp, and his hair stuck to his skin as he rested.

My lower lip wobbled. I'd stayed by his side all night in case he woke up, but I'd failed him. I'd failed him, and worst of all, I'd failed myself. The empty bottle of wine was proof of that, and so was the stab wound that ran deeper than I initially wanted to admit. I should have gone inside with him, armed or not.

Fuck.

And now my sobriety was shot to hell as much as the sacred, protected world that we'd built here.

I let myself cry as I stared at him. I didn't even know if he'd make it or if anyone would know that we needed help. Complete isolation was perfect until it wasn't. And we'd been here for so long, gotten so comfortable, that we'd dropped our guard.

Big fucking mistake.

The thought of losing him forever—truly forever this time—hurt so much fucking worse than a broken heart.

I reached for his hand. Noted his uncanny warmth against my cold skin. His high temperature was dangerous; with my free hand, I peeled back the bandage on his ribs—and cringed.

Blood—so much blood—from that gash. My unstable stitches likely wouldn't hold for much longer.

If he kept bleeding, I'd have to cauterize the wound, but for now it would be fine.

I hope.

I shivered and glanced over my shoulder at the smoldering fireplace. *Shit.* We were out of firewood, and without it I could be of no help to him if we both turned into icicles.

Forcing myself to my feet, I grabbed my gun from the table. At least mine didn't misfire–and hopefully wouldn't. As much as I didn't want to leave Liam, I knew we'd freeze to death if Oliver didn't get to us first—er, again. I slowly layered my clothing, barely taking my eyes off Liam. Barely even breathing.

I leaned down and kissed his forehead. He didn't so much as stir. What I would do to go back in time and plan a weekend away from here, or just to see him give me a reassuring smile or hear his laugh.

I swallowed thickly and made my way to the door, following the trail of blood Oliver had left behind in his destructive wake. The wind whipped at me as I stepped out into the cold morning, my head pounding with every terrified beat of my heart.

Death may be our only escape now. It was just a matter of when it would come for us.

* * *

The throbbing in my head only worsened the longer I was on my feet. I knew I was concussed at the very least, and paired with a wicked hangover, I was in bad shape—but still in better shape than Liam.

I sniffled as guilt wracked me. It was my fault the man I loved lay comatose on the couch. I had been reckless in letting Oliver go. I should've just killed him. Then, at least I could have gotten Liam to a hospital. But now we had no vehicle, no power, and no cell service. Oliver had cut the internet lines. I had confirmed it before wandering off into the forest to gather kindling and anything else I could use for firewood.

Sure, I could walk a couple miles to get cell service, but what if something happened to Liam and I wasn't close by to check on him? Or worse, what if Oliver came back to finish the job while I was away? Liam would have no one there to defend him.

Stupid. I was so *stupid.* Liam was probably going to die because of me.

Eventually someone would come for us, right? I could at least *try* to keep him alive.

I stumbled back toward the cabin with a bundle of sticks in my arms, relieved to find that Liam was still breathing when I returned. Still asleep, but alive. I collapsed in front of the fireplace and arranged the wood like I had seen Liam do hundreds of times. My cold, numb fingers hurt.

It took almost an hour, but I finally got a steady fire going. I breathed an accomplished sigh, looking up at the ceiling and murmuring a silent *thank you.*

Unable to eat, I filled a glass with water, drank it, then refilled it and grabbed a straw. I pressed a finger over the straw opening and pulled it out of the water, then parted Liam's lips and released the water into his mouth. He swallowed involuntarily, but didn't stir.

I repeated the action with the hope that he would stay hydrated until—

if—help arrived.

* * *

Three full days passed, and I was barely scraping by keeping the cabin warm, giving Liam sponge baths, and changing out his bandages. He got worse by the day; that was expected, but it didn't make it any easier to watch. The deathlike pallor of his face was unnerving, and so were the shaky, uneven breaths he took. He never woke up, not even once.

In between my busy work, I couldn't help but wonder how Oliver found us. How was it even possible? The files were confidential, our IP addresses were protected by a VPN, our cover was never once blown, and we were in a tiny and remote town in the mountains on the other side of the country. I mean, people were rarely found once admitted into WITSEC.

The only explanation I could think of was that someone leaked him the information, and I knew that if I made it out of this alive, I would make it my life's mission to find out how the hell this happened.

Someone. Would. Pay.

Looking at Liam now, I felt numb. It was better than crying every time I changed his bandage or pressed a cool cloth to his forehead. I was attempting to protect myself, even if it meant getting drunk in the evening and passing out beside him with a loaded firearm on the coffee table.

Fake marriage or not, I didn't expect *'til death do us part* to happen so soon.

* * *

My prayers were answered on day five, and I could only assume it was because we missed our check-in with the Marshal. If this had to happen at all, I was grateful it happened so close to the meeting.

But God, it did *not* feel close. Five days felt like an eternity. In hell.

I was in the middle of changing Liam's bandage first thing in the morning when I heard the sound of vehicles in the driveway. Frantically, I abandoned my task and grabbed my gun, aiming it at the door. Seconds later, several sets of pounding footsteps came from the front porch, and then our door was kicked in.

I immediately lowered my gun and dropped to my knees in all-consuming relief. The sobs I had been holding in for days broke through at the sight of their familiar faces. Agents Carver and Matthews met my eyes with concern—the most emotion I'd seen out of Carver—and behind them, Sophie and Marshal Rudolph. All of them wore Kevlar FBI vests.

Everything moved in slow motion; their voices sounded like they spoke underwater. Sophie kneeled in front of me, her hands on my shoulders, and I gaped at my best friend in disbelief. I had never been so happy to see her. I sobbed harder, collapsing into her arms as more agents flooded in to assess the situation.

Madelyn came around the couch to feel Liam's pulse, then glanced at me. I shook my head, unable to form the words. She gave me a single nod before calling for paramedics.

At some point a blanket had been draped around me, and thank God because I was bone-chillingly cold—I hadn't gotten around to making a fire this morning. I watched as the paramedics carefully moved Liam onto a gurney and wheeled him out.

I refused to let them take him from me. I climbed into the back of the ambulance and unwaveringly snapped at anyone who told me I had to stay behind.

I would not leave him in his hour of need.

And I was terrified that would be the last time I would see him alive.

* * *

Sophie sat in a chair beside me as Madelyn and Drew—fuck formal titles, we were way past that now—stood in front of my hospital bed. I had been admitted a few hours ago, and the doctor confirmed I did have a concussion and was severely dehydrated.

I was lucky, he told me.

Lucky. Yeah, right.

"What happened?" Madelyn asked softly. It was the most gentle she'd ever spoken.

I averted my gaze. How was I expected to tell them I got too comfortable and had probably broken protocol by doing so?

"I had a bad feeling when I woke up last week. I didn't know why... it had us on edge the whole day," I told them, exhaling sharply. "We came back from the store, and I think we both sensed something was... off. Liam insisted he go inside first because I was unarmed. Oliver was in there, but..." I let my voice trail off as my lower lip trembled. Sophie grabbed my hand, rubbing soothing circles over my skin. "I don't know the details before I got in there. We didn't get that far because... well, because Liam passed out while I stitched him up, and he hasn't woken up since."

"What happened when you did get inside?" Drew pressed.

I told them about the gunshot, then the fight once I was inside. My hand involuntarily flew to my neck, and I flinched when I realized my throat was bruised *again* from Oliver's hands. "It all just happened so fast," I said quietly. "He cut the power and the internet lines, and he stole the car, so we were stranded there. The emergency phone had no more minutes."

I still didn't look at them, and I was certain that was what gave away my guilt.

"So you shot him and... what? You let him escape?" It was Madelyn's typical inquisitive line of questioning, the same tone that had set me off so many months ago.

Yep. Should've known better than to assume I could get away with such a dumb decision without repercussions. I shook my head and said, "No. I made a bad call and now Liam's suffering the goddamn consequences from it."

"Callie... what did you do?" Sophie said.

I turned to my best friend. "Oliver asked for me to let him live and he would leave. I panicked and saw Liam bleeding out on the floor and made an emotional decision. It never even occurred to me he would take the car to escape. I don't even know how he got up there to begin with."

But then… then it hit me, and the missing pieces fell into place. The one person who wasn't here, and absolutely should have been.

"Wait… where's Terry?"

Sophie gave me a disappointed smile. "He was fired. The feds found dozens of cut corners and bad calls that resulted in reckless outcomes. He was money hungry, and his reputation was more important than public safety."

I tried to swallow the lump in my throat, but there was no denying the swell of emotion that rested there. Truth be told, I felt double crossed by the people I had once trusted. First Oliver as my lover, now Terry, the man I once considered a fatherly figure, had betrayed me, almost cost me my life, and may have cost my husband—I mean Liam—his. Trusting untrustworthy people was apparently a personality trait of mine.

"It was him," I stated.

"We know," Drew admitted. "He somehow got ahold of confidential information and leaked it to the public, including your new identities, in retaliation. We called your Marshal the day of your check in to ensure you both were okay when she informed us you had missed it. That's when we all came here."

That betrayal settled in my stomach. My face heated in anger. "He wanted me—us—to *die?*"

Silence.

I scoffed, then licked my lips. "Does anyone have an update on my husband?" Madelyn blinked at me, while Drew cocked his head. I frowned at them both. "What?"

"You called him your husband, *chula,*" Sophia said quietly.

"Oh." I laughed awkwardly, sheepishly. "It must be my concussion." I didn't want to admit the whole truth to them. As it stood, my heart felt lonely not having him by my side.

"Cal, did something more happen with you and Liam?"

I met Sophie's dark eyes with my own teary ones. I let her see it all. She sucked in a breath as she understood. The doctor came in then, and Drew and Madelyn stepped to the side to hear what he had to say.

"Well, Mrs. Blake—"

"Ms. Eden, please," I interjected. "No point in keeping my cover now, Doctor. These are federal agents."

He paused, then nodded. "Right. Okay, Ms. Eden. You're good to go. Just take it easy, and if you feel any pain or discomfort, you can take ibuprofen to help. Do you have any questions for me?"

"Yes. Do you have any updates on Liam Chandler?" I was careful not to say *my husband* again. I didn't feel like being ridiculed or looked at with pity.

His eyes shuttered. "He's out of surgery, but his vitals haven't stabilized just yet. We're keeping him overnight to monitor his progress. In the morning we can assess his condition for visitors. You're welcome to wait in the waiting area until then."

Surgery.

Not stable.

It had been hours.

But at least he wasn't dead.

The doctor turned to leave, but I grabbed his sleeve. "Were there any complications during the surgery?"

"I wasn't in the operating room to say. I will have his surgeon speak with you tomorrow when she's available."

I released him and nodded, mumbling my thanks as a nurse came in to disconnect me from the IV drip and other machines.

Fifty-Eight

Callie

After half an hour of reasoning, Sophie convinced me to come back to her hotel for the night. I took a long, hot shower. The first one in days. And when I was done wallowing in the scalding hot water, I struggled to sleep.

Over the course of the last six nights, I had barely cleared twenty hours of rest. My body ached, my head pounded, my eyes were heavy. But I couldn't help it. Too much had happened that kept me alert and anxious and hurting.

We were quiet on our way back to the hospital the following morning. We entered the waiting area five minutes before visiting hours began, and I impatiently tapped my foot while staring at the clock.

Suddenly, a gasp and a sob caught my attention. A woman rushed over to me. I recognized her immediately, a tattoo of her eyes flashing in my mind.

Liam's mom.

"Are you Callie?" she asked.

I winced, afraid to answer. After all, I was the reason her son was lying in a hospital bed. A man appeared behind her, and I could only guess he was Liam's father.

"Y-yes," I replied.

She threw her arms around me and choked on a cry. "Thank you so much for saving my baby's life."

Stunned, I hugged her back but didn't say anything.

"H-have you seen him?" I stammered.

She pulled back. "I just spoke with the doctor. She said if you hadn't given him those stitches, he would've died."

I blinked at her. "I'm so sorry," I blurted. "It's all my fault."

His mom smiled at me and patted my cheek. "Oh darling girl, this isn't your fault. He knew the risks of the job." She glanced over her shoulder at Liam's dad. "Besides, I think you've been keeping his spirit alive much longer than he has ever cared to admit."

My feet were suddenly very interesting as I avoided eye contact. She must not know the truth about Oliver then.

"I wish we were meeting under better circumstances," I told both of them.

"He talked about you a lot," his father said.

I cocked my head, wanting to probe, but his mom spoke again. "I'm Jackie, by the way, and this is my husband, Steven. We were wondering if we would ever get to meet you." Her green eyes welled with tears, and it woke something in me that I had been suppressing—*yearning*. For Liam. I had no idea that when his eyes fluttered shut as I gave him his stitches, I wouldn't see them again for a while.

Just as I was about to respond, Marshal Randall sidled up next to me. "Ms. Eden, it's time for us to go."

Slowly, I turned my head to look at her. "What? Go where?"

She inclined her head toward Liam's parents. "Mr. and Mrs. Chandler have extended their resort to you for the time being. We will be putting twenty-four-hour security there, posted at your room at all times and around the facilities to protect you."

I wanted to kick and scream and demand how they thought they could possibly protect me at this point, given how their very own program, designed to protect at-risk individuals, epically failed us. But I didn't.

Panic clawed at my chest as I glanced back at his parents. "That's very kind of you both. Thank you." I was about to protest leaving when a doctor came into view.

"Mr. and Mrs. Chandler, we're ready to take you back to him now."

"It was lovely to meet you, Callie. You're more beautiful than he described. We'll see you back in New York, okay?" Jackie said before she turned and followed the doctor out of the waiting area.

My panic tripled. I bent over and rested my hands on my knees, trying to breathe properly. I was leaving, and I wouldn't get to see Liam again. I didn't even know if he was stable.

Marshal Randall put her hand on my back and ushered me out of the hospital, panic attack and all.

Fifty-Nine

Liam

Everything was dark and cold for what felt like an eternity.

My final moments before I entered this abyss were consumed by Callie. Tears stained her cheeks, her hands quivered as she attempted to patch up my stab wound. A pulsing, searing, never-ending pain in my abdomen that felt as though it had been lit on fire when she poured vodka on it. A rough tugging on the wound as she stitched my skin back together.

The edges of my vision were receding and I felt cold. *So fucking cold.* But I tried to stay strong for her.

I accepted I was going to die; at least it was with her by my side, and I could tell her how I felt. That I saw my future with her.

Obviously, the icy depths of this eternal pitch blackness meant I was in hell. I probably deserved it after everything I'd done. Getting divorced, letting Callie cheat on her partner with me—although he turned out to be a serial killer—hurting Callie, cheating on Kelsey, sleeping around, substance abuse… the list of my sins could go on.

The only reprieve I got was the sensation of Callie's touch for a while. It would come and go, and I would lean into that warmth as much as I could. But it was gone now, and there was no sign she would come back.

Then I was drawn to a light, and I felt myself floating toward it, orbiting it, being pulled as if on an invisible thread. I reached for it so desperately that I feared it would be snuffed out before I could get to it. It didn't; it only grew in size and brightness until it consumed me, and then I was surrounded by a rhythmic beeping.

I winced at the loudness. *Jesus.* Was someone holding a smoke alarm in need of batteries next to my ears? My head was fucking pounding.

Wait.

I forced my eyes open, hoping I could see past the thick darkness I'd been staring at. I blinked at the harsh track lights above me. The fluorescents, the beeping, the smell of cleaning chemicals… I was in the hospital.

I blinked, very slowly. *How is this possible?*

Everything came rushing back. I was alive. *But how?* There was no power, no service, no car, and I was bleeding out…

A nurse entered the room and paused when she saw me, then retreated and called down the hallway for a doctor. She came to my bedside. "Mr. Chandler? Can you hear me?"

I nodded, then frowned and looked around the room for the first time, praying I'd see Callie. But there was no one.

Oh God. Did that mean…?

"Callie," I rasped, my voice nothing more than a harsh whisper. My throat was dry and scratchy, my lips chapped.

The nurse picked up a glass of water by my bedside and held it out to me. I took a thankful sip out of the straw, then another, and another, until the glass was empty. I spoke again when she set the glass down.

"Callie. Is she alive?"

She opened her mouth to respond when a doctor strolled in. "Mr. Chandler, glad to see you alive with some color in your face. How are you feeling?"

I frowned. I was in the hospital with a stab wound. How the hell did she think I felt? "Fine, thank you. Is Callie okay?"

"I'm unaware of your wife's current condition. I'll call her doctor once we wrap up here," she replied, her words clipped.

Wife.

I looked down at my left hand, comforted to see the wedding band still there. It had pained me two years ago to remove one off my finger, but now all I could think about was how to keep it on permanently.

"If you wouldn't mind. Thank you," I murmured.

She shone a flashlight into my eyes and I followed the light.

"You were given a second chance at life, Mr. Chandler. You're very fortunate your wife was there during the attack."

I snorted, because how did that make any sense? She could have *died.* "Fortunate? She broke her sobriety to take care of me." That small detail made my heart squeeze, and not in a good way. To think she was under so much duress that she'd cave to her temptations—her old toxic coping mechanism.

"You should be glad you're both alive." *Thank You, Jesus.* "What I mean is, she acted quickly, and because of that, you're sitting here today."

"I'm not following, Doc."

She sighed. "You lost a lot of blood. Enough that some people don't live through it. But she sterilized the best she could and stitched you up. Granted, the knife missed major arteries and organs, but she still saved your life. She changed your bandages multiple times a day, and her efforts paid off. They prevented infections in the wound. She even managed your fever and kept you hydrated. Most people in her shoes wouldn't have known what to do. She has to be the most level-headed and resourceful person I've seen come through these doors."

I smiled through dry lips, because yeah, that sounded like my Callie.

Drew and Madelyn popped their heads in. "Doctor Prashant?" Drew queried. "Would you mind if we asked Mr. Chandler some questions while the events are still fresh in his mind?"

The doctor waved the agents in. "I was just wrapping up my assessment. I'll be back later today to check on you, Mr. Chandler. Sound good?"

I nodded.

"You guys are a sight for sore eyes," I teased, but the joke fell flat from my scratchy voice. I cleared my throat.

"I could say the same for you. You good, man?" Drew asked.

I raised a shoulder in a shrug, then flinched when pain lanced through my abdomen. "Do I look like it?"

He chuckled.

"She's okay, Liam," Madelyn told me. My eyes snapped to hers. "Physically she's alright. She has a mild concussion but other than that and a few bruises, she's okay."

Physically.

"Thank Christ. But is she… you know, *okay?*"

"She was stranded there with you for five days thinking you were going to die. She had to figure out how to take care of you and make fires to keep the both of you from freezing. So no, I don't think she's *okay*," she snapped.

I gulped. "Five days?"

"Dude, you looked awful when we showed up. Pretty sure you were on your deathbed." Drew cracked a half-hearted smile.

I stayed quiet as I let that sink in.

"Do you remember anything that happened prior to falling into a coma?"

Everything.

Sighing, I told them my side of the story, pausing as I got to the part when Callie ran into the cabin after my gun had discharged. "He put his hands around her throat, and I got sloppy. I told myself if he ever did that to her again, I'd kill him. I let it cloud my judgment. I got him off her, but he threw her into the coffee table, and next thing I know he's stabbing me and twisting the knife. It was right after that that Callie shot him."

"So then Oliver got away, and that's when she stitched you up and you passed out?" Madelyn probed.

I nodded.

They exchanged a look.

"Listen, Liam." Drew rubbed the back of his neck, and my stomach churned. "Frankford found your location because Terry obtained and leaked it after he was fired."

I felt the impact of the news like a hit directly to my stab wound. "*What?*"

"I know he was a close family friend. We didn't disclose the information to your parents. Figured you might want to."

I shook my head to get a hold on my jumbled thoughts. "I need to see my w—Callie. Where is she?"

"What exactly is the status of your relationship with her?" Madelyn wondered. Not for professional purposes, but out of sole curiosity.

I opened my mouth to respond, but hesitated. "I don't know. We never defined it. Together? Sometimes it's hard to differentiate between our worlds. They just bled into each other at some point, and we accepted that for what it was."

Madelyn gave a resigned sigh. "I'm sorry shit went awry, Liam. This should never, *ever* have happened. We're working on figuring out who leaked the information to Terry. WITSEC files are highly classified. And honestly, we didn't even have details on your whereabouts." She pushed her blonde hair behind her ears. "Callie's on her way back to New York per the Marshal's orders. We no longer have any say in next steps for you guys. Everything is kinda… up in the air."

I shifted and winced when I felt my stitches pull. "What do you mean?"

"The Marshal and her supervisor are working on a different plan for you guys. They're talking about another WITSEC cover, possibly overseas. That's all we know," Drew chimed in.

Fucking hell.

* * *

The door to my hospital room swung open and my parents followed Doctor Prashant in. My heart swelled when I saw them, and my eyes burned. God, I missed them. Aside from the Police Academy, I had never gone more than a couple weeks without seeing them.

My mom threw her arms around me. I groaned in pain, which caused her to jump back and apologize profusely.

"I'm glad you're okay, son. Your mom and I have been worried sick about you since we got the call," Dad said.

"I'm sorry to have worried you."

"Does this mean you'll quit your job and join the family business?" Mom asked with a longing look.

I rolled my eyes. "No, Mom, I don't plan on quitting because of a minor setback."

She shook her head defiantly, but Dad put his hand on her shoulder before she could say anything else and said, "We met Callie."

My face lit up. "And?"

"She's lovely. She clearly cares very deeply for you. Poor girl looked like she hadn't slept in days, but she's more beautiful than you described," Mom told me.

I smiled. "She is, isn't she?"

"What's between you two… is it still complicated?" Dad pressed.

I rolled my lips, unsure how to answer that. I never gave them all the details about WITSEC—just that a serial killer we'd been chasing was now targeting us and that we were both entering the program. I didn't have any more time to go into the details.

"Well… Oliver Frankford is her ex."

Mom's jaw dropped. "Honey—"

I held up a hand to stop her. "I know. We did a lot of things we shouldn't have that put us in this position." I gulped before I continued. "The feds just told me that Terry leaked our location to Frankford in retaliation for him getting fired."

"Tell me that's a fucking joke, Liam," Dad boomed. I shook my head.

"But he's attended every anniversary party your father and I have had," Mom said. "He—no, that can't be right."

I reached for her hand. "I'm sorry. He's covered up a lot of greedy mistakes over the years, and this whole case turned the precinct upside down, including every decision he's made during his command. It was only a matter of time before it all caught up with him."

Dad took Mom into his arms as she cried. I couldn't help but feel like this was my fault. Maybe if I had never pushed Callie to re-open this case in the first place, we would all be in very different positions.

* * *

The two feds—AKA my new babysitters—stepped out of my room to give me a few minutes of privacy while I phoned Callie.

I was dying to hear her voice.

With shaking hands, I clicked on her contact. She picked up on the first ring.

"Hey, babe." She sounded out of breath, but her sweet, feminine voice dripped with relief.

I looked up at the ceiling, feeling my eyes burn. *Jeez.* I was not a crier and hated feeling like I was weak for it. "Hi, baby." A moment of silence.

"How are you?" she asked.

I chuckled humorlessly. "Honestly? Not great. I, um, I wanted you to be the first thing I saw when I came to."

Callie sighed, then sniffed. "Yeah, me too. I was there first thing in the morning but had to leave *right away* according to the Marshal."

Shaking my head even though she couldn't see me, I responded, "Fucking shitty of her to not wait five goddamn minutes."

"Yeah, tell me about it. I've been sick to my stomach for days."

"Callie, I'm so sorry. I got sloppy and—"

"Stop. We were woefully unprepared. I mean, witness protection is supposed to be, you know, *secure.* We should have been safe. What's important is that we're both alive."

I swallowed the lump in my throat. "Still. I can't imagine how you felt."

"Worst five days of my life." She laughed bleakly.

"I thought I was going to die," I whispered.

"I held onto the hope that you wouldn't. I love you, Liam Chandler."

"I love you, too, Callie Eden. Don't you ever forget it."

Sixty

Callie

⧫

The next couple of weeks were torture. I was on complete lock down at Chandler Resort & Spa, and while it was absolutely divine—I mean, the place was fancy as fuck—I was going out of my goddamn mind.

If I thought it was hard in those early weeks at the cabin, this agony was tenfold. Here, I didn't have the luxury to just waltz down the hallway to Liam, and I certainly didn't have a way to talk to him whenever I wanted. Between the time difference and the Marshal's order of limited contact until further notice, I didn't have a choice but to hunker down here. I was lucky to hear from him once a day.

This was the worst limbo ever. I couldn't work, and I felt like I was just existing in this world, luxurious hotel and all. I couldn't call my family; there were too many concerns of exploiting my location or putting them in danger.

Thankfully, I had a routine to help keep me busy. Wake up early, workout, shower, and get ready for the day. Grab coffee at the onsite café with either Liam's sister or Sophie—who tried to come visit me as often as possible— read, grab lunch, do yoga, listen to a podcast, recite affirmations, eat dinner. Soak in a hot tub, visit the spa if needed, and so on. Sure, it was a lot of self-care, but my heart ached from the distance between me and Liam and the not knowing when I'd see him next.

One day at the spa, I was tightening the plush robe around my waist after stripping down to go to my massage. A couple of women talking while folding towels openly caught my attention. I paused, listening in on their conversation and tucking myself in a corner away from their view.

"Have you seen his new girl? You know, the brunette with pretty blue eyes? She's, like, living here," one of them said, her tone not very friendly.

Wait, are they talking about me?

"Oh my God, yes. Could she be any more obvious?" the second voice said.

Obvious? About what?

"I know, right? Talk about a gold digger. Staying here and taking advantage of Mr. and Mrs. Chandler's generosity."

My jaw dropped. *Gold digger?*

"Liam's not even here, so why is she?" the second one asked.

I pretended to fuss with my hair and lip gloss while I eavesdropped, my stomach turning uncomfortably.

"Well, word on the street was that they ran away together for six months," the first one replied. *How the hell did they come to that conclusion?* "He hasn't been seen around New York, like, at all. And the most recent update is he was injured in the line of duty, so he's recovering somewhere across the country and the feds sent her here."

The second woman whistled. "If she stuck by his side through all of that, what makes you think she's a gold digger? Sounds like love and commitment."

Yes, thank you!

The first woman scoffed. "Please. If *I* was with a trust fund baby, especially with someone as hot as him, I'd stick by his side through *anything*."

I froze. *Trust fund baby?*

I floated through my massage, my head in the clouds as I mulled over their conversation. I didn't know who the women were, never even saw their faces, but I could assume they were employees. I couldn't be sure of the validity of anything they said, but it still got under my skin.

Even more so when I heard other whispers as the days passed by. Words like *trust fund* and *gold digger* were consistently thrown around in hushed voices, *wealth* and *heir to his parents' empire* right alongside it.

If Liam was willing to hide something as big as this from me, what else was he hiding?

* * *

"How's your head feeling?" Sophie wondered as she sat across the bistro table from me in the resort's in-house coffee shop.

I shrugged. "Physically? Great. Mentally? Meh." She cracked a feeble smile. "But enough about me. How are *you?*"

It was her turn to shrug. "Same old, same old. Living vicariously through your drama."

Grimacing, I said, "My life isn't a reality show for your entertainment." My voice dripped with sarcasm.

Sophie beamed. "Maybe not, but it's almost telenovela worthy." I rolled my eyes just as she looked down at her phone and sat up straighter. "Shit, I gotta head back to the city. I'm helping my mom set up for her Christmas party."

"How's she doing?"

She bristled at the question. "Truth be told, this year has been hard on her." She averted her gaze, and that told me she was hiding something. And there was only one topic that always made her retract into the shadows.

"Soph… does it have something to do with your dad's killers?"

She flinched, and I instantly felt guilty for asking. "A lot has happened since you were placed in witness protection, but that's for another time." She scrambled to her feet, her metal chair scraping harshly against the tile floor. "Love you, *chula.*" She kissed my cheek before bolting.

I turned and stared at her retreating back, wondering what the hell just happened and why she wouldn't want to talk about it with me.

Sixty-One

Liam

I was antsy as I stepped off the private jet with Marshal Randall, the familiar New York winter breeze slapping me in the face. The air wasn't as crisp as the Sierra Mountains. It took a minute for my lungs to adjust to the difference.

Climbing into the black SUV waiting for us, I fought the urge to groan. While I was in good enough health to be discharged from the hospital a week ago, I was still sore.

Randall and I remained silent, not having much to talk about, as usual. The last few weeks mostly consisted of me having to "rest" and doing physical therapy while at least two federal agents supervised me. Eventually there wasn't anything else to talk about, so I had grown used to the quiet.

She handed my phone back to me. "This is yours. Effective now, you can return to the public as Liam Chandler with unsupervised phone time."

I scowled as I took it from her. *Gee, thanks.* The last two weeks had been spent feeling like a grounded teenager because they monitored every keystroke and only allowed limited communication with my friends, family, and Callie, all back in New York. In fact, I had barely spoken with anyone.

It fucking sucked.

I watched the scenery outside change from city buildings, to suburban neighborhoods, to larger, more upscale properties and businesses. Before I knew it, we were turning into the winding drive of my parents' resort. The familiarity of it brought a smile to my lips.

We came to a stop at the entrance. Randall gave me a curt goodbye as I unloaded my bags and walked inside the lobby, where I was greeted by Sophie. She tapped her foot impatiently. We looked at each other warily.

"She doesn't know you're here yet," Sophie said.

"Hey, it's nice to see you too, Sophie," I quipped.

She was not amused as she glanced at her watch. "I don't have a lot of time before I have to leave, so let's make this quick, okay?"

I shrugged. "You're the one here. Did you volunteer to debrief me?"

"Only to intercept you before you could see Callie." Her words were clipped and laced with... something unfriendly. Almost like animosity. Which was unsurprising.

I arched a brow at her. "What's your deal? We've spent months together."

Sophie sighed. "She's guilt-ridden over what happened. Go easy on her."

At that, I tipped my head back and laughed. "Go easy on her? I'm not angry about anything that happened, other than not killing Oliver when I had the chance. She knows that. We're just ready to be together again. So why don't you cut the bullshit and tell me what you came here to say."

Her dark eyes flared. She stepped closer to me, poking a finger into my chest. "Hurt her again and I will personally see to your demise."

"Right. Is that all?"

She blinked. "You're serious about it this time?"

"I was serious last time. I just waited a little too long to tell her. What else do you expect me to say, Sophie? As someone who used to be my friend, I'd like to think that you could see that. But apparently we're not friends anymore, right? You've made that abundantly clear, especially given what happened the day Callie and I left."

Sophie scoffed. "Fuck you, Liam."

I reared back in surprise. "You know, if anything, I should be saying that to *you* after the way you treated me. And in front of her goddamn family, no less. That was so beyond shitty. Do you know how much damage control

I'm going to have to do because of you?"

She folded her arms across her chest and pursed her lips. "Not my problem that you couldn't keep your dick in your pants."

"Um, hello? Last time I checked, there are two parties involved with sex. So, what, you thought it was appropriate to humiliate your best friend in front of her family and then continue to twist the knife deeper when she left the room?"

"I was agreeing with some of the shit Leah was saying."

"By discussing intimate details of her life that were no business of yours to share in front of everyone. Those things should've been disclosed in *private.*"

She rolled her eyes. "Fine. I'm fucking sorry for what I said. Happy?"

"No." I'll be damned if I let her continue treating me this way. "What did I do to you to make you so angry at me? One minute we were fine, the next thing I know I'm the devil incarnate in your eyes. So please, enlighten me on how I fucked up our friendship."

Sophie's jaw clenched before she looked away from me. "You ran away when I needed a friend, Liam. And to top it? You had someone pull a few strings for you and got a *promotion.* As a woman of color in law enforcement, I've had to claw my way into every new position."

Oh.

"Soph, I can't apologize for my promotion, but I *can* apologize for leaving you. It was selfish of me, and I admit that."

Her eyes flickered back to mine, brimming with tears. I had only seen her cry one time, when she came to me about—*Oh.*

"You were the only person I could trust."

It all made sense now.

Sixty-Two

Liam

9 months earlier

Heartbroken and sullen, I reluctantly packed up my desk and studiously kept my back turned on Callie's old desk. It was left untouched, the space around it no longer smelling of her as the surfaces collected dust.

She was still gone. I didn't know where she was, and I didn't think she wanted me to find out.

I couldn't stay here any longer. I toughed it out as long as I could before seeking a new career opportunity back in New York. I had to go back—I couldn't breathe here since she left.

There was movement by the door of my office, drawing my attention to a teary-eyed Sophie sagging against the doorframe.

Concern flared in my chest. Sophie was the queen of deflecting so she didn't have to face her demons head on. We were not unlike each other in that aspect, and it was probably what drew us together in this friendship.

"Soph? What's wrong?"

The vulnerable, haunted look in her eyes had me reeling as she glanced at the boxes on my desk, then stumbled toward me. I caught her just as she threw her arms around me.

"Th-they found the people who killed my father. I mean, they f-found who they are, but not… didn't make an arrest yet." She sobbed, turning her face into my chest while I rubbed her back in a soothing caress.

"How?"

She stepped out of my embrace and wiped her nose on her sleeve. "Some new technology or some shit. I just… I needed to talk to someone about it, but it seems like you're busy…" Her voice trailed off when her attention snagged the boxes again.

Rubbing the back of my neck sheepishly, I felt the urge to probe more, but that vulnerable look on her face was fading by the second. "Yeah, about that. I was going to tell you sooner, I just… I was waiting until it was official, but I'm transferring back to the NYPD."

Sophie blanched, her hands curling into fists. "Are you fucking serious?"

"There's just… There's just too much here that reminds me of her. I need some time and space away from it all."

"So take a vacation, Liam. Don't run away. Don't be like her. She shouldn't have left."

"I gave her every reason–"

"Don't you dare blame yourself or make a fucking excuse for her shitty choice. She should've taken a vacation, too, for the sake of her mental health. But running away? *Dios mio.* If everyone who got a broken heart ran away, the world would be a chaotic free-for-all."

She wasn't getting it. I tapped the tip of my shoe against the ground, my focus on the movement. "Do you want to talk more about your father's case? I know how big of a deal this is, and like you said, you needed to talk to someone. I'm here for you."

She bristled, taking a few steps back. "Forget about it. I'll leave you to pack." She spun on her hees and stormed out of my office.

I called after her, a resigned groan tearing free when she didn't come back.

That day, in my office… I shut down. Told her I was transferring when she was at her most vulnerable. Definitely not optimal timing on my part.

Mentally coming back to the present, I fixed my eyes on Sophie again.

"You still haven't told Callie about your father's case."

She tucked her dark hair behind her ears and crossed her arms. "No. I know she would want to know, but she has enough weighing on her."

"But she's your best friend. I understand you're being thoughtful, but carrying this load by yourself isn't any better." She nodded slowly, so I pulled her into my arms, folding her into my chest. She returned the embrace. "I'm sorry. For everything."

Nodding again, she murmured, "I am, too. I should have never thrown you under the bus to her parents."

I chuckled. "Yeah, that'll be a fun mess to untangle." Releasing her, I gave her a smile.

"Go get your girl."

"For the last time, I hope."

Sophie gave me a dazzling grin that told me all was forgiven before she waved and rushed out the door. I breathed a sigh of relief. Now if only she communicated those things to me *sooner*, we could have avoided some collateral damage. Nothing we could do about it now.

* * *

The lobby was bustling with holiday energy, a loud chattering almost drowning out the sound of Christmas music. I weaved through the crowd, angling my body to avoid an elbow to my healing abdomen. Craning my neck over the throngs of people, I searched for familiar faces: Callie, my parents, my sister...

I spotted them by the elevators. My parents knew I was arriving today, hence their shifting gazes across the crowded room; Callie, on the other hand, was unsuspecting, with her back to me. I wondered how they got her down here without raising her suspicion.

Finally breaking free of the crowd, I stepped into the open. My parents' eyes lit up and they rushed over, fussing over my appearance and asking

285

me how I felt. I barely listened; my attention was on the love of my life, who must've heard the commotion because she turned around.

"I need to see my girl," I told my parents distractedly.

Those ocean blue eyes met mine, widened, welled with tears—and then she was crashing into me.

I ignored the sharp pain from the impact and held her tightly to me, her warmth and familiar scent bringing a sense of home to my wandering soul. I was completely lost without her, and had been since I met her. She was my missing piece, the thing that made me whole, and the thought of a life without her would be no life at all.

As her body melted into mine, I couldn't help the emotions that wracked me. I squeezed my eyes shut, hoping to alleviate the burning in them, and held the back of her head with one hand while the other pressed her into me.

"I'm so sorry, babe," Callie sobbed into my shoulder.

"You kept us both alive. You have nothing to be sorry for," I reassured her.

"I should have brought my gun that day—"

I pulled back enough to look her in the eyes. "Stop. This isn't a blame game. We're both safe and alive and together again." I cupped her face and pressed a gentle kiss to her lips. "We should have been safe. We were *supposed to be safe.* What happened wasn't either of our faults."

A feeble smile broke through the tears staining her cheeks. "I was so scared."

I kissed her again. "I can't imagine what you went through."

Her hands closed over mine, and I felt cool metal press into my skin. My eyes drifted to the band still on her left hand, mirroring the one on mine. "You're still wearing the ring."

Callie stepped out of my embrace. "Of course I am. It's been comforting to keep it on. Reminds me of how safe you make me feel. Plus," she shrugged, as if this were a casual thing she was saying, "I have no reason to take it off."

I blinked.

Blinked again.

Swallowed the lump in my throat.

And felt my heart thump harder in my chest.

I glanced down at my suitcase, thinking of what was tucked away in there that I had picked out weeks ago, before looking at her again. Then I noticed my parents just staring at us adoringly and my sister with her lip curled in mock disgust.

"Get a room, you two," Laurie sneered jokingly, before sauntering over and giving me a lazy hug. "Glad to see you're alive."

I chuckled. "Very convincing. For a second there, I almost believed you." I looked at Callie. "Have you two met?"

Callie grinned. "Oh, yeah. She's been keeping me company and sharing lots of stories about you from your childhood."

I paled. "Laurie, tell me you didn't."

"Oh, I so did. No regrets either."

"Honey, leave your brother alone. He's had a long flight," Mom stepped in, giving me another hug and whispering my ear, "She's perfect for you."

"I know," I whispered back, meeting Callie's gaze over her shoulder. I stepped around Mom to wrap my arm around Callie's waist, suddenly only one thing on my mind, and decided to use my mom's statement to my advantage. "Do you guys mind if I rest for a bit? I'm exhausted and feeling sore."

* * *

Callie leaned into me, her back to my chest, as the elevator doors slid shut. "Did you just make up an excuse to get me alone, Mr. Chandler?"

I smirked into her hair and snaked my arms around her waist. "Shh, my intentions are supposed to be a secret, Ms. Eden."

She giggled as the elevator came to a smooth stop. She guided me to our room—one of the honeymoon suites, which my sister thought would be fitting for us—and unlocked the door. I didn't want to waste another second; after all, we had a few weeks to make up for. I kicked the door shut and spun Callie around, pressing her against the door and crushing my lips against hers. I groaned through the twinge of discomfort from the exertion, and she took that as an invitation to sweep her tongue across mine.

Yeah, I missed my woman *a lot*.

And apparently so did my dick, if my rock-hard erection was any indicator. Being monitored twenty-four hours a day made it impossible to pleasure myself, so she was getting weeks of pent-up sexual frustration. I pushed my hips into hers, and she smiled against my mouth.

"You could at least take me to the bedroom before assaulting me," she teased.

I bit her bottom lip, hard, in response. She whimpered and blinked up at me, and—*fuck*, that look was going to get me into trouble. I grabbed her hand and pulled her into the bedroom, then crossed both arms in front of me to grab the hems of my long sleeve, lifting it over my head and dropping it onto the floor. Her eyes went straight to the angry red wound on my abdomen, scabbed over and starting to scar. The stitches had since dissolved, but the delay in medical attention had been detrimental to my healing timeline. With any luck, I'd be one hundred percent in the next week or two.

"Liam," she breathed, taking a step forward. "God, this looks so much better than before."

"I would hope so."

"Don't be a smartass."

I feigned offense. "It's in my genetic code."

Callie smirked at me. "Is being a chronic pain in my ass also in your genetic code?"

I laughed and grabbed her hips to bring her closer. "Now who's being a smartass?"

She hummed. "Guess you're rubbing off on me."

"Not in the ways I want to be," I admitted, walking her backwards to the bed until she was forced to sit down. I parted her legs and dropped to my knees.

"Wait. Before you do," Callie spoke up suddenly.

I raised my head. "What's wrong?"

Her eyes looked panicked. "I love you. I told myself that if we both survived, I would say it to you more."

We stared at each other for a moment, and vulnerability struck me in the chest like a freight train. We almost lost each other. For a moment, I thought Oliver had killed her when he threw her into the coffee table. It made me see red. And moments later, I was accepting my own death as I bled out. I could still feel her hands pressing against the bleeding wound, the searing pain that accompanied her stitching me back up, watching as sobs wracked her body. If she hadn't persisted, death would've been my fate right then and there. But she had saved me—and I hadn't realized until this very moment that I had been blocking that feeling because it was fucking *terrifying*.

I slid my hands over the tops of her thighs, rising on my knees and meeting her halfway for a kiss. "I love you," I told her. "And I won't waste another day not being able to tell you that."

Callie's lips trembled before she straightened and pushed her hips toward me. "You may resume."

I laughed softly as I pulled her panties off and buried my tongue deep in her, letting her wetness coat it before dragging it up to her clit and swirling. Her familiar throaty moan echoed off the walls. I loved it. I hoped everyone could hear it, because *that?* Yeah, I was responsible for that sexy little noise—and she was *all* mine.

Repeating the move a few more times, I couldn't help but look up at her flushed cheeks and bright eyes. I did it over and over until she was calling out my name and squeezing her thighs around my head. Her pussy throbbed against my mouth, and I couldn't wait one more minute to drive myself into her. Slowly, I rose to my feet and finished undressing myself. She did the same, and I swept my eyes over her, devouring her with my gaze.

We were a tangled mess of desperate kisses as we frantically climbed onto the bed. Callie pushed me onto my back and straddled my hips, settling down over my cock. I hissed through my teeth, not expecting her to take the wheel but not complaining either. I held my breath when she reached the base, giving her a moment to adjust. Biting her lip and meeting my eyes, she stayed completely still.

"Such a tight, wet pussy," I murmured, skimming my fingers up her hips, over her tattoos—the new one I'd caught a glimpse of so many weeks ago, with a cursive *L*, and now another one: two lovebirds sitting on a branch on her other rib. I cupped her perfect tits.

Callie's cheeks turned redder, and I almost laughed. I was balls deep in her and *that* made her blush? I'd never get tired of seeing it, of making her react that way. It was so damn endearing.

But then she moved, and holy hell, that was dangerous. The pattern in which she moved on top of me had every rational thought flying out the window. I could only focus on how good she felt under my hands, how her kiss left a hot trail in its wake. How much I had missed her and how fucking grateful I was that we were alive in this moment together.

In the blink of an eye, I rolled so she was pinned underneath me, her chest rising and falling as she stared up at me with dilated pupils. I grabbed a pillow and growled, "Lift your hips." She obeyed, a curious look crossing her face as I slid it underneath her. "Such a good girl."

Sixty-Three

Callie

uch a good girl.

Those words had a certain erotic effect on me, so much so that an unexpected orgasm tore through me in response. Liam stilled above me as he watched, flattening a hand on my pelvic bone and applying the perfect amount of pressure to make the orgasm drag on. I blinked at him, then took in our new position—something we had never done before.

"I could watch you come around me all day long, baby." Amusement colored his face and he flashed me that godforsaken smile—dimples and all.

I sighed happily. "Keep saying that to me and I just might."

That grin widened. He leaned down and kissed me, resuming his thrusts at this unfamiliar but delicious angle, and damn, it hit me in all the right spots. I almost didn't notice him pinning my hands above my hand, rendering my limbs completely useless. Needing to move to relieve some of the pressure, I pleaded—no, *begged* Liam.

"I need to—I need to move," I panted.

"No. I want you to feel it all."

"Liam, *please.*" I didn't even care that I sounded whiny.

Liam nipped at my bottom lip but kept his punishing rhythm. I mumbled incoherently, moving my head back and forth as I climbed further into oblivion.

"Hold it," Liam growled.

My eyes snapped open to look at him. "What?" I breathed. "I c-can't." My body buzzed with the need to release.

"Fucking *hold it,* Callie."

I whimpered as I trembled everywhere, trying to stop myself from coming, caving to Liam's every demand and stretched to my limit. "Please, *please—*"

Liam kissed me before whispering, "Come with me, baby."

I tipped all the way over the edge, exploding and tightening and pulsing everywhere, Liam chasing his release right alongside me. Stars swam in my vision, my breaths slowly returning to normal. I realized tears were streaming down my face when he let go of my hands and cupped my cheeks.

"Are you okay? Was that too much?"

I shook my head. "No, that was—it was…" I stammered. "Mind-blowing. So good."

He grinned. "Must be if you can't put together a sentence."

I laughed and looped my arms around him to kiss him. I had missed him so fucking much.

* * *

"So… you met my parents," Liam said slowly as we snuggled on the plush bed. As much as I wanted to stay here forever, there was something I needed to talk about.

"I've spent a considerable amount of time with them, actually. They're wonderful. I see where you get your wit and charm from." Our eyes connected, and his gaze heated. I flashed him a knowing smile and shook my head. "Don't give me that look."

"What look?" His lower lip jutted out adorably. I patted his cheek.

"You know what you're doing. You can have more of me later."

Liam groaned and nuzzled my neck. "But we have so much lost time to make up for," he complained.

I turned in his arms, then trailed my hand down his chest, over his sculpted abs, stopping just above his laceration. "Honestly, I'm worried about you. Don't think you can hide your discomfort just because we're in the heat of the moment."

He kissed the tip of my nose; it made me feel giddy. "You're sweet, but there's no way in hell I would let this thing get in the way of our mind-blowing sex, baby." He brushed my hair behind my ear. "Something else is bothering you."

My smile faded. How the hell did he see through my facade?

"You're right." I took a deep breath. "Liam… I've been… hearing things, during my time here."

He frowned. "Hearing things. Like what?"

I sat up. "Like… like you're a *trust fund baby*. I mean… is that—is that true?"

Liam stilled, scrutinizing me with an unreadable expression. My stomach lurched. He huffed a resigned sigh. "I don't really want to discuss this right now."

I paused. "So… it *is* true?"

"Callie, please. This really isn't the right time for this conversation."

"The *right time?* Babe, I'm not trying to start some kind of argument, I just feel like I should know about something like this."

"Would it be so bad if I was?"

I gasped. "It's just that… we've never, I guess… this has never—if it's true, why would you never have brought this up before?"

Liam sat up and raked a hand through his hair. "I wanted to, but… it was a source of many uncomfortable arguments with Victoria."

"Arguments? Why would—"

"She had to sign a prenup, okay? And we fought about it for weeks. And then during the divorce, there was so much contention from it, along with everything else, and I just… I didn't want to put that kind of strain on our relationship."

I bit my lip. That answer didn't do anything for my nerves. Actually, it made me fidget more. A prenup meant… "Jesus, Liam, how much of a trust fund do you have?" His eyes searched mine curiously, and part of my heart pinged with hurt. "I'm not asking because I'm with you for money."

"I know," he said immediately. "It's just that, based on your reaction to finding out that's true, I don't know how you'll react when I tell you."

My eyes widened. "Baby—"

He held up a hand, then reached behind him to grab his phone off the end table. After a moment, he handed me the screen. My heart flopped, and all the air left my lungs as I looked at his bank accounts.

Oh my fucking God.

I threw Liam's phone back at him and scrambled to the edge of the bed, needing a little bit of space to breathe. "What the hell, Liam?"

Liam looked at me like I was a flight risk, or maybe a scared animal. "Baby, it's okay. I don't even touch it. I have no need to."

Inhale, two, three, four. Exhale, two, three, four.

"I'm not…" I shook my head, trying to clear my mind. "How is that even possible?"

He flinched, his eyes shuttering. He climbed out of bed and pulled his shirt and boxers on before returning to the bed with me, his expression guarded. "My parents have built this business. This resort… started as a bed and breakfast. They still have the original location, but they made some smart investments when the real estate market tanked. They own several hotels, and a campground just outside of Huntingdon." He gave me a knowing look at that tidbit of information. "And of course, this is their big money-maker."

Still speechless, I tried not to show that I was panicking on the inside.

"My sister and I were both given career opportunities when we turned eighteen. She chose to work her way up the ladder here, and I opted for a career that satisfied my soul."

Okay, that makes sense.

"But… why?" I finally managed to ask.

He tilted his head to the side. "Because I didn't want this life. Yes, it's nice to visit, and yes I have an affinity for the finer things in life, but it's not who I am. Just like you. You own designer jewelry and shoes. You dress nice.

You enjoy it, but it's not your identity."

I nodded, shifting my gaze to my hands.

"Callie, will you please look at me?"

I turned away from him. "No fucking wonder they were calling me a gold digger," I muttered under my breath.

"Who said that?"

I shrugged. "I was at the spa when I heard a couple of women talking about you. About *me*. How I'm after your money. And honestly… I guess I should have suspected this once I got here and saw how extravagant this place is."

Liam crawled across the bed and took my face in his hands, forcing me to look at him. "Hey. Don't listen to them. They don't know *anything* about us."

I nodded, leaning into his touch. "Why didn't you want this life?"

He raised a shoulder. "Because I had another calling in life. Yes, I knew I could get a larger trust fund if I signed a career contract with my family, but that would have tied me here. So rather than needing to use my trust fund, I make a decent amount of money from being a shareholder. I chose a humbling job and live within the means of that, and dip into my disposable income at my own discretion."

This was all so much information. My head was swimming, I felt a little sick to my stomach, and—

"Don't overthink this, babe. Don't let this take away from these moments we have together."

He's right.

I nodded. "Okay."

"Okay?" He offered me a small smile, concern still swimming in his eyes. "We're good?"

I bit my lip. "Yeah, we're good. That was just a *lot* more than I was expecting."

Liam laughed, and I was so fucking glad that conversation was over with. "Seven figures is quite astonishing to see, yeah?"

I rolled my eyes. "Not-so-humble flex, I see."

"It's all part of my charm, baby." He said with a wink, then pushed me down on the bed.

Sixty-Four

Callie

Two nights later, Liam and I sat across from each other at a private table in the back corner of the resort's restaurant.

My fingers skimmed over the menu nervously. I didn't have a reason to be anxious, yet here I was, a nervous ball of energy. Plus, it was just the two of us. Sort of. I knew all the employees were keeping a close eye on us, and that made me fidget. Up until now, they didn't give me so much as a second glance—even if they thought I was a gold digger—but then the owners' son came back into the picture, and suddenly it was like having a local celebrity in the house.

They never treated Liam's sister like this.

"What's making you so restless, babe?" Liam asked, interrupting my thoughts.

My throat was so dry, I contemplated taking a glass of water from the table behind us. But really, I was itching for a glass of wine—surely that was fine as long as I didn't let it get out of hand, right?

I mean, what was I supposed to say? *Hey, by the way, your confession about your reputation as a trust fund baby suddenly makes me feel inadequate, and I'm not really sure what to do with that information or how to act around you in public.*

Shit.

Did I need to act differently in public?

No, no. Just be yourself.

He had never cared about public relations before his admission, so why would he now?

Goddamn it, I'm overthinking again.

"Nothing," I croaked, and I thanked God when our server appeared to take our drink order.

"Mr. Chandler, it's nice to see you again," she cooed, and I couldn't help but purse my lips as she blushed.

"Ms. Torres," Liam responded without looking up from his menu. Him knowing her by name made my heart settle in my stomach and all the air expel from my lungs. It was not the response I was expecting, but it sure as hell solidified me ordering a glass of wine. Not like my sobriety was intact anymore, anyway.

"Can I get you anything to drink?"

"I'll have a glass of Merlot, please," I blurted before I could stop myself. Both our server and Liam turned their attention to me. The look on Liam's face was one of pure shock, so I dropped my eyes back to the menu I now clutched with an ironclad grip.

"Sure..." her voice trailed off. The hesitation in her voice made me wonder if she was noticing me for the first time. "And for you, Liam— uh, Mr. Chandler?" The familiarity had my spine straightening with an uncomfortable awareness.

"Uh, I will have the same," he said slowly. His penetrating gaze didn't leave my face, as if urging me to look at him. I couldn't bring myself to.

I was definitely on edge. It was the unmistakable feeling of jealousy mixing with inadequacy, and suddenly, old feelings of betrayal and infidelity stirred themselves awake until they had a chokehold on the pit in my stomach.

I had *zero* reason to feel this way; Liam had given me nothing but feelings of love, security, and faithfulness from the moment I returned from Springcrest. That, paired with how he defined the term *dicked me down* before we came down for dinner, made me sure he wasn't going anywhere.

But what happened last Christmas—*oh.* Christmas was now only a few days away, and maybe my body had been subconsciously triggered into fight-or-flight after last year's events. I guess maybe my comfort zone was living in perpetual *dis*comfort.

"Callie."

And just the tone of his voice when he uttered my name made me raise my eyes to his.

"Hmm?"

"What the hell is going on?"

I snapped my menu shut and placed it on the table, finally finding my voice. "We're good, right? You and me?" Confused, he nodded. "Great. Then nothing, I guess."

"Have I done something to make you feel otherwise?" Liam pressed, leaning across the table to take one of my hands in his. I hesitated for less than a second before I opened my mouth, but he beat me to it. "You don't trust me."

Sighing, I relented. "I do. It's just that I'm a little out of my element here." I glanced down at my Tiffany's watch and pulled at the memory I had from wearing it to the Christmas Gala two years ago, where Liam and I first crossed paths. The memory comforted me.

Except... this watch was a gift. I didn't just buy this with my own money, or with my inheritance, or just because I wanted to reward myself. I recalled eyeing his expensive taste in style and liquor when we first collided. Now it all made sense.

The server set two glasses of wine down and left the bottle on the table.

"Are you ready to order, Mr—"

"Please, let my wife order first."

My jaw dropped, but when she turned my way with her lips flattened, I gave her a smug smile.

"I didn't know you remarried," she stated.

"I've never been happier," was his only response.

We rattled off our orders, and as soon as she left our table, I grabbed my glass of wine and chugged half of it. I didn't even care that Liam was ogling at me.

"I didn't know you broke your sobriety," he said quietly.

"Yes, you did."

"What? No, I didn't."

"You don't remember? Right before I stitched you up I downed a sizable amount of vodka."

"I just assumed it was a one-time thing."

I shook my head, shame creeping up my throat.

Realization dawned on his face then. "Is that what's bothering you? Are you, you know, struggling with it again?"

Just tell him.

It was the only way we could move past it. I had to talk about it eventually. Isn't that what all that therapy had taught me? All our heartbreak?

"No." I loosed a heavy sigh and played with the linen napkin in my lap. "I'm allowing myself to indulge every once in a while." I paused. "Christmas is in a few days."

That earned a dimpled smile from him. Would I ever get used to those damn dimples? "I know."

"You know what happened last year."

A brief silence. "If you're worried about a repeat of last year, then I think you're certifiably insane."

Laughter bubbled out of me. "No, no. It is crazy, though. I think I'm experiencing feelings of trauma, so yeah, maybe a part of me is… scared. We're back in the real world now, babe, and we haven't exactly had a great track record with that and this time we're talking about a future and I feel like I just found out this whole other part of you and—"

"Cal, stop for a sec, alright?"

I took a deep breath as he sipped his wine.

"What can I do to help convince you otherwise? To give you confidence in us?"

His questions caught me off guard. When I was with Oliver, he *never* asked how he could help.

"Don't leave me again."

Liam snorted. "Fat chance in hell," he retorted.

"And no more lies or omissions."

"Done. Easy."

My smile faded. "Also answer one question for me." He nodded. "Have you slept with any of the staff here?"

It was his turn to laugh. "God, no. Is this about our waitress?" Silence from me. "Ms. Torres's parents have been working for mine for over fifteen years. Almost the entire time this resort has been open, actually. She followed behind them a number of years ago."

My mouth formed an *O* shape. "Did you know she has a crush on you, along with half the rest of the staff?"

Liam rolled his eyes, green glimmering in the flickering candlelight. "Doesn't matter. The only woman I have eyes on is you." His fingers interlaced with mine, and I got so lost in him for a moment that I think I forgot my name.

"You're still calling me your wife, you know."

"And you're not still calling me your husband?"

I pursed my lips to fight an amused smile. "Touché."

Sixty-Five

Liam

ell, shit.

Somehow I had managed to allow doubt to slip into Callie's mind. Maybe it was all the time apart that had triggered a trauma response, or maybe it was her coming to terms with a piece of information about myself that shouldn't change a thing.

Though truth be told, I didn't know we were ready to talk about that yet. And honestly, it was something that even *I* rarely thought about, because it wasn't all that important to me.

But now I needed to work double time to change Callie's mind. Make her feel confident in us. I knew exactly what I needed to do, but I needed to lay the groundwork first. I nervously tugged on my cufflinks—something she was vividly aware that I wore and then said "only rich people wear cufflinks"—as she disappeared into the bathroom to get herself ready for bed after dinner.

"Did it bother you that I called you my wife?"

She poked her head out of the bathroom, her glossy brown hair now swept into a messy bun. "No. I actually liked seeing her reaction," she admitted. "Why?"

I shrugged nonchalantly, even though my heart was doing somersaults at her response. She turned away from me to wash her face, and I slowly unbuttoned my shirt. "It's funny, with all the time we spent in the cabin, we never once talked about our future."

Callie stilled before patting her face dry and putting a slew of moisturizing products on her face. I had no idea what she needed five steps for, but I never asked. I just enjoyed watching her do her routine as I shed one piece of clothing at a time, waiting for her to respond.

I joined her in the bathroom, both of us brushing our teeth in silence. It wasn't until we were climbing into bed together that she spoke.

"You mentioned it after Oliver stabbed you."

I flinched at the memory. I would never forgive myself for dropping my guard long enough for him to land a jab that had almost cost me my life.

"Mentioned what?"

"Seeing your future with me. After all that time up there, I was *only* seeing our future together. It never crossed my mind to think of us as not being together when all was said and done. I just didn't know what it would look like after," she confessed. I half expected her to blush at the confession, because that was her typical reaction to being honest, but she had never looked more confident and serious.

Fuck, she's so sexy.

I ran a thumb down her cheek. "There is no future for me without you. All I've been dreaming about is building a life with you. I want nothing more than to pick up where we left off."

She grinned, then leaned forward and pressed her lips to mine. When I tried to deepen the kiss, she pulled back. I almost moaned in disappointment.

"You know, until we got to the cabin, I never pegged you as a hopeless romantic," Callie teased.

"You'll be happy to know that you're the only person who's made me like this," I shot back, flashing her both dimples and drowning in how her breath caught at the sight.

* * *

Operation Convince Callie commenced the next day, diving straight into Christmas festivities to replace bad memories with fan-fucking-*tastic* ones.

My parents were experts in capitalizing on every holiday possible to maximize traffic to the resort. With promises of luxury packages and themed events, they never failed to book the resort out. Christmas was arguably one of their biggest holidays, with Valentine's Day being a close second. For Christmas, the entire resort was professionally decorated like a Hallmark movie, and the activity calendar was jam-packed with events.

Phase One: Return Holiday Joy began with building a gingerbread house. I was spectacularly terrible at it, but Callie's control freak, perfectionist tendencies kicked in. She was currently sticking her tongue out as she concentrated on thin lines of icing dropping from the roof, resembling icicles.

"Your concentration is impressive," I told her. Her eyes flashed up to mine, a slow, sexy smile pulling her mouth up.

"Someone had to make it look presentable," she quipped, returning to her project.

I watched her, fascinated. At the end of it, when we carried it up to our suite, I saw a spark in her eyes that reminded me of the woman I met two years ago.

Phase One: Success.

After I pinned her against the wall and fucked her with my tongue, I coerced her into the next activity. She pretended to be annoyed, but she didn't protest when I guided her to the room where it would be held.

It was as romantic as it could get—ballroom dancing lessons.

Phase Two: Make Her Swoon.

She was pleasantly surprised when we walked through the door just as the instructor started speaking. I smiled to myself as she paid close attention, while I pretended not to know how to dance so we could "learn" together. Callie grinnedfrom ear to ear the entire time. We got caught up in the moment, kissing and spinning and moving with the holiday music playing over the speakers.

Needless to say, she was laughing by the end of it. All I could do was press a kiss to her forehead while I tried to calm my racing heart. I loved everything about this woman.

Phase Two: Success.

Callie and I had lunch because we were starving and—unbeknownst to her—we would be working up an appetite later. My parents joined us. It was the first time I saw them interact together, and I was appalled at how charmed they were by her. I mean, sort of—Callie was the definition of perfection, but they *never* treated Victoria the way they were treating Callie.

Plus, my parents were hard nuts to crack, but Callie had immediately broken that barrier with them. I was certain it had something to do with whatever happened at the hospital, because my parents hadn't stopped talking about her since.

Phase Three: Make Her Relax.

We made our way to the spa for a couple's massage on the second floor, which boasted stunning views of the sprawling hills of Upstate New York and the gardens beyond. Lying mere feet from Callie and watching her eyes roll back in pleasure just about undid me, because all I could focus on for the duration of it was taking her into the adjoining bathroom and bending her over the vanity.

It took me almost the full hour to will my boner away so I could stand up without embarrassing myself. Callie stepped in front of me in her fluffy white rob and wrapped her arms around me.

"I know you're up to something. I don't know what it is yet, but I don't mind," she said, snuggling into my chest.

I chuckled. "I have no idea what you're talking about."

She snorted. "Please. You've been having us run from one thing to the next all day long. Did you think I wouldn't notice?"

I mean… I had kinda hoped.

"I'm just trying to give you a glimpse into my romantic side and get you in the holiday spirit."

"If you're not careful, I'll get used to this."

I leaned down and whispered in her ear, "That's kind of the point, baby." Then I ushered her out of the spa so we could get ready for the last event of the day.

When we made it back to our room, I made sweet love to her, then curled into her side for a nap, ignoring the dull ache coming from my healing stab wound.

Phase Three: Success.

Sixty-Six

Liam

❧

Callie looked like the salsa dancing emoji when she stepped out of the bathroom. I was tempted to stay back from this event and rip that red dress off her. Nothing sounded more appealing than fucking her from behind, but she looked too beautiful for me to mess up her hair and makeup with my caveman-like ways. Instead, I only slapped her ass as she swayed past me getting off the elevator.

She yelped. "Liam Chandler!" she scolded playfully as she practically skipped away from the ballroom. "Let's go! I'm so excited." I laughed, tugging her hand the opposite direction.

I was almost overwhelmed seeing all the twirling bodies amid a sea of red, green, and gold. It felt like stepping onto a movie scene, and judging by the wonder in Callie's eyes, I knew she felt the same. She squealed and pulled me onto the dance floor, eager to put her new ballroom dancing skills to the test.

But little did she know that I had *plenty* of ballroom dancing experience, and I was prepared to sweep her off her feet. This is where the final step of my plan came into play; after this, the foundation would be set for my grand finale on Christmas Day.

Phase Four: Sweep Her Off Her Feet.

I admit, Callie had been a fast learner today, but there was no way she would expect my level of dancing. I did, after all, spend a few summers here teaching those very same classes to many couples.

I led, and watched as she kept up better than I could have ever imagined. She let the music flow through her, so I grabbed her hand and spun her around, dipped her, and then pulled her back up so our faces were inches from each other. She gave me a dazzling grin before whirling away from me and following the rhythm of the music.

Good. God.

We danced, never once talking, song after song. I wasn't sure if it was her gracefulness, her beauty, her soul, or the sequence of events that got us here today, but I was so mesmerized by her that I lost sight of my plan. I couldn't tear my eyes off her. Her dress fanned out, her hips swaying under my palm, and her hair followed her every movement.

This carefree attitude looked so good on her, and I wanted to do everything I possibly could to keep her feeling that way.

Everything was going great—perfect, even—with Phase Four. Until it all crashed and burned.

The holiday music ebbed, replaced by more upbeat songs. Everyone cheered as a salsa version of *Hips Don't Lie* began playing. I pulled Callie into me and kissed her, but it was a fleeting touch as she grabbed my hand and began dancing again. Seconds later, she spun back into me, her back to my chest, and turned her face towards mine.

"When did you learn to dance?" she breathed, her blue eyes flickering to my lips.

"Many, many years ago, I learned when they started this tradition," I told her, giving her yet another piece of myself. "I used to teach lessons. It was the only time I was part of the family business."

She giggled and turned to face me. I dipped her once more, and when she came back up, her cheeks were flushed, with lips parted as she breathed heavily, hair voluminous from dancing. She looked awe-inspiring, like a painting you'd expect to see hanging in the Louvre.

I couldn't help myself.

"Marry me," I breathed.

My heart sputtered to a stop.

Her grin faded as shock colored her features, as bold as the red color of her dress. She opened her mouth to respond but was cut off by my parents' voices.

No—I haven't heard her answer yet!

"Bravo, you two!" my mother cheered, the sound of her clapping clear over the music.

Fuck.

Callie glanced over my shoulder and beamed at my parents, releasing me to hug them. I cleared my throat and forced a smile.

"You two looked so stunning out there. Naturals!" Mom complimented, placing a hand over her heart endearingly.

"I see those lessons from all those years ago really paid off," Dad said, winking at me. I fought the urge to barge out of this room with my woman in tow. Now was not the time to be having any sort of discussion with them.

"Well, Liam's a good lead," Callie cooed, wrapping her arms around me. I rested my arm around her shoulders, careful not to tug on her hair. I couldn't read how she was feeling, but she was doing a damn good job of putting up a front for the sake of my parents.

"You two are just so sweet. Callie, I'm hoping you're still enjoying all the amenities here," Mom said.

Callie looked up at me and smiled warmly. *Good sign, right?* "I was before this guy showed up, but I am even more now. Truly. I can't thank you enough," she gushed.

After a few more tedious minutes of chatting with my parents, we excused ourselves to change for dinner. I held Callie's hand as we strolled to the elevator, but she seemed distant. Had I royally fucked things up? Did I misread her signals?

I tried not to be frustrated with myself. I intentionally had conversations about our future so this wouldn't come as too much of a surprise, yet now I was thinking she wasn't ready.

Damn it damn it damn it.

Except, why else would she still wear that fake ring and continue to call me her husband? I was so confused that it sparked a headache, starting at the base of my neck and spreading up.

When we got to our floor, still having not said anything, I turned to her. Maybe if I just gave her a few minutes of space to process what I'd said, she'd feel better. I could go hunt down my sister, wherever she was, and tell her what happened while I waited.

"Do you want me to give you a bit to change and have some downtime? You can meet me down at dinner in an hour and a half?" I offered, ignoring the presence of the two federal agents posted outside the door.

She opened the door to our suite and looked over her shoulder. "Actually, that would be great," she replied, then leaned in to kiss me. "I love you."

"I love you, too."

She closed the door and I stood there for a moment, feeling uncomfortable about leaving her, but forcing myself to anyway. I needed to respect her boundaries, even if it wasn't exactly what I was hoping would happen.

I wandered downstairs and made a beeline for my sister's office.

Sixty-Seven

Callie

Marry me, he'd said.

Marry me.

I kept hearing his voice in my head during the entire interaction with his parents, the whole ride up to the top floor, and whenever he spoke to me after that. My heart was soaring, racing, thumping. My body was quivering—from anxiety, shock, but most of all from *certainty.* I was going to say yes right then and there until his parents called us over.

His parents. They really were amazing people, but they couldn't have had worse timing.

I had spent all of today wondering what Liam was up to, and now I finally understood. He was trying to make me feel secure and confident as we headed into a potential engagement.

I could squeal from excitement—from *love.*

I just needed a moment to process it all.

As I shut the door on an apprehensive-looking Liam, I finally took a deep breath and walked into the bedroom, plucking the phone up to order room service: chocolate cake and a bottle of champagne. Then, I called Sophie. She picked up on the first ring.

"You better be calling to tell me you're having the best sex of your life with Liam," she said playfully.

I cackled. "I mean, yeah, that was a given. But Soph, I have *huge* news."

"They caught Frankford?" I could practically hear her sitting up straighter.

As much as I wanted to grimace, I couldn't fight the face-splitting grin as I said, "No, Liam proposed."

Silence.

Then, "He *WHAT?*"

"He proposed! We were dancing and he just… asked me to marry him."

"Oh my God, Cal! What did you say?"

"Well, I didn't get a chance to respond. His parents interrupted us. I'm back in our room now, but I'm going to say yes, obvi. I just needed a minute to myself to take it all in."

"Let's be honest, you also want to make him sweat."

I laughed. "I mean, that too."

"This is the best news ever. Next time I'm up there, if Frankford hasn't been caught yet, we're celebrating."

I kicked off my heels, giving my poor feet some reprieve as I wandered into the kitchen to grab a pen and paper, scrawling *"She said YES!"* on it while Sophie spoke. I folded it in half and propped it up on the counter, filled up a bucket of ice, and gabbed with my bestie the entire time.

After a few more minutes, there was a knock on our suite door. I opened it, turning away to wave the bellhop in. "Hey, Soph, my room service is here. I'm gonna hop off so I can finish getting ready for dinner. Talk later?"

"Of course. Congrats, Cal! I can't wait to see the rock!"

I rolled my eyes and said goodbye, then hung up. Just as I was about to turn back to the bellhop, their arms were around me. A cloth with a sickening smell pressed over my nose and mouth. It took less than five seconds before I was out like a light.

Sixty-Eight

Liam

I rapped on my sister's office door even though it was slightly ajar, then pushed it all the way open. Laurie looked up and simpered, identical dimples to mine making an appearance.

"Liam! What a nice surprise. I assumed you were with Callie in the ballroom, and I wasn't about to crash your date."

I rubbed the back of my neck. "Speaking of my date…" my voice faded as embarrassment made my throat close up.

She tossed her highlighted, sandy-blonde hair over her shoulder and stood, putting her hands on her hip. "Are you *blushing?*" she asked in mock horror. "Liam Aiden Chandler, what did you do?"

I winced. "Aren't you supposed to be the *younger* sibling?"

Laurie raised her eyebrows, obviously eager to know more.

I scoffed. "Fine. Callie and I had this back-and-forth relationship when I lived in Newark. But before I moved back to New York, things fell apart between us and she left the precinct." Laurie nodded, as if familiar with the story. Chances are, she'd forced it out of Callie sometime in the last few weeks. "Anyway, before we were put into the witness protection program, we rekindled things, and then at the cabin…" I paused and shook my head. "We spent a lot of time sorting things out and getting serious."

"Jesus, you *are* blushing. Whatever you did must be epic, because I can't recall a single time Victoria made you blush."

I huffed in annoyance. "Not helping, Lor. As I'm sure you know, our cover was a married couple. But when we got back here… I think we both struggled with separating the idea of marriage from our relationship, because we've spent the last six months intertwining it into our reality, you know? We've talked quite a bit about our future now, so while we were dancing, I sort of—accidentally, maybe—proposed?" I finished, smiling meekly.

Laurie's jaw dropped before she raised her arm and punched me. "Liam! You *proposed* to her?" she cried out.

I rubbed my shoulder where she hit me. "Fuck, I know! And now I'm scared I pushed her into this too soon. I mean, I have the ring. I was just waiting until Christmas, so I didn't even have it with me. I didn't even get a chance to hear her answer because Mom and Dad interrupted us, so I offered her some time alone before meeting me at dinner. Figured she needed it since she was quiet the whole way back to our room."

She scratched her head. "Mom and Dad interrupted your proposal?"

"Again, an accidental proposal. Very spur of the moment. Can't stress that enough. All I said was *Marry me* after dancing for half an hour. Mom and Dad flagged us down right after."

Sighing, she said, "Liam, your love life is a shit show. After your marriage went up in flames, I was scared you wouldn't find someone. But then all the shit with her ex-fiancé being your serial killer, now this, blah, blah, blah. It's like a fucking soap opera."

"You're telling me. So, do you think I blew it?"

She shook her head. "You should've seen her the entire time you were in the hospital. The poor woman was a nervous wreck. Plus, I've seen the way she looks at you."

I rubbed my forehead, praying she was right.

"So." She wiggled her eyebrows. "I know you didn't tap into your inheritance for Victoria's ring. Did you for Callie's?"

I rolled my lips, trying to keep a straight face. Laurie's mouth popped open. "I wanted it to be special."

"And you were too prideful to do that for Victoria?"

Scowling, I snapped, "Probably, but I also never felt this way for Victoria. I loved her, I just… knowing what I feel now? I don't think I was ever *in love* with her. Isn't that fucked up?"

Laurie raised a shoulder. "I mean, kinda? But also, I don't know that she was ever really with you for the right reasons. Remember the fights about the prenup, and all the meetings with the lawyers during the divorce? She wanted a cut of your inheritance *and* your shares. She did know this about you long before you got married."

Oh.

If I still cared about Victoria, that would hurt to hear. But I didn't.

"Have you told Callie?"

"I did, but not by choice. The staff around here have loud mouths and Callie overheard them. Asked me about it the night I got back."

"Well, she's nothing like Victoria."

I chuckled and rubbed my hands over my face, deciding to move the conversation off me. It had been so long since I'd seen Laurie, and I knew she was struggling with the demands of her job. It was the leading reason I didn't want to start down the path of this business—it wouldn't satisfy me.

So I listened to her talk, finding solace in her presence and feeling grateful I lived through nearly bleeding out.

* * *

My stomach was in knots as I headed to the resort's restaurant. What was she going to say to me? I had no calls or texts from her. Was she upset? Did I misread *everything*? Sweat pricked the back of my neck at the thought.

Ordering a bottle of wine for us to share—while I was still wary about Callie having alcohol, I certainly wasn't going to stop her and would only monitor her—I had two glasses just while waiting. But after two glasses and fifteen minutes past our agreed meeting time, that worry turned into dread.

Did she run, leave? No, she couldn't have, not with federal agents posted at every turn. Maybe she couldn't face me? Ugh, that also seemed unlike her; we'd come so far with our communication. If she wasn't ready to be engaged, she would tell me. Right?

I almost poured a third glass but decided against it and called her cell. It went directly to voicemail. I frowned and waited for the beep.

"Hey baby, it's me, Liam," I said, then mentally face-palmed myself. *Obviously*, she would know who it was. I lowered my voice. "I'm here at dinner and just wanted to make sure you're alright. Call me back, or hopefully I'll see you in a few minutes. I love you." I hung up and glanced around uneasily. Some of the staff were staring at me, and I knew this was going to be a topic of conversation. I could hear it now…

Liam Chandler, stood up at his family's restaurant after proposing to his girlfriend-slash-fake-wife.

The knots in my stomach intensified, and for a moment I convinced myself it was from nerves. No, that feeling? *That* feeling was a hunch. And this hunch was telling me something was wrong. I chugged a glass of water, thanked my server, and quickly exited the restaurant. I had to check on her to at least make sure she was okay. I raced up to our room, nodding to the agents outside it.

"Callie?" I called out as I opened the door.

Dead silence greeted me. I poked my head into the room, thinking maybe she fell asleep, but found the bed nicely made and Callie's clothes folded. My shoulders dropped in relief. *Okay, she didn't run away.* Maybe I missed her on my way up?

I walked toward the living room and stopped dead in my tracks, sniffing the air. That was… what was that? Smelled kind of sweet, but it had a chemical tang to it—

Stepping on something on the ground, I lifted my foot and saw a rag bundled up near the entrance from the hallway to the living room. I flicked on the light, then reached down to pick it up. Brought it to my nose, and that smell filled my head, making me feel dizzy.

I dropped the rag like it was on fire and stumbled away, into the kitchen, where there was a bottle of champagne, a dessert, a note, and a bucket of ice that was starting to melt. My eyes swept over the area, assessing the scene. Inside, I was battling between rational thoughts and sheer panic.

Because that smell… that was definitely—

Oh, God, I was going to be sick.

I just needed to keep it together for a little longer. After all, this was my job; I just had to repress my feelings long enough to figure out what had happened to her. I plucked the note off the counter and immediately felt tears spring to my eyes.

She said YES! was written on it in Callie's feminine, looping handwriting.

My vision swum; I gripped the counter for stability. She was going to say yes before she got interrupted. I knew right away who had taken Callie, I just didn't know *how.* I leaned over the sink to upchuck everything I had consumed, not stopping until my stomach was empty.

When I was finished, I moved back toward the hallway and froze. I had already traipsed through the suite with evidence, touched so many surfaces, and potentially contaminated the scene. Okay, just a little longer, man. Hold it together.

I shakily raised my phone to my ear and tried to control my breathing. "Drew, something's wrong. I think—somehow, I don't know—that Frankford has Callie. She's gone."

Sixty-Nine

Liam

I sat at the breakfast bar with my head in my hands, distraught. I distracted myself any way I could and stayed away from the crime scene. Changed my clothes, folded them, bagged them. Other than that, that's all the privacy I got.

Within minutes, the feds were parading through the suite like it was their life's mission to solve the case. I could do nothing but sit there and answer questions when prompted.

I called my parents and informed them of what happened, keeping my voice as level as possible, but the slight waver made it pretty clear that maybe I wasn't as okay as I made myself out to be.

So now I sat alone, waiting. After an hour, Madelyn and Drew came through the doors. I felt a little better seeing them.

My concern was now not knowing how long she had been gone, and how much lead time that gave Frankford in getting away. But right now, that wasn't my job—it was theirs. And I needed to be clear-minded to be of any assistance.

Drew swooped down to grab the chloroform-soaked rag off the ground with a gloved hand, giving it one whiff before confirming it. "Old school, yet effective," he muttered. I grimaced.

Madelyn plucked Callie's note from the counter beside me, flicking her amber eyes to mine. "Oh my God, you proposed?"

"Sort of. Yes—yeah, I suppose," I told her distractedly as their team set evidence markers around the suite.

"And she said yes?" The disbelief in her voice was palpable.

"Gee, thanks for the vote of confidence," I grumbled. "Judging by the note, I guess she was going to. We hadn't gotten that far. She was supposed to meet me downstairs for dinner, and when she didn't, I got worried. I came to check on her. That's when I found the rag and the note. I put two and two together."

"Well, I think we can rule out her running away," Drew chimed in, forcing Madelyn and me to turn to look at a CSI tech holding up a tangle of brown hair matted with blood.

My stomach heaved again. "I'll be right back." Jumping up, I bolted to the bathroom to hurl the little remaining contents left in my stomach.

Drew followed me. "Hey, man, we're going to find her. You hear me?"

I wiped my mouth and straightened. One glance in the mirror told me I looked like hell. My eyes were rimmed red, my hair was a mess, and my clothes were ruffled.

How did this day go from utterly perfect to absolute shit?

If I had kept my stupid fucking mouth shut, we wouldn't be in this predicament.

"Oliver Frankford is a bold motherfucker for finding a way to break in here and kidnap her," I seethed.

Drew rubbed the back of his neck, clearly uncomfortable with what he was about to say next. "Yeah, listen, about that. Maddie and I pulled the security tapes on our way here."

"And?" I turned to face him and folded my arms across my chest.

Madelyn appeared behind him. "She ordered room service as soon as she got back to the suite. The call logs confirm that. So—"

I held up my hands to stop her. "Hold on. I need a second." That meant Callie knew her answer the moment I left her at the door, and somehow the knowledge relieved a tiny amount of pressure building in my chest. She hadn't needed time to figure out her answer. I nodded at the two agents. "Continue."

"Anyway, turns out Frankford had incapacitated the security guards and was watching the cameras. It's all recorded that he was in the room. Didn't even bother to hide it. So when Callie placed the room service call, he picked up the order and came to the suite."

I blinked. *Jesus.* "H-how did no one recognize him?"

"How does anyone fly under the radar? He dyed his hair, threw on a pair of thick-lens glasses, and grew out a little bit of facial hair. At first glance, you'd overlook him. He's just an average Joe," Drew explained.

I ran a hand down my face in defeat. "Christ. So Callie just… let him in?"

"She was on her phone when she answered the door. Didn't even look at him, just turned away. He pushed the room service cart in, and five minutes later, he reappeared."

Stomach roiling again, I closed my eyes. "Tell me he didn't."

Madelyn nodded. "It's the only plausible explanation that she was in the room service cart."

My eyes burned again when I looked at them. "I'm assuming you already had someone check all the carts."

"We did it ourselves before coming up here," Drew said softly. "We know which one she was in. There was a little bit of blood inside, but she was nowhere to be found. Security tapes have him as a ghost after he goes into a blind spot."

I cursed under my breath.

Seventy

Callie

I slowly opened my eyes, my vision blurry, and was met with an incessant pounding in my head. I could hear faint water droplets behind me, and each drop sounded like a hammer striking metal. Dread settled in the pit of my stomach as my eyes cleared. I was in a dimly lit room, surrounded by concrete and restrained to a chair chained to a cement pillar.

Struggling against my restraints to test the strength of the knots holding my arms down, my muscles felt like jelly and my hair hung around me in damp strands. I blew a breath out in an attempt to get it out of my face.

"Ah, look who's awake," a sinister yet familiar voice said from the shadows in front of me. As he stepped into my line of sight, I felt my heart drop to my stomach.

"Heyyyy," I slurred, my tongue feeling heavy as I glowered at him in hopes that he would scamper back into whatever hole he'd crawled out of.

"Callie Chandler," he purred, slowly sauntering toward me. Mmm, I liked the way that sounded. *Wait, this is* so *not the fucking time for this, Callie.* "I believe some congratulations are in order? To you and Liam." I dipped my chin, not responding. "You know, it took some time, but I finally got you alone."

I pulled once again at the ropes digging into my skin, feeling the strength in my muscles returning. "You creep. What you did at the cabin wasn't enough?" I snapped.

He stopped about five feet away. "I'll admit, I'm disappointed at the outcome of that, but this is so much better. A true public spectacle your disappearance has created, Callie. As we speak, Liam is realizing I took his wife away. Just like how I had to watch Henry take mine away all those years ago."

My head was swimming, and I felt like I was going to be sick. "How do you know what he's doing?"

Oliver gave me a malicious grin before walking off to my right. I craned my neck—wincing from pain—to see there was a wall of shelves and a workshop table that I hadn't noticed on my initial assessment of my surroundings. A laptop was set up there, which he disconnected and walked toward me, turning it so I could see the screen.

And there he was. My poor Liam, standing in the living room of our suite with his arms crossed while watching something on a screen with Madelyn and Drew. He ran a hand through his hair, tugging slightly, before rubbing his eyes and saying something to the feds.

Oh God. "H-how long have you been watching us?"

"If you're asking whether or not I saw you fuck him, the answer would be yes. Many times."

I cringed, my ears still unfamiliar with hearing him swear after being convinced he was a Catholic saint who was celibate and waiting until marriage for sex. Sighing in frustration, I glanced at Liam's distraught image again. "Why would you do this to him?" I choked on involuntary tears.

"Because it's torturing you. I would say I feel bad for the guy, but I don't. You both deserve what's coming to you."

A few tears fell. "Please don't hurt him," I pleaded, even though I knew it was pointless. The man before me was a cold-blooded killer.

Oliver returned his laptop to the table. "It's not him I'm after, Callie. It's just a bonus. I gave him a permanent physical scar he'll have to live with, but the emotional scars he'll have after I'm through with you is enough vengeance to last me a lifetime." The calmness of his voice was scary. A shiver ran down my spine.

It was abundantly clear he was going to kill me. He had finally won, because I once again got too comfortable and got distracted. *FUCK.* When would I learn?

I fought the rising panic, needing to stay calm and rationalize with him as much as I could.

"Let's talk about this," I murmured as he walked toward me with his hands clasped behind his back.

He pretended to think for a moment, his eyes damn near black. "No. Sweet dreams, Sergeant." Oliver whipped out a syringe. I threw myself backwards, but with being chained to a pillar, I wasn't going anywhere. He lunged at me, plunging the syringe into my arm. I yelped in pain, but within seconds I was falling back into a deep slumber.

Seventy-One

Liam

"Uh, Liam, you should come see this," Drew called out. I was in the middle of filling Sophie in, and we both turned at the sound of Drew's voice. He was holding up… something. I squinted my eyes to see better but I had to move closer.

"Fuck," I swore. "When the fuck did he manage to put that up?"

"Maybe he bribed a housekeeper to do it?" Sophie suggested, eyebrows raised in concern at the small camera in Drew's hand.

One of the federal analysts, Kira, paused her clacking on her computer. "Since Callie arrived here, there has been a housekeeper up here once a day. We're talking potentially a couple dozen times that someone would have had access."

There went my stomach again. I didn't even want to think about someone on my parents' carefully crafted staff who would accept a bribe over such a violation of privacy, and to the owners' son, nonetheless.

Another analyst plopped down next to Kira. "I just finished reviewing CCTV footage. There are three blind spots in the parking lot, and I haven't found him on it yet."

I was frustrated, to say the least. A look at the clock told me it was already midnight, and we were coming up on six hours. It was all I could do to keep myself from spiraling at the thought of what would happen if we hit twenty-four hours.

I had seen firsthand what the man was capable of.

"Great. So back to square one," I grumbled, then excused myself to have a minute alone.

* * *

I absently ran a finger around the rim of my full glass of scotch. I was of no help to anyone up there, and I knew I needed to let them do their jobs without tiptoeing around me.

As much as it fucking sucked.

Because I was ready to go ballistic and take matters into my own hands.

I wanted to. *God,* I wanted to. But I feared that's exactly what Oliver wanted.

"Need some company?" Sophie slid onto the barstool beside me.

I shrugged.

"They'll find her," she said quietly as she flagged down the bartender.

That statement alone made me toss my entire drink back.

"Slow down, cowboy. I need you sharp."

Grimacing into my now empty glass, I responded with, "Am I failing her by not being up there right now?"

"No." A heavy sigh. "You're too close to this anyway. It's best that neither of us is involved."

I groaned as the bartender slid us our drinks. "Everything was going perfect, Soph. This is what happens when you let your guard down. I'm so tired of this bullshit. So tired of this fucking case and that fucking asshole."

Sophie patted my arm. "Trust me, you're not the only one. And when all this is over, I don't know what life looks like for any of us."

I turned to look at her. "Explain."

"You know what happened with my dad's case. My job and Dean were the only things tying me to Newark, but with Terry gone, and Callie not sticking around, I don't know what the dynamics of my job will be like.

Dean and I have finally called it quits, so…"

I sucked in a breath. "Those issues never got any better?"

She shook her head. "We fought too much. We love each other, but it wasn't enough to make it work. There's only so much you can do for a person who can't tolerate your success."

We both paused to sip our drinks.

"I don't even know what real life looks like outside of this," I told her. She nodded in understanding. "Callie and I have built this relationship in the confines of our bubble. But now that it's burst, what does that mean for us? Where do we move? Who works where? Who sacrifices what? We never talked about this shit because we didn't know when or if it would all be over." I tugged a hand through my hair.

"You have plenty of time once you're reunited to figure it all out."

"But what if they find her too late, Soph?" Our eyes met, and I figured her expression mirrored mine. Denial and fear. "They were almost too late for me."

Seventy-Two

Callie

I woke up with a splitting headache. Again. I was still tied to the chair, fabric scratched my thighs, and all I could think of was whether or not Liam was okay.

It almost made me laugh bitterly.

Because physically—*yes*, he was. Me on the other hand? Well…

My eyes focused on the white wedding gown draping over my body. My eyes stung. I knew what this meant: my time was close.*

I noticed that a tripod was set up in front of me now. I frowned at it, groggily glancing around and spotting Oliver at the workshop table with his back to me. Taking the opportunity, I bent over to pull at my restraints, but had to carefully sit back up when I felt like passing out from the exertion. Just in time for Oliver to turn around.

"How was your nap?" he asked nonchalantly. What the hell had he given me that made me so disoriented?

Fuck you, I wanted to spit. I was tempted to spew all sorts of other venomous words at him, but I knew that it could just cause him to snap.

"Why are you doing this to me?" I demanded, my tongue feeling swollen and making me sound inebriated. I knew what his answer was, but I was buying myself time.

"Because you couldn't leave well enough alone," he snapped. "Because you cheated on me like the fucking hypocrite you are. You ruined my life."

I shook my head. "You cheated on me, too, with that girl from your church. How are you any different from me?"

His eyes narrowed. "I was only with you to keep you close. It's different." *Yep, saw that coming.* "I was never committed to you like you were supposed to be with me."

I chuckled darkly. "And yet, you couldn't even *pretend.* You never even fucked me!" I shouted brazenly. "You didn't try hard enough to keep your cover in place. Maybe if you had, I wouldn't have cheated."

Oliver exhaled. "That's where you're wrong. There's some sickening, magnetic pull between you and Liam. No matter how many times I tried to interfere, you two always came out stronger than before." He picked up another syringe and my eyes welled with tears.

"No," I begged as tears shamelessly slid free. "Please no. Not again."

"Don't worry, Callie, it's not the same stuff as before," he said lightly, as if we were talking about the fucking weather, before he stabbed me in the arm again.

I whimpered and cringed away from him as he yanked the needle out. This time, I didn't feel blackness pulling at the edges of my mind, but rather the world distorting around me. I blinked a few times and suddenly Liam was before me, just out of arm's reach.

"Callie, we need to talk," he said, his voice trembling.

I smiled at him. "Hi, baby. I've missed you. Why don't you untie me so I can hug you?"

Liam shook his head solemnly. "I can't do that. You're going to have to find your way out of this one."

I pouted. "Well then I better get started, huh?" I joked, giggling.

Oliver appeared behind him, seemingly out of nowhere, and my brief fantasy dissipated in an instant. Oliver wielded a knife, the silver blade gleaming.

"Watch out!" I cried out in horror as Oliver raised his arm.

Liam tilted his head to the side. "Come back to me soon."

Oliver brought the blade down, and I screamed at the top of my lungs as Liam's body crumpled at my feet, blood pooling around me. I thrashed against my restraints, desperate to check on him or stitch him up or *anything*—but the world went black once more.

Seventy-Three

Liam

Sophie forced me to eat dinner, claiming I couldn't think clearly unless I sobered up. As much as I didn't want to, she was right.

We sat in the lobby together, not really talking but existing in each other's company. It was well past five in the morning, and we were both bone-deep exhausted. Neither of us could sleep. I sure as hell couldn't go up to my suite, and my parents' resort was fully booked for Christmas.

On my back on one of the couches, I aimlessly scrolled through my phone. An email notification popped up with a video attachment. I clicked on the email to see if it was a scam or not, but the thumbnail had my heart thumping a little harder. I sat up so fast that I felt the blood rushing out of my head.

"Soph." She turned to look at me, dark circles under her eyes. I showed her my screen, and one look at it had her launching to sit next to me.

"What are you waiting for? Play it!" She anxiously reached across me to tap the screen. I wanted to squeeze my eyes shut in case it was the worst case scenario about to play out in front of me.

Callie was sitting in a chair, her head hanging forward with her hair covering most of her face, clad in—*fuck*—a wedding dress. Behind her was just a white sheet, so I couldn't make out her surroundings, but the lighting was dim. Frankford came into sight and stopped just in front of her, reaching forward to tilt her chin up. Her head snapped up and her eyes struggled to focus on him. Even in the low light, I could see her pupils were fully dilated.

"Don't… touch… me!" she panted, struggling against the ropes restraining her to the chair. "I need to get to Liam. Is he okay? He-he's bleeding out and he needs stitches." Her words were slurred, her voice a higher octave than normal. Not intoxicated, but something else.

A dark chuckle rumbled through Frankford. "Remember what we talked about. Look at the camera and tell them what you told me."

She blinked slowly, as if her concerns faded away. I wanted to vomit as understanding flickered across her face. She was clearly under the influence of some kind of drug. Taking her time, she swung her head to look at the camera. "My name is Callie Eden."

I paused the video. "I can't watch it, Soph. What if—"

"Stop," she interjected. "Don't say that. I can't imagine he'd be dumb enough to send a video of him offing her. Just press play."

I did.

Callie squinted at the screen, and I wondered if she was reading off of something. "And these are my last words before I, too, become a v-victim of the Wring Bearer. I deserve everything coming to me after my many acts of infidelity. My irresponsibility as an off-officer of the law allowed Oliver Frankford to get away w-with murder, time and ti-time again. My incompetence made me blind to knowing he was the killer when we lived together. I'm a liar, a cheat, a bad cop, and I deserve to rot in hell." Tears welled in her eyes before, and her gaze became unfocused again. "And I love Liam. Please make sure he knows that."

Oliver clapped his hands. "Nice work, Callie. Now that you've confessed, I think it's time for you to go to sleep." He stepped toward her with a—*was that a syringe?*—in hand. Callie didn't fight it, she just sobbed until seconds later, her head was lolling back.

The video cut off. Sophie and I raced back up to the suite.

Seventy-Four

Callie

The lines between reality and delirium were blurred. I was no longer aware of what was what. Was Liam actually bleeding out—again? Was Oliver drugging me? Did I admit to being responsible for his actions? Did I imagine Liam dying in front of me over and over again?

I didn't know how much time had passed, but I could still feel the effects of whatever he gave me, although it was wearing off. The world slowly became a little more sharp, my thoughts less of a jumbled mess. I woke up from the drug-induced haze in a startle, rasping for air. I looked around with dim awareness. My body was sweating profusely; I was somehow hot and cold all at once, tired yet completely aware.

I looked for Liam—was his death real, and this was my mind's way of protecting me from myself?

Pushing down the panic that I couldn't see Oliver anywhere, I honed in on the windows at the far end of the room—ones I hadn't noticed before, probably because it had been night, but now the sun was starting to rise. Orange light filled the corners of the room with its soft color. I bent over and pulled at the knots with my teeth again. I almost laughed at how fucking dumb Oliver had been to not tie the knots under the arms of the chair.

I got them loose just enough that I could continue pulling and free my hands. Just as I was about to do so, I heard a door clang open. I whipped my head in the direction of the door and saw Oliver stroll in casually, holding a coffee cup in one hand. I narrowed my eyes, my brain recognizing it immediately, and knew how I could escape.

"Ah, you're up. Ready to die now? The sun is rising, so it seems like the perfect way to start the day," he purred, a devious smile splitting his face in half. I didn't miss the infinitesimal look of disappointment flash in his eyes as he said it. I knew what I had to do—I had to call out his weaknesses and weasel myself into his mind.

Stall.

I barked out a laugh, tossing my head back. "You're not done with me yet. You've been *obsessed* with me," I stressed. "Do you really think you can kill me so quickly? Let's be honest: you'll miss me. You'll have no purpose once I'm gone. You don't want to torture me a little more?"

The last thing I wanted was for him to torture me more—if my delusions were any indication, or the bruises forming all over my body from him hitting me in what I thought were my delusions but was actually real life—I knew it was going to upset him that I called it out.

He set his coffee down and came over to me. *That's it, just a few more steps.* He shook me by the shoulders. "Don't get smart with me."

My already tender body screamed in pain, but I mustered up all my strength, flashed him a mischievous grin, and pulled my hands free of the rope. I brought my first up, connecting it with his jaw. He stumbled backward, and I quickly undid my feet. Oliver wobbled toward me with his hands outstretched, but I broke off a piece of the chair and swung it up. It made contact with the side of his face.

He bared his teeth and snarled at me, blood dripping from his lips. Rushing toward me, he grabbed my waist and threw me against the back wall. His strength felt almost superhuman, and I wondered if this is how all his victims felt in their final moments. My body crumpled when it hit the wall, and I drew in a staggering breath as I shakily rose to my bare feet.

Oliver pounced on me again, but I hit him with the wooden chair piece once more. Blood trickled from his head wound, and I took the opportunity to clumsily run away from him, taking off toward the door. He threw himself at my legs, tripping me as he gripped the train of the wedding dress. My face smacked the ground, my teeth singing at the impact.

He dragged me backwards. I fumbled with anything I could grasp, until my hand wrapped around the tripod leg. I flipped myself around enough to whip it over my head and onto his back with a heavy thud.

"*Bitch,*" he sneered.

I scrambled to my feet again and bolted to the door, relieved to find it locked from the inside. I turned the lock and ran, my feet carrying me across a wide-open basement space and to another door, up a set of stairs. A sudden brightness of fluorescent light made me blink and pause in my tracks. When I could see again, feeling drunk as my vision swam, I careened into a wall. I heard Oliver's feet on the steps below me, and that encouraged me to stumble up the rest of the stairs until my hands felt a door handle.

I nearly sobbed in relief as fresh air hit my face, the sunrise greeting me with the sweetest hello. I recognized my surroundings—the backside of the resort, in the loading bay. Now out in the open, I turned and saw Oliver standing in the doorway. His gaze flicked to the top of the building, and in my peripherals I spotted a security camera. He must be out of view in his current position, and knew that if he stepped outside, he'd be spotted—and so would I.

Smirking, I mouthed *Gotcha* at him. We reached the same conclusion then. He bolted past me, and I took off after him, hiking up the damn wedding dress and wincing as I stepped on glass and rocks. As we rounded the corner of the resort, cars came into view. We weaved our way through them; I dodged one and almost got hit by another. I slid across the hood of the car that nearly hit me, desperate to take Oliver down once and for fucking all.

He made it through the valet parking area, springing toward the back parking lot, and the sudden wobble in my knees made me question whether or not I could catch up.

But finally—*finally,* I caught a break. He darted around a light pole just past the valet area, causing him to trip. I used all the power in my legs to push off the balls of my feet and starfish my limbs to wrap myself around him—dress and all. We both careened to the ground; my knees absorbed most of my fall. I rolled him onto his front, pulled my fist back, and punched him square in the jaw. Suddenly I was seeing red, tears blurring my vision as I hit him over and over again. Oliver's head bounced off the ground with each blow, and blood sprayed the both of us.

A second later, I felt a sharp pang in my side. I looked down to see another syringe in Oliver's hand, injecting it with little energy. I gritted my teeth and slapped his hand away to yank it out.

"You piece of shit," I spat, noting that not much of the substance made it into my bloodstream before the syringe clattered to the concrete sidewalk beneath us. "You goddamn piece of *shit.*"

"Callie!" I heard Liam's distant voice call out. I didn't need to look over my shoulder to know help had arrived.

My hands trembled as I glared at the bloody man below me. He stared back with—*was that fear?*—and surrender, but all I could see was a man who deserved to be in jail. Not an ounce of sympathy tugged at me; I sincerely hoped he would keel over and die right then and there.

I rose to my feet on fatigued legs, not tearing my gaze from him a single time. He wouldn't be getting away under my watch—not again. I nodded at the federal agents that now flanked each side of me, one of them pulling their handcuffs free from their belt loop, and stepped away.

As badly as I wanted to be the one who arrested him—it wasn't my jurisdiction.

Nudging Oliver with my feet so he'd roll onto his stomach, I watched with glee as the agent read him his rights. "Oliver Frankford, you are under arrest. You have the right to remain silent. Anything you say can," she recited, cuffing his wrists together and dragging him to his feet, throwing me a knowing smile over her shoulder as she hissed the next part in his ear, "and *will* be used against you in a court of law. You have the right to an attorney. If you cannot afford an attorney, one will be appointed for you. Do you understand these rights as I have explained them to you?"

Nothing from him as he looked at me with disdain. I snarled through gritted teeth, "Do you understand your rights as she has explained them to you, *Oliver?*"

"Yes," he snapped, attempting to shake the federal agent off.

"Good," the agent replied, pushing him forward into the arms of other waiting FBI agents.

I felt an uncomfortably familiar sensation spread through my limbs. I felt sleepy, like I was crashing hard from the adrenaline of arresting him. I shook it off by locking my jaw and turning to march toward the love of my life, who was gaping at me with his hands pressed together in front of his lips.

My heart soared at the sight of him. Yeah, I was going to be really fucking traumatized from this, but... it was over. Really, truly, *finally* over. Two years of my life, now coming to an end. And all that mattered now was giving Liam the answer I almost didn't get a chance to give him. I didn't want to waste any more time.

Madelyn and Drew gave me a quick nod, the former saying, "I'm so glad to see you're alive." I ignored her, because truthfully I was growing more and more unsteady on my feet and could barely focus as it was. Sophie stood beside Liam as I turned to them, both looking disheveled and exhausted, probably unsure of how to approach me.

I only had the energy for one thing.

"Yes, I will marry you," I told him as I threw myself into Liam's arms, letting the blackness take over for what I hoped was the last time.

Seventy-Five

Liam

I let the rhythmic beeping of the hospital monitors wash over me. I clutched Callie's hand as if she might disappear again. I knew she wouldn't—knew our nightmare was behind bars—but the pain accompanying that thought was enough to put a chokehold on me.

When I saw her beating the living shit out of her ex, I was so stunned I could barely move. She had been in the same building… the whole time? The feds had found where he'd been hiding out; a utility room in a tucked away corner of the boiler room, which explained how he evaded cameras and never left the premises.

So how—*how* did they fuck up finding him? They said they checked every corner. But then again, this wasn't the first mistake they'd made when it came to this.

The guilt I felt that I could have found her if I had, I don't know, *tried*, was tangible. It was suffocating me; I felt like at any moment I would blink out of existence entirely.

Callie was tough as nails.

I ducked my head, wanting to fight the burning in my eyes. This kind of fear was as foreign as it was debilitating.

The doctor slipped into the room; it was the first time I'd seen him since he whisked Callie away for an MRI and a blood panel. She had yet to wake up.

Honestly, I was just grateful she was alive, but that didn't stop me from wanting to see those big blue eyes staring back at me with the love and adoration I had grown so used to.

"Her blood tests came back," the doctor said. "She tested with extremely high levels of flunitrazepam and ketamine in her system. The flunitrazepam at those levels likely caused her blackouts, and the ketamine paired with it probably gave her some vivid hallucinations and paranoia."

I bit the inside of my cheek. "Flunitrazepam? As in the date-rape drug?"

He nodded. "Correct. It's not legal in the US anymore, so he likely got it on the black market. We've flushed her system, and this IV drip will help stabilize and hydrate her. She'll need a few days to recover, but other than that, she'll be just fine."

I cleared my throat in relief. "Understood. Thank you."

The doctor gave me a small smile before looking at her chart once more and proceeding with telling me about Callie's after-care.

Seventy-Six

Callie

The first thing I heard was my own breathing. The second thing I heard was the sound of my heartbeat, loud and persistent in my chest, reverberating through me as consciousness tugged on the corners of my mind. I blinked, noting the muted gray tones of the hospital room I was in.

I slowly turned my head to see a screen tracking my pulse and oxygen levels. The slight movement made my stomach churn and my head throb.

"Ouch," I croaked, my voice hoarse. My tongue felt dry and swollen, my limbs heavy like lead.

"Hey, hey, be careful," I heard Liam's voice say from my left.

My attention shifted to him. He was sitting next to me, his forest green eyes filled with concern. His shoulders looked relaxed, his hand resting on my arm. The events leading to this moment suddenly flooded back as the sleep wore off. I shook the cobwebs out of the corners of my mind as I recalled the torture, the very real pain of watching the man I loved die in front of me over and over again despite it being a hallucination, despite me sobering up and escaping.

"Water," I rasped. Liam let go of me and handed me the cup of water from my bedside table. I took a few grateful sips before clearing my throat and smiling at him. "So you're my fiancé now. My *real* fiancé."

He gave me a boyish, dimpled grin that made my skin flush. One I wasn't used to seeing, but wanted to make him do every day for the rest of my life. "I sure am. How are you feeling?"

I attempted a shrug but got little movement. "Stiff and sore. Head hurts and I feel a little nauseous, but all things said, I'm just happy to be alive."

Liam's eyes widened. "You're feeling sick? Do you want crackers or ginger ale?"

I frowned playfully. "No, I'm okay. I don't think I can stomach anything right now. But you're cute when you're concerned about me."

Of all things he could do then, I didn't expect him to blush. The pink tinge on his cheeks made my heart flutter. Finally feeling strength in my arms return, I pushed myself up to a sitting position, flinching when my ribs protested.

"What's wrong? Are you alright?"

"Just my ribs, but I'm fine, babe," I insisted.

"Well… that makes sense," he huffed. "You're still concussed, got some bruised ribs and wrist."

"That all checks out." I chuckled, flashing a bashful smile.

"You almost just died after being kidnapped and drugged, and here you are, happy as a clam." He stared at me in awe, lifting up my left wrist, a deep shade of purple and blue, before turning it over and giving it a small kiss.

"I just put away my serial killer of an ex-fiancé who tried to kill us both, and woke up engaged to the man I'm madly in love with. What's not to be happy about?" I wondered, searching his face for answers but only winding up more confused. He was acting weird and I couldn't pinpoint why.

Liam opened his mouth to respond but snapped it shut and shook his head. I scowled and dropped my gaze to my hands in my lap.

"I thought I lost you," he said finally. "I blamed myself."

I sighed. "But you didn't. I'm right here. Alive and well. A little banged up, definitely got some mental issues I'll need to work out from all of this, but I'm *here*. With you. Happier than ever.

"None of this was your fault. Not even—let me finish," I responded calmly when he tried to interject. "Not even when you proposed. I was never upset about that. You have to know that. I just needed a second to prepare how I would say yes. The last thing I expected was to be blindsided in our own suite while the feds were posted outside our door. If anything, I blame *myself*. I didn't even think to look at who brought me room service. What kind of cop—what kind of *person*—does that make me?"

His eyes softened as he squeezed my hand. "Callie." It was almost a plea. "I love you. So. Goddamn. Much."

My lips curved into a smile. "I love you, too. Our story? It's just beginning, Mr. Chandler."

Seventy-Seven

Callie

I stood alone in front of a large arched window on the second floor of the Rockwell Museum in New York City. Christmas music flitted through the halls as if it were seeping through the walls, and the faint sound of a chattering crowd could be heard. For the most part, it was dark, save for the glittering views of the city through the windows.

Clad in a long red gown with a plunging neckline and long sleeves—in large part to cover the bruises and needle marks in my arms—I was the epitome of Liam's perfect fiancée. Paired with a long diamond necklace that nestled between my cleavage, an early Christmas gift from Liam this morning, and my signature nude heels, I knew I looked the part.

But I didn't feel the part.

Every inch of my body ached, including my face from all the fake smiles.

I felt disassociated from my body.

I usually loved the Christmas Gala, where I could liquor up and weasel donations out of the rich folks of the twin cities, yet here I was trying to escape it all.

Maybe it was because I was here as Liam's plus one—his arm candy—since I wasn't technically part of the NYPD or Newark Police Division anymore. The thought made my chest squeeze, then posed an interesting question:

What was next for me? I still had a job I could return to in Springcrest, but did I really want to go back there?

No. I didn't. I didn't want a small town life, or an isolated remote job in a cabin in the mountains. I wanted a life in the city, though which city I was willing to settle down in was a mystery. After living in the cabin for half a year and a couple of near death experiences… I couldn't really say I hated NYC anymore. In fact, the fast-paced, overcrowded city was a welcoming reprieve. And if that's where my fiancé wanted to live, I was A-okay with that.

Liam's arms slid around my waist from behind, his lips pressing into my neck. I was so lost in my thoughts that I didn't even hear him approach, but I gladly accepted his embrace and leaned back into him.

"There you are," he murmured, his voice husky and low. I shivered.

"I knew you'd find me eventually. You are a good detective, after all." There was a smile playing on my lips, and all thoughts left my brain when he gently bit at the base of my throat.

He chuckled, the vibrations skittering down me in a delicious way. "You know, we kinda have this tradition at the Christmas Gala…" he trailed off suggestively, one hand wandering up to my chest and slipping beneath the neckline of it to fondle my breast. Heat pooled low in my belly.

Sighing, I told him, "Better find us a place before I let you take me here and now."

He groaned. "Don't tempt me." His hands left my body, and I actually whimpered at the loss.

"What are you doing?" I hissed, starting to turn to give him a withering look, when one hand returned to my hip.

"I never got to do this properly," he said. Slowly, I turned and found him on one knee, and tears sprang to my eyes.

I never expected us to get here. If someone had told me two years ago that the man I randomly hooked up with would be kneeling before me at the same event with a two-carat princess-cut pavé diamond engagement ring, I would have laughed.

"Callie-Ann Jade Eden," Liam started, and I rolled my eyes at the use of my birth-given name. "I may have briefly met you as a teenager, but when you came crashing into my life two years ago—literally, might I add—the last thing I expected was to fall in love again." I was laughing already as I recalled me running into him, and his matching dimpled grin told me he felt the same way. "I was so fresh off my own heartache that I made a lot of mistakes with you. I never deserved a second chance, but you somehow found it within your too-caring heart to give it to me anyway."

I bit my lip, clasping my hands in front of me so he wouldn't see how badly my hands were shaking.

"I've known for a long time that you were my person, the only one for me. You challenge me, you love me despite my tendencies to be a godforsaken idiot, you make me laugh, but most of all, baby, you are my reason for waking up every day. Everything that happened before you and I crossed paths was merely a means to an end. I know without a doubt that there is no one else I want to build a life with, start a family with, and share in life experiences with, for the rest of my life. And while you have already accepted a half-hearted proposal, you deserve a real one. So I ask you, Ms. Eden, will you marry me?"

I had fallen in love with Liam not once, but twice, for wildly different reasons. The first time, he was saving me from the bad place I was barreling toward, and while he broke my heart, that decision ultimately led to me rediscovering myself and coming back to him stronger than before. The second time, I fell so deeply in love with who he was, the companionship he provided me, the way he loved me, and the life we were forced to build together that I was still breathless from it all.

That's why, without a second of hesitation, I knew my answer was an easy one to give.

"Yes, I will marry you, *Mr. Chandler.*"

Seventy-Eight

Epilogue

Liam

13 months later

"Fuck," I swore under my breath, a white cloud puffing around me as I waited in Central Park for Callie. It was cold as hell today, and even with my wool trench coat and scarf, I was freezing. It didn't help that my wife liked to make me wait—got off on it, actually.

My wife.

It sometimes felt surreal for her to be my *actual* wife, as Callie Chandler and not as Emily Blake.

Six months ago, Callie and I had decided to elope. We were both too traumatized for a real wedding—what with a serial killer specializing in dressing his victims in wedding attire, nearly killing the both of us, and changing Callie into a white dress. Besides, I already had a wedding that turned into a disaster of a marriage.

So, eloping in a courthouse with just us and legal witnesses was all we needed. We held a private reception a few weeks later to celebrate the union, and that satisfied Callie's desire for an event to be held in our honor. At this, she was also able to show off her Medal of Valor that she received for everything she did to protect herself, me, and the public from a prolific serial killer. She finally had the moment of praise that she had been looking for from her parents ever since she began her career.

"Hey, babe," Callie greeted from behind me. I turned and saw her rushing toward me, glowing with rosy cheeks and bright eyes. Her hair—which she had since cut to her shoulders—was curled, and she had traded in her heels for a pair of knee-high boots. I would have chastised her if she insisted on wearing heels in this weather. "Sorry I'm late!"

I smiled at her. "Are you sorry?" I teased, reaching for her.

We didn't see each other as much as we'd both like to these days, with our jobs in different parts of the city and our schedules overlapping.

Seeing her in a leadership role was a fucking turn on. Apparently, her knack for being a control freak who liked to boss people around was a perfect fit for her new place here in the NYPD.

Callie melted into me and pressed a kiss to my lips, but broke it too soon. Pity, I was tempted to drag her to our favorite coffee shop and sneak into the bathroom with her. Yeah, I really was that horny around her. Especially when she smelled so fucking delicious and looked so goddamn hot.

"I'm not sorry at all," she admitted, her cheeks flushing further as she held up a small gift bag I didn't notice she was holding.

"What's this?"

"A gift." The obvious *duh* in her voice made me chuckle as I held my hand out for it. Slowly, almost warily, she handed it over. "Before you open it, I just want you to know how much I love you." Her voice was barely above a whisper.

Arching a brow at her, I returned the proclamation of love, then guided her to take a seat on a nearby bench. She anxiously fidgeted with her hands in her lap. I wondered what was making her so nervous.

I pulled the tissue paper out one piece at a time, until my fingers brushed a small rectangular box. It was lightweight; I held it up to my ear and shook it. Aside from a slight rattle, nothing else gave it away. Frowning, I carefully removed the lid and froze, more than I was moments ago standing in the winter breeze—as I stared at what was in the box. Slowly, my eyes met Callie's big blue ones, light with something I'd never seen before.

"Callie, is this real?"

She rolled her eyes. "Why wouldn't it be?"

I couldn't stop the wave of emotions that crashed into me. "But… how?"

She giggled, scooting closer to me on the bench. "Don't you remember our little *tradition* at the Christmas Gala every year? And those antibiotics I was on?"

I paused, recalling the two of us finding a private alcove at the NJ Historical Society and me clamping my hand over her mouth to keep her quiet. Of course we didn't use a condom—we rarely ever did to begin with, and we had no reason to now. I thought it would be hot to have my cum dripping down her thighs for the remainder of the night, so I pocketed her panties.

I wasn't wrong.

It *was* hot.

I also recalled her doctor telling her that antibiotics reduced the effectiveness of the pill, but we both brushed it off.

I looked at the positive pregnancy test again before setting it down beside me and taking her face in my trembling hands, kissing her passionately. This was everything I had been wanting for longer than I cared to admit— something she knew, but I never pressed it. Pulling away, I stared at her through misty eyes.

"How are you feeling?"

Callie placed her hands over mine. "Better than I ever have."

I smiled as I kissed her again. When we stumbled into each other's lives a few years ago, I was in a bad place, heartbroken and lonely and suffering from the termination of my ex-wife's pregnancy despite how early on it was. But this? Being in a healthy marriage, enjoying each day as it was given to us, and now welcoming the surprise of a baby…

We'd both healed from all our pain, and we did it together.

THE END

Stay tuned for Sophie's spin-off, *Built For Mercy*. Will she find love? Find someone who challenges her, cherishes her dark side, and dare I say, *corrupts* her?

Read on for the first few chapters.

Also, notice any foreshadowing with Agents Drew Matthews and Madelyn Carver? That's because their story is one just as dramatic, heart-wrenching, and *hot* as Callie and Liam's—without all the miscommunication. Their novella series is coming soon.